DREAMS OF RESCUE

Also by Laura Shaine Cunningham

DREAMS OF RESCUE

A Novel

Laura Shaine Cunningham

ATRIA BOOKS

New York   London   Toronto   Sydney   Singapore

ATRIA BOOKS

1230 Avenue of the Americas
New York, NY 10020

ISBN: 0-7434-3648-2

First Atria Books hardcover printing May 2003

10 9 8 7 6 5 4 3 2 1

ATRIA BOOKS is a trademark of Simon & Schuster, Inc.

Manufactured in the United States of America

For information regarding special discounts for bulk purchases,
please contact Simon & Schuster Special Sales at 1-800-456-6798
or business@simonandschuster.com

*This book is dedicated to my daughters,
Alexandra Rose and Jasmine Sou Mei,
and in everlasting tribute to my uncles,
Ben and Abraham Weiss*

DREAMS OF RESCUE

In Character

I have spent the winter at my summer place. Every night I watch the tabloid television shows for news of other estranged wives, and the extended coverage on those who have already been murdered.

Each evening I wrap myself in a shawl and settle on the sofa. Then I lie back and stare at the double flicker of the television and the fireplace. I am not operating at full efficiency, but am sustained as if on a dual pilot light. Some nights I play compact disc recordings, always operas, at the same time that I watch television, and the combined sound and light gives the cottage an electric liveliness, an air of camaraderie, as if I were having a party without people.

My summer place makes for an odd winter hideout. I am reminded of the scene in *Dr. Zhivago*, the movie, in which Omar Sharif finds his dacha transformed into an ice palace. Zhivago is freezing, but one senses that the unexpected beauty of his crystallized home sustains his soul. My summerhouse is much smaller than Zhivago's, but it, too, is iced with winter whimsy and offers its own chill consolation.

Can I call it pleasure? Perhaps not, under these circumstances, but my spirit rises to the white vista, the glittering twigs, and cushioned bushes. I love the snow—have always loved it—and now I need the snow in ways I never imagined.

The snow might save me, in every sense. The snow keeps a perfect palette: I can detect if anyone has tried to approach on foot. That is a practical advantage of being snowbound, but the spiritual benefit may prove more significant. To survive now, I must recall beauty, the possibility of bliss. . . .

This house was dedicated to love, to the promise of joy. The house is not an ordinary house; Casa di Rosas was built as a chapel for a single occasion, the June wedding of a tobacco heiress in 1899. The Wedding Cake House, as it is more often called, has always depended on the triumph of charm over practicality. Only its fanciful design—and the increased market for second homes upstate—saved the structure from demolition years ago.

The Wedding Cake House stands at the edge of a bluff, overlooking the lake. The rationale for this picturesque but precarious position was the portico, where the bride and groom could pose, framed by latticework, the blue glitter of Lake Bonticou as backdrop.

From where I lie on the sofa, I can see their original wedding photograph, sepia and further faded from the century of sunlight. The Victorian bride and groom appear formal in their garb and expectation. They are young and extraordinarily attractive, but they look to one another with the solemn intention of the past, displaying none of the abandon of my own wedding photograph. My Kodachrome print fell from its hanging nail long ago and now leans against the wall below the more formal 1899 portrait. The contrast is acute: The unposed picture shows me bare-armed as I look up at my new husband; we are laughing, I remember, because the day was chillier than anticipated, and we tried to feign composure. I am wearing a sleeveless white crepe cocktail dress and trying not to visibly shiver; the camera caught us as we collapsed in laughter. The Victorian couple's decorum and our lack of propriety strike me—as if my husband and I, the interlopers, trespassed to carouse where the first bride and groom exchanged sacred vows.

Now, in late February, the light slices through the rooms. The halls appear as through a reducing glass, angles oversharp and outlined. Even the parquet floor seems heightened and whitened, as if the cold raised wax to its surface. The windows tremble and the furnace roars. Every several minutes the boiler grunts and fires. The house vibrates at the effort of keeping the wind outside these walls.

The Wedding Cake House was never intended to be used in winter, let alone converted to a home. Many years ago, the previous owners inserted a bed, dressing, and bathroom under the eaves, and the heat still travels toward the original vaulted ceiling and escapes through fissures in the attic. The upper story rooms overheat, while the downstairs living and dining area remain chilled.

One of the challenges of this winter has been to stay warm. My husband and I added, at some cost, this fireplace into which I now stare. The leaping flames provide a visual cue, but the fireplace loses more heat than it provides. There is a small radius of warmth directly in front of the crackling hearth, and I huddle toward that. I feel warm as long as I don't move, keep my shawl tucked around me, and sip my hot tea and listen to operas. I hope the arias will, in a magical aural equivalent to the beauty outside, counteract the ugliness of the events that happened here.

I have a mental habit, perhaps it qualifies as a tic, the reverse of tic douloureux, tic of sadness. My tic is the prediction of happiness, or at least pleasure. Before I actually see a person or a destination for the first time, I visualize appealing men and women, beguiling locations. I'm not conscious of projecting these people or places; they present themselves, full blown, in exact detail. En route to the actual meeting or on the phone, I conjure a face, a home, an office.

I'm not always accurate; I'm often disappointed, occasionally alarmed, when confronted with "the real thing." I have no idea why I project these visions, as they run counter to my experience. But I cannot stop, nor do I wish to. I have my successes—perfect matches of expectation and reality and a few spectacular improvements over fantasy. I believe my dreams-come-true, my good fortune, predict that I will be blessed somehow. I have always entertained the idea that, someday, someone will come forward on my behalf and offer me love, in all its most magnanimous incarnations, and I will be forever changed, blessed. It's almost happened, just that way.

Seventeen years ago, en route here for my surprise honeymoon, I "saw" Casa di Rosas in my mind's eye. I pictured a pleasant cottage, nothing fanciful. My projection was specific as usual: I saw a blanched cabin, listing blue shutters, picket fence. A single rosebush, thorny. Hummingbirds. The entire vision was blanched, as in an overexposed print.

We arrived in June. The orchard was in bloom, an aisle of cherry and apple blossoms. The white-veiled trees were bridal for us, as they had been for the original newlywed couple. We, too, walked that blossomed aisle, kissed beneath the boughs of the most bountiful tree, the weeping cherry. Matt and I admired the roses for which the house was named—"antique" roses—white, scarlet, teatime yellow. It was not that there were so many roses; it was their run of the property that charmed me. Roses climbed trellises; they poked up from behind the rusting wrought-iron gate and rambled in hedges round the house. The white roses twined and twisted through the wedding latticework on the portico, then descended the cliff, adhering to the rock ledges all the way down to the lake. These renegade white roses had escaped, domestic joining the wild, and they flourished in aromatic profusion.

I inhaled, sighed. We came to honeymoon, and remained to purchase. It was I who cried, "Oh, this is the place." The house was so inexpensive, it seemed to be a gift, sold "below market" with all "the original furnishings," including the four-poster bed upstairs and the rather sunken sofa, upon which I now recline. Even the rugs remained, faded Orientals, showing bare at the tread of my predecessors. The style, Victorian, with many griffin-clawed, ball-holding furniture feet, was not especially fine, just old. But the bureaus were filled with creamy linens monogrammed AJD, almost my maiden initials. Folded sheets, lace-trimmed shams and cases, embroidered holders for every household object—*Spoons, Buttonhooks.* I was beyond charmed; I felt enchanted.

The house met my criteria at that time—a perfect set, I thought, for romance. I could walk outside naked by moonlight and not be spotted by neighbors. The night we took possession, my husband and I dove naked from our dock into the lake. We laughed as he carried me, nude, over the threshold. Propriety was not a problem then. . . .

Now seclusion has become ironic. My desire for privacy boomeranged; no one witnessed what happened to me here. Yet, even after all that occurred, I still find solace in this place during its winter metamorphosis. The orchard bears blossoms of snow. The lake has become a Lalique; the house itself a confection. True to its conception, Casa di Rosas looks like the bakery's best wedding cake, kept fresh under refrigeration. Icicles double its Victorian frills; frost fern retrace the curtain lace.

Outdoors, the grounds are decorous as a deco lounge, draped in white, dust-covered to stay fresh for the next season. The summer wicker furniture, casualties of my distraction, remains unstored for winter, arranged in conversational circles on the white lawn. The porch swing sways, carrying its plumped white pillows, a wind-sculpted passenger. And over all is the whisper of the snow, the unending snow.

Never before has there been so much snow. The locals, the Bonticouans, as the summer people call the natives of Lake Bonticou, swear that this winter surpassed all records. The snow fell before the leaves, aborting autumn. More snow has fallen than the town plows can push; the roads have narrowed to lunar canyons.

I must be the single person here not to complain about the snow; it serves my purpose. The snow has become my buffer zone, kept my situation on literal ice. The blizzard seems to have drifted selectively: The roads may be impassable, but the wind whisked a magical passageway from my front door to the woodpile, a route along which I scurry several times a day to feed my now continuous fire. I have lost only my driveway; the snow drifted over it, obscuring even the delineation of the road that used to lead to me.

I have had an order of protection since New Year's Eve. The actual order, a smudged Xerox, I keep in an old Bendel box, labeled THE ATTACK. In my mind the order is strung round my property like a red surveyor's ribbon, looped through the gray trees, to define my new boundaries. My husband may not step within a thousand feet of me. If he does, I can summon the sheriff of Lake Bonticou. I imagine the sheriff striding from the woods, with his own order of blue knights, the state troopers.

I should know better than to entertain such visions. I already know the reality: I have dialed 911; I have summoned the police. The squad car, red light pulsing, has skidded up this driveway. I know what actually happened next. . . .

Yet, even after this experience, I am too attuned to fiction to contemplate danger without rescue. I'm infected with optimism. I have seen too many melodramas in which the heroine is saved "in the nick of time." I am conditioned now to expect cinematic salvation. I confess that I am implicated in these fictions, having performed in those movies known in the trade as "FemJep"—female in jeopardy. For sixteen years, in a dozen films, I have played the victim-heroine. The aftereffects have been insidious: Having known the comfort of male, muscled arms, I still expect, against reason, to be carried to safety and, ultimately, to be loved.

Now it worries me that I was so often cast as a victim. What is it about me that I must play the hunted, the frightened? I once asked my friend the casting director, Elsbieta, and she said, "It's your eyes: They widen so nicely in terror. And the pointy chin. . . . You look sympathetic yet vulnerable." She used a word I loathe—*plucky.* I put *plucky* right there beside *spunky,* which is my usual character description in scripts—"spunky but vulnerable." And I am light for my height: I can be carried or thrown without too much stress on the actors playing either my attackers or my saviors.

Of course, I imagined a different career. In fifth grade, we were asked to select a play and dramatize a scene for class. Other girls brought in *Peter Pan* or *Grease.* I enacted the climax of Tennessee Williams's *Suddenly, Last Summer.* I can laugh now at how I flattened myself against the blackboard and recited, in breathy tones, the murder of my beloved bisexual Sebastian: "Against the white wall," I recall saying. "Blood against the white wall." I modeled my performance on Elizabeth Taylor's in the film, American Classics Channel version. The teacher's eyes widened and her jaw dropped, but I was recommended to the drama club, and in a sense never left. Soon after I went out to audition for ingenue roles, I was cast—my first strangulation by a serial killer who preyed on schoolgirls. I recall being bent backward in a school coatroom. My legs kicking. I wore small white boots.

Once cast, my trajectory has been direct—straight to Wardrobe for the costumes that would ultimately rip, to Makeup for cosmetics that would smear, and to Special Effects for the fake blood packets, to be concealed and burst upon puncture. I have, most often, been stabbed. Thirteen stabbings, three strangulations, two drownings, one gunshot to the head, and, most inventively, a single impaling with a decorative sword. I survived all. In that sword sequence I had to do ten takes; I was "speared" for days. I cannot even count the hours I have worked on hospital sets, tucked into beds with artful bandages on my head.

Last year I began to refuse scripts in which I was threatened. Now I wonder: How much was premonition? Was it possible that deep within, in some untapped subconscious from whence all motivation springs, I had begun to question whether I wanted to play victim-heroines anymore? Had I sensed in that core of the self, where all is known, the reason?

I should have paid closer attention to the tabloid news, on which most heroines appear in the past tense. FemJep as genre is, I am discovering, criminally false. The producers themselves should be stalked and shot. I had always supposed that such films were not realistic, but the gap between truth and fiction is wider than I would have guessed, and I have taken an almost fatal fall into the abyss.

The first night under the new order, I flipped the yellow pages to *Security* and telephoned around the county, trying to hire a bodyguard, only to discover that I could not afford one. Even the decrepit, crackle-voiced self-described "seventy-five-year-old retired cop" said, "Have to charge you fifty dollars an hour. And how many hours do you need?"

I have no answer. My case could go on for years; it may never be resolved to my satisfaction. In my economic situation—my bank account emptied, unable to work—I could not be protected for a week. My assets, like my house and grounds, are frozen.

In movies, security cost is no object. In my female jeopardy roles I was accustomed to quality alarm systems and even the occasional high-tech electronically sealed half-million-dollar so-called panic room. In my actual low-budget, low-tech life, the cost of being fully "armed against intruders" is prohibitive. I must settle for sound waves that cover my "main points of entry," the downstairs front and back doors, the ground-floor windows. This arming of doorways strikes me as comical, as if my attacker would observe the etiquette of a polite form of entry.

There is also the fact that several years ago it was my husband who paid for this minimal security system; I have now changed the code and my password, *Dot* (the cat's name), but I suspect this will not be a deterrent. Even in the bygone days of "normalcy," the Be Safe system was more nuisance than reassurance: How many times have mice set off the motion detectors? I discontinued this feature; I was spending my days and nights alarmed by rodent social life.

For true safety I would have to wire every opening of Casa di Rosas and install sound and motion detectors, sensors in the ground, including, I suppose, the cliff. My daily life, given the activity of the unseen critters, would be a series of electronic screams for help and continual false alarms to the Bonticou police.

In a high-budget movie, whenever I played the victim, I was

surrounded by kindly types until the denouement. Then, by orchestrated misfortune, I would be left alone for a few tense moments with my attacker until I could be saved by the man who became my next romantic interest. The kindly cast included two types of cops—gruff older ones who became crinkle-eyed surrogate dads, and lone younger cops who had big noses or enlarged pores but were still appealing and sexually tense. The actor with the nose or the pores (sometimes he had both) would be the one to rescue me.

Also at my side I would have brisk but efficient lawyers, either a snappy skinny girl lawyer or a paternal older male lawyer with E. G. Marshall eyes. I was also surrounded by friends who put me up in million-dollar scenic hideaways, often at the risk and occasionally even the loss of their own lives. Throughout most of the movie I would sit around, worried but comforted, sipping home-brewed coffee or tea in hand-painted mugs in an attractive setting.

In recent years there has been a shift: As a film heroine, I have been forced to become less passive. It has not been enough to be rescued; I must participate and help save myself, either through ingenuity or kickboxing. In the end I may still make love with the large-nosed, big-pored, but undeniably virile man, but I also must prove that I am not helpless. The new FemJep has made an effort to be politically correct. In my last movie, *Stalked by a Strangler*, I am such a powerful, formidable would-be victim that I actually save the big-nosed, large-pored detective hired to protect me. I bandaged his wounds and kissed his chest. He saved me; then I saved him; the would-be killer was caught and the big-nosed cop and I end up in a clinch.

The discrepancies between FemJep on TV and in my actual life have been numerous. I have a hand-painted mug and I sip tea, but that's where the resemblance ends. In my current no-budget life, I am left with fire and smoke alarms and a voice activation system that blares: *"Fire! Fire! Get out of the house!"* when I burn toast.

The police have not turned out to be kindly, potential lovers. They have seemed hesitant about engaging in any rescuing at all. My "real" police officer, the one who responded, as they say, to my 911 call, was scared-looking and surprisingly short. He turned out to be short on time, also, and allotted only a half hour to resolve my situation.

On film, no one who comes to your aid is ever in a hurry to get to something else. And your saviors never kick off the relationship by demanding high fees, which actual lawyers do. My lawyer, J. J. Janis, might otherwise be castable: He has perfected a grumpy but loving grandfatherly style (against type, I had imagined him gray-bearded, plump). In reality, J. J. Janis has bright red hair draped over a bald pate, a single red eyebrow knit over the feature he always calls his "schnozz." I did predict the schnozz—I heard nasality on the phone that forecast enormity and a deviated septum. J. J. Janis would be better typed as a Borscht Belt comic, past his prime but beloved by people who enjoy comedians with a mean streak. J. J. Janis leans forward, doubled over by his suspenders, a peppermint in hand. And he always has an endearment on his thin lips ("Let me see that gorgeous *punim*" is his favorite).

J. J. Janis asked for the remains of my savings, $25,000, as a retainer before he could begin to help me. He also conceded that $25,000 was an hors d'oeuvre, the *"forshpeiz"* that would be "eaten up" pretty fast at his rate of $305 an hour. Indeed, new invoices dressed in creamy high-rag quality envelopes, of the sort I used to associate with formal invitations, have already arrived.

Now I question my wisdom in retaining J. J. Janis. Do I connect his high price to the promise of expertise? Or is it my fear of

Matt, who, though a patent lawyer, can navigate the legal maze so much better than I. Surely, I am influenced by the fact that my husband has connections and has retained a powerful trio of lawyers who seem eager to serve a colleague.

The truth, though, is that I had no time to find another lawyer. I had less than a week before Matt's arraignment, and I didn't know anyone other than the local fellow who had composed my will. So I grasped at the single connection I had: My best friend Nadine had "used" J. J. Janis and she swore he would protect me in court.

"J. J. is a shark, and he feeds on the bottom, but you will see his sweet side," she promised. "He can also do your divorce." In the rush to court to maintain the order of protection, there was no time to find another lawyer. J. J. Janis took my call; J. J. Janis was willing to take my case.

"I don't like what I'm hearing. You're in danger, dolling," he said, displaying what I critiqued as middling acting ability. "You're a nice girl. A heart knows a heart." He charged me for the call. At his going rate, plus Verizon, nighttime, off-peak.

The details fascinate me. I would never have imagined J. J. Janis's legal phone meter, which computes the charges of our tele-phone conversations at the same $305-an-hour rate, including, I suspect, my lawyer's digressions regarding his own slipped disc and a recent trip to Saint Bart.

Now I know the answer to one question: Why does the endan-gered heroine always remain in her spooky abode? For years, every time the character went down into her shadowy, moldered cellar with a defective flashlight, I mentally cried, Get out of that base-ment! Now I have the defective flashlight. I do actually go down in the stone dungeon that is the netherworld of Casa di Rosas, the near-flooded chamber where the lake washes in, bearing its tide of decay and rotted critters. I go to check. For leaks. For suspicious sounds. For intruders. I trip over paint cans and scream. No one hears me.

Why doesn't she move? Why doesn't she flee the isolated, atmospheric place where she is being stalked?

I can now also answer that question with certainty: She doesn't move because she can't.

In many of my films, my character has taken refuge in the homes of friends. My two closest friends, Nadine and Elsbieta, invited me to stay with them in New York. The two women live separate but similar existences in studio apartments. Even as they offered, I heard a weakening timbre in their voices. And who would blame them for not insisting I stay with them?

In so many of my movies, girlfriends die. The supporting actresses usually die in car wrecks staged by my would-be killer, or they are murdered, in my stead, at my on-screen residence. My actual friends have sometimes worked on films with me: Nadine, played a detective in the FemJep classic *Kiss of Death,* and Elsbieta trained me to scream without abusing my vocal chords. My presence in their studio apartments would place them in FemJep as well. I sensed their relief when I phoned down to the city and said, "I must stay up here for the court proceedings."

I could not move down to their tiny apartments in New York even if we all so chose. I have to appear in court here, in Lake Bonticou.

For the first few days after "The Attack," I did consider running away. In *Kiss of Death,* I dyed my hair blond, boarded a cross-country bus, and then lived incognito as a waitress. The killer found me anyway, but it took him a while, and then someone, a cop, killed him. In the genre movie no one mentions that if you press charges, as I have, you are also expected to appear in court. If you disappear, so does your case. No, I must stay here, near

Bonticou County Family Court. What if I lose the case? Then I must reconsider flight, hiding. But even then, where would I go?

In my films, there was always a supporting cast of relatives; not so in my life. Where is the silver-haired character actress to play my mother? My mother is dead, my father vanished. No dear, worn Dad will materialize, bearded and wearing a cardigan as cable television dads do, to offer paternal counsel. There is no ingenue with perky bangs to be a cute kid sister. I am accustomed to this, the sense of being alone. I am an orphan. Closest relative: second cousin, twice removed. The cousin's over eighty years old now, and I have not seen her in many years. She lives in a high-rise, assisted living, somewhere in Florida, where I imagine her enjoying early-bird suppers that are always flounder. Could I visit her?

No. There's no place for me but here, at Casa di Rosas, and no identity to assume but my own. I can only work as Juliana Durrell (née Dubrovsky) Smythe. Even at the best of times, my employment is sporadic—when I'm not possibly pursued. Incognito, I would fare much worse. And what of my Actors' Equity and SAG identification cards, tax bites?

So here I am, stuck in the snow, serving a life sentence as myself. I live in the limbo of adjournments: I have gone to court, only to hear that my case is yet again postponed. My estranged has been arraigned but remains free, doing his own time, I suppose, in our former primary marital residence in the city. He commutes to family court. When the weather is bad, which is often, he takes a room at the largest hotel in town, a double-gabled affair named the John Adams, after a signer of the Bill of Rights.

I can almost smile; that is exactly the sort of hotel Matt likes—polished mahogany tester bed, brass eagles, framed historic documents, and portraits of unidentified forebears. I imagine him pick-

ing up credibility from John Adams, himself, the specter of justice.
I overheard Matt say in court, "I'm at the John Adams," and the way
he said it, you would think *he* was John Adams. He has hired not one
but two Park Avenue lawyers and one local lawyer to defend him.
He has an imported city law firm and a local former DA who is a
member of a legal team known for fierce radio commercials—
"Family Law? Disability? Come to Regan, Roach and MacPherson."

J. J. Janis and the counselors at Bonticou County Family Court
convinced me that my case should be tried here, in family court.
While my husband's actions were criminal, there is not enough
apparent injury for a criminal charge to stick. I've been advised to
keep my case in family court, which will protect me on the basis of
the evidence that I have in my possession. I must maintain the
order of protection at all costs, I am told. It cuts the odds that I
will be killed. I see the order as ephemeral, like the sound waves
that frame my front door and ground-floor windows. Both systems
require the attacker to respect certain boundaries. The assumption
is that my husband is maddened, yet in enough control to follow
the rules of engagement.

"Can't they put him in jail?" I asked J. J. Janis.

"Don't kid yourself," J. J. Janis replied. "That would be nice,
but good-looking well-to-do white men in three-piece suits with
law degrees don't go behind bars so easily. You were lucky to get
an order of protection. You'll be luckier still to hang on to it. If his
lawyers are as good as they claim to be, they will pull every trick
out of the hat. If he can control his violent impulses for a while, he
might just walk."

But what about my injuries? Don't they count? J. J. Janis
answered in his one-two, case A, case B style, peppered with
endearments, salted with cynicism: "(a) *Bubeleh,* they were not
severe enough. Dolling, a woman needs a hatchet in her head

to establish injury serious enough to put a man in jail right away. . . . (b) He's innocent until proven guilty, remember. He is free. Let's hope he's just *mishugunah,* not berserk."

In the deco dark of my bedroom, whilst the neon clock fixes to the witching hour of three A.M., I wonder: How crazed is Matt? Crazed enough to drive two hundred miles up here in a snowstorm to finish me off? Or is his insanity an impulse in the midst of argument? The question that keeps my heart beating in time with the clock: Does Matt know his own behavior? Or does he edit his memory? Does he have an amnesiac reaction after his violence? He does wear those suits; he proceeds in a "proper" mien. I think he believes himself. My tenuous hunch is that he will not break in here and attack me now, just before we go to court: It would ruin his case. Then, again, he might.

I would not have predicted his behavior on the final night of our marriage, so I cannot speak of him now with any certainty.

My estranged husband is not an easy villain, an outlaw escapee. He is the person I trusted for seventeen years, whose chest was my pillow and with whom I shared a thousand confidences, all irrelevant in less than a minute on New Year's Eve.

FemJep has one detail down right: the fear. On my first night alone here at Casa di Rosas, I shoved a plank bench against the front door, barring it from the inside. The bench could not have stopped him from entering, but it would have alerted me on the off chance that I lay deep asleep. For the first several days, true sleep eluded me: I went under only for moments, in too-deep dives, as if lowered on a faulty cable. Then I'd be yanked up again in jerking rises, from one level of consciousness to the next, until I lurched to the surface of remembrance, there to stare the blackness in the eye and recall why I had stiffened into sleep on the sofa, still in my shoes and socks.

The memory comes back as a physical symptom, running too fast in my blood. Initially the rush was hydraulic, but another lesson learned in the past weeks is that one can become accustomed to anything, even terror. I can sleep a bit more now, and wake with only a low-grade quiver. Last week I shoved the bench back where it belonged; it would only have prolonged what I dread most: the suspense.

I don't want to lie here, listening for his steps upon the stair. I know how fast he can run up them, and what his steps sound like in that charge that doesn't end at the bedroom door but bursts through it, breaking the latch. I have replaced the latch he broke that night, but I already have proof of its laughable weakness against the weight of a six-foot-tall man going full tilt against the door. It isn't even a question of a better latch; the doorjamb itself splintered against the force.

I've taken two precautions: I carry a cell phone; I have the sheriff's office on speed dial. Of course the cell phone works only intermittently in these mountains; we, the summer people, fought the construction of the cell tower that might have given me a clear channel. I don't regret that: I value my view, the beauty of the undisturbed mountain lake vista, more than I do the convenience of the phone communication. In my business, there is too much telephone, too much computer mail—the cacophony I chose to escape when I found this place.

I do what I can to feel safer. On my first trip into town, I bought a narrow can of pepper spray, formerly illegal in New York but now available on the counter of the drugstore where I buy blush-on. Since then, every night I set the pepper-spray can on my bedside table. Each night that passes without my need to use it makes me feel a bit more foolish. But I do not consider throwing it away.

Friends call from the city and ask, "How do you stand the isolation?" when my secret answer is "How can I maintain it?"
Isolation in the country is another myth. Once the heaviest snow is
cleared, blizzard opportunists appear: a ham-faced man who
wanted two hundred dollars to shovel the snow cone off my roof.
Repairmen in heavy-wheeled trucks fitted with plows have rum-
bled up the driveway, bearing torches to thaw the metal gut of
Casa di Rosas. Oil tankers have rolled uphill as far as they could
reach, extending themselves with hoses to nurse the thirsting
boiler. Even Jehovah's Witnesses trekked in, pushing God. The
Witnesses left a comic book depicting a colorful and unintention-
ally inviting vision of some tropical Sodom and Gomorrah, complete with belly dancers and bunched grapes.

It took two more blizzards and a road closing to secure the
peace I have enjoyed for the past two days and to truly bring the
repairman motorcade to a halt. Even my cleaning "person" canceled.

"I will do a lot of things," she said on the phone, "but I won't
drive in snow, no, no." The housecleaner, Moira, is a young
woman, a just-past-teenager with a safety-pin—pierced eyebrow.
She has the Bonticou love-fear of disaster. I will not see her small
figure, in her uniform of gray sweats and a flannel overshirt, "till
the roads is clear." No, no. Every Wednesday, by habit, I look for
her truck, a high black monster of an automotive creature with
flames painted on its flanks, but she has not pulled into the drive.
No, no. Moira remains wherever it is she lives, in her new double-
wide, at the location she invariably describes as "on the other side
of the mountain."

"I can't go over the mountain," she says. "No, no, not till the
roads is clear."

While the snow settles outside Casa di Rosas, the dust bunnies collect inside. I can write my name on the dresser top as well as etch my initials on the frost. For the past forty-eight hours within my increasingly opaque world, I have been truly alone, with Puccini and an RCA color television. Until yesterday, only a few animals, stressed by the snowstorm, invaded my white-upon-white space.

The skunk arrived first. I watched from my upstairs window as he trudged in a straight line toward my front door. I could see the skunk, a detail in black and white, as he moved through snow higher than his body. When he reached my porch, I ran downstairs to get a better look.

I'd never seen a skunk up close before. While his body was plump and his tail fluffed to Disney specifications, his face crimped into pink irritation, a near-genital look. I tossed him some high-priced granola, which he gobbled without giving me so much as a glance. Then he resumed his trek, cutting straight across the frosted lake. He seemed like a skunk with a destination.

The wild turkeys appeared next, lining up in single file, using the south side of the house as a windbreak. In the past I'd found wild turkeys exotic, but now that they've been hanging around as humped shadows, I view them more as vultures. I know too well their turkey toilette—how they tuck their nude necks under their wings, stand on a single, scaled foot, and fire off turkey pellets that burn green-brown holes in the snow. Seeing the turkeys so numerous, so blasé, I have come to regard them as mundane, no longer members of a precious, endangered species.

I had almost begun to regard myself as safe as well. Then today that changed. The day began with more of the same: an opaque sky, a wind-driven snow. The snow flew in stinging horizontal lines, infiltrating the house and drifting onto the interior windowsills. I was standing inside my living room, scooping snow from the sill with a soup spoon, when I heard a car.

I could see a gray station wagon struggle up what used to be defined as my driveway. The car began a diagonal, backward skid; then, tires spinning, it landed with its rear end in the snowbank. The engine stopped. A man in hooded parka, carrying a gray molded suitcase, emerged from the driver's side. Then, bent against the needling wind, he walked straight and slow, as had the skunk, directly to my front door.

Inside, by the heat and crackle of the fire, I'd been enjoying a simulcast of "La Donna é Mobile" and *Inside Edition.* As Pavarotti hit his high C, I could also hear the television host explain why some men, previously pleasant and even distinguished, could without warning bludgeon or hack their wives to death. He attributed the personality change to " 'roid rage," anger induced by the misuse of steroids. The men bulked up mentally as well as physically; a riptide of hormone swelled their enraged brains. In the ensuing red-out, even nice men could kill.

The "sufferers" of 'roid rage had already been introduced: men thick of neck and narrow of gaze. I could hear them speaking in what struck me as deliberately humble mumbles of their past aggression. Outside, the hooded man reached my door and pounded on it, thudding the brass knocker. I could see him through the curtain lace: a stranger of linebacker proportions. I hesitate, my hand on the chain guard. Should I let him in?

"*Supralux!*" he screams.

Supralux?

"*Supralux!*" he screams again. "We have an appointment, Mrs. D. It's me. Chick."

That clicks. The series of phone messages left on my machine, all addressing me as "Mrs. D." from "Chick Savago"—reminders to service my Supralux 799 vacuum cleaner.

"It's me," he says. "Chick. Chick Savago. I come all the way from Schoharie today."

I stand still, my hand on the chain lock.

"You got my card confirming, didn't you, Mrs. D.?"

I look down at the mail table beside the door. There it is—a service reminder card from Supralux with the time 4:25 P.M. and today's date.

I stare down at myself: I'm dragging my shawl and not truly dressed. I jam my flannel nightgown into the waist of my slacks and open the door to admit Chick Savago to my home.

"No one has been able to get here in two days," I say. "I'm amazed."

"Now you're dealing with me, Chick Savago. Who did you have before—Phil Kneff?" He makes a sound, not unvacuumlike, through both nostrils when I nod yes, it had been Phil Kneff.

Stamping the snow from his boots, Chick Savago shakes himself like a great dog. "Phil likes to sell 'em, but he doesn't like to service 'em." Chick Savago almost fills my foyer. He's football player material all right; he doesn't even diminish when he pulls off the parka and reveals a surprising suit of synthetic green-gray fiber. Without his hood, he turns out to have a polished bald head, not unlike my lawyer's, but Chick Savago's head is set lower on his shoulders, the neck stove in between the blades. For all the power of his physique, he has a baby face, full-cheeked, with a wet under-lip that droops even as he smiles. His eyes are round, blue, and speckled like marbles. He seems hearty and harmless, an innocent emissary from the world where appliance maintenance still matters.

I mentally audition him as a potential bodyguard. As if reading

my mind, Chick Savago instantly offers to perform more than vacuum service. "Hey, Mrs. D., can I shovel your driveway for you?"

I don't say no. "Maybe on your way out. Will you need to call
for a tow for your car?"

"Aw, I'll deal with that after I've taken care of your machine,
Mrs. D." He accepts the cup of coffee I offer and pronounces it "the
best I ever tasted, delicio-*so*." Then I lead him to the Supralux 799,
which squats, hydra-headed, hoses coiled, in the dark corner of my
hall closet. I have long regretted the purchase of the Supralux 799;
it's as heavy and hideous as it was overpriced—a budget-busting
seven hundred dollars. Its cannister looks like an underwater mis-
sile; it has a tendency to overheat and misfire, exploding snakelike
plumes of compressed filth into just-vacuumed rooms.

I'd been talked into the Supralux ("more than a vacuum—a
supercleaning system") by the Lake Bonticou cleaning woman.
The housecleaner refused to use my old upright and insisted that
she needed "to get in the edges and cracks." I have to admit to
Chick Savago that I am almost ignorant of the Supralux's many
functions. I confess that I am not the one who vacuums here—that
my housecleaner, Moira, uses the machine.

"Maybe you should come back when she's here," I suggest.

For a moment I conjure Moira as if I can will her to appear in
the kitchen to deal with Chick Savago. I could just see her as she
always appears, a small girl dressed in those gray sweatpants
with the plaid flannel shirttails out. I associate her presence
with the near-shuffle of her sneakered feet as she drags the
Supralux from room to room. She's young, hardly more than a
kid herself, but she has kids and she knows how to be firm: She
could handle Chick Savago and be sure that he doesn't over-
charge or otherwise cheat, running up a bill for unnecessary
repair.

"You got to watch 'em," Moira is always saying of any repairman who enters Casa di Rosas. "You got to watch 'em."

"Your machine needs servicing now," Chick Savago says. "And
who knows when anyone else will risk coming back in here? When
was she last here? Did she put on this filter?" There's domestic
accusation in his tone; for some reason I am willing to corroborate.

"If a filter was changed, Moira was the one who did it," I say.

When had Moira last appeared? No one has cleaned since The
Attack. She has not been in since the end of my marriage. I lost
track of her missed Wednesdays; a check, scribbled with her full
name, Moira Gonzalez Gerhardt, still rests on the mantel. (Despite
the surnames Gonzalez and Gerhardt, she is not Hispanic or
German but descended, like most people in Bonticou, from the
French Huguenots. On her first day Moira relayed her complicated
heritage: She was "old Bonticou," but one stepmother had "married out"—Gonzalez—and she herself had wed a young man from
"the German side of the Lake"—Gerhardt. The check is for
$120—above-average pay for housecleaning in Bonticou. I tend to
overpay out of female guilt regarding the cleaning itself and in
sympathy for the woman, who bore twins at eighteen and seems as
if she could use the money. The check remains unclaimed since the
snows started. On our "normal" winter schedule I might not see
Moira: She comes and goes on a prearranged pattern, weather and
her own life permitting.

"Car's in the shop," she might say on the phone message
machine. Or: "I got a doctor's appointment." Or: "The kids are
sick," or "I'm not coming in; it's going to storm."

In Bonticou Gothic tradition, Moira is fond of reciting disasters, her favorite being that of the woman who drove off the road
into a pond, sank through the ice, and was not retrieved until
spring: "They found her with her soup cans and soda bottles and

everything." No, no, Moira would not risk a skid on ice and snow.

In her absence my marriage exploded and dust gathered in the corners and under the bed. Even under ideal circumstances I am a stranger to the Supralux: In this crisis I have no interest in heaving around the heavy vacuum; I do not understand its attachments. I have made a few attempts to scoop up the actual dust, feathery clouds that were hard to capture by hand. Half the time the fluff floated back into the atmosphere of Casa di Rosas.

"I never touch the big vacuum," I tell Chick Savago.

Chick Savago examines the big Supralux. "Somebody put the bag in wrong," he says. "If it don't fit good and tight, she can't suck."

Oh, how I wish that Moira could materialize here to deal with him. She would relish this conversation; she would know how to rebut, defend, demand. She's an expert on the vacuum; I doubt that she has, in fact, committed any errors in Supralux maintenance.

Moira herself is an erratic cleaner, but she loves to vacuum. I seldom watch her clean, but I can always hear her. I associate her with the Supralux, a mechanical adjunct to her own body, the sound of her presence in my home.

Yes, Moira would know just what to say to Chick Savago, while all I can do is feign interest and hope the thing works. He is insistent that I observe him. "Watch this, Mrs. D. You see how the hose screws in here?"

As Chick Savago bends close to me to examine the Supralux, I experience something strange: I have a split-second image of him subduing other men. I try not to believe in the occult, disbelieving even what so many in my profession embrace daily—astrological forecasts. But once or twice in my life, I have been given a flash of information regarding a person in close proximity. I do not know how to explain this transmission, but within a second Chick Savago confirms the veracity of my image:

"I'm not really a Supralux man: I'm not full-time. I work as a guard at the prison."

I picture the prison, a rather pleasant-appearing geometric castle that sits squarely a few miles to the west. I know prisons are a major industry here in Bonticou County, employing almost as many men as are imprisoned. The local men seem to be in and out of prison, one way or another.

Chick Savago drops to a squat and opens his molded suitcase. He takes out a plastic cone and attaches it to the suction hose of the Supralux. "Let's see how she picks up." He places four silver balls on the floor. "She should suck four balls. Look. She's barely sucking two."

I try to look attentive. "Can you fix it?"

Ordinarily, Chick says it would have to go "into the shop." But under the circumstances he might be able to "clean the soot from her head" right here in my living room.

What choice do I have? I walk to the counter of the open kitchen. I'm too self-conscious to flop back onto the sofa and stare at the TV and the fire. Personal torpor requires privacy. For Chick Savago's benefit, I turn the volume down on Luciano Pavarotti and click off the news special just as the " 'roid rage" men's wives are murmuring in electronically altered voices of the sweetness of their mates' initial personalities. I take some bread dough I keep stored in the refrigerator and slap it onto the butcher-block countertop and, with feigned energy, begin to knead.

"Oh, Mrs. D., you bake your own bread. I knew it, Mrs. D. I could tell over the phone."

How? I think, but say nothing, and continue my slap-slapping of the cold dough—which, according to my cookbook, should feel as cool and damp as the flesh of a corpse when fully kneaded and ready to rise. For a few minutes we work in silence, side by side: Chick kneeling, cleaning the Supralux; me kneading the bread; Pavarotti swelling to his impassioned finale. There is something domestic in our parallel endeavors—a man and woman working together in a snow-covered house. Custodial Adam with Eve in an arctic Eden.

He probes under the sofa with the vacuum extension. "She isn't sucking; she's coughing it back. Look at this. . . ."

Chick Savago points to the twin husks of two mummified mice whose light corpses have been drawn from below my sofa. These mouse mummies are so desiccated, they do not seem to require burial. Chick moves around the butcher block, close to me, and tosses the two flattened mice into the trash.

"How old are you, Mrs. D.?" I don't answer, and he makes a laughably low estimate. In lieu of speaking, I snort and move away, rattling bake pans.

It's not unusual; it's maybe even common for some element of flirtatiousness or sexual tension to enter the house with a lone repairman. I had experienced remarks and attitudes from a window washer, who smirked as he used his squeegee and offered, "I do backs too." But the border—the line of etiquette that governs such situations—was never crossed as it is when Chick Savago continues and says, "Your husband's a lucky man. You're my ideal woman. Maybe he doesn't appreciate you. A marriage's no good unless the man and the woman make it together."

I can feel the electric pulse of the house in the silence that follows. I have nowhere to go except outside in the snow or upstairs to my bedroom; either choice seems a mistake. I inhale and say, "I don't think that's an appropriate remark."

He can't agree with me more.

"Oh, God, I'm so sorry, Mrs. D." His marbleized blue eyes bulge in contriteness. "I was just complimenting you, saying your husband is a lucky man."

"He'll be home soon," I say in what I hope is a convincing tone, without the built-in irony.

"Maybe he's stuck in the snow somewhere," Chick Savago says with a slow smile.

"Look," I say, "I don't really care about fixing the vacuum today."

His eyes widen as if I had uttered sacrilege.

"It's a bad day to be on the road. I don't want you to be stranded here." I don't add but mentally complete: . . . *and have to spend the night.*

"I'll do what I came out here to do. Chick Savago never leaves without satisfying the customer."

I do not have a clue as to what to do. I look out the window at the gray shape of his wagon; already a pillow of new snow tops the roof.

"Let's call for a tow," I suggest, moving to the phone.

As I pick up the telephone receiver I'm not surprised to hear only static on the other end. It's that kind of day. The static seems the aural equivalent of the gray, horizontal snow outside the window. Knowing it will be futile, I pick up the cell phone. An even more graveled sound, as if the storm is in the system itself. As I stare out the window, the grayness thickens into night.

Chick Savago snaps the Supralux back together and is vacuuming the living room. "Sure wish you'd told me about these stains, Mrs. D.," he says in a neutral tone. "I would have brought along some stain removers. There's no stain I can't get out, even blood."

"It's fine. The stains don't bother me."

"Look how she sucks now, Mrs. D." He demonstrates: The corner of the rug appears to levitate, inhaled by the machine.

"Wonderful," I say. "Thanks so much. I'll give you a check."

"That's not necessary yet, Mrs. D. I want to do your upstairs. I want to vacuum your bedding."

"My bedding?"

"We all lose skin every night, Mrs. D. I say this not to disparage you, Mrs. D., because I am sure you have excellent sanitary habits. But we are all covered with nematodes; our skin dies and is crawling with microscopic organisms that live and feed on our dead scales. That is why it is important to vacuum your bedding at least once a night. Let me do your mattress. You will be amazed at what I pull out of there."

"No . . . really. Maybe next time."

"You know, Mrs. D., I don't want you to think that I am trying to sell you a new machine. But next year the 799 will be obsolete. We are going to a new system: HydroBag. All your dirt and effluvia will be sucked into a water sack. It becomes a sludge, Mrs. D.," he says. "A sludge that you can pour down your toilet and your home is purified."

It strikes me that he is uncomfortably clean-looking and that he is not bald; his head is shaved. Despite having been out all day in the snow, there does not seem to be a smudge or crease on Chick Savago's clothing or skin. His face has the pink shine of a new scar.

"My husband," I stress, "will be home any minute." I gesture to the door. "There is a shed right outside, with shovels and sand. Why don't you see if you can dig out of that drift?"

Chick Savago stares at me and says, "They come at me with sharpened spoons, Mrs. D. One tried to gouge my eyeball this morning. I had to subdue him, Mrs. D." He demonstrates, bringing his forearm across his own throat in a chokehold.

My low-grade quiver rises to the surface of my skin, and again I feel that racing sensation in my blood.

"I could help you dig out your car," I volunteer.

"I wouldn't hear of it, Mrs. D. I'll give it a try when it's time for me to go."

I want to say, "Do it now," but something stops me. The room has taken on the hyperreal appearance of a place where a crisis is occurring but in which, so far, the only action is internal. My blood runs but I stand still, my hands on the cold bread dough. I stare at the culinary clutter at my counter—the copper pots, the braided chili peppers, ropes of garlic. Oh, to be inanimate at such moments. To be safe as an object.

During the final confrontation with my husband, I looked to the jumble on my bedroom dresser—a collection of perfume bottles, lipsticks, hand creams—and mentally addressed them: "So this is it. This is how it ends."

Now I set the dough in the bread tins, drape them with dishcloths. The next hour passes in stop-and-start conversation, with the enforced intimacy of interruptions to go to the bathroom. I feel an acceleration that makes me nearly dizzy as Chick Savago's accounts of his life move further and further from what is deemed acceptable. He tells me that he is divorcing his own wife, whom he suspects is unfaithful. He can tell by the smell of their sheets.

"Women got to provoke the man," he says. "They have to wave the red flag in his eyes." As punctuation, he interjects compliments to me: "You would never do that. You're nice."

The bread rises, swelling under the dishcloths. The aroma of yeast sweetens the air, mingles with the arias and Chick Savago's discordant song of himself. Although he is not drinking liquor, his voice begins to slur, as if a residual alcoholism, associated with these revelations from his past, can still produce symptoms. He doesn't seem to expect a reply but looks to me for reassurance that he is on track:

"You know what I mean? You know what I mean?"

I nod, although I don't know, I don't know anything except that I am becoming very uneasy. He seems more intoxicated by his tale and leans across the counter, listing toward me, breathing hot dissatisfaction in my face:

"People won't let me be nice."

The entire time he is speaking, I am thinking: *Should I run upstairs? Or will that be the trigger?* When he leans toward me, I inch back.

"They push you and push you," he says, "so they can laugh at you when you lose control, and ha-ha, you're reduced to this animal, smashing them in the face. That's what they want. . . ."

At that, I become too frightened to remain in the room, so I move off my chair and walk backward, slowly, toward the stair that leads to my bedroom.

"I'm going upstairs now," I say. "I hope your situation works out for you."

There is a subtlety to a stalk. During the next hour, I lie attuned to nuance—the sound of his breathing downstairs, his step on the stair, the creak of a door, the flush of a toilet. It seems to me that I can hear him think; it's like the electric pulse in the walls, the tick-tock of my mantelpiece clock.

There is a sexual sixth sense, also: I recall it from being sixteen and at the movies or in the backseats of cars: My girlfriends and I could perceive even the most minute motions of aroused males in our vicinity; no gesture was too tentative, no intake of breath too restrained. We knew who was touching himself or trying to graze our thighs "on purpose," no matter how surreptitious the movement. Ions seemed to rise in the charged air. My best friend said she could tell from several feet away, under cover of darkness, when a man ejaculated: She claimed she sniffed ozone in the air.

I could swear that Chick Savago makes not one but three trips to my bedroom door, hesitates there, then descends. I am sure, too, that some sort of sexual release occurs at some point during these tiptoed ascents and descents. A clichéd prickle raises the fine hairs at the back of my neck. I pick up the slim can of pepper spray and hold it, prepared to blast his marbleized blue eyes if he bursts into my room. But he does not try to enter—although once, it seems to me, the doorknob trembled, as if he were testing it from the other side.

I sit and hold the spray can and stare at the stacks of memorabilia that now mount in evidence as the debris of my personal life. For all around me, in hastily marked cartons, are the documents requested by my lawyer: the Bendel box labeled THE ATTACK and the files that contain the history of my long marriage. In a carton on which I'd scrawled *Evidence* I have the single piece, what I call "The Thing in the Box," that I know will prove my case in court. On top of that, in a file folder, is " 'The Synopsis of My Marriage' by Juliana Dubrovsky Smythe."

My lawyer demanded that I assemble this synopsis. The synopsis covers my life from the age of eighteen, when I first met my husband, until New Year's Eve, when we parted so definitively. The evidence seems lopsided, for the letters document a happy marriage rather than a doomed, violent one; I do have The Thing in the Box, but even that will have to be explained in court when the time comes. It's harder to dismiss the correspondence—a hundred love notes for every single scrawled apology: "Sorry for the psychodrama last night. I don't know what got into me."

My husband doesn't know (or at least he claims ignorance) and I don't know "what got into him." I know only that he had sudden mood changes, but until The Attack these events seemed more peculiar than threatening. His anger exploded at unlikely moments: I could never predict what might upset him.

One afternoon last July, I had gathered a bouquet of the roses for which Casa di Rosas was named, and instead of being pleased, he screamed: The roses were in a pitcher meant for drinking water, not a vase. Before I could speak, he smashed the pitcher, and it lay in shards at my feet.

My estranged husband's rage revolved around minute matters of housekeeping or personal propriety. With hindsight, as I try to understand what happened, I remember more odd moments. Last August, as I smoothed suntan lotion on his shoulders at the public beach, he hissed: "Not here—people will see you."

I could not comprehend: Why would this trouble him? We were married, and even if we weren't, what was wrong with my touching his back and neck in public? The series of inexplicable piques soon grew into a full-blown permanent rage. By winter I was dialing psychiatrists and therapists in two counties. It didn't matter: Matt would see no one.

"They're all charlatans," he said.

I accompanied him, over his protest, to a woman psychiatrist's office in uptown Bonticou, and he disliked her sandals: "How can you expect me to listen to a woman who wears sandals like that?" They were homely, heavy-strapped, studded with nails. Whatever her footwear, I wish we had stayed for the full hour. Maybe I would not be sitting here now, holding a pepper-spray can.

Is Chick Savago dangerous? Or am I spooked by the finale of my marriage?

On Christmas Day, I found my favorite hat outside, sitting on the trash. It had been more than a hat; it was an insignia of myself—an old black velvet hat with a brim. I had not only loved it, I had been loved while wearing it: My husband was forever tipping that brim back, teasing me, kissing me—"You and your old hat." It was a sweet joke between us, and when I saw the hat on the garbage pile, I knew he didn't love me anymore, and I shivered: With so much love gone, what could fill that void but hate?

I had never known what it was to be hated, but I found out. From that day until the end, only one week later, I felt his hate every second that we were together. If I spoke, he frowned; if I was silent, he screamed.

Now, sitting alone on the bed that we shared for so many years, surrounded by stacks of our letters, I suffer a reprise of my last night of marriage. Once again I sit behind the latched door, waiting for a man to break in. I stare at the splintered doorjamb, my laughable latch.

I cannot help but relive The Attack, see the latch and doorjamb shatter, remember my husband's forced entrance into this room. I was holding the phone, dialing 911. He ripped the phone from my hand and smashed it to the wall with such force that its innards had spilled multicolored electrical entrails. The disemboweled phone lay on the floor. He seized me by the shoulders, screaming. What had he said? "I love you, I loved you from the minute I saw you. . . ." But all I saw was the blood spouting from his left nostril—not from an injury but, I suppose, from pressure. And all I could feel were his hands on my arms. . . .

I shut my eyes, listening now for Chick Savago. Can I foil him as I had my husband? On New Year's Eve, I fled, knowing the 911 call had registered; I heard the operator pick up. She would automatically trace me: I know that much about 911. I fled this house, knowing the police would be arriving. If they drove fast enough, over the ice, around the curves of Serpentine Road, they could save me. If I could just evade him, long enough . . .

The snow had been high that day too.

The police had a lot of calls, but they dispatched a car, a single patrolman. I remember him, Officer Little. The name fit: He had been . . . little. Hippy in a holster, a tiny man; he intercepted me, almost too late.

I shut my eyes. I do not dare remember what Matt did to me now. I will have to recite the details soon enough, in court—if I survive this night and get to court. *Here I am,* I cannot help thinking, *with another man in this house.* I am sitting on the same bed, by the same ruffled sham, staring at the same roses on the faded wall, feeling my heart hammering, my palms sweating. Hair really rises on the nape of the neck; I note. I have the objectivity to note my objectivity: Why must I always observe? Is the actor in me learning more nuances? Am I not already overrehearsed for terror?

"No one turns their back on me!" Matt screamed. *"No one walks away from me!"*

Now I am "the complainant" and my estranged husband "the defendant," which reverses the roles of our final days. Yet, what good is my defense of myself? I still sit shivering on the other side of my bedroom door. Have I stopped being afraid of one man to become afraid of another?

No. I have not come through this strange season for this finale. I look to the window and see that the snow is lessening. As I prepare my next move I hear, once again, Chick Savago's light tread on my stair. I can almost feel him breathe—he is here, on the other side of the bedroom door—and as the clock on my mantel chimes he speaks my name.

Nothing more. But not "Mrs. D." My actual first name. And the sound of it trips off my last alarm, and I say: "It's time for you to go now. The snow has let up."

"Aren't you going to open the door?" he asks.

I clench the spray, aim it. "No."

He waits there, on the landing, for what seems like minutes. Then I hear him descend, this time with what I consider normal, heavy footfalls. A few minutes later I hear his car engine start. Then, most blessed of all sounds under the circumstances, the sustained roar of the motor as he navigates down my driveway in reverse.

I wait an hour to feel certain that he is, indeed, gone. The snow does stop, as if by the necessity of my need. The moon rises. I look out the window and see by a wild cobalt light, the now deserted driveway. I detect something moving behind the evergreen trees. Then I realize: It is a deer. I can't see the head or body, only the ankles and hooves as they pass, dainty as a dancer's, beneath the skirt of the hemlock tree.

Downstairs, the main room is freezing. I reach, out of habit, for my shawl, which I'd left draped on the sofa. I stop in mid-motion as I feel the dampened mohair—viscous and filled with what I suppose is Chick Savago's effluvia and intent. I pick up the shawl, avoiding the wet spot—evidence too troubling to even consider, let alone save—and ditch the whole package into a trash bag.

I reach for the phone. The line is still dead. I'll call the police when power is restored, I decide. I don't look forward to another chat with Sheriff LaBute. Even I cringe from reciting the details— the repairman, the dampened shawl, the fact that he moonlights as a prison guard. No crime has occurred, has it? Will this distract the police from my main case? Will I be dismissed as a woman prone to suspicion? Cast doubt on my credibility? But shouldn't someone know?

I walk outside Casa di Rosas, the snow crunching under my boots. I sling the trash bag into a garbage can and shut the lid. From somewhere not so far away, a siren sounds, a volunteer firemen call to the scene of yet another car accident or woodstove blaze. The siren alerts the wild animals in my woods; the coyotes yelp and howl, adding their indignation to the chorus of emergency. The deer that I glimpsed before appears from behind the hemlock tree, and I gasp: It's not the dainty doe I imagined but that rarely sighted creature, a buck. There are so many hunters in Bonticou, the bucks are usually shot, shot young. I myself have never seen a buck until now.

The stag seems massive, twice the size of a doe, and he wears a rack of antlers with—I count—nine points. I study him and see that a tenth point has been broken off at the base. His gaze is irregular also: He stares at me through a single brown liquid eye; the other eye appears opaque. The stag has a cataract, one whitened orb, the right, which adds intensity to his left eye as he seems to study me in return and offer some insight.

I imagine he is an old stag, an expert in survival in these woods. Is he my single witness to this night? I note the vapor from his nostrils, his expression of animal sanity. Then he bolts, raising high his white tail as he leaps back into the grove of evergreen.

I stand there, trying to pick up a sense of the nearest human presence. A black cloud scuttles across the face of this night's moon. The truth is that no matter how far you go, you are never so far from what we call civilization. I look off to the east and can see the insomniac glow of the state thruway, and if I concentrate I can hear its distant diesel thunder. I stand there for a long time, until the snow begins again to fall, this time straight down, in lacy flakes. I think of the other lives that have passed through this place, from the first bride to myself.

The snow continues to fall, and gradually even the far-off light and traffic sounds are absorbed by it. Soon the snow fills in the tread where Chick Savago's station wagon stood. The snow covers the footsteps, first his, then mine, leading back to the house.

Within an hour the snow has feathered and filled every declivity and erased all trace of our crisscrossed encounters. The new blizzard blows in undulant veils, obscuring the winterscape.

Upstairs, I fall prone upon the eiderdown duvet, sink into its billowing warmth. It is safe now, I think, safe to dive down under and succumb to the whiteout of sleep.

Glace Noire

L ast night I dreamed of rescue. It is the same dream every time. I am falling from a great height. I see the ground below. It is as if I am hurtling toward a bull's-eye. Surely, I will be killed on impact. But just before I would smash to the ground, I am caught—*swept up,* as if by Superman himself. I am saved. An instant before certain death, in that damned "nick of time."

This morning I woke clutching the pillow. In the predawn dark I was sorry to see that I had arranged three pillows alongside me, to mimic a human form. Not any human form, but Matt's, my husband's. I have sworn to remember this: I must not forgive him, must not let him return, no matter what he says, no matter how persuasive. I must remember what happened, not revise or edit my recollection so that détente is once again possible.

You would think that the memory of violence would be vivid, that you could never forget. But in fact painful recollection is the most transitory, because you will it away; you do not want to retain the information because it is information that will force you to reinvent your life. Maybe this is similar to the pain of childbirth, which they claim women forget in order to have more children: "Oh, once you hold that baby, you can't remember any-thing but joy." So many women have told me that, and I always felt an ache at their words. Did I worry all along that I would not conceive in my marriage? How much truth did I hide from myself? My recall is better for love, for my husband's embrace, the animal safety of the long-term marriage bed. Even now I must concentrate not to forget the details, not to expunge the record of a marriage that I admit gave me, until now, more solace than pain.

Perhaps the agony of what they refer to as "spousal abuse" in Bonticou County Family Court can be forgotten, to allow a woman like myself to remain in her marriage, to permit the formerly smooth surface of her "beautiful life" to proceed as if nothing has happened. Amnesia serves this purpose; it's convenient in my situation. I am almost certain Matt can erase his behavior in his own mind. Can I do the same? I suspect myself of obliterating details from my distant past: What have I forgotten? Has this happened before? What was the first sign? Was there some warning? When did he first flash that strange rage?

How many marriages proceed, after incidents? "Oh, what was that—some aberrant impulse, a night to forget? Everyone goes crazy once in a while." I know these incidents occur to other women, in other marriages, but they are covered over, forgotten, pushed away: "It won't happen again." Or will it?

In the court I have heard other cases dismissed, the charges dropped. At the family court, so many of these wives have babies; I see the women cradling them as they come and go. After dropping charges, the reconciled couples leave court. I have noted that the women have a curious, grim smile: The husbands are courteous, chastened, sometimes with a foolish smile, as if to say, "What was that about? It's all silly, isn't it?" They transfer the baby to the car seats with special care, open the car doors for their wives with belated chivalry. It is the etiquette of postabuse. I shiver: *No*.

Now, almost two months after The Attack, I have dreamed of rescue and know without seeing who my faceless savior is. Oh, it's dangerous, a sweet anesthetic, something similar to what I imagine a nitrogen-chilled injection to be, just a bit too much painkiller. This hope, this doubt of reason: Can I be wrong? Is his behavior still somehow within limits? I have heard couples laugh after fights: "Oh, we almost killed each other." "She throws a mean right."

I must not relent; I must not drop charges. Maybe other couples can fight physically; maybe their wars are farcical. What I remember does not qualify as "a fight." There is something too dangerous in my recollection; I must guard it, as a diamond, the hard truth that will cut me free. I must stay calm, do what I have to do, and remember what I wish to forget and proceed in court. Even my shuddering falls and recalls to consciousness serve a purpose; I have not trembled like this since my mother died. My response defines the seriousness of the event—irreparable.

I hate that I roll these pillows to simulate his body beside mine. How well we slept together—not so much the sex but the actual sleeping. Whatever our differences had been by day, we'd performed like synchronized swimmers by night, rolling over in unison, assuming our favored sleep position.

"Spoons," he always whispered in my ear as he snuggled up behind me, his belly to my back, the warmth a glue strip sealing us together.

"Den animals," I'd whisper back. Our winter nights were warmed; we were reluctant to wake; the sleep comforted us, kept us close. Often the pose melded us together. We could be joined this way, half-unconscious and wake to our own crystalline conclusions, trembling and gasping in the dawn.

"Worship 'n' adore you, worship 'n' adore . . ."

This night, alone here, I suffered a fitful sleep, grappling with the triple pillows, the mock husband, made of down. I am too aware of the night sirens, the screams of the animals outside. I awake and stare into the deco dark of my bedroom. Without warning, I see sparks. What appear to be tiny shooting stars flash past my peripheral vision. Miniature lightning zigzags across my pupils.

I am going blind. I note something new—a fine hair across the lens of my eye—but as I swipe at my face, there is no hair. The flaw is within my own retina.

Blindness, I recall, often starts this way, with flashing lights and floating specks. I wonder if the phone line is repaired, if I should call 911, if an ambulance can even reach me? The main road, Serpentine, is closed. They wouldn't chopper in a medical helicopter for a woman seeing sparks, would they?

For a split second I long to call my husband. He would know what to do.

No. I must not. As the dawn bleaches the blackness and my window begins to appear as a square of gray light, I force myself from the bed, pull a parka over my flannel nightgown, and plunge my feet direct into my husband's oversized waterproof boots. I try not to study the designer box labeled THE ATTACK, which rests on my bedroom bureau, or the shopping bag that now holds the evidence, my Thing in the Box. But as I run a comb through my hair I can see the first page of the synopsis I've been asked to write for court:

"I met Matt Smythe in college, in a senior acting class. He was twenty-four and I was eighteen. He was the first boy with whom I was ever intimate, and we quickly declared ourselves in love and became engaged."

Habit dies hard. For seventeen years I depended on him at such critical moments. Now, by dawnlight, I look at the synopsis I must bring to court when it next convenes on my case. How can I put these personal memories on paper? I can't. I settle for statistics. *"He was older; he'd served in the marines. He was different. He saved my life."*

I am drawn to love stories that contain this theme of rescue, true accounts. You would be amazed how many people fall in love with their rescuers, actual saviors. There was a famous case in New York—the woman crushed by the construction crane. She fell in love with the surgeon who put her back together. The great playwright Samuel Beckett married the woman who knelt over him after he was knifed by a man. It was a true love that lasted. Many men marry their nurses. There is something profound in rescue, beyond compassion, toward what? Gratitude melded into love? The profound intervention of fate? Utter dependence?

To hold another's life in one's hands changes everything, for both parties. Of course, in Asia, saving a life, a rescue, makes one responsible for that person forever. Have I not seen countless movies in which the rescued Asian person lisps gratitude forever: "But now I berong to you, you save my rife." Hollywood convention or fact? The news features rescuer/rescuee love stories too: "He pulled me from the wreckage." "She gave me mouth-to-mouth resuscitation." Women fall in love with the firemen who carry them from burning buildings.

Matthew Allen Smythe saved me—twice. Our marriage was a rescue of a sort. I was living alone, attending college, in a furnished room. I was only eighteen, but old, I think, for my age. I had no family; my mother had died five years before, when I was thirteen and she was thirty-six. I was just free of the foster-care system; I was "on my own."

I remember but cannot force myself to write for the courtroom the hollowness of those days before I met Matt—how, when I ate alone from a container of yogurt in my room, my spirit sounded new depths. I started buying baby-food jars (not the truly putrid stuff but acceptable fruit purees). I told myself it was for economy of price and condensed nutrition that didn't require refrigeration. My thoughts often assumed the context of a one-sided conversation, synchronized to my spooning up the infant serving. "If you could see me now having plum with tapioca for dinner" . . . To whom was I talking? My mother, who would have cared? My father, who apparently had not been interested enough to stick around?

If only you were here, I would think, addressing the unknown "you" who turned into Matt. If only you . . .

Then, walking across campus, he, the unknown "you" appeared and the ache disappeared, the half-conversation ended. I wrote in my diary, which I will not transcribe into the court record: *"He makes the entire difference in my life. Where once I was cold, now I am warm. I am not so alone in the world as I thought."*

Falling in love crosses the border of before and after—Before Matt, I trudged on, after, I skipped forth . . . We raced toward each other at the close of every day—eating, laughing, sharing my single bed. There were such simple pleasures, resting cheek to cheek, watching television, taking walks, riding our bikes. It's a cliché, but clichés are based on truth—Our separate lives had been ordinary; joined they were ecstatic.

There was no joy too small to be shared—I took ridiculous pleasure in listening to "our" music, sleeping "in" all day Saturday, sharing popcorn, making pudding, folding our laundry. I felt I had been admitted to a club I had never before been allowed to join— the formerly closed society of couples, the contented. When I wasn't with Matt, I was planning to be—and he must have felt the same. In the beginning, he occasionally returned to his own room, on the other side of the quad but he would phone at bedtime, and say "I think it's time to cross the campus."

I remember the night we decided to stay together forever—We had kissed goodbye at the corner. It was snowing, and I felt that state of grace, imparted by the lacy veils then, as I do now. Maybe it was the snow that sealed our pact. We had kissed goodbye, and as I walked away, I felt a tug to turn and see him one more time. I had anticipated seeing his back, that Matt would be walking, swift as he always walked, away. But instead, he was standing in the cone of light under the street lamp, the snow falling. I ran back to him, and he held me. "Whenever you turn around, I will be here," he promised. We went back to his place. It became our game after that—The look back, the run into the embrace. There would be no permanent farewell. And in the circle of his arms, God help me now, I felt safe.

It was magical of course—One day, I was alone, the next day, I wasn't and it seemed I would never be alone again. I was not a religious person, but I said my thanks to whatever is my God.

So, yes, he saved me from—I won't call it loneliness, as solitude was a state I was accustomed to—from my aloneness. At eighteen, loneliness feels temporary anyway—I was escorted by anticipation. And yes, my visualization of my future husband was accurate, one of my first successful projections: He was tall, blue-eyed, black-haired, with those Scots-Irish good looks. In a dream, I had seen his eyes, fluctuant blue, framed by the dark eyelashes. In real life, Matthew Allen Smythe surpassed the handsomeness of my vision—Surely, I thought, he was one of the handsomest men in the world.

I won't write that it was his handsomeness that drew me, as well as his talent and what the yearbook called his "outgoing personality." Matt has those features, sculpted as if by an artist:

the cleft in the chin, two deep dimples when he grins. Lips that always appear sunburned somehow. Oh, he is handsome all right. The classic male; a profile for Marc Antony, a gladiator. And under his clothes, the body I know by heart—the wide chest, flat belly, muscles that don't appear worked for; although of course, he is somewhat vain and runs, goes to the gym. He's a fortunate physical type; the muscles don't bunch like the 'roid-rage men. I loved to touch him, kiss the length of his body. We joked that we covered every section, that there was no part of him unkissed, and no section on my body, uncaressed, unloved. Defined by touch of fingers, brush of lips, wasn't my body beautiful, then?

Now, unable to sleep, I fill in what my synopsis for court will omit—how I would sit in class and stare at him, trying not to be obvious. All the girls in the drama department were in love with him too.

Matt had not been serious about his acting; he'd quickly defected from the theater to law school, from there to a job with his family business, Smythe and Smythe. Matt became an expert in patent law, because his grandfather had invented a simple gadget, a device now installed in most washing machines. The grandfather, Matthew senior, was an untutored man, a repairman, but he made a great deal of money. I think Matt studied law to protect the family interests; the family spent most of their time fighting patent infringement. I often argued with him about the business, wishing he'd remained with me in the arts. As an actor, he had talent—how much, I am still beginning to learn.

I cannot forget we met as scene partners in Acting 401. We chose to play out the resolution scene between Brick and Maggie the Cat in *Cat on a Hot Tin Roof*. We brought more than we knew to the interchange, but what the acting instructor saw was sufficient. We were both awarded high grades, for the moment of damaged passion that passed between us.

As Maggie the Cat, I vowed to give my handsome stage husband, Brick, his life back to him, "like something gold" that he had let go of. . . .

Don't remember that, I order myself. Or those first months of love, of being together in his dorm room, joined, it seemed, by the hour. We'd been ravenous for snacks, wine, and one another.

"Party of two," he said, toasting me that first night. "The best party of all."

The party could not end: We married almost immediately.

"We married," my report continued, *"having known each other only eight months. The wedding was almost an elopement, as his parents disapproved."*

In my synopsis I didn't say we chose, by serendipity, a great cathedral on New York's Fifth Avenue, or that the pastor seemed charmed and gave us the small but special chapel filled with white lilies. I did not write that I was so in love, I ran down the aisle. Or that when we emerged, minutes later, man and wife, we both burst out laughing as we heard the choir in the main church ring out in practice, Handel's *Messiah:* "Hallelujah, hallelujah!" *Hallelujah.*

I was poor; there was no money. To my naive eyes, his family seemed rich, because they lived in a house, owned two cars.

Matt bought my bridal gown, a child's choice of a wedding costume: the sleeveless party dress, which I paired with an overlong, not-well-matched veil and an extravagant sparkly tiara. He paid for all the trimmings—my dress, the veil, the tiara, even my white satin pumps and sheer stockings. I still have the entire getup in the attic, stored in acid-free tissue.

Could I have loved him more? The wedding album, now also in the box with the police report, shows a series of images with one theme: I look up at my new, tall, handsome husband as he beams down at me. *"Worship 'n' adore you, worship 'n' adore you."*

Even now I wonder what would have happened if he had left me then, as an eighteen-year-old in love. I don't know that I could have survived such a loss at that age. Teenage love burns so intensely; it can self-ignite. It is dangerous to love so much at that age. Remember Shakespeare's classic. Matt and I were well rehearsed for that famous play of doomed young lovers: We stood in the wings, not playing the leads in that last college production, but members of the court. Our eyes would meet as the final speech was spoken. "Can there be a tragedy any sadder than that of Juliet and her Romeo?"

Saved. Spared the prospect of heartbreak—not a leap from the dorm window but a run up the church aisle. I was saved, and I knew it.

It sounds childish now, but that was how I saw it. Then, only a year into our marriage, Matt saved me again—in literal terms, physically. He carried me, bleeding, in his arms to the emergency room. Now, as I prepare to fight him in court, I must acknowledge I would not be alive to do so if Matt had not acted quickly when I had the accident.

We were here, on our first married summer vacation. The honeymoon ended abruptly: While riding a bicycle, I was struck by a station wagon speeding on Serpentine Road. You cannot begin to know what the impact felt like—like hitting a wall, not even metal but stone. The gnashing metal, the twisted bike. I flew upward and bounced onto the car hood; I bear forever a dent in my right thigh from the hood ornament. I lay still on the road. The single motion then was inside my skull; my brain moved as in an aspic. Concussion, they called it. Actually it was a fracture. Cracked my head like an egg. I was a long time coming "back," as they say, from some distant place where I dove to stay still and safe.

There had been no ambulance, no police. No time to wait. Matt had been riding his bicycle behind me; he saw it happen. I heard his scream, not mine. Matt picked me up from the pavement, carried me in his arms to the emergency room. He was weeping and crying.

"I love you, I love you." I loved him, too, then, but I will tell you this: When you have head trauma, you are not romantic. I concentrated on returning to life, to stabilizing myself. The gelid feeling in my head was very unpleasant; I didn't want to be touched. Every motion set my brain back into that liquid motion. I know what it is to feel life fade, the way you must fight to return to the surface, concentrate to get your breath, keep your own light from being extinguished.

Soon there were drugs, wonderful drugs that stopped the cracking and aspic sensations. In Bonticou Hospital, Matt lay on the floor beside me, his hand reaching up to hold mine, and he watched the doctors and nurses, to make sure that there were no mistakes or lapses. He slept there, on the floor of my hospital room, for two nights. During that time I drifted, floated in transit. Now it strikes me that I had never felt so protected and loved. Maybe injury was the price I had to pay. When I look back, Matt was never so demonstrative, before or since. Maybe he could only fully love this way, when I lay possibly dying. I lay in danger yet wrapped in comfort. Was that when we began to deviate? Did my condition and his response deform our deepest love then? Were our feelings clearest when I was injured? Is this why I still fear some ultimate moment of truth? Was my near-death worth the reward of certain love?

I felt so loved for so long. That was the first time we stayed up here at the lake for any length of time—the whole summer here, months, at Casa di Rosas, recovering. If I glance up at the top of my bedroom armoire, I can see the wicker breakfast tray, now opaque with dust; it rests, unused, on the bureau.

I must face this—whatever is causing these visual sparks— alone. My husband is no longer the man with the breakfast tray, the bud vase, the fresh-squeezed juice, and the fluffed yellow omelets. He is somewhere out there, in the darkness, somewhere beyond the radius the Bonticou court decreed. Wherever he is, I feel certain, he nourishes his grievance against me; he roils with rage. He plots to . . . what? Hurt me? Kill me?

Where is he? I strain to see in the dark bedroom, illuminated only by the sizzle within my eyeball. I'm too tired to sleep, too scared to dream. I sit here, my belly clutched, my blood running, and concentrate on the sounds outside. . . .

I hear a single, distinct animal scream: the death cry. Followed by a mass yelping, a communal howl. The pack devouring their kill. *Coyotes.*

I know my panic is foolish. Coyotes do not attack people, although they could chase down a pet. There are no predators here to threaten me. Even the black bears that den in the mountain rock declivities on the cliff side of the house are said to be timid: "They're more scared of you, than you of them," the townspeople always say. "A bear might break in for honey, but he won't hurt you." No, the only one to fear here is the man who married me.

Now, the parka over my nightgown, the nightgown tucked into my pants, I stumble out of The Wedding Cake House. Half dressed, my feet coming up in his outsized boots, I walk into dawn, a world gone pink and gray. My heart pounds, my blood runs. Being frightened feels like having a fever: I'm hot from fright.

The snow has stopped; the sky will clear. What I see is the winter blush, the sunlight pink on the trees. The trees themselves appear sealed as if in polyurethane: Ice encases every twiglet and branch. While I slept my uneasy sleep and dreamed my unwilling dream of rescue, the world outside turned crystalline. I view the rosy light cast upon my ice forest. A sharp wind blows and the branches chime.

I have not hiked at all since "it" happened, save for walking the necessary path to the shed for more firewood. In my near fever of fear, my forehead hot, my eyes bleared, I want the woods, the snow, the quiet. I want to escape this house, my bedroom, my mind. For the first time in so long, I strike forth, trying to find the trail under snow. It's not so difficult: The deer have found it first. I follow the many hoofprints, the beaten snow dotted with the deer droppings. A scent of pine is in the air. I take deeper breaths; the cold defines my nasal passages. Yes, my head is clearing, the sparks are fading, the lightning ceases.

I dressed in my heaviest parka, the one certified for the Arctic, and soon I feel even more overheated. The deer trail is narrow, and I smash through crusted snow in places, following the pitch of the slope. A few times I slip and have to pull myself up from a deep drift. I wish I'd used my old cross-country skis: I could glide over the snow, be downhill in moments. . . .

Below me, on the wide lawn that leads down to frozen Lake Bonticou, the snow has left a white canvas upon which has been recorded the night's activities. While on the house side the snow drifted and obliterated all sign of Chick Savago, his station wagon, and our footprints, another story is told on the flatter grounds of the lakeside. All night this has been a killing field. There are signs of struggle; the multiple paw marks in the snow, the competition for fresh flesh. For an instant I identify with the predator, imagine

I can feel how the tooth breaks skin, the first burst of blood. Then I wonder: Why? Why don't I identify with the prey?

Then I remember seeing a red-tailed hawk dive and swoop to grasp a squirrel right in front of me. I'd seen the hawk's talons curl, his beak open; heard the kill scream; felt the beat of his wings in the air. A raptor, a bird predator, grasped his victim and left me with this sensation, this identification. Maybe for once I chose the other part? I cannot explain it, but it stirred too the half-memory of dreams of flying, seeing the forest as through those falcon eyes.

I've always loved the tales of the Native Americans, especially the Algonquin who first inhabited this place. The Algonquin could be possessed by the spirit of such an animal, fly high with that hawk, or, in a reversal, stare through the eyes of its kill, the rodent, about to go limp. This week I have witnessed death here— a rabbit surrendering, offering his throat. Is it an instinct in the victim to yield, to sacrifice itself? Does that foreshorten the torture?

Don't think of this, I order myself, but the blood trail leads me into these imaginings. Kill or be killed: That is the law of the land, the story writ red on the white snow. And I have an instinct so strong I would call it a premonition—if I believed in such things, which I don't—that there will be a death here. Mine or his?

There are so many tracks, it looks as if there must have been a traffic jam of critters in the night: dozens of deer, their V-shaped hoofprints crisscrossing to and fro, while on the diagonal the wide-pawed marks of the coyote chart his run for the prey. Curious, I follow the tracks.

At the shoreline I see the snow polka-dotted with red, the blood spots of the kill. The remains of the victim are still apparent: a wild turkey, his tailfeathers, only a clutch remains, like an unglued headdress. The turkey, seeking safety by my house, misjudged his ability to flee and was brought down right here and devoured by the pack.

From nowhere a procession of deer appears. I count eighteen; they prance in single file like reindeer. I note that the deer know exactly where to cross the lake, where the ice is most solid. They tiptoe off the promontory called Crow's Nest and cut a diagonal across to the opposite shore. They avoid the north-end corner, where the creek feeds into Lake Bonticou.

Sometimes to, what—tempt fate?—I have walked to the edge there, to that treacherous north end, and stared through the ice to watch the rivulets perk and bubble below. I know the movement of the water makes the ice unstable. For some reason—an instinct tied to my dreams?—I now find myself walking toward this corner to check the ice. Over the years here I have become an expert on ice, especially the ice that forms nearest to Casa di Rosas. There are many reasons for me to judge the ice, to depend upon it, to find excitement and even my rare moments of serenity upon its surface.

I am thinking, longing, for the ice condition that the natives of Lake Bonticou, many of whom are descended from the French Huguenots, call *glace noire*. *Glace noire* is their term for the perfect ice condition, when a hard freeze seizes the ice before the first snow falls. The ice is allowed to form without the usual creases and bumps.

I first saw *glace noire* the initial winter weekend that my husband and I stayed one November. We had been enjoying ourselves, the snug sense of being at the house off-season, and had decided to prolong the pleasure by staying an extra day. When we saw the lake frozen that first time, I caught my breath: In my mind, the mind of a city woman always, the lake had become a deco ballroom, black as onyx, polished to a turn. . . .

My husband and I waltzed on that clear black ballroom of a lake. We were wearing our ordinary street shoes, but we could "skate": We glided together, danced, decided to return by moonlight. We built a fire on the shore and we danced again by its glow.

If I think of that night now, I will weep, so I must not remember that . . . or how we screamed in pleasure when we discovered the old shed, overgrown, covered in a dead grapevine but intact inside and keeping its secret—a Victorian "skater's chair."

He pulled the old oak seat on runners onto the *glace noire.* I sat in the skating chair; he guided it. We toured our end of the lake. The summer houses that existed then were empty, summer follies all, gingerbread decorations bordering the oval of Lake Bonticou. The winter world was ours, and ours alone.

Is it that night, that memory, that warmth of the fire on the shore, the heat between us—is it that perfect night that set the trap that kept me here? Memories of love and those shards of contentment may be more dangerous than pain, more seductive than fear. If I had not known such happiness here, maybe I could have left in time to avert The Attack.

We stopped coming up here in winter two years ago, when he became shaky. There was no conscious decision, only the inertia of our unease.

Against my will, I am retraveling our history as I walk the border of the lake. By habit I return to the hut. The hut appears as charming as ever, a candied elfin house in its peaked snowcap. The wind has blown hard here, swept the ice and the nearby shoreline as if with a broom. I stare without recognition at a heap of shattered wood and metal that rests outside the hut. Then I recognize the debris as the skating chair, left out on the shore last year, frozen, cracked, rotted—a collection of splayed boards and two rusted runners. The skater's chair no longer resembles itself, any more than the clutch of feathers represented the wild turkey.

The crows screech, at once raucous and a shrill, a summons to the start of the day. I set the debris of the skating chair in a heap; it can be burned someday. The exertion is good for me; I am almost oblivious to my fear when I hear the first crack—a gunshot.

I stop. The shot is close. Damn the hunters. Deer season is past, but that does not stop everyone. I am so far from town, far even from the real road. The local men know they can hunt and hide here. I have seen their tracks as they stalk the deer. I know they have constructed, without permission, a blind at the border of my property. I have never caught the man or men who built it: My appearances here are infrequent; the hunters must feel safe. I always intend to have some men from town come up here and tear down the deer blind. Now, I think, I should leave a sign: KEEP OUT. I should post language stronger than the NO TRESPASSING yellow and black cummerbunds that all my border trees wear for fall. Whoever is shooting here now is breaking the law.

Another shot. Someone is shooting, close, in the woods that border the shore. I look for the hunter, for an orange Day-Glo suit, red plaid, or the green splatter pattern of camouflage clothing. I hear the movement before I see him, the smash of brush and crash of twigs.

Leaping onto the trail, he appears—not the hunter but his prey. The stag—I recognize him: the buck that surprised me last night near the house—this buck is unforgettable for his broken antler and the white sightless eye. In my mind I dub him One Eye. One Eye lands in front of me, so close I feel the blast of his movement, the heat and smell of his breath. His one good eye is liquid, dilated in what I recognize as alarm. He makes a sound I would never have imagined—a snort—then stamps his right front hoof, three times, as if sounding a warning . . . to me? To the hunter? To other deer?

I stay fixed in my position: I feel my own mouth drop open. Oh. Who is more shocked, the human or the animal? I think the deer is more startled than I am. One Eye makes a face, as much as a stag can make a face, and he changes direction, jumping to the side of me, tearing through the old raspberry bushes toward the iced surface of the lake.

"No!" I want to call out to him. "The soft north corner, the bad ice . . . Go back, don't cross there . . . !" But in a second I have a greater worry: The hunter, damn him, is behind the stag. The hunter is not stalking on the path, he is crashing through brush and snow a hundred yards south. He appears, in red plaid wool. I cannot see his face: He is wearing one of those balaclavas, an olive woolen face mask to keep the frostbite from his skin. Hunters often where these—balaclavas are especially common up here in the north woods—but the masks appear ominous: Something there is, that fears a masked face. I try to reassure myself—he is a local man, trying to get his venison; he is a trespasser, an illegal hunter, nothing worse—but I would prefer to see his face.

"Hey!" I start to call out to him. "You're on my land. . . ."

The loaded gun a few hundred feet from my own face is a serious restraint. The hunter sees me—at least he turns and I think he sees me—but he grunts and moves past, following the stag down toward the shoreline. I see him break through into the clearing near the lake, and everything in me identifies with the deer.

Get away, I pray. *Make it to the stronger ice; cross the lake before he gets you in his sights. Fly to the forest on the other shore, hide, survive. . . .*

I hear the gun crack again.

No. The stag must still be here, on my side, too close. Against all logic I, too, follow. I fall into the uneven tread of the hunter; the smashed crusted drift is rougher to traverse than the virgin snow had been. I am tumbling, falling, feeling near tears. He can't kill that stag, not while I am here to stop him.

"Hey, you!" I call.

I know no one can hear. The gunshots come in rapid succession. Blasting the silence of the morning. The crows scream louder, in protest or sympathy.

I reach the edge of the water. What I see makes me want to scream, but I control that urge and utter an odd gagging sound, as alien to my ears as the stag's snort of surprise.

He is standing out on the ice, too close to the north end. I know that even in this cold, below the surface ice, runs that black current. There will be the give, the crash, the frigid drowning.

No, I mentally command the stag. Go back to the center; tiptoe toward the shore, any shore. Your chances are better anywhere than where you are. Another shot. He can't think; he tries to jump. His rear hooves slip; he collapses backward, as if sitting down on the ice. Oh, God, no: Maybe his ankles are broken.

I sense rather than see the hunter moving forward, upshore. He is coming closer for his kill.

I do not plan my response. It is said in theater that your emotions will instruct—that in crisis you will act from your own truth. Your entire life's experience is expressed as reflex. You cannot control this: Your response is the summation of what you have experienced, how that conditions you. Think of a motorist facing an approaching train at a mistaken railroad crossing: Some drivers will accelerate, others will reverse, and some will stop. They cannot plan this: They react as who they are, what they have become. Their lives inform their actions: They accelerate, brake, or retreat.

My shriek shocks even me. The fury, the volume, the hoarse demand: "Get out of here. Go away." I don't know what words I use; maybe there are no words, maybe I am inchoate. Get out of here. You cannot do this.

There is a final shot, as if in answer. Again I sense rather than see the hunter's departure. I watch the branches part as if a wind blows; I see the movement in the brush but cannot discern who or what is crashing through the scrub and snow forest upshore.

I am moving toward the stag. Can I help him, guide him to the safer position? Either direction—toward the firm ice or the frozen earth twenty yards south from the point where he is scrambling in place—would be safer. Each time the buck attempts to rise, he slips down again. Is it the slickness of the surface, or his injuries?

My inner voice instructs, *Don't walk out on the ice,* but it is as if I hear my own thoughts on a delay. I am animal now, as animal as the stag or the screaming crows above my head. Panic is in the sky and on the ice. I follow my instinct and move toward the fallen stag: I am deliberate in staying north of him. If he flees me, he will move to the shore. I want him to move to the shore. *Get off the ice,* I will him, even as I step onto it.

What idiocy, I realize, almost at once: The ice is not stable at all, even where I so tentatively tread. I hear a crack, not on the surface, but several inches below—a shattering, like submerged glass. I think involuntarily of cheap lightbulbs, no bargain, how easily they break.

I try to step lightly, spacing my steps to disperse my weight, but the lake protests, roaring. The deep moans and groans scare me into jumping backward—a mistake. My foot slides as the deer's hooves did. I, too, fall, feel the ice. The cold penetrates the weave of my pants and numbs my backside. I sit on the ice, breathing hard, unable to think. I look across at the stag, who has now risen and stands, trembling. . . .

Go. I will him. *Go to the evergreens. Go slowly, without the force of your leap. You can do it. . . .*

His ears perk as if he can hear my thought. It seems to me that he is telepathically following my instruction. But I do not get to observe his next move: The ice below me cracks, and I fall butt first, my heels rising comically, I suppose, above the ice while I sink backward.

Can I die this way? I wonder. How stupid. But maybe that is what accidental death is: stupid. Why have I ventured out here at all? Deer die in the wood by natural causes; hunters come and go, kill or not, without my intervention. Why not let the life and death on Lake Bonticou proceed without me?

These are my thoughts, but my body fights for itself. I do not will them, but my legs kick, my hands grope. I manage to get myself, while lying on my back, inched up higher on the ice that has not yet given way. And so, unheroically, like an upturned snail, I edge on my back. Every few inches the ice begins to break again, but I make my slow progress till I am almost at the shore. Then the ice shatters in a definite groaning rip, and I fall again. Now I feel it—the water. Oh, no. Then I realize I am in the shallows: There are rocks just below the water, under me. With an effort I heave myself up and crawl like some primordial creature onto the ground.

I stand, panting in place, and turn to see what has become of the stag. Where is One Eye? It's impossible to know his exact fate, but I feel the scorch of jubilation, the blood beat to my face, as I see that the stag, too, has left the lake. His track is clear: He reached the evergreens.

Then, from high on the bluff, beyond the house, an engine roars. The sound is still distant—a snowplow scraping its way toward me. Stiff in my fast-freezing clothes, I walk back uphill, toward my drifted driveway, to intercept whoever has come to "dig me out."

In Wardrobe

They say teeth chattering and trembling are the body's attempts to prevent freezing; if so, I am being actively warmed. My teeth clack like a novelty gimmick in a souvenir gag shop, and my limbs twitch in the weighted cold wet parka, nightgown, and sweatpants. My boots squish with lake slush; my feet burn and itch. I climb the rest of the hill to the house as fast as I can on what feel like stumps for feet, and stagger into Casa di Rosas. I have several minutes before the SnoCat can reach my actual driveway, and I must change into dry clothes. Now I regret the hike down to the lake; what had I been thinking? I should have been preparing myself for court.

If the road is clear, I have no excuse. Today's date is circled in red on my calendar: I must go to court or risk losing my order of protection. As I clamber toward the high ground of Casa di Rosas, I can see in the distance a yellow SnoCat, a mechanical praying mantis, dipping and scooping, shoving snow, clearing a path to me.

I am probably the only person in this area, who does not want to be dug out. The connection to the town, and by extension to the world beyond, is no longer welcome. My buffer zone, the billowing gift of the blizzards, will be punctured.

I peel off the half-frozen layers, leave my parka puddling on the floor. I don't know if this is prescribed procedure for half-frozen skin, but I follow my instinct and jump into the shower. Because this is Casa di Rosas, the pipes groan, the water sputters and coughs up black dust. Then, at last, the shower courses over my beet-red body. The water is hot, thank heaven, and I feel my skin respond.

The shower has the effect of some drastic Finnish treatment; my blood is up, as they say, and some involuntary biological optimism rises to the surface as well. I can do it, I tell myself. I can go to court and get through this. I can, can't I?

Like a child hoping for a snow day off from school, I have counted on cancelation. Now I wonder: Will the other parties appear? Will I have to take the witness stand? Will Matt materialize . . . or not? I try to calm myself. Maybe today will be yet another adjournment, my adrenaline rising for naught, the cost of the lawyer the same. There have been three adjournments already, costing thousands in legal fees but affording me a tiny bit of peace of mind. Just let me keep this order of protection. The invisible barrier. My single solution to the unsolvable.

I step from the shower and towel myself dry. The shiver won't quite stop; I vibrate in place, like some battery-operated toy.

J. J. Janis has briefed me as a director would: We have rehearsed. He has had me recite the facts of The Attack. I am prepared to present The Thing in the Box in a shopping bag as evidence, along with the broken phone and the synopsis of marriage, complete with my husband's apologetic notes. I have prepared a witness list to verify his previous hostile actions. And I hate this collection of evidence, dread its presentation. I don't want to display any of this, but what is my alternative?

Again and again, J. J. Janis has stressed, "They will try to tear strips from you. They will want to leave you in shreds. They will make you seem dishonest, stupid, conniving—whatever it takes to clear your husband. Your character will be assassinated. They will ask you trick questions; they will entrap you into answers that will be fatal mistakes. Do not improvise. Stick to the script. When cross-examined, say as little as possible. 'Yes' or 'No,' not 'I think.'"

This legal, laconic style goes against my training. I will have to bite my lip to keep from adding details, recreating the scene. But there is one step in the preparation that is the same: I have been ordered to wear a costume.

"For court, you must look conservative, reliable. The judge must believe you. You do not want to wear your flamboyant New York actressy clothes."

I go to my closet to choose.

"The best would be a white blouse and a gray or black suit, plain shoes."

In my private wardrobe I favor vintage kimonos, Icelandic reindeer sweaters, and out-of-date French designer dresses. If I have a style, it is Consignment Couture. My favorite outfit of all time is a white woolen riding jacket circa 1898, label from Vendôme, Paris, with a long matching skirt. I love to imagine the original owner of this costume astride English style, riding through the Bois de Boulogne. The jacket has a small rust stain on one cuff and is too delicate to launder. If I wear this outfit to court, I may be regarded as eccentric. Am I eccentric? If I am, I wouldn't know, would I? My hand pauses on the rack. . . .

I love to wear white, but in the midst of a blizzard? Will I disappear walking across the snow-covered court parking lot? Winter white is too chic for real winter in Lake Bonticou. Winter in the real world is not white for long; it is mud and grit, encrusted with road salt.

I am not one of those women with an enormous wardrobe. Choices confuse me, and I prefer to wear the familiar, clothes that reassure me. At home I like old stretchy pants or jeans that don't squeeze. A soft sweater or an old shirt. I often wore Matt's outsized sweaters or even his frayed dress shirts. I always slept in one of his outsized T-shirts. There was something I liked about how large they were; they made me look smaller, my legs thinner. When we were content together, which now seems in another century, wearing his clothes was a secondary embrace.

Now his clothes are jammed to the rear of the closet. In court he has requested permission to come home to reclaim this collection of gray and navy suits, the parka, his jeans, his at-home shirts, the stacks of sweaters, his underpants and balled socks. I know I must face the day that he will be allowed to reenter this bedroom to remove his wardrobe. J. J. Janis told me I must request a police escort to observe.

The image of an officer observing my ex-husband empty his side of the closet would seem silly if the specter of Matt, standing here again in this bedroom where so much happened, did not make the tremor return, tsunami-like, to my blood. I can feel that chug to the brain, the backwash of panic—what is it, high blood pressure?—just at the idea that they might someday let him stand again in a bedroom with me. No.

That can't happen. I must keep the order of protection. Invisible though that strand is, the order wound round this property is all I have. What if I should drop the charges, surrender the order? I think he would barge in to Casa di Rosas and finish what he started.

For a moment I see him once more, charging into this bedroom. His face, so handsome, was hideous. Insanity is disfiguring:

He looked as if a facial nerve had been pulled like bad thread; his face tugged high to the right, the high shine of the maniac glinting off his eyes and teeth. His expression had been impenetrable. His eyes had shut the blinds to his conscience. I had tried to meet his gaze; it was deflected.

Don't think of this now: I will have to look into those eyes again this morning, if court is not canceled. He will stare at me, he will try to break me. He will affect this innocent expression: How can you do this to me?

Insane, I think; he is insane. But if he is insane, how does he manage the other sections of his life? Why is he crazy only with me? Since that night Matt has carried on as usual: He goes to his office, he conducts his business. He showed the presence of mind to empty our joint accounts, leaving me financially stranded. He was thinking, planning.

Hurry, don't brood, I order myself. Just dress for court.

Through my bedroom window I can see the red Honda with the U.S. MAIL sign on top, like an automotive headband, and the SnoCat ahead. They are closing in on my driveway, the final approach, the circular turn to the front door.

There's no more time. For an instant I catch my reflection in the bureau mirror. I see myself naked, white and mottled red, goose-pimpled. I have an unbidden thought: I look like a victim. It is the blotches, caused from the cold. I have a pang: When did I last see myself as beautiful? I used to dance here, naked for joy.

"Do your 'dance for happy,'" he used to invite. I displayed myself, this same body, with the breasts he said were "just right," the indented waist he liked to enclose with both hands.

"Perfect," he used to say. "Perfect for me."

A loved body looks different, I can't help thinking. A loved body is defined by touch. This history is writ on my skin.

Don't think. That is the refrain today. Don't think. Just do, do what you have to do to protect yourself. I pull on my underwear, black woolen tights.

The costume. I must wear the right costume for court. Then I see it, in my closet. I cannot suppress an unintentional laugh. This is an actual costume: a black and white dress with a deceptive dickey front. I wore this dress to take the witness stand in *Stalked by a Strangler*. At the end of the filming they gave me the dress and I stored it here, at Casa di Rosas, never imagining I might need it for a real court appearance.

Perfect, I think. I put on the dress; I look like a substitute teacher, or a housewife on her way to apply for a bank loan.

"Downplay your glamour," J. J. Janis instructed.

What glamour? I feel I have none. Makeup cannot cover my expression. I see it in the mirror—the dilation of my pupils, the smudges under my eyes, the puffed lids of my sleepless nights. Funny how my eyes react separately to suspense; my left lid is raised higher than the right. My eyes are shot, the whites scribbled red.

"No colored eye shadow," the lawyer said. I cannot apply eyeliner; nature has done this makeover. I outline my lips in a natural blush color: This is not the time for Really Red. I add blusher, but the mauve pressed powder rests on my skin as cosmetic stigmata. I cannot conceal my actual face beneath makeup. My real face shows through, pale, plain.

In the few film reviews that commented on my appearance, I have been described as "a quiet beauty." The word *beauty* always made me giggle. I never felt like a beauty. In retrospect—which is how I now see everything—I didn't look so bad. With the light but right makeup, I looked okay. Without the makeup I have always had a slight Ellis Island quality, the Eastern European immigrant look. The only role I ever won without makeup was in a revival of *Fiddler on the Roof.*

Sedate enough? I'm not sure. I stare at myself, can't bear what I see: This is not me. Why should I look like this? I have not committed a crime. Why do I have to drab down? A rebel idea surfaces; I blush natural pink: Yes, why not? Fly my colors. I grab the white wool vintage riding ensemble. Why not? If the judge, the court, rules against me, let them. I will go down as myself, playing myself, not disguised as someone I am not. The hell with it, the hell with J. J. Janis's advice: I want to look good, not false. I am telling the truth—I will also present myself this way—as my true self. I pull on the outfit, close the tiny covered buttons: There are twenty-three of them. I must hurry; there's very little time.

As I button the 1890's riding habit, the ancient covered buttons half-disengage in my fingers. This outfit is beautiful; I can't quite describe the pleasure it gives me to wear it, the relief from my every day, but I have to admit the old wool is disintegrating. One wide gesture and the seam will give way under the arms. The jacket has a delicate trim, and the silk piping, too, has become partially undone. I plan to stitch it, but there are signs of disintegration that are unrepairable, the fraying of the fabric itself. I vow to wear this riding habit till it falls to pieces. I have never had a fitted jacket that followed the lines of my waist; it could not adhere better to my frame if it had been custom-made by the greatest couturier of France. I must not further stress its fragile wool. I think of the woman for whom it was designed: the single clues are *Vendôme, Paris* and the cut, which is 1890. A costume designer friend inspected it and said, "Perfect for Chekhov." I can see Anna Karenina wearing this also; didn't the Russian nobility order custom-made dresses from Paris? The skirt is also lovely; it has a special cut to allow the original wearer to mount and ride a horse.

The skirt allows for such wide motion, but also falls straight and becomingly, adhering to my hips, yet not exaggerating them. I love that it reaches exactly to the floor; the length is perfect. I like my reflection now. That must count. I will be more confident than in the dowdy outfit. I button the final button; it is loose and dangles. No time to sew; I better hurry now.

If I am late for court, will decisions be made against me? Is it like failing to appear in traffic court? Do you automatically lose?

I slide on my ex-husband's boots and carry my dress shoes in a plastic Safeway sack. There is a problem choosing a coat: I can't put on that half-frozen wet parka. My dress coats are all inappropriate, designed for evenings out, or city interviews and auditions. I want to appear as myself, but it would be stupid to sport a coat with ostrich collar and cuffs: Madame X, I think.

Then I see it—the navy coat from *Till Death Do Us Part,* a movie in which I starred as a Mafia wife who is innocent of her husband's wrongdoings but cannot leave him. In a twist of fate the mafioso is murdered and she is suspected.

Here is the Mafia widow coat. My character wore this boxy navy wool coat to the mafioso's funeral. I can't imagine why I saved the coat; I intended to donate it to the Salvation Army. The coat is well made but unbecoming double-breasted navy gabardine, and too short to flatter my legs. The Mafia wife had been kept deliberately dowdy, so as not to attract rival males. Her coat will have to do for my court appearance, even with the mismatch to my white riding habit with its impracticably long skirt.

I pull on the navy coat, imagining the color will not be that apparent in the brief interval of my entrance to the court. The coat rises up, as if it has interior hackles: It's been constructed to include high foam shoulder pads. *Till Death Do Us Part.* That had not been a bad title. For some reason I suffer a fashion flashback: I can see myself, awkward in this squared-off coat, kneeling, feigning grief at the mafioso's funeral. *Till Death Do Us Part.* That title may be apt after all; perhaps Matt has taken the marriage vows literally. *Till Death Do Us Part.*

As I stare at my now linebacker's shoulders; I hear the roar of the engines—my cue to open my front door. The tractor, with the mail car behind it, reaches the front driveway. The little red Honda brings the mail. Moving slowly, my heels rising in the too-large boots, I move across the cleared driveway. Walled in by the snow that rises to my padded shoulders at some places, I have an image of myself in this incongruous bulked-up "city" coat as I traverse the lunar lane. I call out to the driver of the Honda.

"Hey," I say, "how's the roads?" I hear myself affect the local Bonticou accent, grammar. Why? Do I wish for more local approval?

"Town is buried solid," calls out the mailman, Jake Taylor. It has taken the men twenty minutes to reach Serpentine Road from the main highway, Route 27, which slices across Lake Bonticou from the Northway. His voice cracks with the exhilaration of disaster. Nothing energizes Lake Bonticouans like a storm or other catastrophe.

From the door I call out, "Are the county buildings open?"

I hope not.

"Yes, yes, the post office and the court, they are open for business. Schools is closed."

Jake Taylor drives over to me. I have never seen him emerge from the red Honda on these missions: He appears an extension of the car itself as he thrusts a bundle of mail into my hand. His head, topped in a matching red plaid cap, pops from the driver side window. Jake has a long jaw and a big smile, but he is missing several key teeth. I don't know if there is a man over fifty in Lake Bonticou who has the requisite thirty-two teeth. Jake seems to have four teeth, spaced. He represents the local disdain for dentistry, or at least dentistry more sophisticated than extraction. It doesn't stop him from smiling.

In typical Bonticou fashion he relays the night's disasters: "Been a three-car pileup on Mountain Road, two injured bad"; they've been extracted from the wreck by the Jaws of Life.

The Jaws of Life. How apropos to everything.

"Yes, yes, they have been choppered out to Albany. And a woman up on Bone Hollow Road was found this morning froze to death on her porch. Must have forgot her door locked. The old Smithson Place, down on Snyder Lane, burned, leaving only the chimney and some pots melted down so you could hardly tell what they was. Oh, yes, yes, that's gone; nothing left."

Jake Taylor likes to keep me informed of tragedy, and he also gives me updates on those people who are near me, or whom he regards as kindred in some way. This is why he usually reports on my nearest neighbor, a man also from the city, who stays alone in what Jake Taylor calls "the new glass box" across the cove. "That guy, Winsten, from the city, had his whole house buried again. He had to dig himself out the front door with the fireplace shovel."

Jake laughs; that man Winsten was a city fellow who could be counted on to do foolish things.

"I knew that you couldn't build a glass house with a flat roof in Lake Bonticou. Just askin' for it to be buried under snow."

I guess Jake Taylor feels the same way about me, that I am this actress roughing it at a summer place on the lake. But I am glad to see him. I know it would be easier for Jake if I were not here, so far out at the lake; he would have no need to drive Serpentine Road, which leads to me. Casa di Rosas could be ignored, as it has been every other winter.

"Need help gettin' out?" Jake offers. He waves toward the final custard-tipped drift that presents an obstacle between my car and the cleared section of the driveway.

"No, I'll be fine." I can swing a snow shovel with the best. I gesture, grabbing the red metal snow shovel I keep by the door. In about a minute, as soon as the men have driven away, I regret my pride in saying that I could dig. The snow is heavier than it looks, and I am dressed in the damned riding habit; the vintage sleeves bind me, and the Mafia lady coat also weighs me down. I peek in the car window and check the clock (I never wear a watch): I have only a half hour to get to town before the start of court. I heave the snow, which compresses into white cement. I have to use my elbows to knock the pillow of snow off my windshield. Where on earth is my ice scraper?

I start my car, and pray. This isn't our good car; this is the old car, an ancient Saab sedan, my college car. The Saab carries a few dents, as I do. I am counting on its game Scandinavian engine. I don't much like cars, but somehow I got attached to this one, and when Matt drove off in his Infiniti, I was glad I stored this old car up here. She (yes, the car is definitely female) is all I have. She occasionally stalls, but other than that, she has yet to fail me. She steers on snow, thank God, somehow recalling Sweden.

As I unveil her, the snub-nosed white Saab reemerges, engine roaring to life, heater emanating inner rays of warmth. The FM radio blares news from the BBC. I can hear the cultivated English female voice describe world disasters. It's funny, I think, how the English accent softens the news. As I climb into the front seat I hear how atrocities have again been committed in the Middle East, but the broadcaster's modulated tone somehow distances danger, even death.

A civilized world remains, her voice seems to instruct; we can handle anything if we keep calm. She inspires me, this unknown Englishwoman, reporting on murder for the BBC; she is helping me. Even my dread situation can be controlled, if I stay level, modulated. . . .

My spirits surface. It's a beautiful day, really. If circumstances had been normal, Matt and I would be clamping on our cross-country skis and gliding into that pink and mauve forest for an all-day excursion. We would pack a winter picnic too. Now I must meet him in town, at court.

It takes almost twenty minutes to drive to the Bonticou County Family Court on Duane Street at the four corners of Bonticou, Main, Spring, and Duane. As anxious as I am to be on time for court, I cannot resist the charm of the town's winterscape, a Christmas village of candy houses. Even the cars, loaded with snow on their rooftops, look like gumdrops. All is whimsy and wonderland until I reach the courthouse.

I am most sensitive to architecture; I enjoy the Victorian frills of Lake Bonticou's cupolaed mansions and Victorian office buildings. Bonticou is filled with fanciful structures, but the courthouse was built only five years ago, on what must have been a pitiful budget. The courthouse is faced with false brick the color of Spam. The design bastardizes both French and Dutch style. The mansard roof sits atop the building like an oversized hat. The imbalanced-appearing structure is surrounded by a mammoth asphalt parking lot to accommodate the many cars and pickup trucks of the dysfunctional families who must convene here as well as the more expensive vehicles, the Buicks, Lincoln Town Cars, and Mercedeses driven by their lawyers.

As I pull in to this vast lot I wince, unable to accustom myself to the awkwardness of the design. Even the snow cannot camouflage its ugliness, as it had on my initial visit. On that first day in

January, I skidded to a stop here. It was snowing hard. I didn't see the NO PARKING EXCEPT FOR THE HANDICAPPED insignia: I parked over the obscured blue symbol of the wheelchair and was rewarded with a bright orange ticket that I discovered when I emerged.

I am fighting the ticket, along with the entire situation. I expect common sense will prevail regarding the ticket: No one could have seen anything on the macadam. It would be reasonable to dismiss the charge of illegal parking. I am less certain of the outcome of my marital situation.

Now I eye the parking lot, seeking the familiar silver Lexus driven by my attorney, J. J. Janis. Yes, he has arrived: The Lexus, bereft of snow sits agleam beside the court entrance. J. J. Janis is entitled to his handicapped parking: He has a bad hip and is postponing replacement. I park as close as possible, beside a caved-in Taurus with bandaged door handles—even this family's car appears battered, I note—and walk inside.

Rehearsal

Inside, the beige walls give way to a patterned gray linoleum floor. Upon entering, there is a photograph of a slain wife, mounted as message, not decoration, on the main wall. On January second, the day after New Year's, when I first saw this photograph, I viewed the image of the murder victim as a statement, an allegiance: This woman should not die in vain. But dead she is, her legs and arms splayed at unnatural angles, her eyes open and blank, her hair a black tangle reminiscent of my own.

Body double, I think, in the habit of the business. *I could play her, or she could play me.* A police officer sits at the front desk, reading the *Bonticou Crier,* which features the headline THREE AREA DEAD IN ICE STORM. The cover is a split photograph: a mangled car, fender gnashed into a tree on one side; a body bag being carted off an icicle-encrusted porch on the other. The subtitles: *Wreck on Bonticou Road Takes 3 Lives* and *Bonticou Woman Found Frozen on Front Porch.*

As I walk down the corridor I am forced to remember my arrival here in January—how I entered, shaking. Even then I could not quite believe I had to resort to the court of law, to the police, the judges, the system. Somehow I had hoped I could control Matt's escalating rage.

No one could imagine how I resisted coming in here. Earlier in the Christmas holiday, I had driven to the highway headquarters of the state police and sat in my car, mentally rehearsing my statement: "I cannot handle my husband's anger. I am afraid he will hurt me." But no matter how I prompted myself that afternoon, I could not force myself to enter the police station. I had retreated to Casa di Rosas, where Matt sat, Scotch glass in hand, by a roaring fire, Beethoven playing. . . .

"Where did you go?" he asked. "You look so unhappy."

Seeing that slain wife photo portrait brought the first visit back to me with a smack of recognition. I'd entered and given my name. A woman interviewer had been summoned. She took me aside to a blond wooden desk. The woman—I assumed she was a counselor—had affidavit forms and handed me one.

"Put down as much as possible—anything he ever did that was violent, dangerous or wrong. Write down as much detail as possible. This will be the official complaint: Get it all down."

The woman counselor for domestic violence cases was my age, I could tell, but she looked older than thirty-six. Her face had sagged; even her freckles extended into splotches. Tiny cysts hung like permanent tears from her eyelids. Her sadness had taken the physical form of this bagginess, her eyes shadowed as a hound's.

"I been there," she said to me, as though welcoming me into a sorority of sorts. I did not think to ask her credentials. She must have been a paralegal or a lay volunteer. If she was a lawyer or an employee of the court, she was startlingly undercostumed: She wore an acrylic sweatshirt with a Disney logo; I recognized the cartooned face with scowling black brows as belonging to a character, a woman warrior Mulan. Her pants, polyester turquoise stretch, clashed with the pink of the top. We could not have looked less alike.

On that occasion, for my first appearance in this building, I was wearing, for morale, my French designer black skirt and sweater, neat pleats, and good little black shoes from Paris. I had put on makeup, base, and blusher, but forgone lipstick. I was not quite put together, however, as I had shoveled snow for a good half hour that day also, to get to my car. Road salt had splattered the nice little shoes, and a few streaks showed white on the suit. My hair had looked better; it frizzed with static electricity, as if my brain could conduct its fear to the follicles.

"Remember everything; write it down now, because you will forget," Miss Mulan had advised. "And the past, too, the last two years especially. Were there other incidents?"

Incidents? I could feel my brain curl in my skull, retracting from memory. No, I did not want to remember. But only two days before, lying in the snow, I had sworn to myself: Never again: I must remember this.

"On other occasions?" the counselor had asked. "On other occasions?"

"No," I said. "Nothing really."

Then I mentioned the cracked vase, the fallen flowers, and the odd behavior with the sun oil at the beach. I had to take a breath before I added, "And the cat. Dot. She was a white cat with a black dot on her forehead. I think he . . . I don't know. I loved her and she disappeared on Christmas Day, just before he . . ."

"Do you have proof that he killed the cat?"

I shook my head. The truth was that I spent most of my time trying to convince myself that Matt had not hurt the cat, that she had wandered off—even that a coyote had caught her. I would prefer to believe anything other than that I had a husband who was a killer, of cats or people.

"He used to love the cat," I said. *And he used to love me . . .* I wanted to add.

The counselor shook her head. "Forget the cat, although if he did hurt her, it fits the pattern. Often abusers injure animals before they turn on people."

Was Matt now in this category? It was hard even for me to accept that a man who had seemed only "normally" complicated—with family and temper issues that I believe are commonplace—was moving into the category of killer. He had surprised me with the cat when it was a kitten, for Christmas seven years ago. He had tied a red bow to her narrow blue collar. We had played with her endlessly, as couples without children do: She was our four-legged, furry "baby." I remember her mew. The way she tagged along on our walks, stepping neatly in our footprints, her tail straight up, nose bright pink in the cold. . . .

"Evidence?" she asked. And with sorrow I told her about The Thing in the Box. She nodded. "Bring that to court, have it entered into evidence."

"I will," I promised. Then, because of my theater background, I felt I should offer some motivation. "He was beaten as a child," I told the Mulan lady, who looked unsurprised at this. I went on, not realizing this was when I set the trap, the spring in the Pandora's box.

"He was beaten, but many children were beaten. It was almost accepted then." I didn't add *in the dark age of his childhood* for fear of sounding melodramatic. "You know how spanking and hitting were not so uncommon. It's only now we know how much damage. . . . His mother used a child harness on him. For years. I don't think that would be approved of now, but back then companies manufactured child harnesses." I didn't want to say straight out that there was instability in his family. Truly, I am not one to judge families so harshly. What family doesn't have someone who cracked under stress? I said only, "I believe there may have been a genetic tendency, a biochemical imbalance. His father and mother both have psychiatric histories. I believe a grandfather also. I suspect that this may be genetic."

"Put it down," Mulan instructed. And so I wrote in the names of my in-laws, not realizing as I did so, with the cheap ballpoint pen, that I was writing my in-laws an invitation into the case.

"You need more specific incidents when he hurt you or threatened you," Mulan said.

I told her: "Matt began to act strangely last year. That was so odd, with the suntan oil at the beach, when he said I couldn't rub it on his shoulder. That was when I felt it truly started."

The counseling woman did not seem impressed. "The business at the beach is just weird, so skip the beach. But the broken vase— did that vase break near you?"

"Against the wall."

"Could it have shattered near your face?"

Possibly.

The counselor said, "Concentrate: Whatever he did must be on this complaint. This is the document that the court will always refer to. So, we have an assault in your driveway, the unsafe driving, a family history of violent breakdowns. Did he threaten you?"

"Yes," I said. "He said he wanted us both to die."

"And other dangerous actions?"

"He hurt my arm, shoved me out of the car. Then it happened. . . ." I told her the worst of it, the specifics of The Attack. She nodded and looked surprised only once; then she nodded again. She scribbled what seemed to be a computation on her notepad and instructed me to write the details on my complaint form. "An arm twisting—"

"Squeezing," I corrected.

"Arm squeezing, then the shoving, the death threat, the push from the car"—she hesitated—"and then the attempt on your life." She described it in flat detail. "Anything else?" she asked.

"I think there was more," I said. "But it happened so fast. It was seconds. . . ."

The counselor said, "You should put in about the vase. The cracked vase. That could have hit your face."

I wrote down, *Threw a vase two years ago, could have hit my face.* Anything else?

"The sun lotion is no good," the counselor said. "It isn't violent. You want to remember the violent actions. Think hard."

How impossible it had been, even the morning after, to recount the exact quality of the behavior that had frightened me into taking legal action. My husband loved me . . . or so he said. We had been going through a rough patch; he was upset about something I had done. It concerned my work: "You walked away from me, and something snapped. . . ."

Yes, something snapped.

Remember this, I ordered myself. I looked at my arm where he had gripped me, in the car: The bruises had deepened the next day, turning odd yellows and purple, the colors of orchids, irises, not especially shades I liked.

Remember the bruises, I remind myself now. *Do not let your memory fade with the bruises.* Now I'm glad that I consented to the photographing in the hospital emergency room, odd as it seemed at the time. There's my proof: the photographs on file at the emergency room and the physical evidence, The Thing in the Box. As much as that bit of evidence horrified me, I'm grateful that it exists. I have proof—Proof that Matt is insane, that I have been threatened. And there have been witnesses to some, if not all, of his unstable behavior. I have a list of names—a short list, but a list. Witnesses will testify for me. If I can keep paying J. J. Janis and stay the course in court, I should be able to hang on to my order of protection and make my charges of "a family offense" stick.

Walking down the court corridor, I check the wall clock: ten minutes to nine. I run to the plaintiffs' waiting room, where I know I will find J. J. Janis. On the way I pass the court nursery, for the children of battered wives, where the toddlers play as their mothers seek justice upstairs. The babies are tended by volunteer grandmothers, who, in this section of the state, are not so old.

Passing the open nursery, I glance through the door; I see a grandmother, who looks younger than I am. She's holding a baby the size of a spider monkey and rocking her. I cannot suppress a shudder. Who brought this scraplet of humanity into the world? The baby must weigh six pounds, and she is already in family court. Her custody must be in dispute. For an instant the baby's eyes meet mine. She swivels her head, but I am sure she doesn't "see" me: They don't see at that age, do they? I have heard it's all a blur.

I hurry past; the tiny baby in this world of grown-up woe unnerves me.

My heart pounds; I am not yet accustomed to these court reunions with Matt. I do not know what to expect. At the arraignment he was pale, drawn, and apparently contrite. He contested nothing and stood alone, without counsel. I appeared with the local lawyer who, ten years ago drew up our wills—an unrelated service, I hope. That lawyer, Seamus O'Leary, is known for his good nature and own fair share of DWI citations.

Seamus O'Leary seems to hold his own court in the plaintiffs' waiting room. I see him as I approach—an appealing man, just five feet tall, with ginger hair and handlebar mustache.

Character actor, I think. *Irish repertory.*

"How are you today? Terrible?" he greets me.

"Oh, yes." I smile. "Just terrible. And you?"

He grins. "Bloody miserable. Welcome to hell."

Seamus O'Leary, despite his "thirst," finesses all and is well regarded in the community. I wish he had not been disqualified to serve as my attorney, but at Matt's initial arraignment the judge said that O'Leary could not represent me or my husband—a conflict of interest because of that routine will, drawn up so long ago.

The will, I think: I must remember to change it. I leave everything to Matt, and he leaves everything to me. Who can I name now? Who will benefit in the advent of my death? Logic decrees it should not be Matt. Once an orphan, always an orphan? I have no parents, and now I will have no descendents, either.

Should I leave my estate, such as it is, to my girlfriends? Charity?

"Dolling," J. J. Janis greets me. He is quite a vision in Bonticou Court.

He's wearing at least ten thousand dollars' worth of couture cashmere, and he doffs an imported fedora revealing the red strands of hair draped over his pate. The fluorescent light bounces off his skull.

"It's like having a pit bull, but a pit bull who loves you," Nadine had said when she gave me the referral. "You'll see his sweet side, but he will keep Matt against the wall. He will tear strips off him. You won't have to be afraid."

J. J. Janis has that prizefighter's face: Matt has already referred to him, on the phone, as my "Mob lawyer." I have to admit, J. J.

Janis looks the part, but he's also *haimische*. ("A heart knows a heart," he is always saying.) A *haimishe* hatchet—perhaps what I need. The double-edged sword to sever the marital bond and cut me protective orders in this court.

He tugs a luggage cart with legal cartons filled with the growing piles of paper pertinent to my case.

"Dolling," he always addresses me. "I feel I know you all your life. A heart knows a heart. I saw you stalked by the Pantyhose Strangler on TV. What was it, *He Is Watching?*"

"*He Watches*," I correct him.

"You're prettier in person," he says. "The gorgeous *punim*."

Now J. J. Janis kisses me on both cheeks (he often vacations in Provence). I am certain I will pay for his next trip, or at least a case of vintage champagne.

"In here. . . ." He leads me into the actual plaintiffs' waiting room. He limps, listing to the right. He is scheduled for hip replacement when my hearing is over. I am sure, somehow, I will also finance the Teflon ball for his new hip socket. There are a few lawyers already inside, crouching beside their clients. A teenage kid, incongruously freckle-faced and fresh, stands against the wall, observing. I wonder what he is doing there: He seems too young to be a lawyer, too cheerful to be involved in a case. He is the only person to smile as I enter. I take him for a cub reporter. Smile back. I wonder if he recognizes me. God, no publicity, I think. He looks at me curiously, as if he might place me, but is uncertain.

Maybe I am prettier in person or plainer, I think. I walk past and find a seat in the plaintiffs' waiting room.

There are two waiting rooms, protocol to accommodate the violent and their victims. This first room, the plaintiffs' waiting room, is for wives; the defendants' waiting room is for their husbands. Perhaps on other days the sex ratio breaks differently, but every time I've attended, the men were the defendants, the women the plaintiffs. In the larger, sunnier room, the wives and girlfriends chat in small clusters. In the second, windowless parlor, the husbands slouch, their legs stretched out in sullen fatigue, carrot-colored boots extended. Each group darts in and out of the building to a designated smoking zone against the fake brick wall. Outside they observe the segregation also, fuming in opposite directions.

I recognize the hollowness in my fellow plaintiffs' eyes. I must admit, I may look different, better heeled, and more educated; I am even, perhaps, slightly famous. But am I so different?

This is my first true look at the "real" citizenry of Lake Bonticou off-season. In summer, with the second home population ensconced, the average income rises into seven figures; the horses race and the ballet dancers jeté. In July and August one could have the impression that this is a wealthy area, but now I see how poor the local people are. These are the working-class couples who fight one another. The women wear parkas in pale pastel colors, violet, turquoise. There is some matching fake-fur dyed trim. The men favor khaki lined in red or navy blue. Some men wear full body suits, khaki, with zip fronts, designed to withstand Bonticou winter.

In the plaintiffs' waiting room, I take my place among the women, feeling self-conscious in my navy wool Mafia wife coat. The women are chatting, Bonticou style, of the morning's horrors: the icy roads, the death toll. On one side I hear "The air bags didn't open," while on the other an elderly woman is remarking, "It's been a while since anyone froze to death; used to happen all the time. Poor Jane Baker, who'd a thought she'd go out that way. Froze solid. I heard they couldn't bend her to fit in the morgue drawer. I'm glad her mother isn't alive to see this."

"Welcome back to Yekaterinburg," I say. J. J. Janis looks askance at the lineup of plaintiffs. Last week he was in the Virgin Islands. Now this "tundra," as he calls Bonticou.

"When this is over, give yourself a break and go to Saint Barts," he suggests.

He pulls up a chair beside me.

"Love the coat," he says. "And, dolling, I must love you: I drove from Larchmont to Yekaterinburg." He always calls Lake Bonticou Yekaterinburg. "There's no snow in Larchmont; there's no snow until a mile south of Bonticou. And here you could use an airlift. What is this *mishugunah* place, the Arctic? Yekaterinburg, Siberia?"

"Yes," I laugh at his joke. I wonder if he will bill me for his driving time.

"Well, dolling, surprise, surprise," he says. "You're on today. Your lovable husband is trying to overturn the order of protection. He has filed a motion. He wants the right to return to your house."

I feel that dizziness, the heat under my forehead, a squeeze in my belly. I envision Matt running up the steps to the bedroom, breaking down the door again. Matt, back in the house . . . No, it must not be allowed. He must not come "home."

As if on cue, Matt appears. He is dressed, I note, in his best London gray woolen suit. He wears a gray silk tie. He is fresh-shaven, scrubbed, and smiling. He holds a bouquet of roses. He looks, for all the world, like a man going to meet a special date. The white roses recall the bouquet he bought me on our wedding day.

I had forgotten how handsome Matt is when his face is not distorted by rage. He really is one of the handsomest men I have ever seen. We all have our weaknesses; mine has always been this susceptibility to extremely handsome men.

Handsome is as handsome does, I think automatically, like a child recalling a Sunday-school lesson. In his rage attacks he is hideous. Toward the last few months of living with him, I would stare at his perfect profile and curse it. If he were not so handsome, could I have resisted him from the start? Would I have left him sooner?

Now here he is, handsome again, maybe more handsome. He has lost weight, which brings up his cheekbones, giving an odd delicacy to his large hands. I try not to look down at his hands, because I always find them attractive: His hands are large even for his tall frame, and the veins show. There is something heavy, sensual about Matt's hands, his thick fingers (and yes, there is a correlation). He is, whatever his failings and flaws, an "all-guy" guy; the testosterone is expressed in all the usual ways, his ropy hands, the Adam's apple . . . the rest, discreet in his well-cut trousers.

When he walks in, he has that masculine alpha quality; the other men react, shift in their chairs, or stand, straighten, as if to appear taller. The women touch their hair, fluff. No actor can achieve this through technique; this is what is "given"—the presence, genuine virility. He enters and everything pauses. His posture is excellent; his hair curls, a bit wild for the straight suit, curls just over that collar at the back. I remember thinking even at our wedding, This is a wild one—not the kind you marry, the kind you know in the dark of a hotel. Everyone seems to experience his attraction by reacting with interest or discomfort.

Women always comment, "Oh, your husband is so good-looking." In Hollywood, when Matt escorted me to agency offices, the agents popped from their doors to ask, "Who's he? Who represents him?" If he'd wanted, Matt could have been a film actor, maybe a star. His features are classic—the bridgeless nose . . . His lips are unusual, too, full, and always look chapped. When I first saw him, I thought of kissing him. When he did kiss me, his lower lip split a bit and I tasted the salt of his blood. I know why his lips are always chapped: He loves outdoor sports, sailing, skiing, and he refuses sunblock. Matt is forever windburned; the tan exaggerates the blue of his eyes; he is prematurely crinkled round the eyes, a detail I used to find attractive.

I must be immune to him now, even though his eyes seem innocent, clear. The shade has lifted. I know, because I know him so well, that at this moment he is not insane. I have finally learned the hardest lesson, and the lesson is that his clear gaze, his sanity, is temporary: The constant is the roiling anger that lies below. Inconstancy is the constant.

I have a reflex to go to him, have him hold me. I can feel the length and strength of him. His body is very fine. I know him too well, and I will never be able to disassociate sex, physical sensation, strength, from Matt. We were together too long. I know the breadth and smooth planes of his chest, the hard rungs of his abdomen.

I know his body better than my own; I slept pressed against him, covered his skin with my kisses. His body is, to me, more than a human body; it is the landscape of my marriage. It will take years, I think, if ever, to forget the scent and taste of him. If I close my eyes and concentrate, I can still feel the exact pressure of his lips. His lips are calloused but his kisses are light and noninvasive. He isn't like the boys I dated before I met him, or some of the actors I've had to kiss on-screen who jam their tongues down my throat; I never understood the appeal of that.

Matt's a pleasing kisser, maybe a better kisser than a lover in the fullest sense. Desirable he has always been, desirable and desirous—a desire that, despite our long marriage, has never been satisfied. Is this why we stayed together—because he held back, and I did not know, until too late, why? Was the kind of sexual behavior he wanted a sign or a symptom?

He has a way of walking: He moves lightly, on the balls of his feet. There is a spring to his step; he is conditioned, an athlete. That sense of control of his body used to be so attractive; now I know what it is to be caught in the centrifugal force of his spring when he is all instinct, attacking. He is like the cougar, capable of the killer pounce. He is staring at me, staring and smiling, walking closer.

Don't think. Turn away. Don't meet his eyes.

"Come on," he says, approaching me, "let's just get out of here."

He reaches for my hand. "Come on, let's get out of here. We don't belong here with the trailer trash. I don't want to say what I would have to say about you if we go into that courtroom." He is proffering those white roses. I step backward, avoid accepting the flowers. The other plaintiffs eye the bouquet.

From a blond wood desk, a receptionist blares our names: "Smythe versus Smythe, courtroom three."

J. J. Janis jumps to his feet like the prizefighter he appears to have been.

"You don't belong in here," he says to Matt.

Matt stops, turns from me to J. J. Janis. "This is all your doing," he accuses my lawyer. "You've distorted the facts; you've filled her head with ideas. She is not a battered wife, because I am not a wife beater."

"Oh, yeah?" says J. J. Janis. "What about her bruises?"

Matt doesn't blink his long black eyelashes. "She fell. I was trying to save her from falling out of a moving car."

For a moment then I lose what residual feeling I have—my pity, all the softness that had risen in me at the sight of him and his bouquet of flowers, that habitual affection that mandated doubt: Oh, give it up. You might be wrong. Maybe you have over-reacted. Maybe he's not beyond redemption. . . .

But "falling"? This is not open to interpretation. He is lying. He stares into my eyes, as if this could convince me of his candor. His eyes are very blue, burning, like the fire of gas jets.

Oh, no, I order myself as I hear my name called: *Remember this.*

In Court

D id you bring the papers?" J. J. Janis demands.

We are almost ready to enter the court; he has his dolly of files, pushing it like a stroller. We pause in an alcove of the hall, by a window with a view of the smoking zone. I have a view of the smokers, the estranged wives and husbands. For a moment, inside, I feel as they must: If I hadn't given up smoking, I, too, would light up. Kill a cell; inhale, exhale. Feel something, numb up. Smoking suits the situation, with its long wait periods, the need for action when there often is none. Even the smell of burning, and the forceful stubbing out of the singed butts. Grind an ember under your heel or bend it into a soda can. Sizzle and ash.

"Of course." I reach in my bag and pull out "The Synopsis of My Marriage."

"The witness list?" He has asked for witnesses before, on the phone. "Yes, I have the witness list." Nadine saw something, and Elsbieta, the casting director. I was sure they would remember Matt's odd behavior: They had visited the weekend before The Attack. He had been acting out.

But now I picture my two friends. Elsbieta is older, a bit maternal, and we are entwined professionally. Nadine is volatile, hardly impartial: She is that person to whom I tell all—almost all, anyway; my best friend. I now wonder if I should call them into court. It seems inconsiderate at best, dangerous at worst. What if Matt turned on them for testifying against him? FemJep might become more apropos. I have a flash of Nadine in that last thriller: She was no stranger to slashers, either. Matt always seemed ambivalent toward Nadine, in the way many husbands resent "the best friend."

"I'm not sure I want to call friends and business associates in to testify," I say to J. J. Janis. "I don't think it's fair to involve them."

J. J. Janis cuts me off at the start of this line of thinking: "Don't be ridiculous. You need everyone you can find to help you. You have the burden of proof. You need these people to confirm your account. Nadine will be sensational on the stand."

That's certainly true, I reflect. Nadine is a performer of the first rank. And of course J. J. Janis already knows her: She is the person who recommended him. I give Nadine mixed reviews now, but I did ask for her recommendation. She was the only person I knew who had been divorced and who still spoke to her attorney. Now that I know Janis a bit, I think he is a better match for Nadine than for me.

Nadine and I are not much alike, but we've been friends since we were nine years old. She is the only friend I have who can still remember my mother. That matters, I think, to us both. I saw her through her divorce, and now I suppose she will see me through mine. But her divorce was about money and her apartment: Nadine never did get that attached to her husband; the marriage lasted only two years ("and the last year was unendurable"). He had been unfair; anyone could see that: Her husband staked a claim on the two-story artist's studio apartment she bought ten years before meeting him. Nadine hired the somewhat legendary Hatchet of Westchester, J. J. Janis, and won what she needed to win. Her ex-husband was left "in pieces" in a rented room in Weehauken.

"You'll change your mind," J. J. Janis predicts. "I'll call Nadine, and give me the other woman, this Elsbieta's phone numbers: I'll pre-interview them."

"I really feel it's wrong: It's too much to ask," I say. "Elsbieta is someone I know professionally."

"Do you have other witnesses?" he demands. "Someone, anyone, who saw something—anything?"

"The house is so isolated, I don't think anyone could hear when I screamed or see me when I ran."

J. J. Janis can be cryptic. "People see and hear more than you know. You'll see: There will be more witnesses. Meanwhile, I want you to quiz anyone who works for you—the cleaning woman, the mailman, the man who came in to shovel your roof, the oil delivery man, any repair people. Someone saw something," J. J. predicts. "Someone is always watching."

I find that concept almost as unnerving as what we face in court. "What do you mean, 'Someone is always watching'?"

"I just finished a case," J. J. Janis confides. "The woman was being observed, without her knowledge, through a baby monitor by a man parked in a car across the street. Signals can travel."

"I don't have a baby monitor," I say. "I'm a quarter a mile from my closest neighbor—and he's in a house across a frozen lake, buried in snow."

"Talk to him," J. J. Janis advises. "He may have seen something, heard something."

"That's impossible," I repeat. "No one comes through my place, except the mailman and the cleaning woman."

"The furnace man, the oil delivery, the guys who want to shovel snow . . . Jehovah's Witnesses—interview them all. Someone saw something. Start with the cleaning woman. Cleaning women know everything. They make excellent witnesses."

The image of Moira Gonzalez Gerhardt passes through my mind: She hasn't been in to clean for weeks, but maybe she had noted the breakage from Matt's earlier rage attacks. The vase, the upturned lamp.

"Maybe she noticed the breakage. Would that help?" I ask.

"Anything that can corroborate your story."

"I don't like to bring innocent, uninvolved people into this mess," I say. "Can't we go with the evidence we have? The physician's assistant photographed me in the ER, and there is . . . you know what I have in the box."

"You have it with you—the evidence?"

My hand gropes at my side for the Bendel bag, with the wrapped Thing in the Box inside it. I feel the breath suck out of me. I have the bag, but inside it is only the broken telephone, the one Matt ripped from our bedroom wall when I dialed 911. The smaller bag, which I was sure I had tucked inside it and which holds the box, is not there.

"You forgot it," J. J. Janis says.

How could I forget it? Almost the only piece of evidence: physical proof of the destructive force of my husband's rage. Where is it? I could have sworn I was carrying it, in the big Bendel bag.

Did I leave it in the car? No, I'm sure not. The house, then. Yes, of course. When I opened the door to leave, I was holding the bag, my purse, and the attaché case with the papers. I must have left the shopping bag in the vestibule of Casa di Rosas.

How could I forget something so important?

"Can I go back to the house?"

"No time. You haven't lost it, have you?"

"No, no." I couldn't have lost The Thing in the Box. I came straight here. I didn't get out of my car. The bag, with The Thing in it, must be in the entrance to my house. I saw the mail car, the tractor. I was intent on digging out the car, getting here to court on time. Calm down, I order myself. The box must be sitting there, where I left it, in the front hall of Casa di Rosas.

Now I can see how I had such a lapse: I was holding too many things; I was agitated in the rush to get to my car, to reach court. Understanding this oversight is no excuse, even for myself. I could have screamed, kicked the Sheetrock walls of Bonticou County Family Court. Whatever is done to one is not nearly as upsetting as a serious mistake one commits oneself. Inwardly, I was cursing and now off balance for whatever would happen next in the actual courtroom.

I had that Thing in the Box. I had it with me . . . but now I didn't.

Damn. Apart from the photographs of my bruises and the testimony of a few witnesses, whom I am reluctant to ask, that evidence is my case. I have a few apologetic notes from Matt, but I still can't find the most incriminating letters. I know they exist, that I saved them, but where did I put them?

"And you do have the incriminating letters?" J. J. Janis asks. God, is he psychic? He is rough, but he may in fact be the legal genius he claims to be.

"I brought the broken phone," I say, sounding lame even to myself.

"The broken phone doesn't indicate anything abnormal," J. J. Janis says. "It's a broken phone."

"He broke it during The Attack, to prevent me from getting the police."

"It's a phone," J. J. Janis says. "It doesn't talk."

"And The Thing in the Box?"

"That is better; that is truly unsettling, and who knows what forensics could make of it?" J. J. Janis speculates. "Well, it's not here. Bring it next court date. We'll have to go with what we have. And find the"—he uses an alliterative expletive—"letters."

"They were love letters," I say.

"Were," J. J. Janis corrects. "Now they are evidence. Find them and bring them in next time. You need everything you can get." He frowns, his red eyebrows angling toward the schnozz. "Don't go soft on me," he warns. "You show too much forgiveness. You are in the funhouse now. You will come off as a willing victim."

I am calling myself names as J. J. Janis scrutinizes me, shaking his head. I feel hot, a bit woozy, from my errors. I start to take off the Mafia lady coat.

"What the hell are you wearing under that coat?"

"A vintage riding habit," I say, my voice small. "Victorian. It's my favorite—"

"Are you crazy?"

Am I crazy?

"You don't like it?"

I slide the coat half off, revealing more of the beautiful woolen jacket and matching skirt. I know it becomes me; it is "me," as they say in the business.

"It's fine if you want to lose your case and end up in the state mental home," J. J. Janis snaps. "I told you: conservative."

"Look," I say, weakened by my oversight with the evidence bag, "I am innocent. I am injured. I am the one who deserves the protection of this court, no matter what I am wearing. Why should I have to wear a disguise?"

J. J. Janis takes my elbow and grips it hard. He steers me against the wall, near a soda machine, and hisses in my ear.

"You're in family court," he says. "You are the plaintiff and your husband is the defendant."

"Exactly," I try to interject. "I am the innocent—"

"He's innocent until proven guilty," Janis interrupts, breathing in my face: I can smell his Nicorette gum, vending machine coffee, an acid gust of legal disgust in me, the client.

"Do you know what that translates as?" J. J. Janis doesn't wait for my response. "It means you are guilty until proven truthful. Everything you say is suspect. Your charges are unproven, baby."

"Don't call me baby," I say. I will pay him $305 an hour but he can't call me baby. "You know I'm telling the truth; you know he's crazy."

"Yeah, baby, now prove it."

"To you?"

There's no time to answer: We hear the clock chime. He steers me by the elbow. I now sweat beneath my coat but do not dare remove it. J. J. Janis has my entire savings in his account. I will owe him what? Two thousand dollars more for today. The meter is running.

I think about Legal Aid. Would the public defender be as ineffectual as everyone says? Would the court then, as J. J. Janis warned me, throw out my case? Would I have to crawl home, a ward of my husband, into the privacy of his custody?

"Look confident, composed . . . no matter what happens," he is saying. "If you take off that coat, find another lawyer."

J. J. Janis turns to me just as we reach the courtroom. "You do not volunteer information. You answer yes or no. You do not explain. You do not show emotion. Got it?"

He reminds me of my least favorite director, an elderly Brit who actually hit actors. He gave line readings too. "I've directed more living-room plays than you've had hot suppers" was a favorite saying.

"I don't always take direction," I answer.

We walk into courtroom three. The room is paneled in fake wood, and the witness stand and judge's bench appear to be of the same Formica-like "walnut." The entire room seems flimsy, perhaps temporary: One wall looks removable, the other side is an obvious partition. I have seen better mock courtrooms on soap opera sets. The high-quality cable television courtrooms are far better built, with more convincing synthetic wood. The small town court sets favor golden oak. And on feature films we shoot on location, often in historic courthouses with mahogany paneling and marble floors. This may be reality, but it "reads" fake.

I now notice a thin young woman in a navy contemporary career woman's designer suit. The suit is a costume that J. J. would approve. Her grooming also is above reproach, while I can feel my hair curl, out of control, drying in the heat of the courtroom, frizzing in the steam.

She, the lawyer, is blond and quite pretty; I feel a reflexive sting of jealousy: She's a type Matt might like. But why should I still care? Let him like her; let her like him. She'll find out, then she can defend herself. I assume, from her manner and her dolly of legal files, that she is a member of his defense team. I note that her wheelie cart is stacked with legal cartons. This is a detail I have not seen in my films: how burdened the lawyers appear with their legal luggage, rolling along.

Our dirty laundry, I think, glancing at Matt, is their baggage now. I catch myself with that marital *our*. No, "we" are no longer "we." It is him against me. Although we have made love so many thousands of times—although for years he has been my favorite person on this planet—he is now the enemy.

Hate him, I order myself, then feel queasy. I cannot. Why? Why can't I hate him?

She holds more files and walks just behind him. I almost laugh: Matt has a habit of preceding women, in violation of conventional etiquette that decrees the man walk alongside a woman as a proper escort. His rushing ahead always irritated me; I spent seventeen married years running to keep up with him. Now I see this young woman (I judge her to be in her late twenties, thirty-two tops) taking quick steps too. For a moment I feel another sort of jealousy: She looks neat and smart, with her hair aswing at the exact chin-length bob, her eyeglasses set low on her nose. She looks perky and full of spunk, like a television lawyer.

She puts out her hand to J. J. Janis.

"Betsy West," she introduces herself.

Betsy West. A television name.

Betsy West has a brisk, good character-actress manner. She confers with the clerks in a whisper that is both sibilant and deep, so that what I hear across the room is a series of *sshhhshhhshhh* sounds.

J. J. Janis and I sit at one gray metal table; Matt and Betsy West sit as far from us as possible, in the row of metal chairs. With the legal dollies beside them, we would appear as a foursome waiting to embark on a journey—not a bad analogy. The double date from hell.

Betsy West and Matt confer in a whisper, and J. J. Janis whispers too. A collective hiss seems to penetrate the close interior air, synchronizing with blasts of actual steam that escapes from the pressed air heating vents.

As we whisper and watch, another figure strides into the room, a man bundled into a silver parka over his business suit and wearing a plastic-covered fedora. His outfit is a good match for my Mafia wife overcoat.

This new heavyset man is obviously from the city. He has a broad red face with thick features. He looks like a chuck steak wearing a suit. J. J. Janis recognizes him: "Keith MacPherson, former DA from Queens," he says.

"You know him?" I ask.

"Went to NYU Law with him." J. J. Janis looks pleased to see Keith MacPherson. Marvelous, I think. They get to have a chummy reunion. While I pay.

"Uh-oh," J. J. Janis says. At this point a younger man wearing black-rimmed glasses that look like prop glasses (he would be cast as a nerd) walks in, and joins Matt, Betsy West, and the former Queens DA.

"All rise," announces the clerk.

The judge, Cynthia Sintula, whom I recognize from my initial appearance here ("Help me," I asked her. "I am afraid to stay in the house with him") and the arraignment ("I am issuing a temporary order of protection") appears and takes her place at the raised bench.

I had appreciated Judge Cynthia Sintula then, of course. I look to her again in hope. She was sensible; she perceived me correctly when I entered her courtroom on that snowy Monday after the holiday. She recognized a woman in true distress. She knew I would not appear there, discarding my cloak of respectability, admitting the lie that my marriage had become, if I were not telling the truth. Judge Sintula believed me then; she would continue to believe me.

She was the only person I could trust in this situation. She had issued the original order of protection, the membrane that separated me from my husband's wrath and uncontrolled impulses.

Now, looking at Judge Sintula, I think: Good casting. She was an exact duplicate of my projected judge, down to her straight auburn hair. Sensible face. Just the right amount of makeup, clear-as-water gray eyes. Portia in upstate New York. A good-looking woman in every sense. I have a sense of her being a bit hippy, as if she rather filled her robes. She seems careful not to smile, maintaining a judicial frown.

I remember Matt's expression when she issued the original order of protection—how careful he was not to show what I knew was rage underneath. He had given a detached smile.

"Court is in session: All rise." Judge Cynthia Sintula appears to be in my age range, thirty-four to thirty-seven. She gives her stern look to both attorneys as they approach the bench. She has a faintly exasperated manner, as if the dramatics of the courtroom tested her patience.

"Your Honor," begins the former Queens DA, Keith MacPherson, "my client strongly denies any wrongdoing. He has been barred from his home for eight weeks now. He would like to go home and attempt reconciliation with his wife. Failing reconciliation, he still claims a right to remain in the marital domicile. We move to vacate this order of protection."

I feel that tremble in my blood; an actual shiver runs through me: Matt, back in Casa di Rosas. I turn toward my lawyer: *No . . .*

"Never look stricken," J. J. Janis directs me, sotto voce. Preparation for court is not so different, I am discovering, from rehearsing a play. He has told me this before: I must be "neutral, confident, yet injured." In an instant I have forgotten his direction and allowed a look of dismay. First the evidence in the box, now my composure—all forgotten.

"That will cost you," J. J. Janis whispers.

J. J. Janis is up on his feet. "I object Your Honor. I respectfully submit that this court did see the necessity for this order of protection and that it not be vacated. The defendant seriously assaulted his wife, threatened her life. We would like some time to prepare our case. I respectfully submit that to vacate the order would put my client in immediate jeopardy."

Matt looks at me, the rueful smile again: Oh, this was so silly, his expression suggests. But something contradicts his smile: the small bead of blood that begins to drip from his left nostril. I can feel my own intake of breath at the shock of recognition—blood pressure. Whatever causes his attacks of rage also precipitates his nosebleeds. The anger, biological, is percolating through his system. I see him dab with a linen handkerchief. He tilts his head slightly backward.

The others don't seem to notice, but then, no one knows him as I do. The invisible link, the telepathy that exists between man and wife—between Matt and me—exerts its tug. His gaze catches mine; he knows I see the blood. He knows what I am thinking.

I have spent several hours giving J. J. Janis the background and my own theory—that Matt suffers from a mental illness, similar to the one that landed his father and, before that, his grandfather in psychiatric hospitals for brief stays. It is, to my mind, a daisy chain of pain: Matt is forty, the very age at which his father suffered his first breakdown.

"Midlife onset," the woman psychiatrist I consulted had hazarded as the diagnosis.

"Midlife malarkey," Matt said. We were not so far down the road then; he laughed and I did too. Now no one was laughing. The first casualty of madness is a sense of humor. No sane person could engage in the farce of physical chase and assault. Matt does not talk about his childhood; he is not one of those people who continually rework the wounds of the past or even try to understand what occurred. He told me the story only once, the first night I went out with him. It makes me ache to recall. We were both so young, we didn't even know we were young. We thought we were old. I thought of him, especially, as older, seasoned. He had just returned to college after serving in the Gulf War; he had been sent to Kuwait. It was a period of time he didn't choose to discuss; it gave him, to my eyes, an aura of being worldly-wise, saddened by experience. When I met him, he seemed thrust back into youth, a wearied man on a kids' college campus.

Our first date to a "peanut night" at a live music café. I can see us still, as in a photograph—him wearing a blue crewneck sweater and jeans, me in a red sweater and long skirt. He sat next to me in that class, Acting 401. I had recognized him as the unbelievably handsome boy I'd seen crossing the campus. I prayed but did not believe he would ask me out, but when I rose to leave at the end of class, he asked, "Do you like the blues?"

Yes, I liked the blues. What if I didn't? I would have gone with him, anyway. He was not just handsome; his eyes crinkled when he grinned. Definitely a bad-boy grin, an I'm-going-to-get-you grin. I smiled back at him. I was so distracted, I had to plot my words as I walked alongside him across campus. I was happy; I could not believe "it" was happening. Make it last, I remember wishing.

I often think of that night, when we were strangers but able to share secrets better than we ever would as husband and wife. Did marriage come between us? Do husbands and wives have to keep some distance? I suspect that they do. Why? Why is that?

That first night—why did he tell me those raw stories? And then forever after refuse to repeat them?

"Ancient history" was all he ever said. But it wasn't so ancient: Whenever Matt took me home for the holidays to Delaware, the formalities gave way to ferocity. Most often Matt stormed out of his parents' house: Every other Christmas, we went home early. He slammed the parents' door; he pulled me out with him. I was always mouthing the excuses: "He doesn't mean it the way it sounds; we'll call you."

I think of Thanksgiving and Christmas as the gunning of his car engine, the over-the-limit swerves to the Jersey Turnpike, the road home. For the world, I could not see what had gone so extraordinarily wrong back in Delaware. Their family fights seemed to be about form, not content. The father stayed down in the basement workshop most of the time, sharpening things that he said needed sharpening. The mother always got tense over the cooking, the setting of the table. She invariably cried and accused her children of not wanting to be there.

"I don't have to put up with them anymore," Matt always said, leaving his father standing at the doorframe. The father stared after us; their eyes were identical, the same fire, gas-jet blue. I would turn and watch: The father always stood fixed in his position. I always wondered how long he might remain in place. He, too, though, never directly accused: The fight was always, it seemed to be, about the fight.

"Look what you're doing to your mother," he would say to Matt. "She has angina." Then his father, Kurt, would yell, "Get out! I don't expect better from you!"

The holiday was always spoiled, but oddly, whenever I tried to talk to Matt about this, he would jut his chin and his bruised lower lip and say, "My parents are great: We had a home; that's more than you did."

But the night he met me, over draft beer, he said more, he gave more details: the strapping from his father's belt; the thrown furniture; his mother crying but also hitting, striking him with her shoes or—perhaps this was worse—locking him in a room until he "behaved."

On that first night, in his never-to-be-repeated monologue,

Matt relayed his chronicle of abuse. At that college jazz joint he poured it out, downing the tale with draft beer. The story of his father's alcoholism seemed to require beer as an accelerant; I was eighteen and saw no irony or connection—then. Now, of course, I connect the obvious: that both father and son were fueled on alcohol and fired by biochemical anger. And what was his mother's role? Crying and then blaming both father and son, expressing her own distress as illness?

"This is why I need a heart transplant," she was fond of saying, popping nitroglycerin as a chaser to the family arguments, the family feasts. I came to regard her nitroglycerin and digitalis as antacids to rage.

It was not so simple; it never is. Matt's family, even I could see, was not more extreme than many, not even more distressed than their neighbors. They were the Smythes, an ordinary family, with that little *y* in there. Why, I wondered, were they so troubled? Why did they confront one another over what, to my mind, was nothing? And Matt's brutalization had not been limited to his family, to the home. In their working-class neighborhood behind a bottle plant, an abandoned glassworks, Matt had been pummeled by the tougher boys, mocked for his "pretty" face. For self-defense he trained at a gym; he learned to box and wrestle—which now makes him a formidable threat to me. . . .

But on that first date, when he was so young, it seemed understood that he was telling me these sorry stories, displaying his wounds, so that I could heal them. I was happy to do so. How long does it take an eighteen-year-old girl to fall in love? About ten minutes.

We had a pact, unspoken and powerful, that that was what we would do: compensate one another, be reborn in a sense. The first step of course was sexual.

That is the most magical moment, when two people stand alone in a room and somehow decide. There is that sacred silence, the suspense before the first full-body embrace. Then, feeling each other press against each other, bone to bone, we moved into an embrace that seemed to last hours. I felt as if he were branding me somehow as his, and oh, I wanted him to. . . .

When we held each other at dawn, in his attic room off campus, we sealed our bargain. I opened to him, held him; I can still feel my arms around his broad back. I separated a bit from him then psychologically, the way I always do: I saw him on top of me and heard my voice whisper unplanned endearments. I comforted him, rocked him. He held me, too; we whispered each other's name, the new catechism. We were going to save one another, you see.

And now, eighteen years later, in the white winter light of this cheap courtroom, it is apparent that we failed. It is not so easy, even now, to say Matt is crazy; I still feel it, this ache to hold him, to protect him. I alone know his night terrors, his dreams of death, the fear he sometimes feels as he sleeps.

His nightmares were not frequent but they were unforgettable.

"We have to run for it," he said to me one midnight, his eyes unseeing but open, "or we'll be killed."

Rarely but memorably, he sleepwalked. His eyes would be open, but he did not see. I would follow him, almost asleep myself, crying, "Come to bed. You are only dreaming." But he seemed frightened, convinced that he had to flee.

"Listen," I whisper to J. J. Janis. "He needs psychiatric help. Please ask the judge. She can order an evaluation, can't she?"

"There will be an evaluation," J. J. Janis assures me.

Good, I think. Now, he will be forced to get help. For years, of course, I suggested he "see" someone, but he calls psychiatry "the false science." Once or twice I convinced him to make an appointment; we would go together. He always found a reason to cancel or walk out.

Matt Smythe was not going on the couch; he was not even going to take a pill. The rest of the world's population might pop Xanax, Zoloft, Paxil, or Prozac, but he was fine.

So how to explain the mood swings? He called it "temper"— "I've always had a bad temper," he would admit—but now he has crossed the border between temper and terror, and I have no interest in accompanying him further. But I want him to find help; in the new vocabulary of this situation, it is I who repeat the request for the psychiatric evaluation.

"My client would like her husband to submit to a psychological evaluation," J. J. Janis announces. The trio at Matt's table—Betsy West; Keith MacPherson, the former Queens DA; and the nerd, whose name turns out to be Tom Karp—smirk in unison. They shake their heads, looking across at me with a collective expression, so similar to Matt's. You deluded woman, the expression says. Why are you falsely accusing this man?

What has he been telling them? He does not quite look directly at me, but his righteous expression—Oh, poor deluded you—strikes laserlike to the side of my head. He shakes his own head as if in puzzlement at these false accusations. Oh, why are you doing this to me? he seems to ask.

There is a discussion and Judge Cynthia Sintula announces that an order for psychological evaluations shall be read into the record. J. J. Janis then confers with me in one of his stage whispers:

"The evaluations can be paid for by the county, or you can pay for them yourself. It would be five hundred dollars."

I am somewhat startled: Why would I be evaluated also? I have not hurt anyone. But then I see the justice in it: Of course, Matt is innocent until proven guilty. I readily agree to be evaluated, which I assume will be pro forma. I allow the county to assume the cost, which means a court-ordered psychologist chosen by lottery from a pool of such experts often used by the court. I imagine I am saving five hundred dollars, in the hemorrhage of legal costs, but it does raise a concern. I want the best possible psychiatrist to evaluate Matt.

"You're sure we shouldn't just pay for the doctor?" I ask J. J. Janis.

"Not necessary," he says, and of course my husband would also have to agree to absorb the cost. It would not be legal to have one person examined by a court-appointed psychiatrist and the other by a privately paid doctor. The same expert must examine both parties.

In the interim the hearing proceeds. I, Juliana Durrell (née Dubrovsky) Smythe, am called to the stand. I take the usual oath "to tell the truth, the whole truth, and nothing but the truth, I do so solemnly swear." And as best I can, that is what I do, but I know the truth is elusive—that it is open to all interpretation, and that legally J. J. Janis and I are outgunned.

"And you make your livelihood how, Mrs. Smythe?" the former Queens DA begins, after the routine recitations of addresses.

"I am an actor," I said.

At this moment I am puzzled myself by my choice of the traditionally male term. Perhaps it is my female pride, asserting the least sexually prejudiced description under the circumstances.

The former DA, his corned-beef complexion in my face, says, "Why do you use the male form? Shouldn't it be *actress?*"

I look over at J. J. Janis, expecting him to leap to his well-heeled feet and object, but he appears to await my response, so I answer.

"A painter is a painter," I said, "not a paintress. I think it is an attempt to diminish—"

Now J. J. Janis jumps up and I see him admonish me with his eyes. I recall his strong direction: Never elaborate. Say as little as possible. Do not volunteer information. Anything on the record can later be questioned. Do not open sinkholes you will later fall into. . . .

The problem is that I'm accustomed to taking the stage to speak, to improvise if necessary. For fifteen years I've been coached not to be monosyllabic. And so, in my mind, I hear the direction of my acting teacher, the famous Russian Stanislavsky coach, and it is Igor Polishuk who I hear and respond to, when I open my mouth.

"So you are an actor," the former DA says, enunciating the word as if he were saying *leper,* or *whore,* or *phony.* I can hear MacPherson project his contempt, that acting is not a worthy profession. But then, suddenly, he beams and leans forward in a manner I detect as a false attempt at intimacy,

"And tell this court what it is that an actor does."

"Objection," J. J. Janis interrupts. "Irrelevant, and we all know what an actor does."

"I perform," I answer before Judge Sintula declares, "Sustained."

Again and again J. J. Janis objects, but Keith MacPherson manages to squeeze in his remarks, although many are later stricken from the record. We all hear:

"And doesn't an actor have to . . . essentially pretend? Isn't the actor constantly feigning emotion? Isn't an actor involved in make-believe rather than reality?"

I look over at Matt, who is nodding as if in benevolent understanding. Oh, I see: I am the pathetic actress who cannot tell her role from her life, who imagines . . . who invents. . . . I feel the blood beat to my cheeks, burn with anger. Oh, so I am supposed to be this thespian idiot, unable to tell reality, who must then be returned to the custody of her wiser, more mature husband? A ward of the court or a ward of Matt's? If I didn't know it would hurt my case, I would stand and say, "No. No. I will not let you do this to me."

Beside me, J. J. Janis directs, "Wipe that look off your face. You look like you could kill the attorney."

Betsy West leaps in for a new line of questioning. "Can you tell us about a film you made two years ago called *Run for Your Life?*"

Run for Your Life? God, I had almost forgotten that one: I played a stripper in a Northwest lumber town where a psycho has been loose for years, serially doing away with strippers, barmaids, and topless and lap dancers. My character was also a marathon runner. After being attacked, I try to outrace an otherwise successful serial killer. Thus the inspired title *Run for Your Life.*

J. J. Janis objects.

"I object. Do not allow this line of questioning. What does a movie have to do with this actual case?"

Betsy West adjusts her glasses: God, she is good. She emits a small sigh, to show she is patient enough to explain the reason.

"I submit that the events of that film, which were fictional and scripted, exactly coincide with the events the plaintiff has ascribed to her husband."

With a sick certainty I now recall the finale of the film. It is not exactly the same as The Attack—the fictional series of murders had taken place in Oregon woodland—but my character, whom I recall as having a name like Cherylene, did end up trapped in a car with the killer.

I remember filming the scene in a miniskirt, on the brim of a sleet-stung highway, shooting "day for night" and thinking, This is dumb, even for a stripper-jogger. Everyone knows not to hitch-hike. Hitchhiking in winter, in a miniskirt? Not smart. Cherylene had been picked up by the serial killer, who had an engaging way about him. A very nice-looking, rather flirty actor from L.A. who had been too genial for his role, played the sex slayer. The actor never did scare anyone: Off the set, he memorized entire sitcoms from the fifties and sixties. He could recite episodes from *Leave It to Beaver*. All day long he watched TV in his trailer and had to be roused to threaten me.

"Okay," this actor, whose name was Joel, would say going into Makeup and Wardrobe. "Time to strangle, rape, and bludgeon."

I try to concentrate as the lawyers argue "the admissibility": Yes, there are parallels to my complaint and the filmed action sequence. Yes, Matt had driven off the road, then into the oncoming lane, going over ninety miles an hour. Yes, I had tried to get out of the car. Yes, the TV killer (the genial former soap star trying to break into nighttime roles) also seized my arm; we grappled and the car rolled over. As I tried to escape the wreck, my costar knocked me down in the road and began to bludgeon me with a tire iron.

"I was bludgeoned, not—" I say before J. J. Janis can stop me.

Sotto voce, he hisses, "I told you: Don't volunteer, don't argue. Answer yes or no."

The lawyers launch a series of arguments then and finally disappear into chambers to argue a fine point of law. Law books are sent for and carried up from the basement. I sit there, stunned: It has never occurred to me that my occupation could be held against me. I have not invented the story of The Attack; I do not confuse the role on-screen with the actual events that occurred to me in real life. I know reality from make-believe.

"Believe me," I want to say, "I am crystal clear."

Yet, I am unnerved.

When the lawyers reemerge, J. J. Janis tells me that the other team has now officially requested permission to screen *Run for Your Life* for the court.

I protest: This is absurd.

"Keep quiet," J. J. Janis hisses again in my ear. "They probably won't allow it anyway. Unless you keep this up: Then they'll think you are hiding something."

"Motion overruled. At the present time," Judge Cynthia Sintula declares, "we see no reason to admit the film into evidence.

"In fact," she continues, "nothing more will be entered into evidence until the psychological evaluations are completed. Court is adjourned."

"Good," I tell J. J. Janis. "You know, even though I am finished with Matt, I would like to see him get some psychiatric care."

In my heart I have already envisioned his rescue: The right talk therapy in combination with serotonin uplifters. Maybe the boy I loved could still reappear and reclaim the man I fear. I want, still, to save him . . . but not quite as much as I want to save myself.

I watch Matt confer with his legal team; they glance at me, as if I am some demented creature. I overhear MacPherson say, "She has some bizarre fixation that she is hurt," and Matt nods, as if he would like only to help me from these delusions.

"The evaluations will settle that question," he has the nerve to say. "The case will be thrown out."

Then I hear Matt invite Betsy West for "coffee and a bite" as he always asked me. The exact intonation, tilt of his head. I burn, double burn—the backdraft. I hate that I still respond to his actions. Oh, to be indifferent. I should not care anymore. What is he to me? A threat.

As we walk out of the court I ask J. J. Janis, my dubious pro-

tector, "You do believe he's crazy, don't you? You see so many
cases. . . ."

"He has a disease," J. J. Janis agrees. "The cuckoo pops out of
his head. What a Looney Tune. Lunch? Do they have some hot
soup in this tundra?"

I steer him toward Lake Bonticou's one semidecent eatery that
remains open for the winter: Mrs. Schmidt's, a German bakery-
delicatessen with revolving racks of strudel and Kugelhopf cakes.
When we enter the bright restaurant—it is overlit to combat the
darkening, short winter day—my spirit revives as I inhale the
aroma of baking and the pleasant *sssshhhh* of espresso being pres-
surized.

There was once a Mrs. Schmidt: There is a framed photograph
of her at the cash register. Mrs. Schmidt was jolly, with cheeks that
look red even on a black-and-white photograph. She was plump, as
people involved with strudels tend to be. She smiles at us, from the
long-gone past; the curlicue on her forehead marks her hairstyle
from the fifties. I wish Mrs. Schmidt were here now; she seems as
comforting as the sweet, yeasty aromas, the heat emanating from
the stainless kitchen. "Mrs. Schmidt" is now Mr. Schmidt: Her son
runs the place, and he seems to emulate his mother's style.

One time I came in here alone and must have looked the way I
felt. He gave me a bowl of their famed homemade mushroom barley soup, on the house—winked at me and said, "It gets better."
Maybe he is accustomed to refugees from family court coming in
for broth and baked goods. Today he gives me his broad smile.
And a plastic-covered menu with a still life of a strudel on it. I
smile back, grateful for his warmth, the amenities. It's funny, but
sometimes a tiny courtesy can cure a drastic wound.

J. J. Janis and I sit in the window, absorbing more of the thin
sunlight. He orders the barley soup—he watches his weight—but

I give in to temptation and request the cheese strudel with my cappuccino. We are sitting in a booth near the door when we see Matt, Betsy West, the former Queens DA, and the Tom guy enter.

Oh, no, I think, let me have Schmidt's. This is my place. Unbidden, the memory of many breakfasts I shared here, at this very booth with Matt, rises in the steamed air. I remember the long Sunday mornings, sharing the Schmidt's blueberry pancakes, trading bites of bacon for sausage. Coffee, the papers, the coziness of long-accustomed marital munching. Matt must remember too. He has his hand on Betsy West's elbow, steering her past the display of Kugelhopf.

They see us and pause, then look to one another. Schmidt's is the only café left in this part of town. The only other choice is an Irish green neon tavern, O'Malley's, where men and a few women begin to drink at eight A.M. and watch the bar TV all day.

The Matt team confers, then apparently decide to remain at Schmidt's despite the proximity to J. J. Janis and me. Is it my imagination, or does Schmidt sense the situation? He opens an accordion divider and ushers Matt and the opposing legal team into the banquet section, a wide, deserted room. Matt sits down at one of the many square tables with plastic flower centerpieces and faces away from us.

I bite into the flaky strudel but I have lost my appetite. Behind me, new customers are greeting Mr. Schmidt. Many are discussing the morning tragedies. the dead in the car crash, the woman found frozen on Bone Hollow Road. Everyone seems to have known Jane Baker, the woman who froze to death.

"Things like this never used to happen," says a man at the counter. "It's the time we live in, everybody goin' too fast, and going crazy too."

"There were always terrible events," Mr. Schmidt remarks, his tone habitual. "Remember the war. And the Frozen Girls. There's nothing happening today hasn't happened before."

I suppose he means that to be comforting. The Frozen Girls, I think. Who were they? Then I remember the statue at the Bonticou Lutheran Church—the marble maidens, circa 1900, a group of girls who died some terrible death on Lake Bonticou in a long-ago winter. They are some sort of local legend. I found a vintage postcard of the statue in Bonticou Antiques and saved it. It was one of those quaint cards addressed to someone, hand-scripted, dated 1902. I have it somewhere at the house, in a bureau. I was taken with the contrast of the beautiful frozen girls on the picture and the vacation greetings scribbled on the back: "We're having a splendid summer on Lake Bonticou—sailing, canoeing, and sunning ourselves by the hour."

The Frozen Girls. And now there is the Frozen Woman. Maybe Mr. Schmidt is right: Everything comes round again. I look out the window at the crisp day; the temperature is below zero and the air now has that clarity of the cold. It would not be difficult to freeze in Bonticou; the trick is *not* to. I shiver, grateful for the heat and steam of the Mrs. Schmidt's.

I sit and sip the hot, intense coffee, nibble the fresh-baked pastry, reflect that this snack will cost the menu prices, plus $305 an hour.

"Dolling," J. J. Janis says, "I'm going to need another ten thousand dollars. This case should have been over with already. And I hate to tell you this, but seeing the legal force that your husband has assembled makes me think you should also retain a local lawyer."

"You're quitting?" I can't believe it: I've given J. J. Janis my entire savings as his retainer.

"No, I can stay and work with the local attorney for you. But a small-town court like this—the lawyers all have lunch together; deals are made. I am afraid I'm not best serving you if you don't have someone personally known in that courthouse. Betsy West happens to be Judge Sintula's best friend. Of course, she can rise above that, but . . . you hear what I am saying?"

I hear.

Then J. J. Janis gives me a slip of paper with the name of the court-appointed psychologist: Dr. Hubert Lazare. I look at the address. The doctor's office is above our heads, a one-flight walkup over the deli. I get up, go to the pay phone, and call for an appointment. J. J. Janis follows, stands close beside me as I dial.

"Try to pay my fee, dolling: The retainer is gone. . . ." Twenty-five thousand dollars already to maintain an order of protection. I feel queasy, as I always do when talking about money; the cheese strudel backs up as I say, "You know I'm not working. . . ."

"Oh, you actresses always get residuals. I bet *See How She Runs* made millions."

"*Run for Your Life*," I correct. "Thousands for me, not millions."

"We're on again for next week. Choose a local lawyer, get your evaluation. . . . Give a kiss, dolling. Everything will be all right. A heart knows a heart."

J. J. Janis kisses me on both cheeks as I stand, holding the metal cord of the pay phone.

"Sweetie, look right here, under *Attorneys* . . . "

The yellow pages dangle on a chain from the pay phone.

I crack the book open to *Attorneys*.

"J. J.," I say, "help me choose."

"Call five. Make appointments, pick the best two, then call me, dolling, and I'll help you decide." J. J. Janis gives me his dry double peck on both cheeks and departs, going back to what he calls "civilization."

The yellow pages of Lake Bonticou list dozens of lawyers. This strikes me as a large number for a small town. Most of the lawyers have invested in advertisements, many with illustrations. The negligence lawyers depict car crashes, workers on crutches, and silhouettes of paraplegics in wheelchairs. The matrimonial teams feature family portraits torn in half, lightning-divided houses.

I decide to limit the auditions to the five lawyers who feature family law in their advertisements. I rule out the lawyers with the full-page illustrated ads—the inflamed eyeballs or unbalanced scales of justice. There is a beauty shot of a young woman with blond bangs; she is available seven days a week, some evenings. I note her name: Betsy West.

So this is where Matt found her. The low-cut sundress is inappropriate, I tell myself. She looks like an ad for an escort service. Her advertisement features a severed bride and groom staring in opposing directions.

So she also handles divorce. As does J. J. Janis. If I survive, I can sue for divorce. But who can represent me in the small-town buddy system?

I look for good, solid names, unobtrusive listings. I want a Jimmy Stewart or Spencer Tracy type. Katharine Hepburn or Eileen Heckart. I am influenced by every late-show movie classic I have ever watched, and am certain there are charming or at least crusty honest lawyers in Lake Bonticou. Auditioning is something I understand: I almost enjoy being on the other side. I can cast the local lawyer, and there are so many candidates.

As I scan the listings, I fantasize, and (I am embarrassed to admit) romanticize. I have played so many victim-heroines and watched so many lawyer-client clinches in those movie classics, that I half expect that I will fall in love with my lawyer, or he with me. Because of J. J. Janis's peculiar paternal (not to say venal) attitude, I do not nourish such fantasies with him, but I do project them onto the new names in the yellow pages.

My small-town lawyer should have a bow tie (although I have never met a man with a bow tie, even in Lake Bonticou). He is tall and skinny, shy. He has never married but is secretly a virile hetero-sexual. Why he has never married is a plot line that I don't develop.

I have five lawyers' names, and I try to sort for Jimmy Stewart potential: The best name is Cody Laker. I like the idea of a Cody. Jimmy Stewart, Western style? In our future we will raise Thoroughbred horses. We will ride together, leaving my failed marriage, my siege of terror, in our dust.

My first standard for a country lawyer is met on the phone. Cody Laker has a secretary, and she sounds like Eileen Heckart. I picture the small, poor, but honest law office, with leather chairs (real but worn), a frayed rug on the floor, a plant strung to catch the light.

Yes, he will see me on short notice, the crackly character-actress voice assures. I am seeking sympathy in phone voices, and I detect a bit of pity, wry but kind. I ask if there is a fee: I want a lawyer who offers free consultation.

"Oh, no," she says, her voice hearty and honest into my ear as I stand in the prison hospital lobby. "Just come on in. Our first con-sultation is absolutely free."

I take the first available appointment, at four that afternoon. That gives me ample time to get home and retrieve the evidence, The Thing in the Box. I have been feeling its absence the way amputees sense a missing limb. My arm has its own reflex, a near twitch as I repeatedly reach for what is not there. I cannot relax until I get home and find it, as I imagine I left it, set right beside my door. In my mind I continue to project—the glossy shopping bag with the twine handle. It must be there.

I am running toward the door, when I almost crash into Matt. In that odd etiquette of estranged spouses, he holds the door for me. I react, nonsensically, easing past him, careful not to brush against him, in that herringbone coat I know so well. I catch a whiff of male cologne, his personal scent, so pleasant, so familiar, like vanilla.

"Excuse me," I say, without planning to, as I run, my face burning, toward the snow-packed street. Just get me to the car, I think, just get me home. I reach into my coat pocket and fumble for my car keys. As if struck by sonar, I sense Matt has followed me onto Duane Street, that he is standing, exerting his marital ritual. "Whenever you turn, you will see me . . ."

I try to resist the impulse, but I can't—I turn sideways and just catch him, in my peripheral vision. I turn away fast, but not before I see his lips twitch in, I think, a smile.

Good Housekeeping

Safe in the cold shell of the Saab, I check my messages, just in case I'm wrong and somehow lost the crucial bag by dropping it in the parking lot. Maybe there is a message. The automated voice drones, *"You have one message,"* and then I hear it—the low mumble of the housecleaner, Moira Gonzalez Gerhardt. I can barely make out her words, but the mumble translates as "I'll try to come in today, if my car makes it over the mountain."

Instantly, I visualize the old Bendel bag with the evidence, left by my error by the doorway. It could be mistaken as garbage. I imagine Moira Gonzalez Gerhardt with her characteristic shuffle, toting it out to the trash cans, then the massive truck of Bonticou Waste Management grumbling up the driveway, the men tossing the evidence into the grinding mechanism at the rear of the truck. Crunch goes my case. I have too great an ability to envision this sequence. I view, as on film, Moira, in her gray sweats, her flannel shirttail, the running shoes. She picks up the bag, shakes her head: *No, this is trash.* On quick inspection The Thing in the Box would not have value to her.

Oh, how could I have left it there? I try phoning Casa di Rosas, this time to leave my own message, to see if someone—she, Moira Gonzalez Gerhardt—will pick up. I doubt Moira will answer, but I have to try. I speak into the void: I hope she is not there, but I address her: "Moira, if you can hear this, please don't throw anything out. I'll be right there."

No one picks up. I start the Saab, drive without waiting to warm her engine, roar out of Bonticou Court toward Casa di Rosas. Driving at the exact speed limit, fifty-five, which is too fast on the iced and snowdrifted roads. Duane and Main streets are clear, the snow banked along the berm, but Serpentine Road appears drifted. The wind, I suppose, has blown last night's snow across the road. The sky above is bright blue; there is no indication of further precipitation.

I skid on the final S turn before Casa di Rosas. The Saab seems to lift off the iced road, swings about-face, and lands in the (thankfully) empty oncoming lane.

I sit at the wheel, my heart beating against the Mafia lady coat. Catch my breath, yes, the car will turn, and I drive at a crawl, a chastened ten miles per hour up the final ascent to my driveway.

There are fresh treadmarks but no car or truck at the outer circular drive. I pull to the side, where I leave my car in high snow conditions, and walk in the last fifty feet to the driveway proper. I hope that was not the garbage truck; the tread is pretty wide. . . .

I am not the first to walk toward the house. There are several footprints, one set of large boot marks. Moira, I think: Moira must be inside. All footprints point toward the house; no one has left. Someone must have dropped her off and she is inside, cleaning Casa di Rosas.

I stare up at the house, which looks more bridal than ever—a Viennese wind cake, stiff with frosted decoration. The boot prints mark her straight path to the front door. I note how tiny the prints are, the design of the heels, impacted, stamped like brand-name cookies in the packed snow. My body tenses: There is more than one set of boot prints; the others are smaller, but clearly Moira Gonzalez Gerhardt is not alone inside my house.

There is something alien to a house even temporarily occupied by someone else. Music, a country-western song I would not have chosen, blares from the living-room stereo: a woman, claiming to be "Blessed" caterwauls the ordinary joys of a domestic day. I turn the key in the lock and enter. Moira cannot hear me: The music is blaring, the vacuum, the Supralux, roaring. Upstairs, the television squawks. I can't help feeling a touch invaded: Moira has entered in my absence, and not alone. She must not expect me; I have not ever heard her play loud music, or the television. Is this what happens on those Wednesdays when I am not here?

And the worst-case scenario: Where the shopping bag containing the evidence—The Thing in the Box—had stood, there is only a broom and a dust pan. "Moira," I call upstairs. I start up the steps, my heart beating. The Bendel's bag, the evidence. It must still be here somewhere in the house.

Who else is here? I come upon Moira from behind; she is on the second-floor landing, vacuuming the Oriental runner. I see her familiar form clad in soft gray sweatpants and a loose pink pullover. She is intent on her task, and I have to raise my voice to announce myself. She turns at the sound, reflexively screams, then apologizes: "Oh, sorry, Mrs. Smythe, I didn't hear you come in."

"Juliana," I correct her. "Moira, this is important: There was a shopping bag near the door. . . ."

"I thought I better get in while I could; it's supposed to snow again tonight." Moira turns off the Supralux. She hasn't heard my question. "I had to bring the twins; otherwise I could not have come. Sybella! Brianna! Turn that down. Mrs. Smythe is here."

"They're in the bedroom," she explains, "so I could clean. They're real good; I brought along a couple of videos. I hope that was okay, that I brought the kids. My mom couldn't watch them: She's snowed in. Rafe had to drop me off; he's working snowplows today, and he didn't want me driving on these roads, no, no. He'd worry sick over me, in my old car."

Moira has a husband who cares about her safety, I think; then I cut to the chase. Please, God, don't let her have discarded the evidence, The Thing in the Box, in some irretrievable way. I clear my throat and say, "Moira, I hope you didn't throw out a brown-and-white-striped shopping bag? It was near the front door?"

"Oh, no," she says. "I put that out in the woodshed. It looked like something burned."

Relief warms me; the blood actually circulates the good news—what passes for good news—through my body. At this moment I could hug Moira. "Oh, good. Thank you."

"I wouldn't throw out nothing without asking," she says. "And I had to bring the kids," she repeats. "Schools is closed, and this is the only day I could come in for you. The kids are good kids; they won't hurt nothing."

As if cued, the twins appear in the doorframe of my bedroom. They stare—two towheaded five-year-old identical girls. Actually they are not exact duplicates. They are wearing polyester sweatsuits in opposing colors: One is turquoise, the other is yellow. Each shirt has a rubberized embossed bear face wearing eyeglasses. One girl is heavier in a healthy way, as if she had been favored in the womb. The other twin is slighter, paler; she wears thick corrective lenses that appear too large, almost like gag spectacles, on her thin face. The girls resemble Moira—the same fine pale hair, blue eyes; they even seem to replicate her slouch and small lapses in grooming. The twins have identical colds, postnasal drips; their faces appear lacquered where thin mucus has dried like varnish. They contemplate me, and I feel obliged to entertain them.

"I have a stuffed Paddington Bear that was mine when I was little. Did you see it on the window seat?"

They nod. They are holding little bags of a fast-food snack, something that looks like fat orange worms. If I weren't so relieved that Moira has not, in fact, thrown out the evidence, only moved it, I might be annoyed at the fine orange dust that sifts from the plastic snack bags.

"Well, I'm about done," Moira says, sensing some incompatibility in the situation of my return and the little girls being in the house. I sense that she had hoped to come and go and I would never know that she had brought in the twins.

"It's all right," I tell her.

I cannot help but be struck, as ever, by her prettiness. I don't know her exact age, but I would guess Moira Gonzalez Gerhardt is about twenty-three. She must have given birth to these girls when she was hardly grown herself, a mother at seventeen. She has eyes as round, china-blue, and childish as her daughters'; her forehead is a bit protuberant and her lips full and heart-shaped. She wears no makeup; her skin is white, poreless. In another era she could have been a Marilyn Monroe type, the same soft skin, a rabbity tremble to her mouth and lips. For decoration, I suppose, she pierced that left eyebrow; a metal pin goes through it. I know it is the style for her generation, but unbidden, I have an urge to extract the thing. At best, the pin looks like some adjunct to her job, an afterthought to remind her of some task. I think the piercing spoils her looks.

Moira could be beautiful if she believed her reflection, but she has a downward cast, an off-to-the-side indirection. That slump to conceal her breasts is so profound, it perpetuates itself in the droop of her head, the slant of her hair, half curtaining her face. She droops even when moving, and seems not to lift her feet from the floor. Her entire body language suggests avoidance. And indeed now, as I approach, she seems to slink backward, pretzeling her rather outrageous figure: She's got that large, soft, bobbling bosom and extremely narrow hips, almost as if she were shaped in a funnel. Her legs are short but muscular, I suppose from her tasks.

Though she is a great cleaner, Moira herself is not neat: Her natural blond hair appears darkened at the center part—grease—and the hair hangs lank. The dust that she eradicates from the house seems to cling to her person, and I can see white flakes on her scalp.

There is something about Moira, something I can never explain, that unsettles me. I always wonder if she resents me. No woman is a heroine to her housecleaner, I suppose, and I have sometimes read disapproval in her manner as she picked up my scripts, the jumbles of clothing, used towels. *Dislike* is too strong a word; I don't dislike her at all. I simply feel more comfortable when she leaves. In summer, whenever our times overlap, I feel as if I am on stage, my movements choreographed, my voice strained. She is a witness to my Wednesday mornings, so I have to play myself.

For most of the past year I arranged not to be present on her "days." This was not personal: I always prefer to be alone in the house, rather than make enforced conversation. Moira Gonzalez Gerhardt expects a bit of a chat, and that often expands to an hour or so. She starts off usually with the virtues of a particular brand of cleanser, then segues to disasters. Moira, like most other Lake Bonticouans, relishes the ongoing reportage of car wrecks, foul weather, freak accidents: "Man down the road saw lightning hit his barn; he died right there, just seeing it." She is high on electrocutions, the kicker being the double electrocution of a husband and wife who were incorrectly installing storm gutters: "Their neighbor found them both on the lawn, stone dead."

Moira includes tales of emotional upset as well. ("Here's a good one. Woman next door to me found her husband with her sister-in-law: They were performing sodomy behind a billboard on Route 27 while everybody else was having ribs.") Moira has a wide acquaintance of women who are always "catching" their men cheating, or drinking, or "beating up on them." She recites these tales so often, whilst leaning on the long handle of the Supralux or pausing while holding a dust rag, that I have actually begun to wonder if there isn't something inherently "domestic" about domestic abuse. Her sister-in-law was pushed against a washer-dryer, her best friend slammed into the refrigerator. I have always taken a role of near mute sympathy to these sagas, standing in position at the door to my bedroom "office," saying, "Oh, that's too bad; that shouldn't have happened. Uh. Uh. Uh."

Maybe this is my comeuppance: to end up as a Moira story. I had unconsciously perfected a plan in which I seldom crossed paths with her and I would arrive at Casa di Rosas to find the house gleaming and scented with citrus spray. She would leave little notes, most often: *You're out of paper towels and lemon oil. Buy S.O.S pads.*

Upon my homecomings, I could see that Moira Gonzalez Gerhardt seemed to take vicarious pleasure in my stead as mistress of Casa di Rosas: She would make up my bed, especially, in a manner more "romantic" than I customarily did. Moira not only plumped the pillows, she would drape my best negligee on the covers and position the designer pillows, embroidered linen sheets, hand-cut Victorian shams. The intimacy of her handling my clothes, opening the drawers, "designing" my bed, unnerves me a little, but I suppose that she enjoys this as a more artistic aspect of her job. I, too, love handling these linens, smoothing them, tucking down the several layers. And I will concede Moira shows talent: She could have worked as a stylist for historical romance novels, or those "shelter" magazines that feature frilled Victorian bedrooms.

I am perhaps oversensitive to the fact that she cleans for me. I have never been able to make many specific requests, especially regarding the unappealing tasks. I just can't mouth a line like "Can you scrub the toilet?" I do the bathrooms myself, and we've had an unwritten understanding that her job consists of what she wants to do. And those tasks she does extremely well, especially the vacuuming.

Now she notes her twins have sifted the cheese curl dust onto the just-cleaned carpet runner. "Oh, I'll vacuum that up, Mrs. Smythe."

"Juliana," I remind her. "And I won't be 'Mrs.' much longer." I have to explain to her that I am "in the process of divorce."

I recall J. J. Janis's instruction: There are more witnesses than you realize. Housecleaners are among the best witnesses, he said: They watch for detail. They observe changes. They salvage things; they clean up messes. I must ask: Has she noticed anything out of the ordinary?

Moira stands in the accustomed pose, holding the handle of the Supralux. She is truly interested, I see. It is hard to say something so personal. I know every word I say changes everything: I will no longer be the Juliana Durrell Smythe, the actress who employs her. I will be yet another woman in marital trouble. Grist for the Lake Bonticou domestic horror mill. Now I am someone who must ask if she noticed any of the debris of my husband's rages.

"Moira . . . do you remember the vase, the green one with the big roses? It must have been last June, because the peonies were in bloom; it was filled with the peonies. Do you remember the day you came here to clean and the vase was shattered? I remember you asking what to do with the pieces."

She does remember. "You said it fell."

"It didn't fall," I am now forced to inform her. "My husband threw it." I give an edited synopsis: He has been angry, becoming violent; that is why I cannot live with him any longer, and we . . . we have a case in court.

"So that's why you're staying here all winter?" she guesses. "Not just coming up weekends?"

"Yes," I tell her. "Until . . . the court case is resolved."

I have one of my flashes: I see myself, returning here to Casa di Rosas when the ordeal is over; I see myself as triumphant as one can be after such personal disaster. Matt is in jail, or under psychiatric care. I do not have to be afraid. It is summer, and I walk inside, replacing roses in a new version of the shattered vase. The light in Casa di Rosas is summer light, filtered through the greenery outside. The green tint seems to permeate the downstairs, a cool minted shade. And I smell the roses, the white roses.

Unbidden, as if on a second track, my mind plays an alternate scenario: Matt is vindicated, unbound by the court order, and we return here alone together, to this house, for the dance of death. I lose my case but win posthumous respect: The world will know the truth, but the definitive evidence of my case is my corpse. I see myself framed and mounted, another slain wife in the photomontage at Bonticou County Family Court.

"I may have said the vase fell," I clarify, "because I was embarrassed. He, Mr. Smythe—Matt—threw it." I don't add—I just can't add—"He threw it at me." I have to take a breath. "So, if you saw anything, noticed anything out of the ordinary, that made you wonder if my husband might, well, might be . . . irrational . . . you can tell me. . . ."

"Irrational?" she asks.

"Crazy," I translate.

"Just the time he came up alone."

What? "He came up here alone?" Not that I ever knew. . . .

"Yes, between Thanksgiving and before I cleaned for Christmas. He was here without you, and I came in to clean. I didn't actually see him, but there were signs of him."

"Signs?"

"Yes, the liquor bottles, the vodka that he drinks."

"Bottles?"

I knew Matt likes a drink, vodka especially, but bottles, plural?

"Well, I was always finding them in the shed, in the recycling. And there was a new empty one when I come . . . and his clothes were out in the bedroom, the bed wasn't made up, and he had hung sheets up over the window. His car was here but he wasn't. I thought maybe he was cross-country skiing, like you two did."

This gives me pause. Do I know him at all? My husband up here for a few days, drinking, with the windows blacked out? That detail—the sheets over the window—rings an alarm. At the very end he did nail a bedsheet over the bedroom window. He insisted that "people could see in," although the bedroom view is the frozen expanse of Lake Bonticou, and the nearest house a half mile distant, on the opposite shore.

Now I am trying to think, reverse the mental calendar. . . . Yes, I was away, in California, for three days in early December. It was supposed to be my last trip before . . . We had made our New Year's resolution—the irony cuts like acid—to start what he called "our family." I was uneasy; he was already fitful, impatient with me. I did not feel loved, but when he talked about a baby, his voice softened and he implied that our childlessness was the root of his despair. "Everyone has babies," he said.

I am not the first woman deluded enough to dream that a baby may be . . . *may* be the answer. I had stopped birth control, prayed for love to return, perhaps in human form. I would take the final business trip before, we hoped, a pregnancy would intervene.

While I was in California, Matt had called me several times. He seemed to be calling from New York, from his office or the apartment. Of course now, with mobile phones and call forwarding, he could be calling from Timbuktu. According to Moira Gonzalez Gerhardt, he was here, on a drunken bender, and I never knew him to do such a thing. The single indicator that I could recognize was the business with the bedsheet over the window. "People can see in," he kept insisting. "People can see in."

I try not to betray too much shock at her report. I ask if there were any other things she thought I should know.

"Well"—she takes a pause—"I don't know that I should say." And then, instantly, she does say: "He seemed to have messed himself in the bathroom." Then she adds, with a martyred tone, "I cleaned it so you'd never know."

I somehow can't ask for details on "messed himself." What— vomit? Worse?

"And I don't know if I should say," Moira adds, "but I think there may have been . . . someone else here. I mean, not you."

There is a pause. I just look at her. I can hear Matt's antique clock tick on the mantel. It gongs the hour. Someone else. My mind curls into my skull, retracting. Is he crazy *and* unfaithful? Or can there still be an explanation? I ask Moira: How does she know there was another person here?

"Well, your hiking shoes were used, and so were his. I noticed 'cause there were two pairs, tracked mud; the shoes was kicked off in the entry. But I knew you were in California. I only come in 'cause you called me, to ask could I clean before Christmas? Because you and him were having a special holiday here."

A special holiday. God, did I tell her that? It had been special all right: I did remember calling her, from Los Angeles from my hotel room.

"And I come right in, and he's here but not in the house—but somebody had been wearing your shoes. There were lots of dishes in the sink, too, more than I would figure he would need, eating alone. Liquor glasses too."

If time had stopped on New Year's Eve, it now seems to rewind. My mind spins, unable to sort these details. The drinking, the secret visit, someone—another woman?—wearing my shoes. Is the world off its axis, or am I?

I feel an actual dizziness; in the past, when stunned, I have fainted on occasion. In college I fainted in science class, at a frog dissection, and I fainted in the hospital hallway when a surgeon described my mother's fatal malignancy. I remember what to do when dizzy: Sit down and hang my head between my knees, let the blood return to my brain. I sink onto a small claw-footed love seat that sits in the hall. I lower my head and fold my arms as if being punished at school.

"Are you okay?" Moira asks. She sounds very concerned.

"Yes, fine," I answer, raising my head. "I just don't know what to think." Despite everything, I still have my pride. I cannot ask about the bedsheets, the towels, my bathrobe. But now anger is heating my face. How dare he? Did he? If so, was his rage staged on New Year's Eve? Is madness a ruse to end a marriage? Is he actually involved with someone else? Is the marriage really being derailed by adultery? Is this his covert way of forcing a divorce? I don't want to think this, but the sex had been strange between us for the last six months. Or the other possibility: In his madness, is he also acting out in other ways?

"I wasn't expecting to hear all this," I confide in Moira. "It may be important in court. Would you . . . I hate to ask . . . but would you . . . testify?"

She is a pale girl, but she seems to blanche.

"To what? To what would I testify?"

"Nothing more than what you just said. It's strange, and it might help me. I think the marriage is over, and he must never come back here."

"Well, I suppose, if that's all I'd be saying. I never really saw him, though," she adds. "But he was here. I saw his suitcase, his things, his leftover food and laundry. It's a shame: Everybody's getting divorced," she remarks, "except me and Rafe. We're just doin' life, I guess." She smiles, as if embarrassed by the success of her marriage as opposed to mine.

For a moment I envy Moira: She is loved. I think of her husband, Rafe; he's so concerned for her safety. Today he dropped her off, and he will also pick her up, to spare her the risk of driving the unsafe roads. She sometimes mentions other protective details—that he doesn't want her walking in the woods, that sort of thing. "He's always worried something will happen to me," she says.

"Lucky you," I cannot help but say.

"Yeah," she agrees. "Me and Rafe, we're okay. Come on, girls," she calls to the twins. "It's time to go. Daddy will be here. It's spaghetti night."

Spaghetti night. I can see Moira is looking forward to returning home to her double-wide on the other side of the mountain. She is better off than I am. The very words *spaghetti night* conjure the steam and bustle of a family dinner, safety. "I'll ask Rafe about the court stuff," she says. "If I can testify. He wouldn't want me to be in danger. . . ."

"I understand," I assure her. "And I understand if you don't want to testify." I almost add, "You came here to clean, but not this. . . ." Aloud, I add, "I can understand that Rafe might not want you to become involved, but it is your decision. . . ."

"Oh, Rafe will probably say it's okay."

As if summoned, Rafe's big black truck, with the uplifted yellow snowplow and two orange lightning streaks painted on the flanks, roars up to the driveway. I see him lower the plow attachment and shove more of the snow into a ruffling bank. Yes, I think, he's a real good guy.

Moira gathers the twins, with their cheese curls, snow parkas, and boots, dragging "blankies" and assorted stuffed acrylic bears and bunnies. They all file downstairs, struggle into snow boots, and go out the door.

I watch as Rafe scoops up Sybella, and holds out a steadying hand to the other twin Brianna, who looks back at me, her stare magnified through the corrective lenses. Rafe is bareheaded, his thick, waving blond hair catching the clear winter sunshine. We have this in common, I think: We both married unusually handsome men. Rafe would look like Errol Flynn if Errol Flynn were dressed for a role as an outdoor laborer. Rafe is weathered, soiled from work, and his winter jumpsuit is darkened with oil. He has a particular quality no actor could emulate: For all of his twenty-something years, Rafe has absorbed the elements; he has a quality of being permanently soiled, not dirty; he is past being able to be cleaned. I am certain his padded winter jumpsuit is laundered, and he must shower; but the dirt and tar have been incorporated into the texture of his clothes and even his skin, so that no washing can remove the stain. He wears no gloves, and I can see his hands, darkened, purple-gray from the cold. Many men in Lake Bonticou don't wear gloves; it's some sign of pride. In fact, their fingers don't seem to freeze; they are hardened, like plants, to the frost. His hands have become his gloves. I shook hands with Rafe Gerhardt once, the first time he picked up Moira, and I remember his touch: He felt almost inanimate, his palm was so toughened. Moira mentioned that she bought him gloves and he refused to wear them. She buys him hand cleaner, too, the industrial stuff that comes in cans, but even those products named after pumice and lava cannot remove the ingrained grit. For an instant I wonder what his hands must feel like on her soft white skin. Once she said Rafe was highly sexed, "a maniac," but she smiled.

One afternoon last year, I dropped Moira off at their home when her car broke down and Rafe had been out, helping a friend with an emergency tow. I had been shocked that Moira could live in the double-wide, which I regarded as a white plastic box, and that she had allowed the builder—if you could call someone who deposited prefabricated homes, a builder—to set the house onto the high flank of Mount Bonticou. Their lot appeared to be a slash in the side of the mountain, the driveway a raw mudslide, a near-vertical, slashed zigzag to the busiest road in our area, Route 27. It had struck me as a precarious place, perched at so high an angle that it could be transient. Above and behind the house rose the forested side of Mount Bonticou, with two hundred-year-old pines, hemlock. Now, watching the family hurry for home on a cold afternoon, I thought it was probably cozy for them inside the white vinyl rectangular box; they were their own Christmas present, left under the living Christmas trees.

I follow Moira and the kids to the end of my driveway. I watch Rafe hoist his girls into the truck, one by one. They all fit in the front cab. I hear him say that he rented a movie for tonight.

"Great," she says. "I'll make popcorn." Lucky you, I think. Lucky you.

The instant the truck pulls out, I run to the woodshed and I catch my breath. Yes, there it is: The Bendel bag, so incongruous, smart, with its glossy brown-and-white stripes, rests next to the bark-covered logs and stacks of kindling. I open the bag, reach down, and touch the box. I open the box just wide enough to check that The Thing is still in there, and when I see it, the evidence, The Thing in the Box, despite my relief I begin, for the first time since everything happened, to weep.

Pewter Mountain

Having a legal case such as mine, I am discovering, is a full-time job. Protecting the order of protection is my new career, I think.

There is no time for crying; I resist the urge to go upstairs to my beautifully appointed bed. I have only seven days before I must reappear in court, with a new, local lawyer at my side. And I must also schedule my psychological evaluation. It's in my interest to have that evaluation right away. In fact, I hope to jump in as soon as possible with Dr. Hubert Lazare; I should speak to him before Matt has his interview with the psychologist. I know, more than anyone in the world, how convincing Matt Smythe can be. He convinced me, didn't he?

I have that single free consultation set up with a local lawyer, Cody Laker. Standing at my wall phone, not pausing to consider, I call two more law offices. As always, I am interested in a woman, and there is one female name with a discreet ad, a Susan Sachs, who has a family law practice near the courthouse. I will see this Susan Sachs, Cody Laker, and one more, for insurance. I pick the third name on a hunch—Joe Gromolka from my own Bonticou yellow pages directory. Joe Gromolka, a good character name. I imagine a basset hound sniffing for truth, a big shlumpy guy who will shuffle around town, collecting the right evidence. A Joe Gromolka would be unimpressive physically but houndlike; he would get the job done. I call Joe Gromolka, and his answering machine sounds exactly as I might have predicted: a deep, low, muttery voice, "This is Joe Gromolka . . ." He isn't in, but his machine promises my call will be returned "promptly."

Susan Sachs answers the phone herself; even her "Hello, Susan Sachs" is fast, hyperthyroid. I picture big eyes magnified by eyeglasses, a tiny, wiry, metabolically fired body. She wastes no time setting up an appointment: I will see her at two, before Cody Laker.

Now the evaluation. I have the voucher, but I must go to a destination listed on the slip of paper as Pewter Mountain to have it approved. As always, I picture Pewter Mountain as a set from a film classic such as *Spellbound*—Ingrid Bergman in the white lab coat, striding through an ivy-covered, slightly downscale rural sanitorium. Pewter Mountain must be an upstate version of Silver Hill, or McLean's, that sanatorium in New England where so many celebrities have gone to heal the cracks. I also imagine the mental institution where Natalie Wood is sent in *Splendor in the Grass*—a place of basket-weaving craft workshops and lawn chairs, folksy psychiatrists with uncluttered calendars. Endless time to chat and heal, partake of country-club–like meals.

I can't help fantasizing that Matt will be committed to such a place. In visiting Pewter Mountain, I am taking perhaps the first steps toward his recovery. Thank God, they ordered the evaluation; he would never consent to a voluntary psychological testing.

In my past films, people are put away quite efficiently. Would-be killers are soon slathering behind mesh or talking through slots, straitjacketed and confined. In character, I have never been dispatched to the local county "facility" to have my court voucher for the evaluation approved. So much for FemJep, and another dose of reality for me.

I drive through the now cleared streets of Lake Bonticou, trying to feel some relief in the pale winter light. Just keep going, I instruct myself. Do what must be done today. Get the voucher, interview the lawyers, and pick the winner. The slip of paper I have set in the ashtray reads *Pewter Mountain.* I have directions to drive all the way to the outskirts of town—a series of left turns, up a slanted access road, well paved and plowed. I note that the zoning of Lake Bonticou must dictate that such institutions be kept hidden, beyond the sight lines of the tourists and summer people.

The driveway is discreet, the chain-link fence set back from the entrance. I have been near here—the racecourse is within earshot—but I have never noticed Pewter Mountain until today. At first glance I could mistake this for a sewage treatment plant. But from the condition of the clear roadway and the packed parking lots, the winter people, the actual inhabitants of Lake Bonticou, know this facility well.

Pewter Mountain is not, as I pictured, a private mental hospital: Pewter Mountain houses a prison and medical facility. Pewter Mountain is not on the Lake Bonticou map—the chamber of commerce doesn't list it as an attraction—but Pewter Mountain does boast one historic building, a redbrick Victorian fortress that looks as if it might house the Mrs. Rochester of *Jane Eyre.* Its barred windows, overlaid with concertina wire, suggest uncontrolled, grimacing maniacs behind the facade. The other buildings in the compound appear more routine, fake-brick "sister" buildings, adjuncts to the courthouse in downtown Bonticou. The same lack of symmetry, the gawky mansard roofs set too low on the blocklike structures. The entire complex appears almost false, like an artist's rendering by an amateur.

I'm startled at the expanse, the number of the brick extensions: The Pewter Mountain complex spreads out, flanking a quadrangle. Like the courthouse, the structures are old-new, 1960's. Spam-can ugly. I go inside, clutching my request voucher.

As I stand on line at a tellerlike window at the lobby, I hear two women ahead of me discussing evaluations. "I just hope you don't get Lazare," one is saying. I realize I have crossed the border into another Lake Bonticou. This town coexists with the resort as I have known it; now the facade has been struck, like a set at the end of the stock season. In this off-season I am seeing the bones of the town, when the local preoccupations are alcoholism and abuse. The wall is covered with notices, listings of the Twelve Step program, Alcoholics Anonymous, Al-Anon, Overeaters Anonymous, Parents Without Partners . . . Sufferers of SAD Syndrome.

I sit down in a molded orange fiberglass chair to wait for the voucher to be signed. Women on each side of me have cases. I do not understand their references, but the overheard snatches of conversation are enough to alarm:

"They won't be digging in my backyard," says one woman.

And another remarks, "I consider an electric knife a weapon."

There is more Bonticou Gothic: Here, too, the waiting room offers copies of the *Bonticou Crier: Bonticou Woman Found Frozen on Porch,* and the women on line trade theories: "She went out to smoke, the door locked," "I bet it was a stroke and she froze unconscious," and "See if it turns out to be an accident; she was separated, it says."

There is something almost invigorating in the news story of the frozen woman: She takes my mind off my case. In the photograph she appears in a fetal curl, naked but discreetly so—her position obscures her private parts, her breasts—a marble statue of herself, white and stonily dead. There is speculation that her clothes were removed by animals. "She would have been eaten by coyotes," one of the women remarks, "but she was froze solid."

It is quite horrible to think of her on her own porch, trying to open the door. But why didn't she break the window? And didn't she have a car? A garage, or a barn? Wasn't there some alternative to curling up in a ball, naked, and freezing to death in a blizzard?

"Maybe she had Alzheimer's," the second woman says, and that sounds like the most feasible theory so far. How sad it is, I think as I wait for my psychological evaluation voucher to be approved, that I have come to welcome grotesque distractions from my own situation. I would never wish such a fate on any person, but the image, the speculation, of the frozen woman has taken the grip off my own case for a few moments. It is a relief not to run through my rosary of fears.

The woman ahead of me receives a slip of paper at the window and turns to the woman accompanying her. "Damn, it *is* Lazare. They won't change it: He's doing your evaluation."

Why not? And why is it bad to have Dr. Hubert Lazare? I wonder, but I hesitate to intrude on their conversation. Dr. Hubert Lazare. I already like the sound of him, his name. I am imagining a kindly psychiatrist in upstate New York, handsome, silver-streaked beard, quizzical gaze, tweed jacket, maybe a pipe. Without any effort on my part, a fully fashioned potential romance presents itself: Dr. Lazare analyzes me, falls in love with his subject. I end up married to the psychiatrist who comforts me and diagnoses my ex-husband. Matt is sent on his way, healed but disqualified to be in my life. I wish him well, but I am safer with Dr. Lazare.

The only smooth cog in the wheel is getting the voucher: The county will, in fact, pay for the services of a court-appointed psychologist. After a half-hour wait on line, I am given a rush appointment for my evaluation, 11:00 A.M. tomorrow with Dr. Hubert Lazare.

I am so buoyed by relief, that, as I walk from the building, I almost miss seeing someone arriving in the parking lot. By chance I glance across the rows of parked cars and trucks, and there is no mistaking: It's the hooded man in the parka, carrying the molded suitcase.

Chick Savago. The Supralux repairman. Of course. He said he worked at the prison; I assumed he meant the maximum-security prison ten miles away, the geometric castle, not this complex of hospitals and jails. Is my life so derailed, I now travel on a security circuit? A route frequented by the victimized, in which not much is left to chance? Must every moment now be charged with the nature of my new situation? Fear must be infectious.

They say it is the scared mouse that is eaten, the ailing deer that is brought down. Predators find the prey, wherever they are, and they know the weak, the wounded, are easiest to kill. To be very young or very old is a disadvantage in the wild, but nothing endangers one as much as being frightened: The scent of fear functions as a lure.

Instinctively, I duck my own head and try to walk sideways, so as to be less visible, toward my Saab. But of course that weird energy that sparks the air, alerting the nervous systems of those involved in a stalk, signals him. He turns as if beeped—and sees me.

The memory of the previous night rushes back, like a nightmare willingly forgotten, now retrieved in all its alarming detail.

"Mrs. D.," he calls from across the parking lot. He smiles. He is pleased to see me.

I nod and try to rush, without seeming to run, for my car.

"Mrs. D., where you running? You're just the person I want to see. . . ."

He moves so fast, without seeming to run. Here we are in a vast parking lot, the winter sun glancing like so many lances off the metallic rooftops of cars and SUVs, and yet, he is blocking my passage.

"Mrs. D.," he says, his voice even. "Not so fast. You'll slip and hurt yourself. Watch for icy spots. I think I left something at your house last night."

My mind flashes, as if viewing a slide—my crumpled shawl.

"No, you left nothing," I say. I refuse to avert my eyes. Meet the challenge: Show him I'm not scared, even though I am.

"Oh, no, Mrs. D., I am sure I did. Remember when I was testing your Supralux 799? How she didn't suck the balls?"

I can't believe I'm hearing this: Is he attempting to bait me? In social reflex, in the momentum of the moment, I hear myself agree, "Yes, I remember. . . ."

"Well, the damnest thing, when I got back to my trailer, where I've been since I left my wife . . . I checked my case, and two balls are missing."

"They're not at my house," I say, firm as could be. I am modeling myself now on Allison Crowe, the survivor of *Buried Alive!* Tough, a no-nonsense style. One does not argue with her or seek to elaborate. Allison Crowe dug herself out of a coffin and nailed her assailant. She was my last FemJep role: I can still do her intonation.

"Oh, but I think they are, Mrs. D. You know what I think might have happened to those balls? I think they may have rolled right under your bed."

"You didn't vacuum upstairs," I remind him. "And I have

checked my home thoroughly. There is nothing of yours remaining."

"It's all right, Mrs. D., but I am sure they are there, maybe under your sofa. You were my last call last night, and the balls were missing this morning when I opened my case. When I'm next in your area, on Serpentine, I'll just drop by and check. I can give you a complimentary rug shampoo while I am there, Mrs. D. Remember, I have better stain removers than what I took with me yesterday. I will bring the one that takes out everything. . . ."

Even blood, I recall.

"That won't be necessary," I say. "In fact, I have to ask you not to return to my house."

There is a moment of silence.

I walk past him, keeping as much distance as I can, and proceed to my car. I do not have to turn around to know: Chick Savago is still watching.

The Auditions

Proceed as planned, I instruct myself. Now more than ever, I want the best local lawyer I can find. Forget Chick Savago. He's just a creep, I comfort myself. He's not my problem.

In the car I have the list on a piece of yellow legal pad paper on my dashboard: Cody Laker, Susan Sachs, and the phone number for Joe Gromolka.

Susan Sachs offered the earliest time slot, just ahead of Cody Laker. Their offices are next door to each other, on what turns out to be an unofficial "advocates' row." This is another aspect to the gingerbread town: I did not realize how much of the quaint business district known as the Stockade is devoted to litigation.

As usual, I project the image of the ideal legal office. However misguided, the extreme focus of my predictions comforts me. The more specific details I attach to my destination, the less fearful I feel. Duane Street contains several landmark Colonial clapboard houses, a cluster of cobblestone former forts, a Revolutionary War tavern. It is easy to imagine a structure for my lawyer that will add a sense of security. Everything in the Stockade district has been here for centuries.

I want that innocent exterior, shuttered, with an interior that is shabby but clean. I see a respectable small-town office: a braided welcome mat for leaking, frozen boots, maybe old china stands for the snowy umbrellas, an easy chair for me to sit in while I sip complimentary coffee and spill the secrets of my case.

The first address reads well: 11½ Duane Street. The ½ promises small-town charm; I imagine a split twin Colonial townhouse. I drive down Duane Street, which is near the courthouse. Duane, I now learn, is the gauntlet of lawyers' offices. The gingerbread mansions and miniature Colonials that line Duane Street's cobbled lane function as facades for dozens of legal firms; many share buildings with psychologists or psychiatric practices. Are the services allied in some way I don't yet comprehend?

At 11½ Duane Street, I find a miniature Colonial sliced into picturesque halves: One side has red shutters, the other blue. The Susan Sachs side has batiste curtains, the red shutters, and a red enamel door with a knocker. A plaque decrees that Benedict Arnold slept here. Brass umbrella stand, a mat for the boots. A hand-painted sign reads KRONKITE, BAUER AND SACHS, ATTORNEYS AT LAW.

Inside, the walls have been removed and mammoth Xerox and computing machines added. There is a banklike teller window that turns out to be all too apropos. A young girl sits at this window, and I announce that I have come in to see Susan Sachs. "It's two hundred dollars for the consultation," she tells me through the speaker hole.

On the phone Susan Sachs had sounded like a firecracker: "We'll get him, we'll get the sunofabitch. . . . We'll put him in Pewter Mountain. What? What? What did he do to you? Sonofabitch. We'll nail him; we'll crucify him; we'll hang the sonofabitch." I had taken heart from her anger, although as an

actress I thought she seemed a bit too ready with the denuncia-
tions, a tad overrehearsed.

In person, Susan Sachs is eerily as I imagined: not quite five feet
tall, under a hundred pounds, bug-eyed behind glasses that mag-
nify her stare. She drinks three cups of coffee in the half hour that I
am in her office. Her office is mint green. The room itself seems
almost empty, inhabited only by more copying machines and her
version of the spitting fax.

"I'm too busy for free consultations, Ms. Smythe," she begins.
"And, quite frankly, in this town you get what you pay for." In
addition to the two hundred dollars for the consultation, she wants
a serious retainer, $7,500, to share my case with J. J. Janis.

I sit there and my ears pick up a dripping sound: She has paint
cans set out, to catch leaks.

"Snow dam," she explains. She has one of those nasal voices. I
detect a personal unhappiness, a dysfunctional whine; her mechanism is straining. She wants this job.

"Write the check, I'll get started." She is setting out her legal
pads, ready to take my case. "Which judge? Sintula . . ." She is
moving fast, as if I have agreed to retain her. "Which psychologist?
Lazare? Don't keep the appointment. You need me."

I pause. Too much push.

"I'll let you know," I say, rising.

"Big mistake," she says as I leave. "You're running out of time.
You'll come back to me, and it will be harder then."

Cody Laker's office is next door, in a restored fort. There is a
miniature cannon in the yard and a plaque, 1777. The building
itself is stone, with Delft blue shutters. He has a musket on the
wall and a cooking kettle on a crane in his unlit hearth.

The charm here, too, is a false front; within the postcard historic exterior are more "renovated" rooms awhirr with electronic

buzz, histories of cruelty, crime, and neglect. From what I can discern, the files are crammed with complaints; his fax machines spit depositions as I stand there, in the foyer. Everyone in this county must be in litigation, I think. I have a moment of longing for the years gone by, when a winter walk on Duane Street meant going to The Bonticou Inn for a hot supper with Matt. Oh, why did this have to happen? We had held hands, on this cobbled lane; our greatest indecision whether to eat French or Italian. . . .

"Can I help you?" the receptionist asks.

On the phone, the character-actress–sounding woman (Cast Thelma Ritter? Eileen Heckart? Eve Arden in her later years? I choose Eileen Heckart) had seemed so kind: "Of course, the consultation is free. You just come on in." It was the "come on in" that drew me. Now, in person, the Eileen Heckart soundalike appears as a heavy woman with a sprayed upswept hairdo. She looks all right, but she, too, sits behind a glass window at a tellerlike position at the entry. "Just take a seat and fill in the forms on the table," she invites. "Sucker?"

"Excuse me?" Can it be this direct? Is she joking?

"Do you want a sucker?"

Oh, now I see it: butterscotch candy, offered in a cellophane twist.

Financial disclosure statements are fanned on his coffee table. How can I walk in off the snowy street, sit down here, and divulge the intimacies of my bank accounts? Am I too cynical in my suspicion that his bill will approximate my net worth? Am I still idiot enough to expect the Cody Laker of my imaginings, the Cody Laker who is handsome, honest, and kind, who will take me under his wing and into his heart? Do I really believe this man is still a possibility behind the closed Colonial-blue-painted pine door?

The door opens; he steps forward to greet me, invite me into his office. Laker is a good-looking fellow with a trimmed beard, wearing a tweed jacket and jeans and cowboy boots with silver tips. We settle into leather armchairs, studded. He flatters me at once.

"You won't get much money from your husband," he says, "because you could not have been married very long."

"Seventeen and a half years is long to me," I say. "And this isn't about money. This is about protection from violence. . . ."

Cody pulls a sad, sympathetic expression.

"Battery," he says. "Seeing too much of it." He stares at me in what I interpret as feigned admiration. "My God," he cries. "You look ten years younger than you are. I thought you were twenty-five, tops." He winks. "Very pretty. I've seen your movies."

My vision of Jimmy Stewart is extinguished with the wink. This man is a bit of a con, but he does have small-town con charm. "I saw you in a movie at the mall last spring."

"Yes, with a knife through my heart, probably," I suggest. "I'm trying not to let life imitate art, such as it is. . . ."

He orders in soup, the famed mushroom barley soup from Mrs. Schmidt's. I enjoy him but cannot bring myself to write a check from my dwindling account on the spot. I have that piece of paper with the name Joe Gromolka scribbled on it. Maybe Joe Gromolka is the Jimmy Stewart type. His office is out there, across the street at number 14½.

"I'll let you know," I say, shaking his hand when I go.

"Don't take too long," he advises. "I'm not taking many new clients. But I'm interested in your case."

I had wanted to like Cody Laker or Susan Sachs, but somehow they canceled each other out. As they say in casting, I am ready to go "in another direction."

Across the street I pull out my cell phone and call Joe

Gromolka. Joe Gromolka answers, the deep mumbly, bumbly voice. I visualize the basset hound face, the shadowed eye bags, drooping suit, heavy shoes.

Gromolka's office, Gromolka and Gromolka, is in a frilled peach-color Victorian, almost as fanciful as Casa di Rosas. "Come on over," the basset hound invites on the phone. "I can squeeze you in. I just came from court: We were adjourned."

With some anticipation—Gromolka and Gromolka has the prettiest house—I walk up the steps of the Victorian but within, I find the familiar fluorescence. The hall wafts a faint mold smell. Joe Gromolka is "my second choice," as it is known in casting.

He is sitting at his desk, and rises to greet me. He has big hands; I feel the heat of his palm. I almost laugh. He is identical to my image of him, down to the sad brown hound eyes, the ambling gait. He does have large ears, with pendulous lobes and corresponding jowls. He is the basset hound with the suit jacket tailored to hide his girth and elevator shoes to add to his height.

"Do you charge for this consultation?" I ask, worried now about my checkbook balance. I can't afford to audition more lawyers, at cost.

"Oh, no, I'm free," he smiles, as if he is admitting he should charge for his time.

"And the retainer?" I now know the ropes, and a free consultation might mean an inflated retainer. No bargain.

"$3,500," he says, "and you can pay in two installments, if it's difficult for you."

Really? That is as appetizing as the homemade doughnuts and hot coffee that he proffers. The china mug has a painted Dalmatian on it.

I sit and sip and study his desk—Gromolka has a baby picture of a laughing boy in a sailor suit, and another photograph of him-

self embracing a wife in a hammock. He has an aura of less pros-
perity which, in his line of work, might indicate he has a heart and
doesn't overprofit. Or am I just cold and tired? Do I need to
believe in him, because I have run out of time and money to interview other local lawyers? I won't know until we go to court.

"It's a shame," Joe Gromolka says as I repeat the now familiar
litany. "A shame. You should not have to go through this. Your
husband (a) has to be legally restrained and tried and convicted,
and (b) has to get psychiatric help."

"Oh," I cry in what approximates delight these days, "he's
being evaluated tomorrow, and so am I."

Joe Gromolka's pencil pauses on the legal pad. "Who's doing
it?"

"Dr. Hubert Lazare," I say.

I wonder at the pause that follows.

"Oh," he says, "that's too bad."

Why? Why is that too bad? I am getting an actor's instinctive
dread now of Dr. Hubert Lazare. The lawyers and the women on
line at Pewter Mountain all said his name in a tone I recognize—
the intonation that actors use when they mention certain directors,
even other actors—and it always means: Bad news. Watch out.

"Is there a problem with Dr. Lazare?" I ask.

"I don't wish to prejudice you," Joe Gromolka answers. "Some
people feel, well, that he is biased in favor of the husbands. His
evaluations tend to favor the husbands."

"Even the abusive ones?" I ask.

"Only in certain cases," Gromolka answers.

"What sort of cases?"

"When the women are . . . well . . . I don't want to prejudice
you. Go in, see Dr. Lazare. Do the best you can to convince him of
the veracity of your account."

"But it is true. Do I have to work that hard with the truth?"

"Try to avoid becoming . . ." Gromolka searches for the word, ". . . hysterical in any way. You want to sound just as you have with me: creditable, level. I think I can help you."

His maroon eyes meet mine, questioning. He holds his pencil poised. Are we on? Will I retain him? I reach for my checkbook, scribble $1,750. If he fails, have I cut my losses or thrown good money after bad? If he succeeds in my case, he is a bargain, and a hero.

Gromolka accepts the check, sets it in an "out" basket. He eyes my outfit with fresh scrutiny, now that I am officially his client. I am still wearing the Mafia widow coat over the 1890's riding habit.

"Do you have a white shirt and a black skirt?" he asks, suggesting the same costume that J. J. Janis wanted me to wear.

"No. I don't," I say.

"I like the coat," he says. "Keep it closed."

The Evaluation

The MMPI is the abbreviation for the psychological evaluation test Minnesota Multiphasic Personality Inventory. On the day of my appointment with Dr. Hubert Lazare, I sit in the small waiting room of his third-floor walkup above Schmidt's Bakery and Delicatessen. Although the bakery smells were pleasant, almost euphoria-inducing when I was actually inside Schmidt's, Dr. Lazare's office must be on line with the rear air shaft where cooking odors vent: A stale smell of grease and overspiced meat permeates the little room.

I try to concentrate on the test, but I am still thinking of the strange persona of Dr. Lazare and the awkwardness of our interview. The pages before me offer a long list of statements:

I am a special agent of God.

Lightning is one of my fears.

I often memorize numbers that are not important.

I have had black tarry bowel movements.

The list is perplexing, but both Joe Gromolka and J. J. Janis told me the test would reveal significant aspects of both my personality and Matt's: J. J. Janis cautioned me against anticipating the gradings:

"Don't try to be too 'goody-goody,'" he instructed. "For example, you will be asked if you ever stole anything. Be sure and say yes, because everyone has stolen something. If you say no, you will be graded as lying."

I am fascinated by fire, I read. I mark off the box, with an X at the negative—indicating that I am not especially fascinated by fire. But then I think about it: Fire is very beautiful; how many nights have I stared into the hearth of Casa di Rosas, mesmerized by the fluctuant oranges and blues, liquid, leaping yellows? Haven't I enjoyed the crackle, the smell of woodsmoke? Am I not, then, fascinated by fire? But if I check yes, am I branding myself as a firebug?

I leave the mark that I am not fascinated by fire, but uncertainty has set into my mind, like gas gangrene. The interview with Dr. Hubert Lazare unnerved me. Nothing was what I anticipated.

I like to keep people guessing what I am going to do next.

Bad words, often terrible words, come into my mind and I cannot get rid of them.

Almost every day, something happens to frighten me.

Dr. Hubert Lazare was sitting behind his locked door when I arrived. A woman, a scarf wrapped around her head, scurried out as he opened his door: She seemed to be fleeing. She looked as if she has been crying.

"Come in, Mrs. Smythe," Dr. Lazare invited without a smile.

I looked at him: He is a bear of a man who fills the open slice of doorway in which he stands. His gut protrudes, a stained necktie splayed almost horizontal on the bulge of his gut. He has a graying blond beard and thick eyebrows that are knit in a scowl as he regards me. My romantic vision of the kindly psychiatrist is replaced by the reality of a most unappealing and angry-looking middle-aged man. He seems to have soup noodles caked in his beard. No wonder he hates women: No woman would want him.

I am often afraid of people.

His mouth is round, red, and wet, an open orifice between the hair of his mustache and the beard. There is something lewd about his mouth, I am sure of it.

Sometimes people disgust me.

"Come in," he repeated. He gestured to a chair and a tape recorder on the table beside it. "I'll be taping your interview."

It is almost impossible to describe the dichotomy that followed. While he questioned me, he maintained an even tone of voice, without inflection. As an actor, I recognized his vocal control. But the entire time his voice rolled on, fluent, almost mellifluous and neutral in expression, his face contorted as he stared at me. His heavy brows held the scowl; his wet lips twisted in a lascivious smirk, and at one point he even bared small yellow teeth (pointed) in a grimace of utter and impersonal hatred.

I often wish I were dead.

I know one thing: Matt has been in to see him; Matt managed to snare the nine A.M. appointment, the first of the day. I can imagine how my husband achieved this, saying in his earnest way that he had to "return to work in the city." I can almost feel his presence still in the room—and sure enough, there is a stubbed-out cigarette butt, Matt's brand, in the ashtray stand. So he was here this morning, took the same test, gave his interview, and left. In the interim, only the frightened-looking woman in the head scarf had passed through this room. The impressions of Matt's version of our marriage and The Attack must be very fresh on Dr. Hubert Lazare's mind.

This bothers me, because I know how convincing Matt can

be. What has he told Dr. Hubert Lazare to induce such contempt for me? Oh, maybe *contempt* is too strong a word.
Skepticism? Not only has Matt gotten to tell "his side" first, he
also appeared in his most normal guise: the good businessman
on his way back to the office, dragged upstate to deal with an
unbalanced wife.

It could be presented that way, and I sense that it has.

"Are you a psychiatrist?" I ask Dr. Lazare.

"Psychologist." He glares. I can see he does not like having the
roles reversed: He wants to interview me, not vice versa. But I have
learned, in auditioning, that it is clever to seize an element of control at the start. Directors and casting people respond when an
actor is not entirely passive. My friend Nadine, who is cast quite a
bit, says her trick is to interview them to see if she wants the job:
"So you're shooting in Canada?" she'll ask. Okay.

The same strategy can apply to an evaluation. I am not the one
who will be pushed around. I wish Dr. Hubert Lazare had more
degrees. He is not impressive. I suppose there are excellent psychologists, but he doesn't seem to be one of them. He looks like an
uncivil servant, parked in a public job, because he might not fit in
the private sector with his open hostility. But I always win the
roles I go after, so I am sure that I can also swing Dr. Hubert Lazare
to my side of the case.

I know I can turn this around. The man is a psychologist after
all. He will be able to discern who is telling the truth and who is
not, who is sane and who is in the midst of a breakdown. Matt
must have taken this Minnesota Multiphasic Personality Inventory
also, and I can only imagine how he responded to *I have killed small
animals* and *I sleepwalk* and *I have often imagined my parents as corpses*
and other touchy topics.

During the interview I am careful to keep my tone level, my

gaze direct. I do not weep or in any way give in to my emotions. A few times I bite my lower lip to keep it from quivering.

I recite the facts of The Attack as simply and accurately as I can. I look at Dr. Hubert Lazare when I finish; he consults a list of questions he has scribbled on a pad.

"You had a difficult time at adolescence, didn't you?"

I hesitate. What does he mean by that?

Doesn't everyone have a difficult time at adolescence? Isn't that what adolescence is?

I wonder how he knows that? Has Matt gone into my background? At what length? And with what distortion?

He asks me more personal questions then, about my childhood, my parents; first my father's absence from my life, then my mother's death after what was called "a lingering illness."

"So you were orphaned at thirteen," Dr. Lazare says. "You must have felt very sad, very alone in the world."

I'm startled: This is the first sign of compassion from this man who is rumored to dislike women. I feel a surge of faith. He believes me; he has become sympathetic.

"Yes," I answer. "Of course I did."

"And the series of foster homes were not entirely satisfactory?"

Matt has told him, I realize, of the unhappy years before I met him. He has probably told him how I fled the last place, a raincoat over my nightgown . . . how I begged to be placed in a group home, and finally was, at seventeen, on the college campus.

"It was not that bad," I say to Lazare. "It was pretty routine; I was only in foster care for a few years, until I went to live on campus."

I didn't want to go into the details of the indifferent, self-serving foster family, the Hedges, who kept me for the stipend. Or the Gates, who were even stranger and wanted me to convert to their fundamentalist version of Christianity. I am half Catholic, half Jewish, and that leaves me, questioning organized religion but with some faith, which I cannot name, of my own.

"You were abused?" Dr. Hubert Lazare is asking. Is it my imagination, or does he seem to anticipate, hope for, a positive answer. What has Matt been telling him?

"No," I say, "I was not abused. I was given adequate care after . . . when the foster parents took over."

"But it was not the experience you had with your mother?"

Why do tears spring to my eyes? Twenty-three years after she died, I am still stunned into this inconsolable grief.

"She's been gone a long time," Dr. Lazare comments. Is it my imagination: He seems . . . disapproving. He jots down in his notebook, the pen scratching.

"What caused her death?"

There is a pause; I sense he is expecting an answer. What has Matt said about my mother?

"Cancer," I say, my voice cracking. I know it is not the entire truth, but I am in no frame of mind to confide in this man. Matt is the single person on earth to whom I have talked about my mother.

"Do you miss your mother?"

Hey, I think, this feels like an inquisition.

"Yes," I answer. "Yes, I miss my mother."

"You're feeling some rage?" Dr. Lazare asks, pen ready.

I am—directed at him.

"No," I repeat. "I miss my mother."

"How would you describe the care she gave you, as opposed to the foster parents?"

Why is it as painful to recall tenderness as cruelty?

"More loving," I answer.

"Speak up, I don't think that recorded," Dr. Lazare instructs.

"More loving," I say, then almost shout, "More loving!"

He looks at me, his face changing, the beard even seeming to shift. Well, he has gotten a rise out of me, if that's what he wanted. Yet, if he meant to break me, he has failed. The repetition somehow strengthens me.

"More loving," I repeat, and I draw sustenance from the words and the past and my mother, that woman who had the misfortune to lose her life at the age I am now. For a moment I conjure her as I last saw her: her dark curling hair, the heart-shaped face, the pointy chin; I resemble her enough so that people who knew her gasp at the resemblance. "Eva," they breathe. "Eva."

My mother was lovely; she failed at her work—figurative painting—but only in the world of commerce. And she was denied her great romance: My father left and never returned, immediately after my birth. But she succeeded in one most challenging arena: She could give love to her only child. And she gave me something more. . . .

I am beginning to lose myself in the reverie of my mother, when Dr. Lazare interrupts my thought. "For years you suffered from nightmares, you walked in your sleep, you were drawn to morbid thoughts of dying young?"

"No," I say, truly shocked. Has he shuffled the notes? That is Matt. Matt has the nightmares, the sleepwalking, the preoccupation with the idea that he will die young.

"You're certain of that?"

"Yes, absolutely certain." I can't resist interjecting, "I think you are describing my husband. Matt has very dark dreams. He walks in his sleep. I always hoped I could help him recover, but—"

"This isn't about your husband, Mrs. Smythe, this is about you. You had nightmares."

"Everyone has had a nightmare. I don't often have nightmares." This is not the time to describe the falling dreams. I have only had these dreams since The Attack. The whooshing fall from my window, the descent just short of bull's-eye, earth—then the rescue, the upswing in the man's strong arms.

"How do you feel this situation will resolve, Mrs. Smythe?"

"I think . . . I hope we will . . ." I cannot control my response. ". . . both be saved."

"How is that?"

"I feel this crisis is a chaos based upon nothing tangible—that it is fear and violence emanating from a chaotic chemical imbalance. In a way we are at a war over nothing, and I cry for the waste—of his life and mine. He needs your help, and so do I."

This seems to give Dr. Hubert Lazare pause. He takes a breath before resuming.

"So you were miserable in college?"

"I wouldn't say that." I transferred from a college near the Canadian border to return to New York City. Yes, I was lonely there, but my grades had been excellent. And I was the star of the Drama Department. I played Shen Te in *The Good Woman of Szechwan*. "It wasn't so bad. I was homesick."

"For a city where you had no one," Dr. Hubert Lazare remarks.

"Well, I met Matt when I was seventeen."

"Yes," the doctor confirms. "And he seemed the answer to your problems, your acute sense of aloneness."

It's curious, but somehow the psychologist does not wound me with these words; they strike me as the first truth he has uttered.

"Yes," I answer. "I fell . . . we fell very much in love."

His eyes seem to soften and I wonder: Does he respond to this long-ago love? Does he feel its loss as I do? Does he mourn for our happiness just a bit—regret our descent into the violence that brought us here, to this third-floor walkup above Schmidt's?

Am I a fool to think I have touched him?

I leave the office believing that I have.

The Bath Scene

These days sap my strength; the effort of fighting back seems almost too much. I plan an evening to recover. A hot bath, I think, with bubbles. My warm robe and an early sleep.

Of course, I remain conditioned from my film roles to know that a moment of relaxation is the antecedent for another attack. Who can forget the shower scene in *Psycho?* Not I, as I head toward the bathroom. In this instance, however, life will triumph over cinematic tradition: Casa di Rosas is secured. The alarm system is active—there are sound waves invisibly securing my main points of entry—and I have every law enforcement agency in the area on speed dial, not only the sheriff but the state police, on my new answering machine.

I imagine Matt has returned to the city; tomorrow is a workday. It is not snowing; in fact the night is crystal—sharp stars against a black heaven, the orb of a bright white moon. The snow has drifted over the roads, and I feel anyone attempting my driveway would be well announced by the squeal of tires if they could drive this far uphill.

I need a few moments of solace, some seconds to simply soak in a tub. To relax and forget. I barely eat these days, and only what is quickest; dinner was the same as breakfast—scrambled eggs and toast. I love to cook, but there's been no time.

My single culinary effort was to bake the bread that rose the night Chick Savago was here. The bread was another casualty: It had risen too high and filled with airholes, and its crust is crackled and hard. I will toss leftover bread to the hungry winter birds in the morning. I don't set food, even crumbs, out after dark, as any sustenance attracts the bigger animals.

I do feel entitled to a glass of wine tonight, although it feels luxurious, even wasteful, to open a new bottle. I uncork a good Shiraz and let it and myself breathe. I carry a full goblet upstairs. This is a really good idea, I congratulate myself.

Upstairs, my bedroom waits, so beautifully cleaned and arranged by Moira Gonzalez Gerhardt. She has outdone herself: Every ornate pillow sham has been set out, my best linens, the embossed duvets. Twin pillowcases embroidered with bluebirds with *Hers* and *His* on them in script are in place. In the bathroom the long towels are set out, fluffed and ready. My tub boasts an improvised shower—a brass halo that held the curtain and a central spout—but I opt for immersion. A real bath.

It's bliss to peel off the frozen black woolen tights. My feet are numbed; my boots failed. I take off the plain black wool dress I've worn to Lazare's. (I knew better than to sashay in there in my riding habit; he would have asked, "Where's your crop?") I see Moira has hung the riding costume on its padded hanger to dry. It dangles from the shower ring, still somewhat retaining the shape and movement of my body.

It's strange what can assuage this pain that has been so constant now for the eight weeks since The Attack. The beauty of my view; the sight of that old stag leaping; the intricacy of my hand-sewn riding ensemble. I need to see such perfection, to know that my life is not the unremitting ordeal, this excavation of the netherside to human experience that it seems to be. Let's have a reprieve, I think, an hour to surrender to bath salts and scent.

I light a candle in a Victorian frosted glass holder—there are etched figures of cherubs . . . or are they angels?—and draw my bath by its glow. Oh, to sink under the warm suds, inhale the lavender of the aromatic oils. I enter stiffly, like a person who has been injured. My cold and ache are a kind of injury, and I crave this . . . down, down, until only the tip of my nose is above the surface. Hydrotherapy, aromatherapy—the benefits of these age-old treatments cannot be exaggerated. Tonight, I find it pleasing to recall Bonticou's origins as a turn-of-the-century spa, famed for its mineral waters and sulfur springs. I am enjoying the latter-day products made up of the local salts and minerals. The lavender grew right here, on the property. The soreness of my muscles, the hollow in my heart, the near-nauseous buzz that is my fear . . . all is soothed, warmed.

A few bath beads mimicking pearls dissolve in the hot water with me. My tub is Victorian, claw-footed, a deep porcelain well with the original fixtures—brass mixing taps with porcelain handles. Feeling my first pleasure and relief in two months, I twist the Hot tap and let the water rise. The heat in the small bathroom mists the windows; the medicine-chest mirror fogs.

Forget. For a few minutes forget the marital disaster, court. Let go of fear. Submerged, I do not so much as fall into a dream as I lose consciousness. The descent is profound, as if my mind needs to dissolve, to release the toxic truths of the day. Underwater, I dream, dream. . . . It is summer here, and I am diving off our dock, into the warm waters of the lake. Matt is here, but he is the "old" Matt, the loving and sensual Matt, who dives naked from the dock, swimming after me. It is August and our night shore is lit by fireflies; the fog is a scrim for the musical comedy performance of the bullfrogs, who are accompanied, on natural "strings," by the cicadas. Nature's summer in concert, the outdoor symphony underscored by lapping water. . . .

Fish splash and so do we. There is no demarcation between the fog and the surface of the lake. We dive as if into nothingness, to erase ourselves in pleasure. I feel our joy, the perfect peace. This is a dream, but it is also memory.

My new bedside phone rings; the alarm seems to shoot up my submerged spine. I bolt upright, disoriented. What? I have fallen asleep in the tub? What's happening?

The phone shrills, shrills. I rise from the deep tub, grab a large towel, and wrap myself, then stumble through the door to my bed. On the bedside table, the replacement phone, a utilitarian white answering machine, is shrieking its electronic scream. I miss my old phone, the old-fashioned peach one with the dial that called to me with a bona fide rotary *ring-ring-ring-a-ling* that always made me feel like Barbara Stanwyck answering. I am even nostalgic for my original answering machine, the separate black box that had connected to the peach phone Matt smashed. The answering machine itself wasn't damaged, only obsolete, and for some reason I haven't thrown it away; it still sits on the floor under my bedside table, although it's been replaced by the electronic phone, which performs both functions.

I am surfacing, like a diver with the emotional bends. Who would call here tonight? Lawyers, on their phone meters. Is it J. J. Janis or the newly retained Gromolka on the line?

On the phone is a man—I assume the person must be male—breathing. . . .

There is the lickety-slickety sound of lubricated friction. A man is working his flesh into the receiver.

"I know who you are," I say, unrehearsed, "and I'm reporting you to the police."

Slam. Click. Down with the receiver. It rings again, in my hand . . . and I simply hold it, trembling. The machine clicks on. More breathing, more lickety-slickety sound effects, moistened frictions.

This time, at the end, he speaks: "Juliana." Just my name, but now perverted into an obscenity. "Juliana."

I cannot recognize the voice. Can it be Chick Savago? A reprise of his performance at the house? Now I regret not calling the police when the phone was repaired; I'd moved on to what I considered my more pressing crisis, the court. I had made a note to call them, and the vacuum company, to ask that Chick Savago not be sent here again, but I had yet to attend to reporting him.

Is this Chick Savago now? He had breathed my name also, on the stairs outside this door. Much as I wish to assign an identity, the voice doesn't quite match. Of course, he could be disguising his voice. But I am trained to pick up intonation, timbre: I have an instinct that this is a new caller. Surely not Matt—not my husband. We were married too long for his insanity to take this form. Unless, unless, he means to unsettle me.

Whoever the caller is, he succeeded: I am unsettled. The contentment and comfort of the bath dissipates faster than the steam that wafts from the open bathroom door. This time I shall not procrastinate.

Dial *69, I recall, to retrace the phone call. I do, and a woman's electronic tone says, "The number you have reached is private or unavailable at this time."

I call the police. "Listen," I say, "I have just received an obscene call, and I am in the midst of a difficult personal situation. I have an order of protection. Can you trace?"

I stand in my dripping towel, beginning to feel chilled, as a series of referrals takes place on the line. There is a special number, an office, for threatening or obscene calls.

"They have to call three times," the woman operator informs me. "After the third time, we can take some action."

"But how will you know? If they call three times? If it's the same person?"

"We retain the number of the person who called you, but we cannot release that. If there are three calls, then you will have the right to pursue the case for harassment. But we do not give out the number of the person who is dialing you."

"Thank you," I say, and hang up.

The phone shrills again. This time it is Gromolka. For a dizzy second I wonder if he is also the obscene caller. His voice timbre is similar. Oh, no, he couldn't be. . . . He is proceeding, in a hearty tone, "You need to put together a witness list. And I want your witnesses here, in Bonticou, in my office, so that I can interview them."

"Interview?" I am confused. I am standing in a puddle of now cold water. I reach for my big bathrobe, hanging over the door; it is an oversized unisex, one size fits all, true Egyptian cotton terry. Matt and I had matching robes, for those past evenings of shared baths. His robe is now shoved to the rear of the closet, waiting the day of his police-escorted visit to retrieve his wardrobe.

"I take a statement," Joe Gromolka explains, "so that I know, when we are in court, exactly how your witnesses will behave. What they say, how strong or weak their testimony will be. I can guide them, also, to be more effective witnesses."

Witnesses. This is the part that has always bothered me. There really are no witnesses that I know of—to the main events, at least. But in following J. J. Janis's advice, I now wonder if, indeed, people saw more than I could have anticipated.

"There are always witnesses. People notice more than you think," Gromolka says, echoing J. J. Janis's words.

Moira. She had noted the broken vase, and now there was this new and upsetting possibility—I was still not willing to accept it as absolute truth—that Matt had been here at Casa di Rosas with someone else just before the holiday. She could testify to the out-of-control appearance of this bedroom, the signs of a wild bender, the covered window . . .

I look to the window: Why would he cover it? The expanse of glass looks straight out at the water. No one could possibly see into this bedroom. I feel tears start again in my eyes. What had happened in here, in my absence? Even after the violence, my own decision to divorce, the image of Matt here, in our bedroom, with another woman, conducting some secret affair is excruciating.

From where I stand, I can see the open closet door and the two sets of hiking boots, Matt's and mine. Moira has left the footwear lined up in perfect order, pointing toward me—Matt's size eleven masculine boot-shoes, and my own, smaller, narrow hiking shoes. My shoes are old, like most of my wardrobe, and even at a distance, I can discern the odd little bumps, deformations of the leather, that conform to my exact podiatric anatomy.

Somehow the thought of an alien woman's toes in my shoes is as invasive as any other action taken in infidelity. She must have small feet; my feet are tiny, size five, and narrow, triple AAA. If she squeezed into my shoes (and my life) she is also tiptoeing around on very small feet.

"There may be new information," I whisper to Joe Gromolka. "Since I saw you, I was able to interview Moira Gonzalez Gerhardt, the women who cleans for me. She says that it's possible my husband was involved with someone. . . ."

There is a long pause on his end. "That changes things." For a moment I reflect how difficult it must be to be a lawyer on a case like mine, having to enter in medias res, as it were, to offer reactions to someone whom he met today. He sounds shocked, as if I were his kid sister, and he conveys a sound of betrayal.

Very good, Joe, I think. Not a bad actor. Better than J. J. Janis, whose delivery is slick, loaded with ethnic jokes, and spiked with demands for more cash.

"That's terrible," Gromolka commiserates. "Fidelity in a marriage is everything. There must be trust."

I agree. "I did trust him; I thought we had terrible problems, but they were between us. I didn't imagine a . . . a third party."

"Changes everything," Gromolka says.

Yes, I think, that changes things.

Gromolka urges me to pursue my own investigation, or hire a private investigator.

"I can't afford one," I protest.

"My son is one. He's young but he's good."

An image of a miniature, skinny Joe Gromolka appears in my mind—I visualize Gromolka junior—light acne, protuberant Adam's apple, one small earring.

"I can't afford him," I insist.

"He might be really cheap," Gromolka says, and I suspect he is drumming up business for the son. "He's training for police work."

"How old is he?"

"Eighteen," Gromolka answers.

My discomfort is increasing as the conversation proceeds. It is one matter to defend myself against attack, another to investigate my husband's sexual activities. And yet another to employ an adolescent to sniff into our most private lives.

Was Matt faithful? I wonder. I never knew him to have an affair, but of course no marriage is without its mysteries: He traveled, I traveled; sometimes, he was not in his hotel room, or even at home, very late at night. I consider 3:00 A.M. very late—past the witching hour, as it were. I did not demand excuses, but he offered them: "The group went to a club to hear jazz," or "I slept through your call. . . ."

I'd been grateful for the explanations then, but now I wonder: Would an innocent husband offer the excuses? Wasn't Matt always a bit overexplained?

"The witness list?" Joe Gromolka reminds me.

"Two women who visited me before the holiday, in the fall. They saw him act out. He *was* strange. He threw things. And that was the weekend the cat disappeared, the cat I am afraid he . . ." I cannot say *killed*. ". . . did something to. . . ."

Unbidden the image of Dot, my little white cat, returns to me as she often appeared in life—curled in a ball, on a pillow on the bed. I see Dot, her eyes shut, nose quivering in her sleep, long fluffed tail, repeating the curve of her back; her entire small, furry body rising and falling with each purr. She was a white cat trimmed in pink—pink paw pads, pink tongue, pink inner ears; even her gold eyes were ringed in pink. I can see her as she usually appeared, licking her paws, swiping her face. She was always freshly washed; she kept herself groomed. Dot always looked prim, dressed in a narrow blue collar.

In the same instant I can see Matt's hand knocking her from the pillow: "Get off!" His voice had been rougher than required, even for an irate husband who didn't want cat hair on the bed. He had been jealous, I realized, jealous of a little cat, because I loved her.

And where was Dot now? Was she bones in the woods? Under the frozen surface of Lake Bonticou or tossed from Matt's Infiniti power window as he drove off in that fit of rage he had at Thanksgiving? Awful as the information would be, I longed for certainty. I need to know. I also need to be certain that Matt has, in fact, crossed the border to complete madness. I must have some conclusion to my fears, some final definition of the perimeters of pain. Was Matt evil or crazed? Was he both? Or was he a sane, unfaithful man, deliberately alienating a wife he wanted to desert but for some reason would not divorce by conventional means?

I recite my short witness list to Joe Gromolka: Moira Gonzalez Gerhardt. My best friend, Nadine Jagoda, the famous character actress, and my older friend, Elsbieta Andrews, who had come along that weekend, more by chance, to drive Nadine. Elsbieta Andrews—that will be a tough call; I know Elsbieta professionally. I dread telling her a personal tale such as this and then recruiting her to participate in the case.

"I'll talk to the witnesses first," I say, "to prepare them for your call."

Only Nadine knows the situation. I have kept a low profile in the business, not informing anyone of why I am holed up here for the winter. I am not anxious to spread the news, whatever it is: Either way, this is not a story I want to see in print or hear in whispered gossip at my next major event. There is shame to being a victim; I feel it now. I wish I had known, when I played the victims on film, how embarrassing it is to be the target of violence. The burn of shame could have informed my performances.

I call Nadine Jagoda first. She answers.

"You mean you need me to come up to the Adirondacks to testify that Matt threw a turkey leg at you on Thanksgiving?"

Nadine cuts to the chase in her inimitable way. She started as a stand-up comic. She makes me do something I would have thought impossible: I laugh.

"Yes, that's what I'm asking."

"I'm there," she says. The truth is, Nadine has never liked

Matt; they were wary with each other. He always made a face when I said she would join us for the weekend, and he was polite to her when she did arrive—but just barely. Again, I think, someone I love . . . whom he resented.

"Do you remember anything else from that weekend?" I have to ask. "Concentrate. He was out of his head and throwing things."

"I think he dented the car," she reports, "But you'll have to ask Elsbieta. Her car had a big scratch along the side; it looked deliberate to me."

"And my cat?" I am forced to ask. "Did you see him . . . mistreat Dot?"

"He kicked her when she tried to run back inside your house," Nadine says, "but you know, a lot of men do that. I had a boyfriend who threw my cat out the window—eight stories. She landed on her feet, of course." I can hear Nadine pause to purr to her own cat, Kitty, and say, "There, there, pussy-wuzzy fuzz face. That was bye-bye to that boyfriend."

Nadine adds an epilogue I have heard her repeat in the past. "Boyfriends come and go. The cat stays."

I warn Nadine, that this will be difficult, maybe even dangerous. She says what she always says when I broach anything fearful: "Don't go there." Nadine has been a veteran of many Twelve Step programs, and she is forever quoting sayings such as "Don't borrow trouble from the future." She also believes in past life regression, rebirthing, and all manner of New Age practices.

And now Nadine is perhaps a bit too happy to help me divorce my husband. They had been natural enemies. Nadine had disliked Matt on sight; in fact, she had sensed he was unstable.

"I don't like men that handsome," she's fond of saying. "They're spoiled at best." She used the word *psychotic* early on, but Nadine talks like that: Everyone is psychotic, or "working out issues from their family of origin." True perhaps, but I loathe the lingo. Give me the Bard with his "tale / Told by an idiot, full of sound and fury; / Signifying nothing."

"I think he's psychotic," I say to Nadine now; I am wrapping the phone cord round my body in a nervous gesture, and untangle myself to stumble onto my bed. I can still see my candle, aglow by the bath. Nadine and I can talk for hours in that emotional way that old friends do, saying everything and anything that comes to mind, reluctant to say good night even when we are both exhausted and our conversation stalls and our voices rasp with hoarseness.

She will attend my court hearing; she will bear witness.

"What a friend," I say.

"Don't mention it: I owe you so many dinners," she says. "Get your sleep." We finally say good night—it is early morning—and hang up.

I look at my bed, so beautifully arranged by Moira. I curl under the down comforter. White on white. Snowy eiderdown, inside this house and out. . . . I can look out the lakeside window opposite my bed: I see the snow spread across the frozen lake, drawn taut as these bedcovers, scalloped by the wind. I hear the wind: *Woooo,* it calls from beyond the window glass. *Woooooooo . . .*

Again I wonder why Matt draped the bedsheets over the window frame. Did he not want to look outside? Or did he fear someone, something, was observing him? And someone else? Was there really someone else in my pristine marriage bed?

I shudder: Even my bed may not be sacrosanct, a true refuge. It may be the scene of another sort of crime. Someone else may have been in here, sleeping, if that's the word, with my husband.

"Don't go there," I can hear Nadine say. "Don't go there." That's another way in which we are not alike: Nadine loves slang, and I don't. But tonight I mentally obey her, and refuse to "go there."

I feel my body warm the sheets; I nuzzle into the pillow. I can forget for a while, can't I? Then I realize the candle is guttering in the bathroom. I rise, drop my feet to the cold floor, and run to fetch it. My bedroom is dark, and when I return, something catches my eye at the window.

I look out across the lake. Because the night is clear, I can see a distant light; it must be that glass house across the lake. I extinguish my candle and look back to the window and am stunned to see that the light on the opposite shore has gone out also. It must be a coincidence, I think. Following an instinct, I strike a match and relight my candle. Instantly a faraway glow can be seen, all the way across Lake Bonticou.

I repeat the procedure, blowing out the candle, then relighting. Each time the sequence is repeated in the window across the water. How strange, I think. Is it a child imagining I am signaling? What would be the purpose to this exchange of light flashes, at two A.M.?

I blow out the candle; this time it will not relight. The wick is almost gone, submerged in the hot paraffin. Just as well. I look out the window. Across the lake, there is darkness.

I try to forget the strange exchange of light. The point is to rest tonight, to recover. I must face the ongoing case again tomorrow.

I almost throw myself onto the pillows, clutch them, the twin bluebirds, embroidered with *His* and *Hers,* in a body hold. I need to descend into unconsciousness again, to recover my dream. And for a few moments I do. If there were another person here, I would hold him in a bone-aching embrace. Is it fear or loneliness—or some combination of both?

I reenter the summer world of my sleep, where all is warm and the orchard is in bloom, the cluster of cherry and apple trees white and palest pink in flower. The lake is not frozen but asparkle in the sun. Matt is not the mysterious Matt of today but the man I used to know. . . .

We had two old wicker rocking chairs on the boat dock. White paint flaking on gray willow, decomposing ever so slowly, sagging more each summer, becoming more organically part of the decaying dock . . . graying. I imagined we, too, would go gray together this way, naturally, in the order of things.

We faced the sunset every evening. He would bring a tray with coffee or, if it was too hot, lemonade. He smoked and I sighed. I baked then, often pies from our own fruit—the blueberries that grew all around us; small, frosted-looking little berries, tart rather than sweet. . . . Our all-time favorite was sour cherry, from the queen of the fruit trees, the oldest tree, the one beside the kitchen window. That tree produces thousands of bright red cherries every June, and they have a taste that no sweet cherry can replicate. Every year the juice stains my fingers as I pit the cherries, but the effort is always rewarded by hot, bubbling pies that waft cherry aroma and give off a flavor beyond any commercial cherry. I can't say that the queen cherry, as we call her, is beautiful: The tree is old, gnarled, stooped from years of fruit-bearing, but I prune her each year, cutting off the dead wood. The reward is always to see her aflower in late spring and, just a few weeks later, to pluck her fruit. We ate the cherry pie as dessert, most often down on the dock. We forked the last sour-sweet bits into each other's mouth.

Apples came later, but they were wonderful too. The apple trees bore three kinds, all "old-fashioned" apples—Granny Smith, Winesap, and Northern Spy. We liked Spy the best—"Spy for pie"—but all those trees gave great apples, and I baked the apples into puffed, sweet pies.

We celebrated each fruit in its season, and last of all were our vintage grapes. I can still laugh at our attempts to harvest: We worked for a week to secure a single bottle, a homegrown merlot. We drank it almost immediately instead of letting it "mature." We toasted one another. It was our last anniversary.

That was the way it was, wasn't it? Didn't he reach out and hold my hand? Didn't I touch his thigh?

I want to enter this dream, recover my lost evenings, reverse time and let Matt and me become that couple once again. But the descent to sleep is always too steep now, and I am yanked back, as if on that faulty cable, to face the blackness of the window glass, the iced truth of tonight's situation. The tremors seize me then, reverberating with the violence of The Attack.

Is this why I see—surely it is an optical illusion?—a face pressed against the glass.

Before I can scream, or fully awaken, the white visage vanishes . . . and with it, my dream.

Someone Is Always Watching

What possesses me? I wake to the sun streaming over the duvet, to a brighter morning, and yet I cannot banish that specter from the windowpane. I know it must have been an optical illusion—the reflection of the moon. A literal man in the moon. The moon was full last night; doesn't that mean something? Magic? The tidal pull? Lunacy?

I must go across the lake and question the man who lives there, the man in the glass house. I have never met him, but I know so much about him from Jake Taylor, the mailman. His name is Winsten; he, too, is from the city. "He's some kind of writer," Jake once told me. But mainly I know this man Winsten is in over his head—in the actual sense: His flat-roofed glass house is not suited for this northerly clime; each blizzard buries him, and he comically tries to dig out with the tiny fireplace shovel.

I have to meet him now, today, and know why he is signaling me. What other explanation can there be for the flickering light, synchronized to my own?

I am incurable, I suppose, in this romantic tic—the visualization of heroic men who might save me, then love me. I wonder if he is flirting. I conjure a Mr. Winsten, who is exactly right for me, a bit older, a streak of silver in his hair, handsome, well built, if ineffectual against blizzards. A bespectacled and kindly man who will take me to his chest and put his arms around me and let me, for one minute, rest. That is my dream for the day: a moment of peace in a man's embrace. Maybe it isn't even sexual but soothing: Can comfort exist between men and women, without another motive? In the movies, comfort—let's face it—is the prelude. Very few women are comforted on screen without having sexual congress shortly thereafter.

In my own scenario this man Winsten says, "I signaled you because I sensed your despair and I wanted to hold you." In reality he has an unlisted number.

Of course, with a fantasy like this, I can hardly wait to cross the lake. If I had a dogsled, I would be in it, scooting over the ice. But, especially in my current circumstance, I am a great respecter of privacy. I settle for running out to meet the mailman, and slip Jake Taylor a note to deliver on the morning route: "I live across the lake. I saw your lights last night and would like to speak with you. As your phone is unlisted, here's my number."

Jake Taylor accepts the letter but issues an advisory: "Mr. Winsten, he don't like to be disturbed, no, no; he got Keep Out signs all over the driveway, and puts a chain on, too, except when the garbageman or the town plow need to come through. Sometimes, even then, he don't take the chain down. That's how come he stays buried," Jake concludes, with a rustic cackle. "I wouldn't wait to hear back from him."

Which of course, I do. I wait. Is it possible this Winsten watches the house? Might he have seen something on New Year's Eve? Could he be my witness?

"Someone always sees," Gromolka said.

As it stands, I realize the existing witnesses are weak. I need them, but none of the witnesses saw The Attack. They will bear witness to actions and mood swings that were the precursors—if, indeed, the witnesses will "cooperate."

"It isn't like on TV, when witnesses come forward and corroborate your story," Gromolka has warned. "Most witnesses hide and try to leave town. No one wants their ass on the line."

So it is with some trepidation that I call my only other possible witness, the famous Transylvania-born theatrical legend Elsbieta Andrews (née Ionescu). I've known Elsbieta professionally for eighteen years. When I first met her she was still acting, and gave lessons in her loft in Chinatown. We were great friends then, despite the age difference: She is over seventy now. Eastern European, she was famous for her interpretations of the classics. Her distinguished good looks, the long, then prematurely silver hair, her aquiline nose and blazing gaze, made her extremely castable for Greek tragedy. She won an award as Antigone.

We got on famously in the capacity of pupil and coach: It was Elsbieta who corrected my vocal habits, who taught me to scream without stress and project from my diaphragm. Then her good fortune—she was tapped by an entertainment agency to head their casting department—placed a slight strain and created distance in what had been a very close friendship. There have been times when I was not called in to read for a part I would have liked. But then, sometimes, she did seem to favor me. For the past ten years there has been a gingerly quality to my relations with her; I never, ever feel entirely relaxed, even when we meet for tea or have the occasional dinner.

Elsbieta has become very imposing as well—a personage. She wears hats—I mean *large* hats—with veiling, not lowered but draped up over the brim. And dress gloves. She is ladylike, but her

pale eyes are always flicking, going over me for details of grooming, signs of aging, perhaps, or fatigue.

Are you right for this? she always seems to be wondering.
Whenever I am in her company, I have a sense of an ongoing
appraisal. For all this, Elsbieta is an excellent judge of character
and of acting technique. She might be an extraordinary witness.
She might prove my case. Her clear, almost white-blue eyes miss
nothing. I can't even begin to imagine what she noticed between
me and Matt last Thanksgiving.

Last Thanksgiving weekend—God, was it only four months
ago?—Nadine had been the invited guest, but she needed a ride,
and Elsbieta had offered to drive her up here for what was supposed
to be a pleasant fall weekend. What had I been thinking? Having
guests? Matt was already half out of his mind. We had the actual
Thanksgiving Day dinner with his parents in Delaware, and he'd
slammed out, as was his custom, in a rage over something his parents said. We'd driven here in record time and were supposed to
take the rest of the holiday to "relax."

He hadn't wanted friends; he'd been clear about that: Casa di
Rosas was a bit small for overnight company. One guest would
have to stay upstairs, on the daybed in my tiny study, right off our
bedroom; the other would have to take the downstairs couch. It
promised to be awkward at best, without much privacy for anyone,
but the truth was, I was already afraid to be alone with Matt, especially on a holiday. Events proved my intuition correct.

Elsbieta Andrews had been the innocent bystander, but she
had seen the catastrophe unfold. Maybe she would not mind
bearing witness. If she refused, of course I would understand. I
tried to imagine the roles reversed: What if I saw someone's husband become violent? Would I want to appear in court to testify? Would I find it too intimate? Too dangerous? Would I be

one of those witnesses who flee until the court procedures have passed?

I dial Elsbieta, imagining the woman in her rooms at the residential hotel where she lives now. As soon as she became prosperous, she left that soy-scented loft I loved in Chinatown and moved to Fifty-seventh Street, into an ornate building with a rococo facade. The building became infamous: an actor murdered his wife there and then took his own life. He got the big obituary, I recall. He was usually referred to thereafter as a tragic suicide, a depressive, and very few people remarked that he had killed his pretty young wife.

I apologize again and again to Elsbieta: "I'm so sorry to involve you in my case. . . ."

"I'm casting a revival of *The Iceman Cometh*," she begins, an unpromising start. How many pseudo-drunken Irish character actors can she find in time? She seems to be suggesting she is too busy, but then Elsbieta surprises me by saying, "Ay, marriage. Divorce. I went through much the same at your age: My first husband, too, went, crazy. He broke a milk bottle over my head at a lovely breakfast place on the Danube," she confides. "I had to call the police. With my second husband it was all the time jealousy, with knives. He held a knife to my throat and said, 'Confess.' I was innocent, but I confessed to sleeping with everyone. I didn't want to push my luck with the knife. You never know what makes a man slip."

"Then you understand?"

I try to explain that I don't know the perimeters of Matt's rage: I don't know if he might endanger her.

"Eh," she says, "I'm seventy-two. I've been through two revolutions—Romania and Cuba—and two crazy husbands of my own; I can handle your crazy husband."

At this moment I well up with appreciation for this older woman. This is beyond the call of our friendship. I had been braced for her to edge away from the request. I would be the first to understand if she had refused. She had the misfortune to observe Matt at his near worst, and now she was willing to repeat what she had seen, in court.

I felt my old love for her surface; I had been wrong to sense some distance, reserve, in our friendship. "Thank you," I whisper. Then I have to ask what she saw that holiday weekend.

I hope she had been more aware than I was, had registered the telling detail that would be effective in court.

"He drove like a maniac," she recalls, "and he tried to run over your little white cat. She was quick and jumped out of the way. I'm sure he scratched my car; the mechanic said it was 'keyed': Someone ran a key along the side. You know how that goes these days: two thousand dollars for a scratch. Insurance paid for it. I didn't accuse him; I had also parked at a rest stop after dark—so it was possible that it happened there, on the Northway—but my instincts tell me, he did it. I didn't like the expression on his face when he looked at me: I could see this is a man who hates his mother."

"You're astute," I say.

"Well, it's my job," she sighs.

"Did you see the business with the food?"

"When he threw it?" she asks.

"Yes: the turkey."

"I heard it go," Elsbieta answers. "Nadine saw a leg flying. . . ."

I didn't think I could laugh again but I did. Bless her, bless Nadine. Thank God, I do have friends.

"So tell me when to be there, I'll be there," Elsbieta concludes.

"I feel so guilty. It's so far, such a long drive, in terrible road conditions. There have been seventeen blizzards."

She says what she always says: "Eh, I'm used to it. I walked to Hungary."

I'm so happy I have witnesses, I will agree to any condition; so when Elsbieta asks, "One favor, please," I say yes before she asks:

"While I'm there could you show me, the famous place, the Moldavian Colony? You must have heard of it: It was established in 1878, on the shore of Lake Bonticou."

The Moldavian Colony did sound vaguely familiar: "A Victorian bungalow colony? A religious kind of campground?"

"Yes," Elsbieta answers, "what they call a psychics' camp. They were all mediums."

"Mediums?"

"Yes, you know—when you need to reach the dead?"

"Uh-huh," I say.

"I'd like to see it when I'm up there," Elsbieta says, "if it's not too much trouble."

I say the only thing I can, under the circumstances: "No trouble." But it is a bit of trouble: I have to prepare for court, I must still search for more evidence, witnesses. I am not truly eager to go seek out a defunct psychic community in the frozen cliffside of Lake Bonticou. "It won't take long?" I ask, my voice weakening. I know I should be glad to indulge her: She is doing me such a huge service by speaking at the court hearing.

"Oh, I don't think so," Elsbieta answers. "But I must go there, if even only for one moment. I must go there. . . ."

I grit my teeth. If there is anything I find hard to subscribe to, it is my fellow thespians' obsession with the occult—the telepathic coincidences, premonitions, astrological forecasts.

The phone rings in my hand.

I wonder if it is the mystery writer from across the lake.

"Yes," a man greets me. "You sent me a note?"

The Man under Glass

On the phone, Gideon Winsten sets a series of ground rules for my visit: I am to appear after two P.M., so as not to intrude on his "writing time." And I may remain for only an hour, as he is not well and will need to rest.

"Oh, I'm sorry," I say. He does sound clogged. His voice quality is odd anyway—thin and reedy, and now he is congested. My initial mental image of Winsten—the handsome, bespectacled man in the checked flannel shirt; a touch of silver in his hair; his long, lean body—is revised to a hunched-over neurasthenic. Now I envision Winsten as short and shriveled, with an overlarge head, and foreshortened arms that end in stubby fingers. He is not attractive, and now I predict that he is controlling and hypochondriacal. Yet, he might be a witness. He has a direct view of Casa di Rosas—distant but direct—from across the lake. He doesn't sound as if he is a man likely to come to the rescue, but, on the other hand, he has responded to my note.

"I've seen your films," he tells me. "In fact, *Kiss of Death* is based on my novel *Mortal Coils*," he informs me. "You probably didn't realize that. I also had a writing credit on *Run for Your Life.*

The best dialogue is mine. The rest was atrocious. I took my name off it."

Oh, now I realize why his name rang bells. *Kiss of Death* was filmed ten years ago, but I assure him, "I read your book, of course, to prepare for my role." The truth was, I tried to read *Mortal Coils.* I found the descriptions of the victims upsetting in their detail, and his prose a bit florid. He leaned heavily on a third-person protagonist, Angelo, who struck me as irritatingly omniscient. *Angelo knew in his soul that Michaela was not real, that she was a phantom, an imaginary extension of him, Angelo.*

If I had to choose, I would say I preferred *Run for Your Life,* because my character had the gumption to sprint at the end. "I like my character in *Run for Your Life,*" I interject fast, fearful Gideon Winsten will hang up to use nasal spray.

My compliment is habitual, a courtesy of the business. I didn't much like *Run for Your Life.* And I am taking an instant dislike to the whining man on the other end of the line.

"You were excellent throughout most of the film," he says in a flat, clogged tone.

Don't think I didn't catch that "most of the film," I silently respond.

"Forgive me if I don't effuse quite enough," Gideon continues. I hear a honk as he blows his nose, which I now picture with oversized nostrils, untrimmed. "I'm going out of my mind here today with sinusitis, on top of my cold allergy. Apart from that, we know no civilization will get through the Adirondack Pass for days, so there goes FedEx." There is an interruption as he suffers a sneezing fit.

Oh, well, maybe he is very sick and unable to sound more animated and pleasant today. A mystery writer, a FemJep source . . . Now, I am very curious to see the real Gideon Winsten.

Benefit of the doubt, I instruct myself. *Give him the benefit of the doubt.*

"I'm so sorry you are ill," I begin. "Do you need anything there? Juice? Aspirin?"

Maybe he will turn out to be a friend and neighbor after all.

"No. I have everything," he answers. "Maybe a *New York Times* and a *New Yorker,* if you have the latest. Mine wasn't delivered. Otherwise, I have absolutely everything that I need. Come over if you're not a germophobe," he invites.

And at two P.M. I can confirm that, indeed, Winsten has every known cold remedy: On his open kitchen counters, there are hundreds of tiny homeopathic vials, cards of sinus tabs, Tibetan nasal cleansers, humidifiers, and jugs of fresh-squeezed organic grapefruit juice. I can see the rows of medication from a hundred yards away.

The house is as advertised—glass. A glass box. When it was built seven years ago, I resented the construction of the house. Not only did it distract from what had previously been an unobstructed view of the opposite cliffs and forest, but the actual construction had been so noisy: It echoed to my place, and ruined the tranquility of an entire summer. More than just a construction nightmare, the house replaced a picturesque ruin of the original manor house of the Deschelles estate. There had been a charred stone foundation, but I had always found it romantic to imagine "my" bride and groom sailing across the lake from The Wedding Cake House to their mansion. A futuristic house on the location seemed architectural sacrilege. I remember how the birds screamed when the demolition job began; the crows shrieked, and the turkey vultures, animate shadows of the ruin, had flown over my house, casting a chill.

The square glass house is my nightmare: There is no cranny unexposed, and the flat roof is, as Jake Taylor described it, topped off with a ledge of snow. Although the rear of the house is still

buried by drifts, someone has "dug him out" up front, and through
the sheer wall I can see, from a hundred yards away, Winsten—the
real Winsten, who is unlike either of my imagined versions of
Winsten—blowing his nose into a hankie.

I had decided to approach his house on foot—across the lake.
On foot, crossing the lake is a shortcut. The lake road, Serpentine,
winds uphill, then descends again, adding a half mile. I love to
walk the frozen lake. The ice is solid. The temperature is below
zero, and the wind has blown the snow to expose the surface. Not
glace noire, the ultimate, but an opaque, bumpy, granular white
surface—rock hard.

I can use the exercise, I tell myself, but maybe I want to measure
this distance between this man and me in a new way. We face each
other across the narrow north end of the lake, and my guess is that
Gideon Winsten is barely a quarter mile away as the crow flies.

The short hike does invigorate, although it instantly numbs
my feet through my warmest fleece-lined boots. I have had to force
my feet into these boots. Had a strange woman really been wearing
them? I put that idea from my mind: innocent until proven guilty;
maybe Moira's own children had worn them and she is too embarrassed to say. In any case, they are my best boots for this surface;
the soles have traction and I feel secure enough as I march across
Lake Bonticou toward the glass house. I can't help wondering
about my neighbor. My experience with playwrights has been that
they are very idiosyncratic. Gideon Winsten is a novelist, a new
breed to me. He built a house I hate, wrote some scripts I can't say
I admire, and now he may be flashing signals to me at two A.M.
What will he be like in person?

"I can't abide orange, it's too sweet. I get sugar shock" are his
first words to me as he opens his door, partially, greeting me with
a glass of grapefruit juice in his hand. He has been struggling with

a bottle of antihistamines, and I note toothmarks on the child-guard cap.

For all his display of textbook hypochondria, I find Mr. Winsten in person quite good-looking. He is not as appealing as my initial mental projection, but he is not a troll. It is almost fun to discover him, appearing somehow like a fifty-year-old toddler in his navy blue running suit with a winter coat draped over his shoulders in the well-heated glass house before a fire that blazes in the futuristic copper funnel-shaped hearth. The room is hot, but apparently he is cold. Gideon Winsten is tall, over six feet, with my initially projected silvering hair with a bit of curl, a longish pale face, brown eyes, and a thin body with a kind of torque. He twists in place, averting his gaze from mine even as we meet.

"Juliana," he greets me. "I'll stand back. I'm quite contagious."

It's all right: A cold would be the least of my problems.

"I'd offer you something to eat, but I'm fasting, trying to rid myself of yeast."

What does that have to do with my not having something to eat? I wonder. I have worked up an appetite stamping across the frozen lake. I can inhale the steam: He has a kettle on high, near whistling.

"Tea?" I suggest. Maybe he will offer a yeast-free biscuit.

"Noncaffeine only," he answers.

Winsten is handsome—or would be, if he were not so neurotic. The neurosis actually bends him: His body keeps arcing in various insecurities. His constriction extends to his windpipe—the voice is what makes him less male, less handsome; it is reedy, barely aspirated—and he utters each word tilting, neck cricked, as if it cost him some agony to utter a simple sentence. The general unhappiness of his face, too, detracts from his regular features—the wide white brow, smooth skin, squared chin. Movie-matinee-idol material, save that he is afflicted by neurosis, the way you see invalids spasm with palsy. His pelvis has a concave look, too, which projects a negative sexual energy. Nothing going in that department, my female instinct tells me. I scold myself for being this uncharitable. He's ill, after all. Maybe that sunken pelvis corrects itself.

I look around the glass room. It is so odd: I feel as if I am in a display case, yet I concede there is an undeniable drama, an *Architectural Digest* high-tech chic; the white expanse of the frozen lake seems an extension of Gideon Winsten's decor. I have to admire his taste: His furniture is handmade, twisted gray willow, Adirondack-style. The concept—winter woods continued within the glass box—is striking. The house is small but seems larger because of the glass—the effect is of wall-lessness. At the rear, where the house backs into the woods, he has set a wall-sized mirror in a thin silver frame. The light is brilliant inside, glancing off all the glass and that mirror, which doubles his view of the lake.

The mirror. Of course. I stare into it and see . . . my house, the little white wedding cake, miniaturized at this distance on the other side of the lake. I stare into this mirror for a moment, in shock, as comprehension hits: I am looking at my own house, reflected, in the distance.

I realize now: That light I saw last night, it's my own light, reflected in his mirror. His gas lamp had not been synchronized to my candle: It was my candle.

I drink the juice he offers, with the assurance "Don't worry, I washed it in the sanitizing cycle. The tea will take a bit to steep." His hand—it is cold—grazes mine as I accept the juice glass.

His hands are oddly small for his six-foot frame, adding to his aura of compromised strength. He has a total loss of energy also, and soon sags into what is obviously his accustomed seat, a posture swivel leather armchair beside the hearth.

I notice a smaller willow chair, angled toward him. "Your place is stunning," I compliment him. "I admit I somewhat resented it when you went in—the construction, and the destruction of the ruin. . . . But now that I am here, I see what you have done."

"I hated to lose the old ruin," Winsten agrees. "In fact, I incorporated a few retaining walls behind the house. I had to work within the setting. I inherited the land, and architecture is an avocation of mine, so I decided to go bold with the plans. I have always admired your house: It's a perfect example of Bonticou Gothic. You're my view, one of the reasons I chose the site."

"You're my view," he said. I am thinking: How much did you see? But how to broach the topic? I don't want to ask: Did you notice when my husband tried to kill me?

Winsten has papers and architectural plans piled beside him, on a library table, and more on the window seat, next to a folded telescope. The room is neat, but there are stacks of things—books, papers, file folders. I check the bookshelf to discern his interests. There seems to be a preponderance of local history. And there are also stacks of newspapers, clippings, Xeroxes, faxes. I catch the headline from yesterday's Bonticou Crier—the Bonticou Woman Found Frozen on Porch. Winsten catches me eyeing the headline.

"Reduced to the local news," he admits. "No Times?"

"No, I couldn't get hold of a paper. I don't think the Times made it into Bonticou since the snow yesterday."

"I'm in a terrible withdrawal," Winsten says. "No Times since

Friday. No Sunday, no nothing. I didn't mind Monday. But today is 'Science Times,' my favorite."

"Mine, too," I say.

"You know," he says, suddenly staring at me, "most actresses are not really beautiful in person. They are photogenic. The beauties are no beauties, I find. They have bad complexions, mostly, and they are shorter than you would think."

So? What am I supposed to think? That I look less attractive than on film? Winsten surprises me.

"But you're really beautiful," he continues.

"Thank you," I say, as stunned by the compliment as I would have been by an insult. There is something so precise in his attention as he studies my face.

"You died well in *Kiss of Death.*"

I didn't die, I think. I escaped. Should I correct him?

"Thank you," I say. "But as I recall, I survived. . . . Actually, I have never been 'killed.'" Yet.

"The studio insisted," he corrects, "in my script, you—your character—died. They hired another writer to do that scene when you open your eyes. I didn't need to see that. What I was referring to was that work you did, as the life seemed to leave your body, the way your pupils changed. . . . How did you do that? They actually seemed to harden, the way a corpse's would."

"Technique," I answer. I know I should feel complimented; no one has ever commented on the exact transition that I achieved in that scene, but his attention makes me uneasy. I notice he is staring at my feet.

"Your feet must be cold."

I realize I should have removed my wet boots; they must be tracking, dripping in his immaculate abode. "Oh, I'm sorry," I apologize, and undo the laces, wriggle off the boots. I am surprised when he almost leaps up to seize the wet shoes. He sets them near his wood-burning stove. I wonder if the boot toes will curl, as my real ones are. . . .

"I feel a little silly coming here," I say. I don't want to add, I thought you were signaling me at two A.M. "I'm in a marital situation and I thought, perhaps, you had witnessed"—I hesitate—"an incident during the holidays." I stare out the glass wall: Could Winsten have seen anything on New Year's Eve? There, not so far away, across the lake is my house: The Wedding Cake House looks like a dollhouse at this distance, a fanciful miniature. But the view is direct; Winsten would have seen the police car. Could he have seen me run out my door, Matt in pursuit? We would have appeared as tiny figures, but we would have been visible. As I stare toward my house, I see the deer, unself-conscious, trot across the snow-covered beach area. I imagine I see One Eye en famille.

I have to give him a brief synopsis of my problem. "I'm in court," I explain. "I've brought charges. . . . My lawyer wondered if you might have heard screams or seen anything odd . . . ?"

"No, no, nothing at all. In fact, I look at your house and admire its . . . its stillness. If you didn't have the one light burning upstairs, I'd assume it was unoccupied."

He notices I am still staring at the now-familiar photograph on the *Bonticou Crier*—the Frozen Woman, curled in her fixed position that suggests prayer—and the headline *Bonticou Woman Found Frozen on Porch.*

"Actually," Winsten says, holding up the front page, "this story is of interest. It's terribly written. I can't tell if she was eaten by coyotes or stripped or was walking around naked on her porch, but it ties in to something I am working on. . . ."

Why do I shiver? Another of my odd premonitions? I reject the sense of dread I feel as he continues: "I happen to be researching a new book on a series of murders that occurred here at the turn of the century, when Bonticou was a sportsman's paradise, known for great parties in summer and ice sports in winter."

"Yes, when Casa di Rosas was built—"

"For Amie Deschelles's wedding. June 22, 1899."

"Very good," I say. "You've done your research on the entire community."

"Amie was one of the victims."

I feel an all-over body tingle, the odd rush of blood through my body, that chug of fear. . . .

"Victim of who?"

"Well, that's what I'm trying to discover. . . . More than a century later, I am trying to solve . . ." Winsten takes a breath, and I see him smile for the first time; I notice that he has odd, pointy incisors, exaggerated canines—another factor that keeps him from being handsome.

I can see he is delivering his title with relish: ". . . *The Riddle of the Frozen Girls.* Do you like it? Would you read it? Would you buy it? Will you star in it? You'd be perfect: You have such a quaint, period look."

I can't return his smile. Frozen Girls. The original bride, for whom my house was built—was she a victim of Victorian FemJep? I am quivering.

"From 1897 through 1899, there were seven beautiful young girls, all of impeccable social credentials, who were found naked, frozen, on Lake Bonticou. There was never a murder weapon or an apparent injury. The killings were never solved, but it is believed to be the work of one deranged, sexually frustrated serial killer, who stripped his victims and then watched them freeze to death. There's one other really great detail. . . ."

"What's so great?" I ask.

"Oh, you'll love it." He looks animated for the first time, almost chortling and rubbing his hands near the fire. "They were always found in positions of prayer."

I can't tell him how unsettling this story is to me. I feel faint, as if I might again have to lower my head to redirect the blood supply.

"Do you mind?" I ask, indicating the second chair, the gray willow armchair with a white linen seat cushion.

He looks concerned. "Are you all right?"

"Maybe not," I have to answer as I sink into the chair. He moves quickly for his small homeopathic vials. He holds something near my nose.

"Smelling salts," he says. "I bought them for research, but they work."

I take a whiff and my nostrils burn. I do lower my head, and I can still see the room sparkle with gold dots, a sequined scrim to my unconsciousness. I do not want to black out, not here, with this man. . . .

"Vasco syncope," he diagnoses. "I suffer from it myself. 'Oh' syndrome. Low blood pressure. You faint often?"

Thank goodness, not now. I raise my head and refocus. At least he looks concerned. He is no hero, no savior, no muscular-armed rescuer, but he looks like he is worried. At least, I reflect, he is only neurotic; I have been dealing with a psychotic. I suppose this is better.

"The ginger tea?" he invites.

"Yes, thank you." This is better; he is neurotic but not to be feared. The story of the Frozen Girls is upsetting, but it really doesn't concern me. The man is a mystery writer; it is not abnormal for him to take some enjoyment from grotesque tales of this sort. And if you look into the history of any area, you can find a string of mysterious deaths.

I sip the fragrant hot tea; he has proffered it in a fragile German china teacup, the bone china so fine, I can see my pinkie finger through it as I hold the cup in the prescribed, ladylike manner.

"This woman," Winsten says, indicating the dead cover girl on the *Bonticou Crier,* "she doesn't fit the profile. She is lower class, for one thing, and no beauty, for another, and whoever killed the Frozen Girls lived over a century ago. So that person could not have killed her. Unless," he giggles, "he can also return from the dead. I'm sure this will turn out to be, the woman is an alcoholic or an Alzheimer's case who just wandered outside in the blizzard, in confusion, and passed out before she could get back in her own door. But it's curious, isn't it—her pose. Almost as if she is kneeling, with her hands clasped. . . ."

"Someone who is cold would fold into that position," I volunteer.

"True, true, true," Winsten agrees. "Well, I don't care about her. It just caught my eye. I have my seven victims, and I am determined to 'solve' the case . . . even though"—he giggles again—"the trail is cold."

He inhales from a nasal sprayer. "God, don't you hate phlegm?" he asks. "I feel as if I am underwater. Well, I am sorry I can't help you. I didn't see or hear a thing from your place on New Year's Eve."

"It's all right," I tell him, rising to leave; for some reason I am anxious to get away from him now. I pull on my boots; they have stiffened as they dried and feel hot from his hearth.

He sees me to the door, his back curving to maintain his odd, distant body language. "And I must be honest with you, Ms. Smythe: Even if I had seen something, I don't know that I would volunteer to come forward and be a witness at a court proceeding. I hate divorce; I've suffered through three, myself. I find it best not to take sides. The truth is in the middle," he says. "I like plots without heroines. We're all guilty of . . ." He smiles again, revealing those lupine incisors. "We're all guilty of something."

"This isn't a question of sides. This truth is not in the middle," I say. I am surprised at the heat that rushes to the surface of my face. "There was an attack. I was hurt. If you saw something—anything—I would appreciate it if you would just tell me. I just thought you might have seen—"

"I didn't see anything," he answers. "Good luck with it. I wish you well."

I am out the door and up the narrow, snow-packed footpath, when it hits me: He has a telescope there, in that room. I spin round and see he is closing the door. I run back. There is a strange energy now in the air; he directs his stare to the telescope, which is pointed innocently at the ceiling. I don't even have to ask: I look at it, and he says, "I stargaze, Ms. Smythe, I stargaze."

Then I am out of there, almost running. And my blood runs, too, faster and faster inside me. I don't think I mentioned the date: How did he know the attack happened on New Year's Eve?

I am still straining my recent memory—did I say New Year's or not?—as I run back inside Casa di Rosas. My feet are numb, but I don't stop to remove my boots. In the entry, from the pegboard, I grab Matt's birdwatching binoculars and race up to the bedroom. And there—as I somehow knew would happen—when I train the glasses across the lake, my double, magnified gaze meets the lone orb of Mr. Winsten's telescope.

Witnesses

Now I consider hanging the bedsheet across my window—and writing a message, MIND YOUR OWN BUSINESS, on the side that faces Mr. Winsten. I call the sheriff's office and explain the situation.

"Is he bothering you?" the sheriff asks.

Is he? "It bothers me that someone has a spyglass trained on my bedroom window." There's nothing, I am told, that can be done unless he disturbs me in some more tangible way. A man has a right to gaze out his own window. If he harasses me, issues threats in any form—in person, by phone, or by mail—I should call the police.

The phone rings as I am draping the sheet across the window. I pick up and am not surprised to hear the hoarse whisper "Juliana . . ." and then the slickety, clickety sound effects of someone, I assume a male someone, working himself toward release into the receiver.

"This call is being traced," I announce in a distinctly non-amorous tone. Then I slam down my phone. That's twice. One more call from Mr. Slickety-Click and they will be able to pursue charges against him. I stare at my now opaque view and wonder in the direction of Mr. Winsten: His voice, disguised? He had seemed too neurasthenic to be a breather, but everyone has urges, and perhaps his desires are directed in this manner.

The single benefit to my situation is that I have no time to brood. I must continue to prepare my case. Joe Gromolka wants to preinterview my witnesses, so there will be no surprises when we return to court. Now I am looking forward to the hearing, to getting it all out in the open: The court will read Matt's psychological evaluation, have him referred for psychiatric help, establish just cause for maintaining my order of protection. When all the evidence, including The Thing in the Box, is presented, I will be able to go on with my life, without this court procedure shadowing my future. I anticipate my return to work the way people long for a vacation: Oh, to be engaged in professional pursuit again, to have impersonal days and nights, to lose myself in a role . . . I take it as a good sign that my morning mail, unopened in my haste to see Mr. Winsten, contains a residual check for my work in *Run for Your Life*. The movie is being shown on Japanese television. The check is considerable, but I look at the numbers on it, and feel certain that there is a god, a god of freelance females, who has come to save me, at least financially. I can pay J. J. Janis, I can pay Joe Gromolka, and I can buy a new outfit for court and a bottle of fine wine to celebrate what I feel certain will be my turnaround in the justice system. I envision Elsbieta and Nadine, one of our shared toasts, this time in relief. I will be saved, I can feel it. . . .

Elsbieta is arriving first, by train. She is arriving in the evening, to be here in time for her interview with Gromolka in the morning. I drive to meet the five o'clock train at Bonticou Station. We will be able to eat dinner together, I think, my first friendly, civilized meal since this ordeal began. I've been living, I admit, like an animal in Casa di Rosas: There have been no amenities. I, who used to cook hearty four-course meals and bake all those pies from scratch, have been eating standing up at the stove. The skillet, with its scrambled egg residue, sits congealing in the kitchen sink; my laundry is undone.

Most nights I have opened a can of soup or fried more eggs. I've eaten canned beans, too, and been drinking mineral water straight from the bottle. Except for the single glass of wine I poured to relax last night, I have abstained, to stay alert. I exist on coffee, strong coffee, and I can taste the espresso on my tongue; I exhale its bitterness, my roiling, acid belly growling gut fear. My daily work has been my defense, in a sense—the sorting of correspondence, the scrounging for more evidence, the interviews with the prospective attorneys. FemJep, in real life, is a full-time job, a job I can barely keep up with. On my last trip to the attic, searching for more incriminating letters from Matt, I was overpowered by exhaustion. It was so hard, for some reason, to sit in the attic and read through the trunk of correspondence. I felt as if I were being mugged by memories: Most of the letters were so loving, and ultimately, they saddened me into sleep. I woke on the unfinished floorboards, feeling I had been "gone" for hours, but, by the clock, only moments had passed. . . .

Yes, I think as I drive down Serpentine toward the station, it will be civilizing to sit, dressed, in a café, across from an old friend, an emissary from my professional life, and have a real meal.

There is something inherently charming in meeting a train. At Lake Bonticou this is especially so: Not only is the train station a Victorian peaked-roof red building, with fanciful gingerbread and a hand-painted sign that reads Bonticou Station, but the approach from the south affords a spectacular view of the entire mountain valley. The northbound train is visible a long way off as it ascends. It's hard not to feel one's spirit rise with the sharp toot of the train whistle and at the sight of the silver train snaking round the bend. I wait outside on the platform to enjoy the view. In the sharp cold I stand, my hands jammed into the pocket of the Mafia lady coat. I have decided to maintain my public appearance in case anyone from the court should happen to see me. In a town as small as Bonticou, I am likely to run into people connected to my case. I have changed clothes and wear plain black pants and a sweater underneath, but on the surface I still want to project what both lawyers agreed I should: a more conservative look.

Elsbieta alights, the train conductor assisting her. She emerges like visiting royalty, in a full-length deep-purple wool coat with matching gray tight-curled Persian lamb collar and hat. Elsbieta knows how to dress herself in high style, and she wears kidskin charcoal boots with quite a heel. What a beautiful woman she must have been, I can't help thinking; what a stunning person she still is. . . .

She holds herself so well; her posture is textbook. Elsbieta strides along, sees me, presses her face, fresh and cold, against my cheek. I pick up a whiff of her perfume, Je Reviens, and the combined scents of femininity that seem to accompany women of her lineage: the smell of pink pressed powder, fruit aroma from her plum lip gloss, something else that is fragrant, indefinable: a scent I associate with the past, lavender, rose water. . . .

We meet at the exact magic hour, so beloved by film directors and cinematographers: The sun is setting and the horizon is rimmed in fuschia. The sky is a deepening blue, and the white snowcaps appear ultralucent. Although it is still light, the full moon is already rising: A gauze globe materializes in the sky as the hot, swollen sun sinks.

And for a moment I forget my pain and rejoice in the evening and the warm embrace of a friend. I am about to suggest we go to a Swiss-style bistro that caters to skiers on the edge of town, when Elsbieta says, "Can we go straight to the Moldavian Colony?"

I remark that it is almost dark, and I am uncertain of the Moldavian Colony's exact location. "I have a map," Elsbieta says. "It's very near here. This may be my only chance to go there."

Of course I agree to take her to the colony. She is here, after all, to do me a difficult favor. How can I refuse her anything? She won't even accept my offer to reimburse her for the train fare.

"I'll explain when we get there," she says, "but I must go. And I have to return to the city tomorrow, immediately after I see your lawyer, as I must be in my office in the afternoon. So this may be my last chance to see the Moldavian Colony."

I drive, following her directions. She reads from a map that looks antiquated itself. I have the vaguest recollections of the colony; there is a burned shell of what once a rambling Victorian mountain house resort, The Moldavia House, that is something of a local site of interest for long-distance hikers and cross-country skiers.

I have no idea if the place is accessible in winter by road, in a car. I drive, following Elsbieta's instructions, ascending all the way. The moon rises, seeming to accompany us, on the right. It is fortunate, because the moon illuminates the woods, almost as if under klieg lights. . . .

There must be dozens of abandoned bungalow colonies scattered through this mountain ridge. In the 1890's, straight through the 1950's, the mountains here were popular with city people seeking to escape the asphalt summers of New York. Husbands remained in the city to work, and wives and children settled in these clapboard clusters, cottages grouped around a central beach on the lake or perched high on the ridge.

Now the colonies sit listing in similar states of decay: The tiny white frame buildings sag; most roofs have long ago caved in, and the driveways leading to them have become half obscured by wild overgrowth. Here and there, a painted sign still stands, half the letters missing, offering a Scrabble challenge, sometimes in a foreign language: Ukrainian Lodge, Green Cottages, the Spruce Colony . . .

"It should be this next turn, at the top here," Elsbieta instructs. I take the right and pull the car a few feet into a steep driveway. The snow has drifted here, and I cannot drive any farther without risking being stuck. By moonlight I can read a white chipped lettered sign: Moldavian Colony. Some of the letters are missing, so it reads: Mold olony. Oddly, the second sign, mounted on a stone pillar, is engraved on a bronze: Certified Mediums, 1879. The remains of a shattered lantern sit atop this column. The glass is long gone, and the lantern is packed with snow. I look to the left and see that there was once a matching pillar; they were a pair, guarding the entry. The second column has crumbled and its lantern is missing.

The entry between these columns is drifted with snow. The lake wind has blown the snow here, leaving a narrow walkway similar to the paths carved out at Casa di Rosas.

"I guess we can walk in."

Elsbieta is already opening her overnight bag and pulling out a pair of serviceable mukluks. Off come the delicate charcoal kidskin boots and on go the snow boots.

I follow her lead: Has she been here before? She is moving swiftly, in eagerness. . . . We pass the ruin of the hotel; only one wall stands, with its empty window sockets. The stone walls have been stained black from ancient soot. I think it must have burned decades ago.

From the empty hotel a deer emerges, tilts its head: Yes?

"Somebody's home," I say. Elsbieta laughs.

The deer looks faintly annoyed, leaps from the hotel, and goes crashing through the woods. *Great hideout,* I think.

"The cottages should be here . . ." Elsbieta says, leading me up a path to the cliffside. The colony must be on the same side of the lake as Casa di Rosas; I recognize the view, only we are about seven miles south, where the lake widens, and it is almost impossible to see the opposite shore. The view, if anything, is even more dramatic than my own . . . but so is the wind, which is blowing straight in our faces.

The wind picks up surface snow, and some of it stings like sand as we continue toward the cliff. There, at the edge, is an Adirondack gazebo, painted white, with a built-in seat. I am startled to see the sign, Readings, still legible, nailed to the entry of the little shelter.

"Look there," Elsbieta says. I follow her gaze . . . and catch my breath. A cluster of ornate gingerbread cottages forms a semicircle, also facing the cliff. The wind has worn the paint from the lakeside of each cottage, but the rear walls are still visible in surprising pastel colors—apricot, lemon, lime green. I try to envision these frilly little houses in summer; a century ago they must have been festive.

Beyond them, however, are the silhouettes of tombstones, and one statue of what appears to be a dancing angel. "The colony graveyard," Elsbieta tells me, "But, of course, no one here believed in death. They call it 'the transition.' Do you know about mediums?"

"They claim to be able to be in touch with the dead."

"The Moldavian Colony was founded in 1879 for licensed mediums. . . ."

Who licenses mediums? I can't help but wonder, but I listen respectfully. "They had a carriage trade: People came from all over this country—and many from abroad—to establish contact with their dead loved ones. The hotel was booked with the guests. Bonticou Lake was called Spirit Lake then, and the cottages were the summer residences of the mediums. For a small fee, the guests could contact their dead family or friends or lovers and receive messages."

My cynicism rises, but I can see Elsbieta is sincere.

"What was the fee?" I ask, out of habit. I am now so accustomed to inquiring as to cost.

"I think it was ten dollars a message," Elsbieta answers. Her eyes are darting across the moonscape. "I must go to my great aunt's cottage. . . ." She leads me farther up the path. We go to the final cottage, the apricot-colored one with the sagged porch, closest to the cemetery.

"Let's go inside, out of the wind." We step carefully over the rotting porch boards; even so, they have a soft, sick give. I wonder about the advisability of this venture. What if we fall through the floor? No one knows we are here; we'll be sending and receiving messages all right, if we break our legs in this place. We may be found in the spring thaw, by hikers. . . . I think of my little white Saab, pulled discreetly off the mountain road. Yes, we could be here a while.

We do make it inside, and I am surprised to see that some furniture remains in the cottage. I suppose the player piano and the breakfront were too heavy to dislodge, and move backward on a now overgrown track. But the little mohair settee, with its cut-relief fleurs-de-lis—you would think someone would have stolen it by now. I sit down, and the sofa springs arch under my buttocks, almost popping. I suppose the piece hasn't been worth stealing for many decades. Elsbieta moves to the player piano and taps it, eliciting a few discordant notes.

I wonder if it has played in the past half century. "This was my great-aunt's cottage," Elsbieta explains. "When the war began, the First World War, one sister migrated, the other remained in the Carpathian Mountains. My great-aunt Eleanna came to the United States; very quickly she began to seek a place that would remind her of home. Here, in the Adirondacks, she was able to recreate her home village of Bunesti, in Transylvania. The family had faced prejudice there . . . because it was suspected that they were part Tigon . . . Roma . . . Gypsy—very disdained there. So my great-aunt felt she was fortunate to escape to America. She joined the Moldavian Colony, because it was made up of many people with her own background: They were Moldavians. They were mountain people, very secretive, and hardy, and of course they all had the gift. . . ."

They could commune with dead, or so they said. Sitting on the morose mauve mohair settee, I could not dismiss her story. I resist the occult, but there is a mood here. . . .

The story Elsbieta tells is a sad one: of her family massacred in Romania and her own trek to Hungary and eventual migration here. She had long ago planned to visit the extinct Moldavian Colony—she felt a spiritual obligation to do so—but the opportunity had not presented itself until last fall, when Nadine had asked her to accompany her to my country house for the remainder of the Thanksgiving holiday.

She had intended to visit the cottages then, but my marital conflagration—Matt's explosion at the Thanksgiving table—had driven her off. Now, because she was summoned to testify, she felt it was a sign that she must return here, to the ancestral medium's cottage, to receive a message.

And this is my first witness, I think, *the descendent of Gypsies ousted from Transylvania.* I wonder how well Elsbieta will do when she must take the witness stand. I don't doubt her sincerity, but how will she play in Bonticou family court? I also can't help wondering how well she would score on the Minnesota Multiphasic Personality Inventory.

Aloud, I say, "Would you prefer to be alone in the cottage for a few moments?" I sense that she would, and she does.

"Thank you. . . . Yes, but I must be alone in here just for a minute. . . ." She looks into my eyes. "I'm sorry, it's so cold out there."

"It's cold in here," I say, trying to lighten the atmosphere in the Moldavian cottage.

Outside, the moon is higher now, and the woods could not be more lit than they are: The forest is black, skeletal, casting a duplicate forest onto the snow. I go a few feet away from the cottage and find myself face-to-face with the stone cut angel. How long has she been dancing here, caught in midspin, her stone chiton furling, her arms outspread?

Since 1899, I note. I shiver. The date is the same as today's: February twenty-seventh. A coincidence. Still, I move closer to her, note her nose is forever snubbed, the stone chipped, and her eyes appear blind—more wind abrasion on the marble, I suppose. She has been nicked by time, weather, and perhaps a vandal or two: There are red initials, CFS, painted on her pedestal.

Her name is unfamiliar—Frieda Van Deheuval—but her life span sends another shiver: 1878–1897. I figure the dates. She died a few days short of her nineteenth birthday. I wonder if the actual Frieda Van Deheuval was as beautiful as her mortuary angel—-the carved rosebud lips, the curved cheeks . . . She is a beauty, Botticelli-like, in spite of her damage.

I am lost in contemplation, standing absolutely still, when the animals streak past me, unaware of my form behind the statue. A winter weasel, white-furred, flees the larger creature. The big animal is moving so fast, flattened in his predatory leap, that I doubt he is what he appears to be: a silver wolf.

I didn't think we still had wolves here, but there have been rumors for years. Maybe he is a silver fox, or one of the grayer coyotes. Whatever he is, his ears are pinned back, his shoulders and haunches extended, and even I, at a distance of some feet, see the ivory yellow of his exposed fangs. I am so stunned, I cannot even cry out, let alone move. I freeze, as the prey also does. The little weasel turns, its stuffed, sleek stocking of a body upside down, and as I watch, it yields up its soft throat for the incisors. . . . "No," I want to cry out, "don't give him your throat."

A self-sacrifice. I have heard of this—the surrender. When prey acknowledge the victory of the kill. When they foreshorten their own struggle, submit to die quick.

That is what happens, but it is indeed quick, and the spurt of blood and short cry can almost be overlooked. The wolf, if it is a wolf, carries off the limp weasel, hanging like a toy between its teeth. The killer ambles off; I could swear his tail is wagging: There was no malice, only appetite. He is loping off to enjoy his dinner, perhaps with his own family, who wait in a den nearby, warmed by their own body heat. . . .

I say nothing to Elsbieta when she emerges. She appears pale but satisfied.

"Did you get your message?" I ask Elsbieta, who is smiling.

She nods. "Yes. But it was for you."

"For me? Are you going to tell me?"

I don't believe in such communication, but I can't resist; I am dying, in fact, to hear from the dead.

I wait, my pulse in my throat. What is the message?

"I'll tell you at the right time. When you are ready to hear it."

Plaintiff

If there is a role I resist, it is that of the plaintiff, the complainant. I don't like even the sound of those nouns; plaintive, whiny. I am determined to prevail, to not yield to the marital disaster that has overtaken me. As soon as my reinforcements arrive—Nadine, who drives up in a rented Jaguar, follows Elsbieta the next morning—I feel, despite my friends' eccentricities, no longer so alone. They are witnesses; my account, at least of the preamble to Matt's violence, will stand.

The sight of Nadine alighting from a red Jaguar will jog anyone's spirit. She describes herself on her résumé as "formerly gorgeous," but in fact, she is still "somewhat" gorgeous. She is a big girl, almost six feet tall, and her lack of victim castability is heartening to me under the circumstances. In the films we have worked on together, she is invariably cast as a comic sidekick or a formidable opponent. She often plays "the other woman" because there is nothing wifely about Nadine. She is statuesque, to say the least, weighing in at a shapely but zaftig 150 pounds, with broad shoulders and fairly outsized breasts, or "boobies," as she calls them. She changes her hair color every few months and, like

Elsbieta, tends toward every known superstition or New Age belief system. Nadine has a few innovative spiritual or psychic aspects that are unique: She claims that she can predict earthquakes "all over the world" by a twitch in her buttocks.

"Girl, I am seismic," she likes to say. What I love about Nadine Jagoda is that she will take no nonsense from anybody—and gives none, either. Her warmth overcomes her idiosyncrasy in every situation, and when she arrives wearing a huge scarlet faux fur, with her hair dyed to match, I can do nothing but give in to her heated hugs and outcry: "We'll nail the bastard."

"I don't call him that," I demur. Nadine sees the sexual battle in high-contrast black and white. I see a world in shades of gray. I never saw my husband as "a sunofabitch" or "a bastard"—which was, perhaps, part of the problem. I don't see villains; I see victims of other victims—daisy chains of pain that link the perpetuators to the injured and reverse those roles.

Maybe I also don't choose my friends, but allow them to choose me. I know other women, even a few men in the city, but somehow they are not here in Bonticou as the case comes to court. Perhaps this is coincidental: They are not witnesses; or maybe, as Elsbieta insists, it is all written and this entire story is inevitable, given the characters. I have learned over my long career that the strongest plots arise from character. Is this the case here now?

Whatever. I have been alone, or alone with lawyers and litigation for so long that the sight of a familiar face is welcome. We embrace.

Nadine arrives in time for breakfast, and I make a great effort—my first in recent months—to cook for company. I light the living-room hearth and get a fire going. I edge my dining table closer to the fireplace—no more lounging in petrified torpor on the couch—and set the table for three.

Elsbieta and Nadine protest, but I cook my specialty: omelets crammed with cheese and vegetables. Against all our diets, I fry bacon, for the optimism of its aroma and the sound effect of the smoked meat curling and snapping on the stove.

"Eat hearty," I say. "We have a big day . . ."

Fortified by strong coffee and the big breakfast, we drive down to Gromolka's office on Duane Street. It is strange somehow to be accompanied on what has been my solitary beat. I escort Elsbieta and Nadine into the Victorian office of Gromolka and Gromolka. This time, there is a boy sitting in an armchair in the entry. I know who he must be without any introduction: Joe junior.

The boy is in fact Joe Gromolka, as if all age and weariness and compromise have been sandblasted from the father's face, and the older man has been reduced in bulk to a slim, fresh-faced boy. Junior, or Joey, as he introduces himself, is not quite the kid of my imagination: He is far more appealing; I forget how fresh an eighteen-year-old can be. He has no pimples, although there is an earring. He is cupid-faced, with downy cheeks yet, liquid brown eyes, dimples when he smiles, and a cleft in his chin. When he stands, he unfolds, the length of his body a surprise—so it seems to us both. I have a feeling he has just completed a growth spurt, for he has a child's head on a suddenly elongated body. He flushes when he sees me in the entry but comes right forward with a strong hand-shake. I recognize him now—the boy I noticed at court.

"This is awesome," he greets me. "I saw you in the movies a million times. I have *Run for Your Life* on tape, and *Kiss of Death* is maybe my favorite thriller of all time."

Elsbieta and Nadine laugh: a fan—in all of places, this minuscule law office in a tiny off-season hamlet in the Adirondacks. "No escape," whispers Elsbieta.

"Hey, I'm a star, too," says Nadine.

The boy's eyes widen: "You are?"

His father opens the inner-office door.

Gromolka deposes my witnesses one at a time. I sit in the foyer, sipping Gromolka coffee from the big urn and, against all reason and even desire, nibble his frosted doughnuts.

Elsbieta vanishes inside first, emerges, tells me, "I acquitted myself admirably," and then asks for a ride to the train station. While I drive Elsbieta, Nadine is interviewed.

When I return, I see the door is still closed: Nadine must be inside with Joe senior. Joe junior, Joey, has been waiting for me, a script in his hand. "I've been working on a screenplay," he confides, "and I've written a great part for you. . . . Would you read it?"

How can you say no to a boy? I say yes. He grins and amends, "Now that I actually have met you, I can make your part bigger."

"Thank you," I say, trying not to laugh.

"I appreciate this," he says. "It's beyond my dreams, actually. I want to help . . . on your case. You know, I'm studying to be a PI— private investigator?" He has the habit of his generation, ending his sentences as question marks. "I can do some"—he searches for the lingo—"legwork for you? I might even be able to help you with evidence for court? I've been watching my dad all my life: I know how these cases go."

How do they go?

Why not? I think. What do I have to lose?

"There'd be no charge: I'd be honored to . . . and for the experience?"

Sold. I feel a moment's yearning that I cannot explain. It has been a while since I have been exposed to youthful enthusiasm. I recognize this kind of kid: When I was a teenager I was like him, I think. Enterprising. I held down two jobs after school, and so, I learn, does Joey.

"I write for the *Bonticou Crier*," he says. "Actually, I'm an on-staff reporter."

I want to ask him about the Frozen Girls and Gideon Winsten, but I am interrupted: Nadine emerges. "I wowed him," she says. "This is going to be a walk in the park. I can't wait to take the stand."

Later, when I confer with Joe Gromolka senior, he agrees that both women will give strong testimony to my estranged husband's escalating rage. But he has not heard from Moira, who promised to call for her own interview. While I sit at his desk, he dials her. I see his face furrow.

I would not be surprised if she waffles—all that "I have to ask Rafe" and "Rafe will be so worried"—so I am relieved when Gromolka nods. "She's set to testify," he tells me. "I'll interview her this afternoon. We're just waiting for the psychological evaluations, then . . . and we're back on in court."

Can it be? A court victory in sight? I thank him, and Joe junior walks me to my car. I mention the Gideon Winsten incident and the fact that the writer is researching a famous Lake Bonticou case.

"The Frozen Girls?" The kid's face crinkles. "Never heard of them. But I'll do some research."

"Can you see if Winsten . . . has a record of some kind? For obscene calls or voyeurism?"

"I'm on the case."

Even though I discount Elsbieta's "messages" from beyond the grave, I also ask him for some background on the Moldavian Colony.

He does know about the colony. "The kids goof on that place every Halloween," he admits. "That was one of the oldest psychic communities in this country. It helped put this town on the map. Spiritualism and sulfur baths. Victorian industry." He smiles. I am thinking, *This is my lucky day: What a bright boy.*

He promises me he will come visit and bring his collection of "spirit photographs"—daguerreotypes he salvaged from the burned hotel. "The pictures are really cool: They show hotel guests with, like, Abe Lincoln or Sitting Bull behind them."

I'm delighted—exactly the sort of thing that might distract me. I have to admit, this boy charms me. If I had a son, I think, I'd like him to be like this kid, so eager and sweet.

I see Joey's face go soft when he looks at me, and I realize, Oh, dear, a crush. I wonder how older men can take advantage of young girls. This would be so easy—and so wrong.

If I'd had a baby when I first met Matt, he could be this boy's age. For a moment I feel a reprise of my slight propensity to faint. How did the time go by? I was eighteen when I met my husband. . . .

This sweet boy gives me a soft kiss on the cheek, and I drive home toward Casa di Rosas. I notice the sky is darkening, becoming dense with the possibility of yet another snow.

A t the house, I am surprised to see Rafe Gerhardt's black truck, with the lightning zigzags, parked in the parking slip below my main driveway. What would bring him here? Perhaps he has dropped off Moira to clean, I think, but this isn't her day.

There's no sign of Moira, but Rafe is standing at the front door. He has been waiting. I tense, somehow anticipating that he will tell me that Moira is not "allowed" to testify. I am not encouraged to see that he has brought a weapon, a hunting rifle.

"Here," he says, handing the rifle to me. "My wife says you've been threatened, and I been thinking of you, alone up here, all by yourself at night, and I thought you might feel better if you was armed."

What a conundrum. I don't want to hurt his feelings, but I

loathe the idea of a gun, even for self-defense. "Oh, I'm fine," I say. "I have my cell phone and some pepper spray and everybody in law enforcement on my speed dial."

He does look like Errol Flynn—same fine features, clear blue eyes, waving blond hair. He has the Bonticou bad teeth, however: He isn't smiling, but when he speaks, I can see black gaps. "I think you should take the gun for a while—just till your trial is over, anyway. . . ."

He seems so insistent. But I don't want the gun—any gun. "I wouldn't even know how to fire it," I say.

"I'll show you," he offers.

I can't help but be touched: Here is a protective man, trying to help the only way he knows how. Maybe it would be easier to let him leave the gun. He is already demonstrating how to load: "Now, you don't want to leave her loaded; that's bad: You misfire. She could go off on you. But you want to keep your ammunition handy, by your bed, and the weapon right beside it. . . ."

There's no arguing with him, and the wind is picking up again. I feel the moisture in the air sharpen to a needling sleet even as we stand there, while he demonstrates.

For some reason I cannot stop thanking him, praising him. Maybe I am just so surprised by his gesture, I don't know what else to do. "If it was my wife, my Moira, I'd blow the guy's head off," Rafe volunteers.

Um, a downside, I think. He's just a bit too enthused about this protection. But I am planning to get back inside the house, put on a kettle for tea, take another hot soak in the tub, and get some sleep.

"Fine," I say. And for several minutes he demonstrates: "Lock 'n' load. Aim. Fire."

It is surprisingly difficult to shoot straight. I am aiming at the big dead maple tree, and I can't hit it. "Maybe I can just use it to scare someone off," I finally say, having missed every shot.

"No. I won't go, till I see you do this right," he insists.

He stands close to me, works with my hands on the sights and handle of the rifle. He has an odd, masculine smell: Tobacco has seeped into his wool plaid jacket, even into his blond hair. I feel that leatherlike flesh on his hands; he is, of course, not wearing gloves. I've taken off my own gloves, and my fingers are freezing. I feel them numb, growing colder in contact with the trigger.

In desperation, to end the lesson, I finally score a shot in the dead bark.

"Good," Rafe says. He beams now, revealing missing molars. "Great shot. Now, just remember how's I taught you, and you call me you feel scared, huh?"

"I don't know how to thank you," I say to get rid of him.

"Well, come next fall, hunting season, I wouldn't mind coming onto your property. I know there's a big buck hides out here, ten-pointer. I'd like to get him for a trophy."

One Eye. "My" stag.

This isn't, I sense, the time to mention that I disapprove of hunting, let alone that I want to protect that majestic stag, to whom I felt a mystical connection the day he escaped from the other hunter and then nearly fell through the cracked ice of the lake.

"Actually," I say, "gunshots make me nervous."

"Well, they wouldn't, knowing it was me," he says. His eyes have taken an odd kaleidoscopic inner turn, almost like the sights on the rifle. He has not liked my answer.

"Fine," he says, showing the gaps between his teeth. "When I come here, I'll bring my bow."

Oh, no. Bow hunting is perhaps more ominous than hunting

with a rifle. I have seen the bow hunters: The bows are not simple bows and arrows. They are massive black machines that fire steel arrows at astonishing speed.

"Seventy-five pounds of pressure," Rafe promises, as if reading my mind but misinterpreting my impressed expression.

I immediately suffer a vision: myself, shot through the head.

Do I dare forbid him the bow hunting too? He is looking at me, bouncing from one foot to the other in the cold. I am trying to summon the appropriate remark when I am saved by the bell: Inside Casa di Rosas my phone is ringing, ringing.

"I'd better get that," I say, and run fast back into my house.

Day in Court

The call turns out to be momentous. J. J. Janis, the Hatchet of
Westchester, or the Butcher of Briarcliff Manor—whatever
title one bestows upon Janis, the lawyer is crowing: "We got the
evaluations. We're set for court. Monday. So I'm back in
Yekaterinburg for you, baby. How is the Schmo working out?"

He refers to Joe Gromolka only as the Schmo.

"Fine." I report the status: We have three witnesses—none to
The Attack itself, but to the violent actions that preceded The
Attack—Elsbieta, Nadine, and Moira.

"Don't forget the evidence this time, baby," he says.

The court date is March seventh, which also marks an early
thaw. The winter sun seems faintly stronger; the temperature is
above freezing for the first time in months. I hear the musical drip
of icicles, and the road asphalt gleams wetly from meltwater. My
driveway is clear for the first time in months. And so, armed with
the Bendel bag, this time packed with The Thing in the Box, the
busted phone, and more damning notes from Matt ("I apologize
for my behavior. I was hideous last night . . ."), I load the car and
head for Bonticou County Family Court for what I trust will be the

finale. After this I can expect to have my order of protection in place for a year. If Matt violates the order, his arrest will be automatic. On the drive down Serpentine Road, there is an actual gush of cascading water—the runoff from the mountains—and I feel my own emotional thermostat rise. The sense of release is imminent. As I pass the town waterfall, which has been frozen like a massive white stalagmite, I see the cascade flow below a sheer veil of ice. Shards of that ice are cracking, falling into the creek. And the lake itself is voicing its seasonal excitement, with loud roars and rips, as the ice resettles and prepares to crack and melt. I can sense the bubbling of the unfrozen waters exerting their pressure to break through the surface of the great lake.

Everywhere in Bonticou there is softening, warming. Of course, the real locals, the year-round residents, never optimistic, are saying, "False spring." In the court entrance, I hear the guard quote the *Farmers' Almanac:* "We got two more blizzards due in. This won't last." The groundhog, of course, had not seen his shadow—not in Bonticou, anyway. If a groundhog came out here, I reflect as I turn down Main Street toward the courthouse, something would kill it.

Maybe this is a false spring, but it is also a reprieve—a reprieve from the grip of cold, the incessant wind and snow. I want to look forward to spring, and then summer, to a reordering of my own universe, a sense of returning to "normalcy." Of course, I know that it will never be the same. I dread seeing Matt today. It will be hard on him, I think, to hear his weaknesses, the cracks in his psyche, exposed in open court. But maybe he will get help, and perhaps even, someday, he will be stabilized by some miracle drug, and be able to thank me . . . for, in a sense, saving us both.

I walk past the guards, intent on reaching the plaintiffs' waiting room. I am passing the nursery when I hear a small sound. I peek in: There is that young grandmother holding the minuscule infant; she is burping her. The baby hangs over the woman's shoulder, and the grandmother is patting its tiny back. The baby faces me and opens her mouth in an oval. I wait for the burp or the cry but no sound comes out.

The grandmother sighs and says, "She is too weak to cry," and for some reason this starts the tears in my own eyes. I must utter a sound myself, for the baby lifts her head and looks toward me, directly into my eyes. I could swear this near-newborn is imploring me, but it must be some trick of my imagination. Why would the baby look to me? I am a bit spooked by her. She is the smallest baby I have ever seen, with the most adult gaze. Elsbieta says babies are old souls—that they know everything, and their memories must be erased before they speak.

The baby's mouth opens wider, and this time an almost inaudible cry issues forth. "Is she all right?" I ask.

"Just weak," the grandmother answers. In answer to my other unasked question, she says, "Abused. Do you believe someone would hurt a person this small?"

"It's a shame," I say, and move quickly on down the hall. The world is filled with agony, I think: Suffering is everywhere. Then I see him, Matt, handsome as ever, his thick brown hair curling over his high white shirt collar; he is holding his gray winter coat and escorted by the legal team, MacPherson, Betsy West, and the slumping, bespectacled Tom Karp. I avoid eye contact, follow them in. There is an odd moment when the younger man, Karp, holds the door for me. His eyes, behind what I consider his black-framed "nerd" prop eyeglasses, register some intimate knowledge as he stares at me. What has Matt told them? I believe I see something I do not expect: Pity?

As I enter I cannot help but note that Betsy West, walking

briskly just ahead of me, her blond bob swinging, her derriere snug in straight gray wool, has tiny feet. I can recognize my shoe size from a distance, and I am right behind her. The gray Ferragamos flash with thin brass trim on their heels. Size five.

I would say I was going crazy, imagining this, if Betsy West was not gazing—and I mean gazing—at Matt's profile as they precede me into courtroom three. Oh, this is bizarre, I think. My husband's attorney has fallen for him. But can it possibly be that Betsy West is the woman who was with Matt at the house before Christmas? In that case, she knew him before The Attack.

My mind boggles. I think of Moira and her ongoing monologue of the cheating husbands: They are forever being caught with the best friends, the sister-in-law, even in one case the mother-in-law. . . .

I know Matt's sexual drive, the relentlessness of it, and how at first a woman might mistake that for passion. I myself did not recognize his nature until it was too late.

There's no time to worry these bones. J. J. Janis and Joe Gromolka, Joey junior, are all waiting for me at the plaintiffs' waiting-room door. J. J. Janis is holding a manila envelope, and his gleaming brow is creased with concern. "What's wrong?" I ask.

"Don't worry about it. Just give your testimony. You'll have your chance to describe The Attack. That might be enough. . . ."

Don't worry about what? I have to know. I don't like his expression; Janis is looking at me differently. Something has happened. "What is it? I have to know."

"I'll fill you in later," J. J. Janis promises. "Don't worry about it. Just concentrate on your account of The Attack."

I wonder what has gone wrong with my case. Could it be the evaluations? That strange Lazare? Could he have underestimated

Matt's disorder? "Is it the evaluation?" I ask J. J. Janis. He makes a hand-chop motion: Silence.

And where are the witnesses? I see no sign of Elsbieta, Nadine or Moira. Elsbieta was driving this time, and the two women from the city were supposed to arrive together. Moira had also promised that she would be here.

Just as I begin to feel my heart hammer and my palms sweat in my gloves, I see Elsbieta and Nadine run in the door. They are breathless. "Semi truck trailer crash on the Northway," Nadine whispers. "Sorry we're a tiny bit late."

But where is Moira? She is supposed to be "on" first, when my witnesses are called to verify my account as much as possible. She must testify to the shattered vase, the mussed room, and the empty vodka bottles. There is no sign of Moira when the clerk calls the court in session.

"Don't look stricken," J. J. Janis reminds me. He helps me off with the Mafia lady coat. "Good. Better outfit," he compliments me.

I have broken down and bought a white blouse and full-length black wool skirt. They were hard to find in Bonticou. I panicked at the mall outside town—too many people, too many shops, the lit indoor boulevard with four hundred pound couples, pushing strollers . . . The scene confused me. I drove to the consignment shop at Bonticou Hospital and, as fate would have it, found the ideal costume, size seven. White blouse, long black skirt. I felt fine in it, and I was well rehearsed. The lawyers and I had gone over and over the facts of The Attack and the odd series of events leading up to it.

I am an actress and I know the confidence of being prepared. I am even "off book," as they say: I know my lines by heart. And I remembered to bring the evidence.

"Everything will be okay," Gromolka whispers, and his son smiles too. I feel a bit sad that I will have to recite the melodrama of my marriage before this young boy, but I suppose that he is used to tales of domestic violence.

"Court in session. All rise." As we stand I see the doors open, and a familiar couple rushes into the court and takes their places behind Matt. There can be no mistaking the woman in the harsh black wig and the gaunt, white-haired man beside her: My in-laws have come to attend the hearing.

Actually, it is a bit worse than that. "Your mother-in-law is on the witness list," J. J. Janis whispers.

My mother-in-law? This is grotesque. Can this be legal? My mother-in-law has despised me since "our Matt married beneath him." I shut my eyes. At our wedding she caused a scene. "This is what you want? She's smart, she's too smart." And the kicker: "She's smart about men." She didn't say *slut,* but that was her implication. Since that time, ever since Matt lost his temper at home, she would deliver the kicker: "He was never like this till he met you." She has always refused to see any film in which I kiss another man. She attends the premieres of movies in which I am hurt. Out of habit, I feel my lips twitch into a smile.

"Hi," I mouth. She turns away. My father-in-law, whose name is Bill but whom everyone calls Buck, nods in my direction. I always thought he liked me a little but was afraid to say so. He is tall and well built for an older man; you can see Matt's handsomeness came from his father, the insanity, essentially, from the mother, but Buck had been a drinker in Matt's youth. I never saw it, but the family referred to the period of his blackout binges as The Thirst. The Thirst was history by the time I met Buck, but maybe not the damage he had done with the belt. Matt did not relate the tales of the belt, but he'd told me that first night, the

night we met, how hard he'd gotten hit. He said he lost consciousness a few times when he was a small child. When Matt was big
enough, he fought back. These are his parents, my in-laws. They
are holding hands. Whatever their individual madness, they have
forged an inseparable union.

"Your affidavit," J. J. Janis whispers. "You mentioned the
in-laws' 'insanity on both sides.' They can testify."

I notice they carry a legal file box too. What on earth can be in
that?

There is a buzz at the bench, and I see J. J. Janis present the
Bendel bag with The Thing in the Box: "Evidence, Your Honor."

Judge Sintula asks questions of the attorneys: "And do we have
the psychological evaluations?"

"We do," they answer in unison.

We begin with my complaint. I am called to the stand. I raise
my hand, recite my name, address, and the oath: "I will tell the
whole truth, and nothing but the truth, I do so solemnly swear."

My own lawyers lead me into the familiar tale.

"There was an event on the night of December thirty-first?"
Gromolka begins. The men have agreed between them, that
Gromolka should do the questioning, as he is the local lawyer,
familiar to the judge and the other local attorneys.

I note at once that Joe Gromolka, whatever his good traits, is a
lousy actor. He has no presence whatsoever, stammers, and loses his
place. I'm hard-pressed to start my story properly, because he for-
gets the first question, which would allow me to describe the drive
from Delaware.

"There was a problem when you reached your house on
Serpentine Road?" he asks, when he was supposed to ask, "Was
there anything unusual in the drive from Delaware to Bonticou on
that date?"

I am still composed enough to say, "Actually, the problem began in the car on our way to the house."

J. J. Janis beams at me: I can see he thinks I have gotten off to a good start. I am not happy to report these events; I know the shame of being hurt, but I now also know the danger of trying to deny what has occurred, even to myself.

And so I must go over, moment by moment, the drive from his parents' home in Delaware—how he slammed out of there after having words with them. More than words: He smashed a glass near his mother's face.

"Why can't you act like a normal son?" she was screaming as Matt ran from the house, with me behind him. Then to me: "He didn't act like this until he met you."

I was accustomed to such scenes: On most holidays there was always some sort of blowup. His mother cried, and his father descended to the basement, where he sharpened tools.

"Go on, go!" his mother yelled. And we did go: Once in the car Matt floored the accelerator, and we zoomed up the turnpike eighty miles an hour. I was alarmed, but I thought he would calm down. He didn't. If anything, he accelerated, expressing his emotion with his "pedal to the metal," as they say.

Matt was silent and his expression set. I hunched in the passenger seat, watching the gray landscape flash by, the orange and turquoise Howard Johnson's, the rest areas . . . I suggested that we stop, and get some coffee.

He didn't answer but pushed on. I could see he was heading north, so I assumed the original plan, of going to Casa di Rosas, was still in effect. But he was swerving all over the road. Finally, I couldn't remain silent, and I asked him to please be careful, to slow down. . . .

He said, "You just be quiet"—just like that. Then he took the thruway, and I actually prayed we would be stopped for speeding. But of all the luck, we passed through every radar trap: The police had already snared their speeders. The other cars were pulled over, with troopers scribbling tickets.

Still, I was not fully alarmed until he swerved off the main road after the Northway. I felt the drive would exhaust his anger, but I was wrong: He was building. I could feel it, internally, in my abdomen. I have seen this onstage, when an actor builds toward a climactic act. I had an awful sense that Matt was going toward that second act "curtain"—the death scene.

On the road up from Bonticou to Serpentine, he began to steer toward the cliff. "Matt," I said, "please. . . ."

"You just keep quiet," he repeated. "You just keep quiet."

He skidded on ice, and we swung round and almost struck a tree. He righted the car and prepared to floor it again. "Matt," I said, "if you won't stop, just let me out: I'll walk the rest of the way. . . ."

"You're not getting out," he said. He drove directly into the oncoming lane on a hairpin curve. I held my breath, expecting to die. My mind was reeling: What could I do?

"Matt," I said, "please stop. . . ."

He began to scream then—that he wanted to die, that we should both die. . . . That was when I grabbed my door handle. He pressed the automatic lock. I struggled to click it manually open; I had the door ajar and unclicked my seat belt. We were going too fast—I knew I'd be hurt when I jumped—but my instinct told me it would be better than the head-on crash off the cliff that he was aiming for.

He barely controlled the wheel as he seized my left arm. I could feel his fingers dig into my flesh. I lost control myself then; I was crying, screaming, "Stop!" Somehow he drove this way, the car veering, nearly hitting every tree, almost coasting over the cliff, but ending rear-ended in the snowbank in front of Casa di Rosas.

That was when I did leap out and run into the house. He ran after me, but I raced up the steps, reached the bedroom, and threw the latch. Almost immediately, behind the latched door, I smelled smoke. The smoke curled under the door, and I realized he had set a fire. . . .

I was sobbing, but I had the presence to go to the rotary phone by the bedside table and dial 911. But before I could speak, Matt smashed the latch and hurled himself into the room, splintering the wooden doorjamb. Then he was on me. He was swinging his fists, but I ducked and he missed. Then he seized me around my arms and held me fast, as if to talk some sense into me, and he was saying, "I love you, I loved you from the first moment I saw you. . . ." The blood was pouring from his left nostril.

At this point in my recitation, I look across the court at Matt to see if he is responding, perhaps even spouting the blood from his nostril as he has in the past. But he appears composed.

The interruptions begin then. MacPherson rises: "I object . . . I object . . ." He is undermining everything I report. "How did you know the speed? Did you check the speedometer? How do you know the speedometer was working correctly?"

Judge Sintula repeats, "Overruled . . . overruled . . . overruled," and finally instructs MacPherson, "Please allow the plaintiff to relay her account."

Okay. So I say how I see that Matt has set this fire and I recognize what it is he is burning. . . .

J. J. Janis jumps up and says, "That is the piece of evidence labeled Evidence A. Please let the record show that the object that was burned is in evidence."

He comes forward and opens the Bendel bag, removes the box inside, and takes out the charred wooden pieces that I now must identify.

"And can you please identify this object for the court, Mrs. Smythe?"

Why does this piece of evidence make me weep when I have managed to get through the car scene without trembling?

I stare at the charred wood. No one would recognize the object unless they knew its original form and purpose.

"It's a cradle. . . . It was . . . a cradle. . . ."

"A cradle intended for a baby?"

"Yes. Our baby," I answer.

"Objection: There is no proof that this charred stick of wood was anything, or that this couple intended to have a baby."

I look at Matt now: You know that's what it is, I silently communicate. And you know why you burned it.

"It was his own cradle," I say. "His mother had given it to us . . . in the hopes that we would soon . . ." My voice fails for a moment, my lip quivers, but I regain control. ". . . have a baby of our own."

"Objection: We cannot state the purpose of this piece of unidentifiable debris," MacPherson blares.

I see Matt tilt his head, whisper to MacPherson. Matt is shaking his head, disagreeing with my testimony, I suppose . . . but why? He knows what the charred wood is, he knows it was his own cradle, and he knows why we had it and why he burned it. . . .

"And did something more happen?" Joe Gromolka asks. "Something more that inflicted bodily harm on you on this occasion?"

"Yes," I continue. "I ran from the house. . . . I was able to get a few hundred yards down the driveway, when my husband, Matt, caught up with me, and threw me to the ground. He was . . . berserk."

"Objection: Cannot characterize—"

"Sustained."

Then I remember my coaching: Repeat only the actions; do not characterize. The actions should be sufficient. "He was kicking and punching me, and I was rolling over in the snow, trying to avoid the blows. . . . And he was screaming, 'Nobody turns their back on me! Nobody runs away from me!' And that was when he pressed his hand over my windpipe and tried to choke me. . . ."

"Objection: This is speculation on the part of plaintiff."

"I could not breathe with his hand on my throat," I say.

"And what happened next?"

"I had dialed 911, and even though I did not get to tell the 911 operator, I knew they immediately trace the call, and so I was very relieved to hear, then see, a police car. . . . The officer jumped out of the car and ran toward us, and my husband, Matt, he stopped and ran back inside the house, and I was able to tell the officer what occurred." I describe what happened next—the trip to Bonticou Hospital, the photographs of my bruises . . .

I see MacPherson sneer, and Betsy West places her hand in, yes, a comforting gesture over Matt's hand. Karp is scribbling in his pad.

I am shaken, and accept the glass of water that the clerk hands me.

There is a brief recess, and I feel that I have done as well as possible. Gromolka and his son Joey are reassuring, as are Nadine and Elsbieta. But J. J. Janis seems concerned.

"It isn't over," he warns at recess. "You've given your story; now they must disprove it."

"But they can't disprove the truth," I insist.

"Strange things happen in court," J. J. Janis says, and for once he and Gromolka agree.

I have a sense that the lawyers are keeping information from me. The sensation reminds me of the Minnesota Multiphasic Personality Inventory. Wasn't there a question: *I suspect people have been talking about me before I return to a room . . . ?*

"It's the evaluation, isn't it?" I guess. "Matt finessed it?"

J. J. Janis responds, "Just be glad the evaluation hasn't been admitted in court. You don't want to hear it read into the record."

"Why? I demand to see the copies."

"Against the rules," both attorneys recite.

Oh, I think, there is some terrible secret, and then I recall another test statement: *I know that people plot against me.*

Forced March

It is difficult to assess the damage that follows. What is the worst testimony? The most conflicting evidence?

It is an old legal trick to save the "worst"—i.e., the best—for last. And MacPherson is a skilled and experienced attorney. I wish I had him on my side. He begins with a mild description of how events can appear very differently to "the persons involved." How actions can be "misinterpreted."

In FemJep courtroom scenes, everyone you need as a witness is available and takes the stand. In my actual case, the police officer involved, Officer Little, is on vacation in the Bahamas and has faxed a brief statement, in addition to the original police report, that gives, to my mind, a mild account of what he found when he pulled up to the snow-covered grounds of Casa di Rosas on that late afternoon of December thirty-first. He describes the scene as "a scuffle" between a husband and wife.

As MacPherson reads the police report into the record, Gromolka and J. J. Janis object, and the objections are often sustained. But not before we have all heard an ambiguous description:

a man and a woman "rolling around in a snowdrift." It sounds almost innocent, playful.

But what about the 911 call, the burned cradle, my bruises? I am confident in the strength of my case before the other witnesses are even called—and Nadine, Elsbieta, and Moira will confirm that this is a man prone to sudden mood swings and violent actions. Then the psychological evaluation, which Matt could not possibly have finessed, will also be on record, and the portrait of a man who lost all control and almost killed his wife will be a matter of record.

"Let's start with the 911 call," MacPherson suggests.

Yes, I think, *let's.*

"Shall we play the recording?" he suggests. "As we know, all 911 calls for help are recorded. . . ." He has an avuncular tone.

Go ahead, I think, but my voice won't be on it: I dropped the phone. It was the automatic trace that allowed the 911 operator to dispatch the patrol car.

MacPherson produces a small tape recorder and enters it into evidence. Judge Sintula leans forward, as does everyone else. I suppose any recording device offers a break in the usual court routine, but I know it will only have the sound of a dropped phone.

MacPherson depresses the Play button: I hear not just the sound effect of a falling phone, or my scream, but in a few seconds Matt's voice, quite calm, requesting an officer to come to our address: "Seven Serpentine Road, at the end of Lake Shore, on the bluff. It's a white Victorian. . . ."

He sounds quite calm, almost calm enough to be convincing when he says, "I'm afraid my wife is going to harm herself."

What? Harm myself? J. J. Janis grips my arm.

"Don't react."

"Is this real?" I whisper to my lawyers. "How can he be on the 911 tape? *I* called them."

My legal team gives me the first of its collective squeamish looks. Their belief in the client, as I am known hereforth, is beginning to erode. . . .

The connection then breaks, but the audio damage is done. Matt summoned the police. How can this be? I cannot explain. . . . *I* dialed 911 . . . I know I did. . . .

It sickens me to say this, but I have to defend myself: "What about my bruises? I was covered with bruises. . . . They were photographed. . . ."

MacPherson seems happy to produce the photographs. This is odd, I think. Why doesn't Gromolka or Janis have the pictures? The photographs prove my case. Why does Matt's lawyer have them?

"The defense wishes to place in evidence, the photographs of the plaintiff taken in the late hours of December thirty-first in the emergency room of Bonticou Hospital. . . ."

"Object," Janis hisses into Gromolka's ear.

"Why?" Gromolka whispers.

Too late: The photographs are out of the envelope, fanned out before Judge Sintula.

"Let the record show that these photographs show no bruises on the plaintiff. . . ."

I almost rise. "Let me see that!" Janis glares at me.

Then, as the photographs are being passed to me, I remember: I remember the nurse saying, "Nothing much will show: the colors don't come up till tomorrow. You should come back. . . ."

The photographs are poor quality, and they show nothing but my exposed arms, and one shot of my perfectly ordinary-appearing throat.

I turn to J. J. Janis: Why didn't you look at these before we went to court? In FemJep, lawyers don't make mistakes like this; there are no such serious lapses.

Janis has some grace; he looks embarrassed. "I assumed they showed what you said they would show; we just got them, they had to be subpoenaed. I was distracted by the evaluations, baby."

My fuse ignites, fizzles. I knew J. J. Janis was venal, but I imagined he was competent. "I'm not charging you for today," he offers in penance.

But the nurse—in person, that nurse had seen the red and white impressions, even if they had not photographed accurately. She had seen them, and I remember clearly what she said, "My husband did this to me once. He's out the door."

Out the door. "That nurse should be called in to testify; I am sure she will remember me," I say. And there had to be marks, I think, even then. . . . I saw fingerprints, grip marks—pale at first, but deepening the next day. The bruises were hideous two days later. Oh, why hadn't I returned to the hospital, to insist that they reshoot? But I couldn't: I was terrified, hiding at Casa di Rosas, dialing for lawyers and guards. There wasn't time to do more. . . .

"We tried to find the nurse," Gromolka contributed, "but your bad luck, she had an aneurysm and is in the hospital herself. She's not testifying to anything."

I look to my witness gallery: Even Nadine and Elsbieta look perplexed, at best.

"We're being crucified in Yekaterinburg," J. J. Janis says.

"Don't worry," Gromolka assures him. "We can tear him apart when he takes the stand." His son seems dazed, but he, too, is reassuring: "I've seen things turn around," Joey says.

I hope so.

I'm shaken myself: How deceptive evidence can be. If I did not know, know without doubt, what occurred, even I might wonder. Remember, I command myself, remember. Don't be swayed by legal tricks and optical illusions. There must be explanations. I know what happened. I am telling the truth. We still have my witnesses, and the psychological evaluations will correct the mistaken impressions made by the tape and the photographs. Even if Matt's evaluation is not as definitive as we expected, it will have to show significant abnormality.

As I walk down the hall for the recess break, I pass under the photographic portrait of the slain wife. *I am telling the truth,* I silently address her, *and I'll bet so were you.*

The Cross

L et's see how you do on the cross," J. J. Janis is always saying, and now I am on the stand. J. J. Janis, who coached me for interrogation, is taking a backseat to Gromolka, whose initial questioning I find weak. I feel as if I have been caught in a play that switched directors in mid-rehearsal and has suffered a crucial cast replacement. Whatever J. J. Janis's failings, he did not get to be the Butcher of Briarcliff Manor by lacking power in the courtroom. He always prevails, is granted his stays, recesses, adjournments. What J. J. Janis demands, he gets from the judge. It is Gromolka who is weak, going "up," as we say, on his lines, meandering, and ultimately floundering. Even I am giving Gromolka poor reviews: As the local lawyer, why didn't he demand an adjournment until that police officer, Officer Little, was back in Bonticou? Even I know that that cop should be here, not his statement, which seems inconclusive. The officer saw me lying there. He knew. He did see what Matt did to me.

So what now? Even I am not confident that Elsbieta and Nadine, testifying to a thrown turkey, will save this day in court. They will both be regarded as "city people," exotics who have dif-

fering standards and who may not be trusted. Moira's testimony
will be stronger, if only because she is local—but where is she?

I walk to the plate-glass door and see that Matt has joined the
other defendant-husband smokers in the smoking zone. He puts
out a butt under his shoe. Even though he lights up again, he
appears relaxed, confident. Betsy West walks out, joins him.

There is a primitive instinct, I feel it rise in me now, that tells a
woman when another woman has been with her husband. I watch
and there is a body language, although they do not touch. An ease
of being . . . I would put money now on her being the woman in
my bedroom.

When she precedes Matt back into the courthouse, Betsy West
avoids my gaze. The telepathy, similar to the thread between Matt
and me, also links me to Betsy. But it's a loose thread I would yank
if I could. Her eyes cannot lie as she looks into mine. She colors,
looks past me. . . . Guilty. As sin.

Yes, I think, she was there, with my husband in my bedroom.
There are women, I reflect, who will sleep with a married man.
Maybe most women would, under certain circumstances—during
their own difficulties or when both husband and wife are distant.
But there are very few women who are low enough to crawl under
another woman's covers and then take a hike in the wife's shoes.

You are the lowest of the low, I silently address Betsy West. She
can feel my words: I see her shoulder blades pin back under the
neat designer suit. Is she going to have the nerve to question me?

I am wondering about this as the doors part and another familiar person enters, in an acrylic parka, wearing jeans and high snow
boots. I am so happy, so relieved to see her, that I could run and
hug her, but Gromolka appears in time to avert this.

"Don't talk to her," he whispers. "She's moved onto the defendant's witness list."

What? This is impossible. "I just spoke with her; her husband was just over at Casa di Rosas, sympathetic and instructing me how to use a rifle." She can't be on Matt's witness list, she can't be. . . .

But she is: Moira is testifying for the defendant. I recite the rest of my own testimony, sick with awareness that there sits Moira Gonzalez Gerhardt, pretty as ever, pale and nibbling her lip . . . getting ready to testify . . . to what? What can she possibly say?

J. J. Janis is upset also. "MacPherson deposed her early this morning."

Has she been paid off? Threatened?

My remaining witnesses, Elsbieta and Nadine, are called, in turn to the stand. I am hard-pressed as to who is the riskier witness. Elsbieta looks more sedate: Dignified, her silver hair gathered up in a French twist, she is wearing pearls and a classic Chanel suit, plain black pumps. She will be fine.

Nadine is another matter: She, too, has been asked to dress discreetly but her idea of discreet includes emerald-green ostrich trim on her sweater, deep-dish cleavage in the décolletage, and a skirt that hugs the bottom of her hourglass figure. She has donned another faux fur and dyed a matching green streak in her hair. Her eyebrows are plucked, and her eye shadow clashes, turquoise, with the fluctuant hazel of her eyes. Her lips are outlined in Really Red. To counter all this irrepressible sex appeal, she is wearing bifocals low on her nose.

Elsbieta is called to the stand first, and we go back to the Saturday of November twenty-fourth, the Thanksgiving weekend.

"Mr. and Mrs. Smythe had invited you for the weekend following the actual Thanksgiving Day, and you and another friend, Nadine Jagoda, drove up to their home on Serpentine Road on

Lake Bonticou," Gromolka begins. "Can you describe the circumstances of this weekend?"

"Well, Juliana invited us for the weekend, and we arrived on Saturday at around noon."

"Did you notice anything unusual in your host and hostess's demeanor?" he asks.

"Juliana was pale; she seemed tired and strained. . . ."

"Objection." From MacPherson.

Be specific, I beamed my thought to Elsbieta. You can't "characterize"; you must cite specific actions and remarks.

"Juliana came out of Casa di Rosas to greet us, but her husband appeared unhappy that we had arrived."

"Objection."

"He was raking leaves in the garden and did not look up or greet us when we arrived. He did not offer to help with our bags or the groceries that we had brought. When we entered the house, he moved past us, kicking a small white cat that also tried to enter. . . ."

My belly clenches, hearing this. It is all coming back to me, that terrible weekend, Matt's time-bomb silences, his rough actions. "Did you find anything unusual about your car in the morning?"

"It was badly scratched, as if scraped by a key."

"Objection."

"Did something happen at the dinner table on Saturday night that was unusual and gave you cause for alarm?"

"Yes," Elsbieta answers. "He . . . Mr. Smythe picked up the turkey and threw it across the room. It almost struck his wife, Juliana. It would have hit her, but she ducked."

"Did any remark or incident precede the throwing of the turkey?"

"Yes," Elsbieta answers. "He—Mr. Smythe—was carving, and he served himself first."

"And then what happened?"

"Juliana, his wife, said, 'Oh, you should serve the guests first,' and that was when he threw the turkey."

"Thank you. That's all for this witness. Unless you wish to cross-examine."

MacPherson loomed at the stand, and I wondered if Elsbieta was thinking the same thing I was: He was not bad casting. Brian Dennehy type. Big voice, imposing manner, but could project gentleness.

"Elsbieta Andrews. Your occupation is . . . ?"

"I am a casting director," she says, straightening her spine.

"Can you tell this court what it is that a casting director does?"

"I try to match an actor to a role. I 'cast' . . . find the cast for a film or a play."

"So you are used to looking for dramatic characterization? To assigning emotional characteristics to individuals?"

"Mr. Smythe is not an actor."

"That is not an answer to the question."

"Yes," Elsbieta answers.

"Dismissed."

Nadine takes the stand, her great bosom quivering like a Jell-O. I have never loved her more or wanted more to drape her in a shawl.

She kept on the glasses, which I appreciated. We had a joke in theater: Need to look intelligent? Wear glasses.

She reprises the circumstances of their arrival, the scene at the dinner table. She corroborates that my last remark prior to the turkey toss was "I think we should serve the guests first . . ." She adds ". . . darling," which I did not recall saying.

She, too, describes the twenty-two-pound headless bird on its flight across the dining table, and its hard landing beside me. I had felt the grease of its passing.

Gromolka is satisfied with her account, but MacPherson cross-examines: "Isn't it possible that Mr. Smythe simply dropped the turkey, or, given that we have testimony that it was basted in butter, it slid from his hands?"

"No, he threw it."

"Then what occurred?" Gromolka asks.

"He said, 'I am sick of being—' He used an obscene verb; may I say 'fucked'? 'I am sick of being fucked with . . .' and he left the house. From the window I saw him pick up the little white cat, which was still mewing to come inside, and he threw her into his car, a black Infiniti, and drove away."

"You saw all this from the window," MacPherson says, "even though it must have been quite distracting at that moment inside, with the headless turkey on the floor. And Juliana Smythe—what was she doing?"

"Apologizing . . . for his behavior. She kept saying, 'I don't know what's gotten into Matt, I don't know . . . what's gotten into Matt.' I could have told her: He's just a sonofabitch."

"Objection," cries MacPherson.

"Granted," says Judge Sintula.

MacPherson seizes the moment. "Thank you. No more questions of this witless." He gives a smile. "I mean witness."

Well, this is a disaster, I think, as we all troop over to Mrs. Schmidt's. The opposing team is also there, behind the folding doors of the "banquet area." We can hear them laugh and chat in a celebratory way.

Joey, the kid, is excused: He is going to do more "research," bless him, but what can he possibly uncover in time? My credability is disappearing faster than the snowmelt outside, under the now unseasonably hot sun. Gromolka senior stays, and it crosses my mind that I am now paying the legal team $480 an hour to eat Kugelhopf and drink coffee: $305 for J. J. Janis and $175 for Gromolka.

J. J. Janis slaps a folded document on the Formica table. "You're not going to like this," he says. "You're not allowed to read it. I can be disbarred for showing it to you. It's your evaluation. I am not going to give it to you . . . but I am going to excuse myself and go to the men's room for quite a while. . . ."

I see. I am supposed to open the file and read it while he is not present. J. J. Janis darts to the men's room. I open the file folder and stare, without comprehension at first. There are two evaluations, mine and Matt's, and the results of our Minnesota Multiphasic Personality Inventories. . . .

It takes one second to see that so far as Dr. Hubert Lazare is concerned, I failed.

As I stare at the psychology report, I face a funhouse reflection. A woman "lost in fantasy, paranoid, fearful, passive aggressive, imagining her husband and others are trying to harm her . . ."

The chronicle of my childhood and life before and after Matt is there, and if I didn't know the truth, this could pass as a "biography." Small matters, such as swiping lipsticks with a friend when I was ten years old, are recorded as "a record of dishonesty" and worst of all, my mother's death, which was assisted by morphine while she died, is listed as "mother, a suicide." The single person on this earth, whom I confided that my mother lost hope at the end and asked to be "let go," is Matt. This is the bitterest betrayal, I think—the privileged information of our marriage, now twisted into this deformed document.

Matt's evaluation, of course, is excellent: "Upstanding businessman, entrepreneur, mature, responsible. Showing, in fact, remarkable tolerance for his disturbed wife." Tolerance.

The graphs of the MMPI are more difficult to decipher. Dr. Lazare's interpretation of them is not: "Subject A, Juliana, is delusional, overconfident, and cannot tell reality from fantasy. Subject B, Matthew Smythe, is well within the range of a well-formed personality." And he says *I* can't tell the difference between reality and fantasy?

Of course I can tell the difference: Reality is worse. And the worst part is, I am shaken. It is impossible to look at a report like this and not, on some level, fold inward, fearing partial truth. One has only to be labeled crazy to become crazy; these are self-fulfilling prognoses.

I can feel myself slipping down in the Mrs. Schmidt's booth. This is too hard to fight: The difficulties have become insurmountable. At the base is my own loss of confidence ("overconfident"?): Why doesn't Matt love me anymore? Why does he want to hurt me? How could matters have gone so wrong?

Gromolka senior is now more forthcoming regarding Dr. Lazare: "There are twenty complaints filed against Dr. Hubert Lazare. Lazare is a hack for the county and it's almost impossible to fire him, but he's been a notorious figure in this court for a long time. Remember I was upset when you said he was doing your evaluation? He has a little bias—he favors men in domestic abuse cases—but if he always stacked his evaluations against the women, he would be in trouble. So he goes maybe eight out of ten anti-women—especially, I might add, women such as yourself. . . ."

"Meaning?"

"Attractive, intelligent, independent. That's the type he gives poor evaluations. . . . He is easy on the unemployed welfare moms. A woman like you, it's fuel on the fire. He's a very strange, very angry man. He belongs to a radical male-rights group in Bonticou, The Pow-Wow Club. They meet in the woods and male-bond and beat tom-toms."

"You're kidding."

"I wish."

"And the tom-toms don't disqualify him?"

"Nothing disqualifies anyone in Bonticou County: We're very understaffed. In hindsight, you should have insisted on a private doc, a psychiatrist. I wish you had retained me first—" Gromolka breaks off: At this moment J. J. Janis returns to the table.

"This evaluation makes me appear like a liar and a delusional mental case," I say to J. J. Janis. "It's the flip side of the truth. A lot of what it says about me is true of Matt—the impulse control, the aggression . . . the lying. . . . You do believe me, don't you?"

But I am wondering? Was I overconfident? I had been warned about Lazare, how he hates women, that he is unfair, that there were problems with him in the past. I had seen him anyway, believing my case spoke for itself. And I had believed that my interview with him had succeeded: It had seemed so calm, so reasonable, after the initial oddness of his scowling. I thought he had been swayed by my conviction. I had been telling the truth, I know I was. I hadn't grasped what the warnings about Lazare had truly meant. Now I recall that woman lawyer, Susan Sachs, saying, "Don't keep the appointment." I had thought she was exaggerating; I thought she was after her high retainer. Now I consider the possibility that she had tried to save me and knew it would take many hours.

"Oh, God," I say, "I should never have kept that appointment."

"It was a court order," Gromolka reminds me.

I look to J. J. Janis: Why did he advise me to accept a court-appointed, lottery-chosen psychologist? He should have insisted that both Matt and I pay for a respectable psychiatrist, if there was such a person in Bonticou.

"This is what happens in towns like Yekaterinburg," J. J. Janis tells me. "Even the psychologist has a screw loose."

At that moment I could have kissed him on both well-shaven cheeks. He was a tough guy, and he'd made some mistakes, but he knew I was telling the truth.

"I believe you, baby," he says. "One hundred percent. Now I need another ten grand."

My Husband Testifies

If I did not know, would I believe him? I am horrified, frightened, to say that I would. It is Matthew Smythe who should be onstage. He is so convincing, I suspect that he has convinced himself. Is it possible? Does he believe his own denials of violence?

I cannot know the answer, but he appears candid, dignified. He has never been more handsome than on this day, when he takes the stand to testify against me. He replays the events of the Thanksgiving weekend, but through the focus of his defense.

"Absolutely nothing happened," he says, having sworn to tell the truth, the whole truth, so help him God. "Thanksgiving weekend, I may have been out of sorts." He smiles: Oh, it is ingratiating, better than a complete denial. "I was tired from a week at work, I was coming down with a cold, and the last thing, truthfully, I wanted was to entertain Juliana's show-business friends. But I agreed, because I knew it would make her happy.

"But we had a series of minor catastrophes: The cat walked through something foul outside—excrement, or maybe a dead animal, whatever. I saw this cat slipping into the kitchen, and I admit, I freaked. It would be so unhygienic, the germs on that

251

cat—ticks, too, probably. We did argue a little about whether the cat would be kept inside or outside up here in the country."

He smiles, showing his perfect white square teeth. The smile is memorable, but it is his entire manner that is so winning—the self-effacing gentle humor, the strength of conviction. His attitude of relaxation, his body language, suggests, I just need to state my case and everyone will understand. It's so simple, really—a true misinterpretation by my adorable but highly suggestible, maybe even fragile wife—smile, smile—whom I love so much anyway. I just want to heal this, and come home.

I am afraid to look up at Judge Sintula. Even I am having a tropism toward Matt at this moment. The sun slants in the courtroom window and lights him, picks up the gold in his tousled brown hair, exaggerates the transparency of his pale-blue eyes. His color is wonderful today, ruddy under the tan, and he appears so fit, vibrant; I can almost see the epinephrine coursing under his brown skin. He has, of course, the magnetic deep voice: he seems to pipe it up straight from his gut, or maybe his groin. All boy, he is—and all the women in the courtroom feel it. I check on Betsy West, and her lips are actually parted; her face looks as if it melted off a spoon.

But how will he explain The Attack? He is smoothly excusing "my poor serving technique with the damned—excuse my language—turkey. The bird just flew. I may have cursed when it hit the floor. I was exasperated. But I didn't curse at anyone, I just"—oh, here comes the most winning grin—"said something like 'expletive deleted.'"

He got his laugh. "I dropped that damn twenty-two-pound turkey on my foot. And then, of course, we couldn't eat it. So we were all stuck with stuffing and fixings, and no bird. Sure, I blew my stack, but only at myself and my damned butterfingers. . . ."

He opens his hands and I want not to look: His hands are amazing, so outsized, brown; with the ropy veins, they are just as sexual as the actual part of him. Heavy testosterone, and it shows in the details. And maybe in the mental aberrations. What about those 'roid rage men on the television? Couldn't his own megadose of male hormone similarly derange Matt?

He was really sad, he says, when Elsbieta and Nadine left early. "Maybe I should have apologized more for what they may have mistaken as an attitude."

Again, he apologizes, he was not in the best of moods. "I had work from the office, and my mother wanted me at the family Christmas, and my wife wanted to come up here, to Bonticou. I was the monkey in the middle." Smile, smile. "I could make no correct choice. So we tried to do both, and it was a mistake.

"I was exhausted; we hit traffic. I lost my temper at a car that whizzed past, and . . . uh . . . again, I may have said something that could be called 'expletive deleted.'"

He doesn't get the laugh this time. Hmm. I think maybe he is appearing overrehearsed, too smooth. They say liars always add unnecessary gestures, and Matt does: He licks that sunburned upper lip of his, and he trains his blue stare, just a bit too innocent and direct, too often at Judge Sintula. She looks interested but not entranced.

"Well," he says, "we—Juliana and I—began to argue." We had, according to Matt, been talking about starting our family . . . conceiving a baby. And he was hoping we could . . . "you know"— naughty-boy grin—"start right away."

You didn't want a baby for ten years, I mentally address him, then suddenly you were furious that we didn't have one and said we had to have one, because otherwise we were . . . lacking.

I was the one who wanted a baby, but feared to push for it. I didn't want to lose you. And, I admit, deep down, I feared something I could never name—that the baby might flip some switch, or be disturbed like Matt's parents. . . . I felt an uncertainty that was profound, that acted as a powerful mental prophylactic against having a child.

He was, at best, ambivalent, but not according to his testimony: "I believe the family is the greatest institution; I would give up my life for my family. I want with Juliana what I had with my own parents. . . ."

God forbid, I think.

"But Juliana was orphaned at thirteen, her father rejected the mother, and her mother committed suicide, so I feared there were certain insecurities in Juliana . . . that might make it difficult for her to be a mother. That was why we waited . . . but in the seventeen years of our marriage, I could see she became more and more absorbed in her career—that, frankly, it began to obsess her—and I often found her vacant and absentee when she was with me."

Maybe I was learning my lines, or maybe you scared me silent, I mentally retort.

"In any case, we had agreed that this holiday was for us to be alone, to really search our souls and see if we could . . . you know . . . go ahead. I wanted a little baby . . . just like Juliana, a little Juliana . . ."

You did?

"But as we drove north, Juliana is clearly becoming restless with the idea of the entire Christmas holiday up in Bonticou—a place I love to go to relax, a place I dream of making our permanent family home. But Juliana springs it on me that she has a job offer . . . that she is supposed to fly out to Los Angeles on January second, cutting short our entire vacation, and yes, well, I was hurt and disappointed."

I was flying in for one day, and offered to take the red-eye home.

"She was abandoning me for the Christmas holiday, essentially junking the idea that we would have a child together. I was hurt and offended that I meant so little to her, so maybe I was distracted and started to speed. . . . I know that's wrong, but it couldn't have been that much over the limit. After all, the troopers were all over the roads, and I would have been stopped if I was going as fast as she claims. She became hysterical and said she didn't want to go to the country, that she wanted to turn back and take an early flight from Newark Airport—forget the entire vacation—and hoped to get the part in . . . Hollywood."

He said the name Hollywood exactly as the townspeople might say Sodom and Gomorrah.

None of this was true. I wanted to go to Bonticou—I always did: I think this place was always more my dream than his—but in any case, according to Matt, I began to cry and became hysterical. He tried to comfort me, but I threatened to jump from the car. When I did, in fact, open the car door as we drove over sixty miles an hour on the Northway, he had to seize my upper arm and prevent me from leaping, possibly to my death, . . . *because I would leap rather than be beaten,* I amend his statement.

At the house, it is more of the same: I am having a wild tantrum and he is beside himself as to how to soothe and placate me. He is afraid I will harm myself. I run out in the snow without a coat. He fears I am going for the cliff. He calls 911. Then he runs after me, must wrestle in the snow to save me from killing myself by hurling myself off the cliff onto the frozen lake.

When Officer Little arrived, that is exactly what he saw—a loving husband restraining a hysterical wife. Of course the photos show no bruises: There were none, just some "pressure marks" where he had to hold me, to keep me from jumping. . . .

I know he cannot believe this version—or can he? Will his mind adapt to the lie, incorporate it into the gospel according to Matt?

Gromolka holds up the broken phone. "She threw it when I said we needed to get help," Matt says.

"And the burned cradle?"

"That was *my* cradle," he says, and he appears to overcome the possibility of weeping. "And she used it for kindling."

Kindling instead of *Kinder.* Not bad. If I did not know this was the big lie, I might accept this distortion of myself: the ambitious, neurotic actress, determined to get a role, no matter what. . . . And now so deluded, that she has to rationalize her own bad behavior, and accuse him.

But, he stresses, even though he is hurt and puzzled, he wants nothing more than to forgive and forget, to take me home, have counseling, whatever therapy is required. Yes, even for him-self . . . whatever it takes, so we can realize the dream and "be a family."

I look at Judge Sintula. She appears shaken, doubtful for the first time. He seems so caring, so reasonable. And, after all, here I am, this actress: Actresses are given to outrageous emotional swings, aren't they?

I can see the possibility: the order of protection "vacated"—removed—and Matt steering me by the elbow, back to the car, back to Casa di Rosas.

What I feel now is roiling fear and anger. How dare he? I will not live this way, I will not suffer, I will not give in and crawl back, returned as a ward of my husband—the poor actress who "broke down" and now lives sequestered . . . for her own sake.

"The evidence, the evaluations," recites his lawyer MacPherson, "support my client's testimony. And we have a witness who will establish that Juliana Smythe has been lying from the beginning. . . ."

The first witness for the defendant is called: his mother.

This could be funny if it weren't so tragic, I think. I try to evaluate my mother-in-law as if I did not know her, know of her hysteria and mood swings.

She appears to be a pleasant woman in her mid-sixties, undistinguished save for the harsh wig that she wears. I don't know why she wears wigs: Her own hair is not that different; if anything it looks softer, more natural. "I don't like to fuss" is the only explanation I have ever heard from my mother-in-law.

My mother-in-law is sworn in by her proper name, Harriet Smythe. Even her demeanor impresses me: She has the grieving expression of a concerned mother. She doesn't appear vindictive or angry, only saddened and perhaps a bit righteous.

The thing about my mother-in-law is, she is unexceptional except for her madness. Other than that, she is indistinguishable from millions of other late-middle-aged mothers who play bingo, shop at malls, heat up frozen dinners.

In a way, her insanity raises her above the crowd. For while her usual persona is ordinary, even cloying—"I decorated the house kind of Frenchy"—when she goes off, she is big time, and oddly poetic: "I dreamed I was a corpse hanging from our American flag pole; the wind whipped through me, all fraying black flesh." She has a few styles of insanity—the morose nightmares (which her son has either acquired or inherited from her) and the frantic spending: She bought six washing machines one summer, and she owns two hundred pairs of shoes. On weekends she does nothing but shop, acquiring more and more appliances and clothing, which she stores in the basement and garage of the family home in Doylestown. Last but not least are the paranoid tirades, in which she accuses her relatives of stealing from her, her son of neglecting her, and me, her only daughter-in-law, of "ruining" her boy. Her tirades are the hardest aspect, but they are not the most dangerous. It is she, not me, who has tried to kill herself. She was taken off a roof in downtown Doylestown one afternoon, threatening to jump.

The box she is submitting in evidence contains her medical records, she claims. She insists it shows no record of mental instability. "The McCrackens [her maiden name] were always good people; she has no right saying different."

I know Harriet Smythe is hoping for divorce; in this, I fear we are now on the same side. Divorce, I think, will be preferable to death.

Whatever she did to Matt, they are sticking together now: His behavior was not at all as I described in my testimony. "We had a lovely holiday, and *she*"—Harriet Smythe gets to point the finger at me—"*she* spoiled it by insisting our Matt leave. . . ."

"Look at her box of evidence," I whisper to Gromolka. "If those medical records are continuous, they will contain a record of her breakdowns. If there are gaps, go to Gracie Square Hospital in New York and see if you can obtain the records of her electroshock treatments."

In a film or on television, the next scene is your lawyer or an investigator hotfooting it to the other city to obtain those records. In this actual case, my lawyers say they have no time to go, and I can't afford to send them. Gromolka has his son root through the box. "It has her blood and urine tests," he reports. "And an EKG."

The next witness for the defendant is called.

All eyes swivel, turn to Moira Gonzalez Gerhardt. She is dressed as I have never seen her, in an acrylic suit, hose, and heels. I would hardly recognize her except for the pin through her left eyebrow and the rabbit-twitch of her lips. She does look embarrassed, I note that. Her normally white face turns pink. She rises, goes to the stand, and is sworn in, "to tell the truth, the whole truth, so help me . . . God."

She recites the facts of her employment: Just two years, cleaning Casa di Rosas—most often when the lady of the house, Juliana Smythe, was away, and the husband, Matt Smythe, also. They were weekend and summer people. She didn't see us that often, but she cleaned the house regularly. I hear the disdain in her tone, for the first time, the resentment—"summer and weekend."

"On a certain occasion, did you happen to notice a broken vase?" MacPherson asks.

"Yes."

"Can you describe the vase?"

"Green, with big roses on it."

"And what was special about this vase? Sometime in June, did you have occasion to discuss the condition of this vase with Mrs. Smythe?"

"Yes, I did. It was broke. In many pieces. It was a shame, because it was very beautiful and it was too busted to be fixed."

"Did Mrs. Smythe say anything to you as to how the vase happened to be broken?"

"Yes, she did." Moira looks at me. "She said it fell."

My God, I did say that. I didn't want to explain the entire marital tension at that time.

"And did she speak with you again—very recently, this week, as the case came to court—about the vase?"

"Yes, she did."

"And what did she ask you to say in court?"

"She asked me to testify in court that it broke when her husband threw it at her."

In a film, at this point there would be a collective gasp. In the actual courtroom Judge Sintula looked over at me.

I nudged Joe Gromolka. "Let me explain," I whispered to him, "that I didn't want to tell her the entire story but that now I was asked for witnesses, and I gave her more information. . . . I didn't lie: I just didn't tell her how it fell. . . ."

Court, of course, is adjourned. Moira Gonzalez Gerhardt rises, looks at me, almost as if to say, "Sorry." I believe MacPherson has gotten to her, coached her, made her feel that this detail is significant and exposes that my entire case is a lie.

I wonder if she intends to come in to work on Wednesday. It's her "day" to clean Casa di Rosas.

Nadine and Elsbieta flank me as I walk past her to leave the courtroom. Elsbieta whispers direction: "Hold your head up. You are above this. Remember: truth!"

Nadine is less sanguine: As we pass Moira, my oldest best friend hisses, "Sneaky Pete."

Weeping Cherry

In times such as this, sleep is seductive. I am burrowed deep
under eiderdown, so many fathoms down in my dreams, that I
can incorporate any sound and explain it in a way that means I
don't have to wake up to investigate the noise. The incessant buzz
I hear is interpreted in my dream as a horde of hornets . . . then a
wild snoring bear. In unconsciousness I seek several solutions, but
the sound ultimately penetrates and I wake: What on earth is
going on outside my window?

I look out. It is still dark, but the moon illuminates a man in
silhouette; he is standing at an angle to my favorite of the trees, the
queen of the fruit trees, the weeping cherry. What he is doing is
too horrible to accept. In my disorientation I can believe it is a
nightmare.

The man is taking a chain saw to the cherry tree.

Safety be damned. I plunge my feet into my boots and grab my
coat and Rafe Gerhardt's gun. I might be murdered, bilked of
funds, humiliated in court—whatever—but no one is chopping
down this orchard. I fling open the door, and scream into the dark:
"Stop! Whoever you are, stop or I'll shoot!"

There is a short burst of sawing, as if in defiant reply.

I open the loading chamber, insert the shells, fire into the night sky. The retort knocks me back against the door, and I drop the damn gun. Whoever is out there drops the chain saw, runs. . . .

The silence is enough. I will go no further. I pick up the rifle and trudge back inside. My heart pounds. I won't know until daylight how much damage is done. Meanwhile my phone is ringing. I look at the clock: It is five A.M.

"Goddamn you," I say into the receiver, "this is being traced."

"Gee, Mrs. D., is that how you say good morning?" I recognize the voice. And who else would call me Mrs. D.

"Sorry to wake you, Mrs. D., but I'm up with the birds. . . ." *The cuckoos,* I think. . . .

"I'm up with the birds," he continues, "and I'll be in your area this morning. I thought I would drop by and see how you was doing, with your Supralux and all. . . ."

"We're fine. I need nothing." I slam down the phone and am not surprised when it rings again. I pick up. "Please don't call again," I say. "This is being traced by the police."

"Gee, Mrs. D.," he says, "I was just trying to be . . . nice. I have information that can help you. I just want to help you."

"I'm sorry—no, thanks."

"Well, I know you have your problems, your husband and all. . . ." Oh, God, now he knows Matt is not here; he knows I'm alone. Now what?

"I'm remarrying," I lie. I think of yelling into my empty bedroom a fictitious husband-to-be name: *Marc!* But I don't have the oomph for it this predawn.

"Oh, I didn't know. Congratulations. . . . You have my number and I'll leave you my pager. . . . Just in case . . . anything changes, Mrs. D. I really think you would benefit from seeing me."

I don't want to antagonize him, so I try to maintain an even tone. "Thank you for your concern. I'll be in touch if I need you."

Click. I sit on the bed, watching the light blanch the sky. I'll never get back to sleep, so I might as well shower, dress, and get an early start on my new ongoing career: my defense.

Casa di Rosas feels emptier than ever: The absence of Nadine and Elsbieta makes me feel more alone than before they arrived. Although they have promised to return, I feel bereft. I have sworn to fight, however, and I already have an appointment with a Dr. Shirley, a rival psychologist whose professional sideline is contradicting Hubert Lazare in court. Joe Gromolka has "used" her before.

"How much?" I wanted to know.

"A hundred an hour in her office, two thousand to testify in court."

Cast of thousands, I think, and one more on the payroll.

"You'll like her," Gromolka promises. "She's worth every penny. And Judge Sintula respects her: She knows Lazare is an oddball."

Hot shower, hot coffee—all work their morning magic, and I am at least up for today's task when I emerge. Nice, "sane" suit, my white blouse, the long black skirt, with a Chesterfield jacket that almost matches.

I run straight to the queen tree and could cry, in pain but also in relief. She has been attacked—her main boughs are severed— but her trunk stands thick, if bent. Several of her lesser branches are intact, thrown skyward, as if in supplication. The weeping cherry has not, after all, been slain. She may survive to bear flower and fruit again.

I check her wounds and make a mental note to buy tree paint. I will ask at the hardware shop garden center how to heal her. I plan to save this tree, no matter what the cost.

Who could commit such a crime—attempted arboreal murder? Would Matt do this? I can't believe that of him, in spite of everything. Matt knows how much I love the cherry and apple trees. I have a lasting and beautiful memory of him standing here, with me, under its veil of flowers, and he saying, "Let's always remember this—remember this moment," but in his nervousness he was plucking the blossoms, and I had to reach for his hand and say, "No. Never take the blossoms: they must turn to the fruit. . . ."

We kissed then, in the intoxicating atmosphere, tented under the flowering boughs. We emerged from that kiss to stare at one another; we could read each other's minds then, and we often spoke in synchronized jubilation: "How did I ever get so lucky?" we said at the same moment.

Would he go out before dawn to kill a tree because I love it? I can see the pattern now—my hat on the trash, my cat tossed, the friends offended at the dinner. Even the cradle, holding my hope for our future. Is this the literal axe to grind—hack away at anything and anyone I love?

Or is someone else harassing me in a new way? I know the obscene phone breather, Mr. Slickety-click, is a possibility, and of course there is the mystery writer across the lake, Winsten. Or maybe it is, as they often state in the *Bonticou Crier,* "unknown vandals."

At Halloween, unknown vandals did quite a bit of mischief— banging mailboxes down, spraying paint on barns, blasting parked cars with shaving cream or, worse, smashing windshields. There was a population that I did not know, composed of drunken or drugged boys, who did such things. Perhaps this was a random act and I am sensitized because of my situation.

As I stand at the hacked cherry tree, Jake Taylor drives over and hands my mail through his car widow. There is a stack of bills and one hand-inscribed envelope without a return address. I wait till Jake has exchanged his pleasantries: "Godawful mud today, was a mudslide on West Lake Road, hit a car with a woman in it. She was choppered out. . . ." Then I open the letter.

I stare, uncomprehending: The envelope contains only a photograph. The photo, which appears to be an Instamatic type, shows a gravestone. On the stone is etched a name. My name, Juliana Durrell Smythe. And my birthdate, which is correct. The unfortunate dash toward the death date is also there, but that date is left blank. Not entirely blank, however: Only the day and month are missing. The year—this year's numerals—is cut into the granite.

There is no message other than that implied: I will die this year.

Someone has gone to great effort for this. This is not just vandals or a Halloween prank. This is a mortuary stone, and a professional stonecutter's work.

For the first time, I think: I really will be murdered; he's going to kill me. I had rationalized that Matt's rage did not extend beyond his in-house tantrums, that he had no premeditated plot against me, that he was the victim of his impulses. He was deranged, I thought, and believed his own innocence. But this tombstone . . . this tombstone meant he was really intent on burying me, or at least scaring me half to death. Unless . . . Could someone other than Matt have carved a tombstone for me? Who? No one hated me as much as the man who loved me, I thought.

This is not a bad day to check in with a new psychiatrist, so I proceed as planned to the office of Dr. Shirley, Dr. Anna Shirley, whose office is as convenient as the lawyers' offices, at the intersection of Duane and Main. As I pull up to the doctor's office, housed in a yellow eyebrow Colonial with black shutters and a white picket fence, I experience a sense of déjà vu. Have I been here before? The building for its surface charm is yet another facade, this one masking mental health services. Then I remember: I *was* here. . . . The building also houses a Dr. Gladys Schultis. Dr. Schultis was the psychologist I went to with Matt in the final days. He objected to her sandals: "No one wearing sandals like that could have anything of value to say. . . ."

Never dismiss a deranged person's observations: When paranoid, they tend to hit on interesting aspects. The amount of misdirection is astonishing—and very persuasive. Dr. Schultis's sandals were indeed homely, heavy-strapped numbers. How I wish we had remained, to truly meet with her. She was a sandal type: African folk-print dress, unshaved legs and armpits, eyebrows joined over espresso-bean eyes. Your typical Bonticou mental health professional. But I had thought she had kind and not unintelligent eyes.

Should I have insisted? I thought I did insist. Matt bolted. How do you get a powerful six-foot-two-inch man weighing 180 pounds to do something he resists? "It's all malarkey, anyway," he was always saying. "They're all charlatans."

Now, of course, he swears by Dr. Hubert Lazare, a man of "acute perception," I overheard him say to MacPherson and Betsy West. How did he finesse that test? Could those evaluations be rigged? How does a psychotic get a better result than the person he attacked? Maybe it *is* malarkey.

Dr. Shirley is one flight above Dr. Schultis, and I walk up the now accustomed listing Colonial staircase to her enameled door. Inside, the waiting room is quaint, with a paisley-covered sofa, small fireplace, and stacks of psychoanalytic reviews. There is no receptionist, and the inner door opens to reveal Anna Shirley herself.

She is a frail woman whose delicacy is in itself a form of beauty. She is petite, weighing well under one hundred pounds, and her features are very finely drawn. She has large green eyes, wispy blond hair pulled back with a hair tie, and a pale, peaked manner. Her voice matches, thin and high.

In a film, what you want is a person of more literal weight and substance. But I feel a bit encouraged: Her eyes are lit with intelligence, and she has my folder on her desk.

"Joe Gromolka sent this over early this morning and I've reviewed it."

I'm pleasantly shocked: two competent actions. I have been so fatigued by people not doing their jobs—the entire, uncaring machinery that has meshed gears over my marriage.

"I just need help for this court case," I begin. "I don't understand how the evaluations could be this way. I know you don't know me or my husband, but I am telling the truth. He attacked me, and now Dr. Hubert Lazare is submitting this report that insists my husband is sane and I have imagined everything."

I sink into the armchair she indicates in her inner office. It has a nice, protective feeling, a wing chair, upholstered in another soft ruby paisley. Dr. Shirley sits at her desk, facing me. The brightening sunlight streaks into the room, illuminating dust motes in the air between us.

Please, God, I pray—and I am not given especially to prayer— let this woman make some sense of this.

This is my lucky day. She makes a face as she says the name Hubert Lazare: "It's a disgrace. He should never be doing this work. There are charges and complaints against him going back several years. It's impossible, unfortunately, to dislodge him."

"He does play tom-toms?"

"In the woods behind my house. He belongs to an extreme

male-rights group. The man hates women. He is married to a mental defective."

I laugh uneasily.

"That wasn't a joke," she says. "His wife *is* a mental defective. It's a very sad story. He has actually reversed orders of protection; mothers have lost custody of their children. Women coming into court for help can be hurt if their case is given to him for evaluation. You were very unfortunate. There are two other doctors who could have been appointed by the county who are reasonably competent. It's a lottery."

"I lost."

"Not yet. Judge Sintula is well aware of his record. She's no fool."

Dr. Shirley studies the graphs, the report, and the complete Minnesota Multiphasic Inventory tests. "I see what he did," she says after several silent moments. "It's very curious, though: Your husband and you actually scored very similarly; his curve is just under the guideline for what you would refer to as a 'normal' score, and your line is infinitestimably above it."

"It doesn't indicate that I'm drastically unstable, delusional, paranoid?" I ask.

Of course, simply asking that question makes me feel unstable, delusional, paranoid.

Dr. Shirley isn't a laugher, but she smiles. "Not at all: You're a very creative person."

"I'm an actress," I say.

"I know," she says. "I've seen you: *Run for Your Life.* But I would guess you were in the arts by your scores here. All this test shows is that you answer in a nontypical, fairly original manner. There is no indication of a pathology or even a neurotic style."

"Really?" I am so relieved, I can now admit to myself that I was half convinced I'd gone mad.

"Not only that," Dr. Shirley says, "your scores would be considered absolutely normal, if Dr. Hubert Lazare had not differentiated by sex. What he describes as 'overconfidence' is an appropriate score for a male."

Now I burn. "So this is more of his sex bias?"

"Exactly."

"And the really good news is, this test is not to be taken as the Holy Grail, either. Even if you had flunked it, it is now regarded as, at best, a dubious tool for evaluation. It's used in prisons, that sort of thing, but I would hardly say this is a cutting-edge manner to appraise a personality."

She squints at the papers. "Your husband's responses border on manic, anyway. Another psychologist might have given him a much less satisfactory report. I think his answers suggest poor impulse control."

She hands me a series of stapled psychological quizzes, and we do a Rorschach as well. I note that her eyebrows go up like circumflexes a few times during the testing.

"So? Am I imagining things? Am I passive aggressive?" I ask.

"You're different," she answers. "Most people fall into . . . categories, patterns. Yours are . . . idiosyncratic."

"Oh. Is that bad?"

"Not at all. There are two traits that emerge that are fairly unusual: You have a compulsion to tell the truth."

"That's true."

". . . and you refuse to give up."

"Is that good?"

"You don't give up when there is no possible solution. You just keep trying."

"There's always a solution," I say, "if you look for it."

"See," she says, "That's what Lazare calls your 'overconfidence.'"

"What do *you* call it?"

She looks at me and whispers, "You've been very frightened, haven't you?"

"I'm too frightened to say how frightened. I don't think any of it is imagined." I open my purse and pull out the Instamatic of the gravestone with my name on it.

Her eyes widen.

"This situation has me unnerved," I confess. "I need your help, but I don't know how much I can afford. I was not at all prepared for the costs. . . ."

"We'll work out a payment plan," she offers. "For today, it's a hundred."

It says something that I am nothing less than joyful as I inscribe her check.

I float from her office: good value received. She will appear at the next court hearing and reinterpret the tests and give her own report—something to look forward to, I'm sure.

She says something wonderful as I leave: "I usually don't comment," Dr. Shirley remarks, opening the door for me, "but I think you have some unusual survival skills—what we call coping mechanisms."

"Thanks, I may need them."

"You have nothing to fear . . . from within."

Boundaries

There are perimeters to pain, and the human soul has an amazing capacity to regenerate. I am feeling as good as a person could, with a tombstone with her name on it. Who would do such a thing? My insomnia is in full force, and I turn the possibilities over in my mind. Matt? Not his style. Chick Savago? Not likely, either. So who else had such destructive impulses toward me?

Winsten? I consider the possibility. This is the work of someone who imagines terror, who is creative and would enjoy a surprise ending. But why? Why would he dislike me?

"He doesn't dislike you," Elsbieta tells me on the phone at two A.M. We may have a psychic connection after all: She called, sensing I might be awake. "I'm glad you have told me this suspicion, because I happen to know, he likes you very much."

"Really?"

"Yes. I cast *Run for Your Life* and *Kiss of Death,* and now you have jogged my old brain, and I remember, because it was unusual: Most often the screenwriter doesn't have much input in the casting, but that time he did. Unless I am getting senile, I am sure he asked for you—insisted, in fact. Said he wrote the part for you. . . ."

I soften a bit toward Gideon Winsten, as only an actress who has been chosen can. He may be odd, but he is on my side. At worst, he is an obsessed fan. He is not the first; I have had a few. I still have the bedsheet over my bedroom window: I do not want to indulge his interest, but I think I understand its limitations.

In the morning, when Joey Gromolka calls in with his own breakthrough, I cut him off to tell him the good news regarding Gideon Winsten. "I think he's just a voyeur," I tell the boy.

"He does like you," Joey confirms. "I was going to tell you: I asked over at the town clerk's office if they remembered anything about when Gideon Winsten got his permits to build the glass house. And they said he specified the angle he needed for his permit: He said he had to have a view of your place."

"So it is not a coincidence, then—the window facing mine across the lake?"

"No," Joey insists. "The plans had to be redone. He insisted on that exact location. It was a big issue for the town because of sewage. It cost him a fortune to get that close to the lake: He has to pump his crap back up the mountain. I mean thousands. He demanded the lot be right on the shore, directly opposite you, at the exact angle that affords him a look at Casa di Rosas."

I feel that cool creep of nausea that is a barometer of truth. This is more than interest: This is obsession. Winsten's gone to a great deal of effort—casting me, building a house. Maybe I am right to get nervous with him. I tell Joey, "Did you check for a police record?"

"Nothing there. No record."

"He's clean?"

"No," Joey reports, "there's just no police record for anyone by that name. There's no record at all, anywhere, for a Gideon Winsten."

We mull over the possibilities; I try to restrain Joey from jumping to conclusions. "So many writers use pen names. That's probably all it is. . . ."

I am so impressed with this boy. He comes up with a plan to search real estate files, the tax office. "I can get his real name if I go back and research the title."

The title. Something snags in my memory; then I catch it: Gideon Winsten, that first day I met him—what was it he had said? "I inherited the land"?

"This may not have been a sale," I tell Joey. "I think the land was in Winsten's family."

"Then the title will reveal his identity." Joey can hardly stay put to hear the rest of my plan. "We'll get him, we'll get him. . . ."

I caution him to proceed with care. We don't know who Winsten may truly be, or how dangerous. And what about his pre-occupation with the Frozen Girls?

Joey has searched the archives of the Bonticou Lutheran Church and uncovered moldered accounts of weddings and statistics. Along the way, he has chatted up every local historian and busy-body in Bonticou. The amount of information he unearthed is prodigious. He is still delving through it. "The stuff is so old, I'm sneezing," he confides.

Joey appears before ten A.M., a stack of documents in an attaché case in one hand, and a bag of still-warm crullers from Mrs. Schmidt's in the other. He is rather adorably costumed in a trench coat and fedora. Playing detective, I think, but playing it well. He is bubbling over with delight, using every known expression from *True Crime.*

I fix him a hot chocolate, sit in my nightgown with my own coat over it, and sip coffee, trying to absorb how he "cracked the case."

"Okay, okay, what do you want to know first—the true history of the Frozen Girls, or who had your tombstone cut to order?"

What a choice, I think.

"Let's stay with the personal emergency: My tombstone is a priority here."

"Professional stonecutter up on Eagle Mountain Road."

"Means nothing," I say. "Don't recognize the road."

"Okay, we check it out. Meanwhile . . ." He dumps the file from the church cellar onto the kitchen table. The papers flake, like old, burned skin, and give off the mustiness of a century. The girls, all seven beautiful faces, peer up at us as if aching to return to life. Their wistfulness is apparent. Whatever the connection of their deaths, in life they were a lookalike collection of ethereal blondes.

"Theosophy! Spiritualism." Joey unfolds a scroll that almost disintegrates as we look at it: I see the faded lineup of the same seven beautiful young girls, in chitons, standing at an outdoor gazebo. It is summer, and the spot appears familiar.

"These are the girls," Joey tells me. "They are the Frozen Girls. Every single girl in the group died and was found naked on the ice."

I have cried a bit for myself; now I am ready to cry for these long-dead young girls. Standing in a semicircle, arranged as if for a dance recital, they gaze out of the photograph. They wear their hair up, with identical tendrils.

"They were murdered?" I ask, feeling horror more than a century after their frozen bodies were found, praying, on the lake.

"Never established murder. No signs of foul play. They went, one by one, to the lake. They all belonged to the Moldavian Colony; they believed in transition, not death. But it is a mystery why they died. They froze fast, always in the same position: hands clasped, praying."

I recognize "my" bride, the original bride of Casa di Rosas: Amie Deschelles.

She is unmistakable—the identical Botticelli face of the wedding portrait on my wall, above the fireplace mantel. I have gazed at her picture for hours. But what of the husband, the groom, John Deschelles? I ask Joey.

"I'm working on that," he says. "I'm hot on the trail." He smiles. "But the trail is cold."

Then, as the pièce de résistance, he fans out the collection of "spirit photographs"—images of actual people with famous ghosts standing behind them. Here again are the Frozen Girls, but this time we see past presidents behind them, even a few actors: I recognize Edwin Booth, Isadora Duncan, Eleanora Duse.

"You cannot imagine," Joey tells me, "how cool it was, in those days, to cross over. . . . The entire community believed in the transition. They talked all the time, through the mediums, to their dead loved ones, and—see—even posed for family portraits."

No, I couldn't imagine. I think the past was very unlike the present, when we cling to life and youth at all cost. The Frozen Girls share their level, grave gaze, looking beyond the here and now. Observing their expression, I have my own theory as to what happened to them, but I don't wish to tell Joey.

He's exuberant, leaping round Casa di Rosas; he feels he can "crack the case," save me, whatever. He does what any eighteen-year-old would do, under the circumstances: He gives me his pager number.

Then he's off, playing Sherlock Holmes. I sit, too emotionally drained to stir my coffee. My house is just as I left it to go to court. The dishes still sit in the sink, the fry pan rests with more congealing scrambled eggs.

This may be Moira's "day," but there is clearly no Moira. It is amazing how fast the house deteriorates in her absence: The dust bunnies are beginning to accumulate again, and that uncared-for look is creeping back into the corners. I contemplate lugging out the Supralux 699 and vacuuming, but as I touch the handle, the telephone rings. For an instant I fear it will be the vacuum man, Chick Savago, somehow psychically connected to his instrument.

"Oh, Mrs. Smythe, Juliana, I'm so sorry." Moira Gonzalez Gerhardt. I visualize her in her trailer, her white face reddened, sobbing into the receiver.

"I'm surprised you would call here," I say, smarting from her testimony against me in court.

"I'm sorry, Juliana," she says. "I just have to tell you . . . I am really, really sorry. . . ."

I don't know what she is apologizing for—her testimony in court, or not appearing here to clean.

"It's all right," I tell her. "I can see how you might feel you had to testify for my husband's side. It is misleading, what I said about the vase."

To my shock, there is the sound of sobbing on the line.

"Really," I say, "it's okay. It won't make or break the case. I understand, honestly. . . ."

"I'm so sorry, Mrs. Smythe, I'm so sorry." I can't understand her: Her voice is inchoate.

"You still have your job here, if you want it," I say, misunderstanding.

"No," she says, her tone suddenly clear and flat. "It's not that. It's not any of that. It's Rafe. He beat me up last night. He was drinking and he really lost it. I had to jump out the window to get away from him. He chased me down Route 27, and caught up with me on Lake Shore Drive on my side of the mountain. I've got two broken ribs, black eyes, and my face . . . he rearranged my goddamn face for me. I can't let my kids see me like this."

I was now more alert. "Where are the twins?"

"With my mother. She was watching them for me. He would have hurt them, too, he was so out of his mind." She adds a detail. "He shot the heads off two chickens."

Shot. The image of his rifle, so gallantly presented, looms in my mind. Is it still in my hall closet? Holding the phone, I open the closet: The weapon is there, pointing up at the hat shelf.

"Where is Rafe now?" I want to know.

"In jail. The cops came and put him in Pewter Mountain. He was DWI for starters, and then they seen me, how bad I look. . . ."

"Take photographs." I can speak, unfortunately from experience, when I give her the rundown on what to do: Have photographs taken, press charges, complete as much of an affidavit as possible. . . . She has only twenty-four hours to get this on the record.

"You're pressing charges, aren't you?"

There is a pause, but then she says, "Yeah, sure. But I'm having trouble getting around. I'm stiff and sore: I don't think I can drive."

I have to take a deep breath before I offer this, but I feel that I must. Who will understand her if *I* don't? I now have the knowledge to assist her through the process I am still staggering through, learning as I go. . . .

"I'll help you. I've just been through something similar. I will walk you through the doors. You can stay here for a few days if you like. . . ."

"You'd do that? After what I just said in court?"

"Yes." These cycles of violence have to stop somewhere. "You know something strange? He was here yesterday and loaned me a rifle . . . for protection. He seemed so . . . concerned and protective."

"Oh, yeah," she says, "that's the other side of Rafe. I call him Jekyll and Hyde. I have to look close at his face to see who I'm with sometimes."

"He's beaten you before?"

"Uh-huh."

"But I thought you two were so happy. . . . Spaghetti night, the twins, the rented movie, the popcorn . . . He was always worried about you . . . your safety."

"Yeah," she says, "nobody can hurt me but him."

"I'll pick you up," I volunteer.

As I drive toward her home on the side of the mountain, I wonder why I have acted so fast on her behalf. I could rationalize leaving Moira Gonzalez Gerhardt to her fate. She is not my responsibility, after all—and in fact, she has just testified for my husband's legal team.

Yet, my instinct is strong to help her. I know how difficult it is to go public with injuries, to admit to the world that the person closest to you has done something like this. I have just learned, unfortunately, "the ropes." I should take her under my admittedly wounded wing for a few days, until her case is well established and she has properly documented the assault. Mainly, I know how susceptible she will be—if no one stands by her. She could crumble, drop the charges, and be killed. Perhaps only someone such as I myself can truly appreciate the ambiguities. . . .

The road is slick with mud, and at a few places mud cascades actually cross the road. I drive slowly toward her house, not wanting to veer off on the steep drop to the lake. The color scheme of the day is shifting: Blue skies giving way to gray. The thaw is in serious effect; the snow is disappearing as I watch, shrinking back up the mountain. The edge of the lake looks gelid, softening.

There it is—her almost right-angle driveway. It is a veritable mudslide. But I see Moira has walked down to greet me, and at the sight of her—huddled in a parka, with an extra blanket on top, her face red and tear-streaked—I feel I have been correct to come collect her. If someone didn't intervene here, she would wait for Rafe to get out of jail, come home, and swing at her again.

"Thank you, Mrs. Smythe," she says in a small voice as she gets into the passenger side of my car. "I asked my mom to watch the twins for a few days. I don't want her or them seeing me like this."

I know from experience: Her bruises will be further discolored tomorrow.

I drive down West Lake Road to loop back on Spruce. I am silent, but Moira is talking the entire time. She is very fearful of the road, the mud. "Oh, watch this bad curve coming up, Mrs. Smythe . . ." and "Careful. See those plastic flowers on the guardrail? That's where a friend of mine died. . . ." While she is in near-hysteria in the car wreck department, Moira refers to the marital assault in a curious, unemotional tone.

"Rafe is okay most of the time," she is saying, "but when he drinks, he is another person. It all comes out. His father is crazy: He beat all of them kids, all thirteen of them. He even tried to drown them. He never hurt Rafe's mom, though, just the kids. This isn't the first time with me, but it's the worst time."

"And the last time," I stress to her.

"You bet. I don't need this. . . ."

Rafe put a hole through the wall with his fist, she tells me.

"You know, he thinks you're part of the problem," she says as we turn up Serpentine Road toward my house.

"How's that?"

"He thinks my attitude is 'cause of working for you. I seen you get rid of your husband, and now he thinks I want to do the same. You're an influence, he says."

I hope so, I think.

At Casa di Rosas, I light a fire in the hearth, put on the kettle for tea, and prop Moira Gonzalez Gerhardt up in my accustomed position on the sofa to watch the TV and the fire. The original simulcast.

While she recuperates, I dial around the county, contacting lawyers, the police, a photographer. Moira's case is going to be done right. The evidence will be tight: Rafe Gerhardt will remain in Pewter Mountain.

"You're so good to me," Moira says, cuddling under the comforter like a big child. "I don't know how I will ever thank you."

"By staying safe," I say.

The alarm system is on. I hand her my semi-useless cell phone.

"Can you fire Rafe's rifle?"

"No," she answers. "I hate guns. I told him he couldn't keep one on our place."

"When did you tell him that?"

"Yesterday."

Oh, now I see: Maybe Rafe was removing the rifle in anticipation of losing control; maybe he had a built-in safety mechanism, like the catch on the gun itself. Or maybe he had another reason to leave his rifle here. If he mistrusted me, resented my influence on his wife, why did he arm me? Or was he looking for her then, and I came home, and he was standing there with a rifle and thought of a quick excuse. Or maybe it was just as it appeared: He wanted to kill the great stag, One Eye, and was buttering me up for permission to hunt.

Concern is the flip side to control; I know this myself. His obsession with safety cut both ways. Is he another schizophrenic, or a brutal young man with a plan?

Well, there would be time to learn the answer, as I anticipated another court hearing for Moira. I wonder if Joe Gromolka will take her case. She would not need J. J. Janis, and he would have none of her anyway, not at his rates. But Joe strikes me as having some heart: How could Gromolka raise such a great boy as Joey if he didn't? She'll need representation. The good part, the part of her case that is so much better than my own, is that her attacker is behind bars, on Pewter Mountain.

All things being relative, I think, that's another piece of luck.

With the DWI, and most likely a high bail, there's no chance a man with Rafe Gerhardt's resources will be out and about, but just in case I call the sheriff.

"It's me, Juliana Smythe," I say. Sheriff LaBute and I have developed a near-jocular informality over my many calls. "The latest is, my housecleaner has been attacked by her husband, Rafe Gerhardt."

"I know him well," the sheriff says.

"How well?"

"It's happened before."

"Then you know he was arrested last night?"

"Battery and DWI," the sheriff says. "He's in Pewter Mountain."

"He won't be let out of Pewter Mountain, will he?"

"Not likely. They got $10,000 bail. He's in. For a good while."

"Do me one more favor?" I ask. "Give me some notice if Rafe Gerhardt is released. His wife is staying here with me."

"Will do."

I actually feel better; one can become more competent at anything, I reflect. I am anticipating the call from Joey Gromolka: I am anxious to know more about this stonecutter who carved my name on that tombstone. And I have also left a message with Gromolka senior, to see if he would consider taking Moira's case on a low retainer.

I sit at the kitchen table, allowing Moira some privacy at the sofa. She has the TV remote and is now watching talk shows in alternation with soap operas. I do something I have never done on film: I sit and pay my bills, scribbling check after check. This makes me feel better, more in control. How long since I paid attention to the pragmatic details of my life? The Central Bonticou bill has a termination notice. I pay the most essential invoices, all the ones stamped PAST DUE in red. Then I open my purse and take out the Instamatic photo with the tombstone.

Where is my "grave" I wonder. The shot is blurry, but there is a single clue: a stone detail behind and to the right of the grave. What is that—the hand of a statue? Yes, I see the marble palm, the extended slim fingers. . . .

I feel the proverbial chill creep up my spine.

I recognize that stone hand. Isn't that the hand on the dancing angel?

An image of the Moldavian graveyard springs into my mind. I see the chipped paint on the cottages, the cliff, the gray cluster of headstones, and that one dancing carved naiad, with the stubbed stone nose and abraded gaze.

So that is where someone wants me to rest, forever—among the souls of those who have not died but are "in transition."

Messages

Do I dare drive to see my own grave? Was the headstone there, that night I visited the Moldavian Colony with Elsbieta? I hadn't noticed it, but then, I was hardly looking for such a thing. Who would want to frighten me this way? Carved headstones are not Matt's style. He is all impulse; this carving had taken time, someone who could cut stone.

Come on, Joey, I mentally summon the kid. Call back. I have to know more before I drive out there. . . .

Maybe I do have powers: The phone rings. Joey. "Okay," he says, "I got it. I called every monument maker in Bonticou and I got the guy who cut your name in the stone. With the dates and everything. Here it is: Emil Yablons."

Emil Yablons? I don't know anyone by that name. "Old guy, family-owned monument company. They did my grandparents' crypt. They are right near the Moldavian Graveyard. Emil admitted it right off. He just did that stone last week, and it was a weird deal. The stone was already in place. They usually carve, then set them, except if it's a couple and the wife is still alive, in which case they have her birthdate and no death date. Or it's a family plot.

This stone was there already but blank. It was set in 1899. The plot belonged to the Moldavian Colony, but it's been in arrears for back taxes. So it's county land."

Emil Yablons. Why would he want to scare me?

"Emil just cut the stone. It was paid for and ordered by a man named Deschelles."

"Deschelles . . ." Now, that did ring the warning gong: Deschelles was the name on the original deed, the name of the bride for whom the house was built. Amie Deschelles. My bride. Her groom.

Could there be a descendent? Was this some sort of real-estate revenge? Did he want to scare me into selling? Maybe this was a whole other issue from the obscene caller, the Peeping Tom mystery writer, the estranged husband, and the insane vacuum-cleaner salesman.

"You may be the focus of some energy," Elsbieta says when I phone her to report. I have to admit an undeniable urge to tell her about the Moldavian Colony graveyard. After all, she has ancestors there as well.

"What was the message?" I ask her. "That night, when you tried to commune with the spirits on the other side of the Moldavian Colony, you said there was a message, but it was for me. . . ."

"The message?" Elsbieta hesitates. I can hear her drink, with ice rattling. I imagine her with her Transylvanian 120-proof tuica, plum liquor that inflames the brain.

"I thought you didn't want to know," Elsbieta says. "Now you want to know."

"I'm curious."

"Both messages?"

I deny psychic communication from beyond the grave. "Yes, both."

"The first is from the cat."

"Dot?"

"She's dead. Thrown from the car at high speed. Your husband, in a fit of insane rage, tossed her. She's in the bushes, at the first turn from your private driveway onto Serpentine Road. Of course, there is not much left. The little blue collar with the tag from the veterinarian."

Sorrow wells up in me. Dot did not deserve such a fate.

"If you walk down your driveway and look under the hemlock tree there, you'll find the collar."

"The second message?"

"Your mother. Eva."

Now I know why people trooped over to the Moldavian Colony. I would give anything to hear from my mother. But I don't believe in such things, as messages from the dead. "What does she say?"

"She's watching over . . ."

I am surprised at the ache in my throat. Oh, I wish I could believe. . . . I have always longed for my mother; if only we could be together, just once again, to speak as women. I was thirteen and she was thirty-six when she died. She chose to exit early, I think to spare us both the wasting and the pain. She died in her best night-gown, looking just lovely. In white. My father had never married her; she had that gown for her wedding night. . . .

"Deschelles," I say. "Does the name mean anything to you?"

"Dead," Elsbieta declares. "All of them dead. But one."

"One bought a grave and had my name put on it last week."

"Maybe," Elsbieta says. "I don't see that . . ."

"All right, the Frozen Girls. Seven girls mysteriously died on Lake Bonticou between the years of 1897 and 1900. They were all found naked, in positions of prayer. The mystery was never solved."

"Ay," says Elsbieta. "This is a lot . . . I will have to concentrate. May I call you back? My meatballs are burning."

"Whenever you have it," I say.

Joey Gromolka has fared better. He has further researched the Frozen Girls and found that Amie Deschelles, the original bride of Casa di Rosas, was the last to die, on March 15, 1900.

"The ides of March," I remark. "What a coincidence."

"Maybe not," Joey says, his enunciation poor in his excitement. "I think I really have cracked this: They were not murdered. They had a pact. They were classicists and believed in the transition. They chose specific, important dates and chose those dates to 'cross over.' The lake had a spiritual significance to them: They called it Spirit Lake, remember? They received messages. They were kids: The oldest was nineteen and a half. They were like me, like the kids in my school. Rejection is heavy. Two had broken engagements, and Amie Deschelles was reputed to be an unhappy bride. Her husband was investigated but exonerated after she was found, on the north end of the lake."

No more information is available, Joey says on the phone, but he will keep looking. We agree to go together to the Moldavian Colony the next day, to examine my "grave."

I spend the next three hours listening to Moira reprise her marriage to Rafe. There has been a lot of violence. It often seems to revolve around his looking for her and not finding her home. "Then he finds me, and he's been drinking, and he starts hitting. One time he bit through my lower lip."

Kiss of death.

I make her a good hot supper—a *boeuf en flammade* I had frozen for Christmas, and an old-fashioned baked potato. Sometimes there is nothing as satisfying as a baked potato. For dessert I give her a foamy whipped hot chocolate with homemade sour cherry pie made from the last of my frozen handpicked cherries, from my own queen tree. I try not to dwell on the fact that Matt and I had picked these cherries together, as we did every season. Sour cherry, I reflect, seems to be the just dessert of the evening. For all parties concerned.

I have never seen anyone cry as much as Moira Gonzalez Gerhardt. She actually wets the front of her nightgown.

What could possibly make her feel better?

Then inspiration: She should sleep in my bedroom. To be honest, I've been ambivalent about it since she told me about the shoes and the possibility of another woman sleeping in there with Matt. Not to mention the view of Winsten's house. I still keep that window draped with a percale sheet, but I cannot block the images from my mind.

Yet, the room looks lovely. The antique bedstead is decked out, by Moira herself, in my vintage linens. She seems pleased by the idea and trundles upstairs holding a hot-water bottle she has brought from her own home.

It feels odd to have a housemate, somehow even odder that it is Moira. "This is a little funny," I say, "but sleep tight."

"Don't let the bedbugs bite," she says, a bit singsong, as if by habit of saying good night to her children.

"Are you warm enough?" I ask.

She doesn't answer, and I peek in the door and see. She has fallen asleep, her face, puffy from crying and the beating, relaxes as a child's would.

The phone rings. I run to pick up before it can wake her.

It is Rafe, calling from Pewter Mountain.

"I want to talk to my wife," he says.

"She's not here."

"I hear she is. . . ." He sounds angry with me.

I wonder how he knows. Who is talking to him in the county jail? I want to hang up, but I have to ask: "I have your gun. Why did you give it to me?"

But then I hear a loud male voice in the background: "Gerhardt, your time is up."

And he is gone. *Click.*

The phone rings again, and this time it is my husband.

His voice is softer, deep with contrition. "Listen," he says, "I'm sorry about what I had to say in court. But it will get worse. I don't want to have to reveal the rest. . . ."

"The rest of what?"

"You know."

"No, I don't know."

"I still love you," he says. "This can all go away. It's too late for us to separate. I'm vomiting. I am bleeding through my nose. It's unbearable to be apart from you. I'll do anything."

You would think that I am wise enough; yet, he affects me. It takes all my will to set down the phone.

Then I go back to sorting my papers for court. The apologetic notes don't seem that conclusive, more like normal married couples' kiss-and-make-up messages after a fight. I know there is one more letter that may be decisive. But where is it? I know myself: I throw out nothing. I must have hidden it and—as often happens with items that are kept for safekeeping—I cannot find it.

Where would I hide something so personal and crucial that I separated it even from my own precious documents? I concentrate and, almost unbidden, I think of the attic, the odd space that was once the interior of the old cupola. Where the wedding bells rang.

Gong. Now I remember: During the last Thanksgiving holiday I went up there to hide—to hide from Matt—and I took with me all that was precious and irreplaceable. I must have been half insane myself, driven by fear, to go up to that unheated space.

Now I force myself to retravel my steps that day. I had some money, jewelry, my important documents. I was intent on saving myself, fleeing. I suspected that Matt had killed the cat. Certainly he had driven off my friends with his scowls and the thrown turkey.

He had a heavy step—a sign—and he stomped through the house saying, "Juliana? Juliana? Where are you? Come out. I know you're here. . . ." I huddled up there, next to the cold metal bell, long silenced, its clangor stolen by vandals. Fee-fi-fo-fum . . . I shook like a child. I had my own giant, ready to kill. . . . What was he going to do when he found me? Was this a fatal game of hide-and-seek?

"Juliana, don't be ridiculous. I know you are up there."

We used to play a game, hide-and-kiss, more than kiss. And when he was the real Matt, the good Matt, his step was light and he would call out in fun, "Where is she? Where's the one it's all for? Where's my girl?"

Now I open the door to the attic stair. It is so narrow, barely a body width—a stairwell that had been constructed, like everything else in the Wedding House, for one time use, as access to the bell. As I climb I feel the brush of cobwebs on my face, the crack of beetle backs under my shoe.

Moira was right: The critters take over. There is no part of a house that is uninhabited; these secret sections are simply lived in by other species. Insects, vermin . . . a large web veils my hair. I brush it aside, continue climbing, climbing.

The stair is as tall as it is narrow, and I finally reach the top and open the second door, leading into the uninsulated attic itself. There is no finishing: The wind whistles through the wainscoting; sleet infiltrates. The single Gothic leaded window is cracked, and the draft through the broken glass is sharp as a knife in my face.

Where would I hide documents? The room is filled with junk, the detritus of our married life, the debris of past occupants, extra materials for construction, odd pipes and two-by-fours, trash bags of old clothes.

There it is: my wedding trunk. Would I have placed evidence inside the old steamer chest? I open it and find a white lace negligee ensnared in hardened black goo. My mind cannot interpret what I see until I discern tiny claws and the webbing of wings: A bat died on my wedding nightgown. When? He seems so rubberized, the creature might have lived a century ago; he is as dried-up as a fig. I throw him, wrapped in my negligee as a shroud, out the small attic casement window. The bat sinks, unseen, into the remaining crusted snow below.

I am freezing; I should have put on a coat to come up here, but I am determined to find what I need for court. It must be here, somewhere.

When I lift the carton that contains my marriage license and letters, I make another discovery—a petrified bird, beak up, its claws in a death curl, wings flat to its sides. I scream; it barely helps that it isn't an especially nice bird, a black grackle. I guess he was the bird who squawked and banged at the gutters in spring. How had the grackle entered? How long ago had it died? I throw the bird, too, like a stone from the window, and it also sinks at once into the snowbank.

As I try to shut the broken window, my hand sticks on the gluey mass of spider egg sacs, a massive future population tucked into the windowframe.

Ugh. I wipe my hands on a shred of curtain that remains. And that is when I notice it—that trapezoid-shaped cupboard door wedged into the angle of the attic corner. The door is low to the floor. It looks like yet another access door, to reach pipes. But now I have a memory of reaching inside there, tucking my papers in that recess.

Gingerly—wasn't it Moira herself who warned me of spider bites? ("Know a woman lost her thumb")—I grope into the opening and, yes, I feel it: a folder and a sheaf of paper. God, I think, I must have been distraught. . . .

I pull out the sheaf of papers and am startled: The handwriting is not mine; the penmanship is the near-calligraphy of Victorian script, page after page, in black india or purple. The feathery scrawl deepens as with force of intent on the part of the writer.

I sink back and sit on my own wedding trunk. I can quickly discern that I am reading not my letters but the letters and diaries of the original bride, Amie Deschelles. Her "So glorious, purest bliss" soon thickens into "John is not home tonight," then "John is increasingly distant" and "John turns away from me now, without explanation."

The paper is of such fine rag content that it is less deteriorated than my own papers when I find them, in the folder. And the content of the 1890's documents is riveting enough to distract me from my original mission.

I cannot decipher some of the script, but one document is clearly a calendar on which are marked important historical dates. Under seven of those dates are recorded the names and a notation to match:

Frieda Van Deheuval, age 16, January 1st, in transition.
Amelia Whithurst, age 17, February 14th, in transition.

Carla Dumont, age 15, March 1st, in transition.
Mary Lee Hallstrom, age 18, December 24th, in transition.
June Lindster, age 17, December 25th, in transition.

And finally, heavily inked, a circle around *March 15th, 1900.* A question mark. *My transition?*

A hand-transcribed poem also by Chidiock Tichborne is scribbled on the margins. It records the feelings of the boy on the eve of his execution in the Tower of London:

"My prime of youth is but a frost of cares . . ."

His youth is an old age, filled with pain, I translate into modern usage.

The rest of the documents are written on lesser paper and almost turn to powder at my touch. There is a garland of ribbon, a wedding veil, and two white silk garters.

A charter, with roses hand-painted, remains intact: "We are the Daughters of the Rosebrier," it states in a floral script. "We know that beauty is pricked with thorns, and we believe in love and life everlasting."

A series of names identical to those on the calendar appear, with the final delicate signature of Amie Deschelles. Beneath her name she has written her vow—and I imagine her voice, and the voices of the other seven girls, as they must have recited: "We swear to escort one another to eternal joy." Are these rust spots or blood drops that dot the bottom of these pages?

I sense their ceremony. Shivering almost mechanically in spasms, I tuck the sheaves into my folder, replacing the letter I have searched for for so long to validate my court case.

Evidence? I do not want to enter a letter this personal, once so precious, into court as evidence, but I have learned that I must do whatever is necessary to protect myself from further harm. Somehow, I have received a message from the past, in the disintegrating elegant script of the Daughters of the Rosebrier—or, as I am sure they are now known, the Frozen Girls. Love everlasting—a scripted colloquialism, or eternal truth? My inheritance from the first bride? And who, then, to escort *me*? Toward what "transition"?

I touch my own letter as a sort of talisman: my letter, though only seventeen years old, feels like silk from being folded and refolded. Why do I reread it? What is it in this correspondence between Matt and myself that tears at me so? I must be compelled, for I know its message by heart. . . .

Grave Matters

It is "unseasonably warm" for March when I meet Joey, as planned, to go the Moldavian Colony. The snowmelt has become a flood, the mountainside streams with transient waterfalls. Lake Bonticou is softening, the gray stain spreading, the fissures cracking open.

Joey has picked me up in his Jeep and we are bouncing along the rutted road to the Moldavian Colony. Even this morbid trip has a slight aspect of an outing, and I have packed a thermos of strong coffee and a few cookies for the boy. He has thought of a picnic, too, and brought along a bag with sandwiches, corned beef on real rye, from Mrs. Schmidt's.

For about fifteen minutes I feel perked up; then we turn onto the driveway for the colony. If anything, the place is more haunted by day. The cottages look more worn, their broken windows even more like empty sockets. Without the cosmetic cover of the snow, debris is revealed everywhere—piles of boards, armatures of a burned central building. There are even the husks of rusted cars and discarded equipment.

A dead raccoon, upturned, bloated, looking more like a furred bagpipe than an animal, is there, a gruesome welcome mat to the entry to the graveyard itself.

Many of the stones look quite beautiful by day, their marble and granite faces worn by time and the wind. There are elegant lettered messages, frilled designs. To the rear we see the stone angel spinning in eternity, a graceful girl in a marble chiton, hands outstretched, a thin smile on her stone lips.

Here it is, I think, my grave. . . . And there it is . . . the stone: Juliana Durrell Smythe, birthdate dash unknown date, this year.

There's more, I notice, than I could decipher in the blurry photograph: an almost invisible, worn-down script in the stone— *Beloved Wife.*

Maybe it is Matt, I think.

It seems elaborate, but he is emerging stranger than I would have ever guessed. Does he mean to spook me into surrender?

Joey finds a stone bench and unwraps the sandwiches. I can smell corned beef and pastrami. Joey and I share this response to an ordeal: appetite. We eat with relish and down the coffee too. Joey is eating the cookies when, on an impulse, I rise and go to "my" stone. Something about it has been bothering me. I kneel and examine it more closely.

The actual ground here is blanketed in last autumn's leaves, a mauve, moldered coverlet. On top of that is the now-porous, breathing snow. In the warm air a vapor rises from the grave. "Look," I call to Joey, "this grave has been disturbed." Even though this is "my" grave, someone else is apparently in it.

"We're out of here," says Joey, taking me by the elbow. "This stonecutter starts talking now." I appreciate my boy detective more now than ever as he drives us straight from the Moldavian Colony to Emil Yablons's family monument business down the road.

Emil Yablons, whoever he is, has obviously run this family business from his home, a small blue frame building, for a long time. Outside are demonstration tombstones, from simple marble wedges to towers and massive double "couple" monuments. The metal orb of a satellite dish pops up, incongruous as a gray flower, among the display gravestones.

Emil Yablons is inside, watching the shopping channel. Joey has been here before and knocks on the door. "Come in," he calls out. "Door is open."

We are welcomed by a thin, bent man with gray hair and a white mustache; he is tilted back in a frayed gray-tweed recliner. His house is stacked with mail-order catalogs, magazines, videocassettes—any possible diversion from the long, shut-in winters. There is a small green cannister, an oxygen tank, at his side, but he is smoking.

He seems excited to meet a new person, but he startles at the name.

"I just carved that," he says. "Your mother?"

"No, me."

We explain that there must be a terrible mistake, or possibly a crime. Could he tell us more about Deschelles? Did he have his address, phone number? What was he like?

Emil has a coughing fit—"Stonecutter's lung," he says between wheezes. Then he gasps out what I sense is his habitual joke: "Making tombstones will get you one of your own."

Yes, yes, he remembers the man: He was an average-looking fellow; paid in cash, though, no check. It was an odd deal, the whole thing. "But business has been slow," Yablons admits. "I couldn't turn it down."

The stone, he admits, was old, too—recycled. It had been found knocked over in the graveyard, the inscription worn off, save *Beloved Wife*.

"I didn't see no harm in it," Emil Yablons says. "This is my livelihood; can't make it on Social Security. And people aren't dying like they were."

He is not good at physical description, and even Joey cannot drag out of him a real account of what Deschelles looks like.

"Kind of pale guy. Didn't seem to be from around here," Yablons says, "but I knew the name. There's Deschelles up there, so I figured it's okay. He had a deed to the plots, so that was all okay. Bought the grave for back taxes."

We ask a few more questions, but his answers frustrate us: "He wasn't tall or short, young or old. No, no, he was kind of an ordinary fellow."

"Bald?" I want to know.

"No," Yablons recalls. "Think he had hair. But then, maybe he had a cap."

There was one thing, though—"He give me a deposit: Says he'll be needing more stones. . . ."

Reconciliation

The drive back to Casa di Rosas is frightening in and of itself. The thaw is accelerating and the mud has become a tide, a flood. A wind is picking up and blowing scraps of previous hidden garbage into the underbrush. Bits of plastic and cellophane are snared in the bushes. All looks dreary and bereft of the charm the snow had lent to this landscape only two days ago.

There is a sense of nature out of whack, a season not in sync. A duck appears, disoriented, walking on the road toward the lake. "He should still be south," Joey remarks.

It is seventy degrees, unheard of in Bonticou for this date.

At one point Joey's Jeep wheels slide, and the back wheel begins to spin crazily in the mud. For a tense ten minutes I fear we won't pull out, but Joey takes off his jacket, sacrifices it for traction, and we push onward.

The atmosphere of violence in the barometric pressure fulfills our accelerating panic. Something is building to a pitch in Bonticou, and without speaking, Joey and I share a foreboding as we reach Casa di Rosas. There's a disorder, even in the sky—black clouds scuttling in, crows screaming. A group of turkey vultures hang like animate shadows in the trees that border the turn to my driveway. As we approach they do not even bother to depart, but hunch and spread their wings in place.

We leave the Jeep at the pull-over place and start to walk in. As we walk I recall Elsbieta's prediction regarding the cat's collar. An odd thing happens then: I pause as we turn the bend and, as if guided, walk to the single evergreen tree, a tenting hemlock, and peer below. There are no bones, thank God, but I do see, left as if for inspection on a final pillow of snow, the small blue cat collar. There can be no doubt: Dot's name, and identification number are perfectly legible on the tag.

He did it. Matt killed her. I knew it intuitively, but here is the evidence.

Unbidden hatred, which is new to me, burns through me, and I do not originate the thought—it also comes unasked for—that I wish he were dead.

This horrifies me, and I rescind it. I do not consciously wish this upon him. I don't wish him dead, truly: I wish him sane.

I am so distraught over the discovery, and my own response to it, that it takes a moment for me to realize that something is "off" at Casa di Rosas. My car. The Saab. I had left it parked at the pull-over spot and now it is gone.

"We'll call the police, report the car stolen," Joey says.

I have a more urgent thought: Moira.

When we left earlier in the morning, Moira was home alone at Casa di Rosas. Now my instinct tells me something has happened. My impulse is to run to the bedroom. Oh, my God, I am thinking, what if she has been hurt, abducted? Fearing the worst, Joey and I run inside. The door is open, a bad sign, but the house is ticking the electric pulse of an empty domicile. No one is home. No sign of Moira, although her suitcase, her hairbrush, shampoo, and body lotions, are all very much in evidence in the bedroom.

"No sign of a struggle," Joey says.

"Call it in," I say.

He is on the phone, calling the state troopers and reporting the disappearance of Moira Gonzalez Gerhardt ("Yes, she is twenty-three, blond, about five-foot-one, distinguishing marks . . . a pin piercing through her left eyebrow"), when the Saab abruptly reappears, sliding to a halt in the mud right outside the door.

I am stunned to see my car returned to me, but even more surprised by the driver: Moira Gonzalez Gerhardt alights, wearing her lavender parka and gray sweatpants.

"Moira!" I cry. "Is everything all right?" My first thought is that for some reason she felt unsafe alone here and had to flee until I returned.

"I've had a very difficult morning," she says.

There's something in her tone I find unsettling. This is not the shuffling, tentative, demure Moira: There's a hardness I haven't heard from her before. And she offers no explanation as to why she took my car. Just "I've had a very difficult morning."

She tosses the Saab keys to me and walks past into the kitchen area and pours herself another cup of coffee. She looks worse than she did yesterday: Her bruises are deepening, shadings of purple and blue. I notice that the ballooning flesh from her swollen eyelids has filled in her eyebrow ring. It's strange how different she seems—almost as if her lips have grown thinner—as she says, "Could you do me one favor?"

"What is it?"

"Could you loan me some money for a lawyer? I don't have a cent."

Neither do I, and I say as much.

There's something in her attitude that makes me bite my lip about my request to Joe Gromolka senior—to take her *pro bono,* without a fee, or to charge as little as possible.

"Well, I thought maybe you get an advance on your credit card or something. I would pay you back, or"—her swollen gaze takes in the house—"I could work it off . . . instead of my wages."

I flinch. This isn't right. If I am to help her, it should be my idea, my plan.

"Well, if you want me to go through with this, I need some cash," she says.

What is she suggesting? That if I don't finance her case, she will drop it?

"Moira," I say, "this is making me uncomfortable."

"It's all right, Mrs. Smythe," she says, in a tone that says it is not all right. "I don't expect anybody to help me. People like me fend for themselves. I don't have a fancy house to run back to, or a movie role to play. I clean the shit out of toilets."

Not all the time, I think, but I don't say so.

There is this uncertain ground, between housecleaner and employer, between two women with the same problem, but are we friends, or simply associated by victimization? I am unsure as how to proceed. Isn't it condescending to suddenly switch this into a friendship? I don't truly know her: She has worked here most often in my absence. But as an abuse victim, I feel for her. I must help.

She sniffles. "You know, I was going to go to Jane Baker's wake. She's laid out down at Vandermeyer's."

Vandermeyer's, the local funeral parlor, with the aluminum awning listing and rusted from snow. The frozen woman of the hour, the woman found on the porch. "You knew her?"

"My mom played bingo with her, and they would bowl some-times."

I wonder that Moira would want to go to the wake; her contact seems tangential to me, but I sense she needs to add that tragedy as collateral to her own. So I will not press her for explanations.

As we leave, Joey whispers, "Funerals are social events here; don't make too much of it. Not that much happens in winter. It's more a chance to get together."

His pager goes off as we walk to our separate cars. "Hey," the boy says, "this could be the answer. I got a source at Town Hall. I bet he found out what Gideon Winsten's real name is. . . ."

Even with all that is happening, I admit to being curious: "Call me if you find out anything—anything at all."

I must go back to Dr. Shirley's for my second session. She is building my psychological rebuttal for the next court date, which is in four days. I cannot cancel. I wonder if, with her expertise, she might be willing to speculate on what kind of man creates a false grave—if in fact, it is a false grave, and not an actual one.

Joey has been talking up exhumation. "After all, that can't be you under there."

At least, not yet.

We depart, in our separate vehicles this time. I have another unbidden thought as I see Moira heading upstairs to my bedroom: *I really, really want you out of here.*

Mistaken Identities

The wind is blowing so hard, it moves the Saab on the road. I veer toward the lake but am able, by gripping the wheel, to stay my course. The wind is making a sound now, at the higher elevation: It sounds like a roaring, mechanical thing—maybe a freight train, if freight trains roared through the sky, just above the trees.

I drive for several miles, but I am reconsidering the trip to town. Tornadoes are not unheard of in the area. One came through last year and blew out the windows of several stores. There is almost sure to be a power failure: the electric and phone lines fail at the first serious blow. A sixty-mile-an-hour gust like this will have Casa di Rosas blacked out any minute.

I see Joey pass me on the road, intent on his own quest. I wish I had my cell phone with me: I'd suggest he turn back. There is a loud crack right after he drives by me, and I see trees swaying in an El Greco frenzy. A sick lime light has come into the sky, and daytime lightning jags through the air.

At a moment like this, I just think: *Home.* I swing into the first pullover and make a U-turn. A smashing evergreen, completely uprooted, its root system quivering upright, just misses the Saab.

I drive on, determined to get back to the house. A slashing rain starts, and below me the wheels slide without traction.

Damn, I might not have to worry about being murdered. I can get killed right here, on my own road. I think about abandoning the car and walking the rest of the way, but it's supposed to be safer to stay in the car: The wheels will save you from a lightning strike. Right?

So I continue to drive, slowly, because of the mud, which feels like a moving sidewalk in an airport. I can actually feel my car being swept along the road. My eye notes the surreal displacements of the storm—a shoe caught in a low tree, a trash bag flying like a flag from another branch.

At last I see the house—and there is no flicker of light. There should be a glow from the kitchen, or at least my night-light upstairs. But there is nothing. The blackout has begun. Casa di Rosas waits like a blind woman, eyes shuttered, at the top of the cliff.

I park at the pull-over and have to lean into the wind, bending to make progress uphill. The rain is slashing me, and I have never been wetter; my Mafia lady coat is saturated, whatever water repelling properties it has lost in an instant, in this soaking deluge. I am so fixed on my progress on the road that I almost miss him: He is standing, discreet, under the evergreen. His eyes meet mine from the shade; he is on the other side of a veil of dripping water. I smell the resin on the pine and grunt a greeting. One Eye, "my" stag, grunts back, several snorts in succession.

"You made my day," I say.

He doesn't bolt as I pass. Maybe he senses I mean him well, or it is just so damned wet, even a deer won't venture forth. I have never been so close to him before: I can see the crenellated, barky look to his antler base, the glisten of his muzzle, and the glow of that single, limpid eye. He watches and I pass.

At the house I have to push hard to get the door open; when it does, I am fairly blown into my own kitchen. The house is dark. It seems as if even the air is black. It is not dusk, or nearly dusk: The clock has stopped but it could not be much past two o'clock.

Where's Moira? I call out, and hear her mumble something, from upstairs. I grab a flashlight. I hear a sound, something awful from downstairs. . . .

My first thought, as I hear the crash in the basement, is that the lake has somehow risen and smashed into the cellar, knocking everything in its path. The sound is loud, violent, and my instinct is to avoid finding out what caused it. But I know there is a storm door, and if I can, I should bolt it from within or the water will roar in and undermine the foundation.

So I force myself to put on waders and descend, flashlight in hand. There is water in the basement; I can actually smell it—that old mildew rot of softening cardboard and decaying matter. But I am relieved to see that the waters have not really entered: It's a puddling flood, only a few gallons, filling a declivity in the basement door. The storm doors are open, however; I assume the wind has blown them apart. But as I make my way, to my shock, the doors slam shut: Someone, something, has closed them from the other side.

What? I can't fathom. . . . Has Joey returned to help me secure the house? Yet, some inner knowledge, some chill dread, has entered me, and I go, with an awful certainty, up the steps to my bedroom.

I hear her: Thank God, she must be all right. It sounds as if she's up now, doing something, maybe up and washing her hands, I think, to explain the running-liquid sound. It's so dark inside now, I don't really see her until I am right inside my bedroom. She is lying on the bed, but her head is limp and hanging off the side. The liquid drip I heard is the blood running from her mouth. In the beam of light, I see the blood as black, her face as white. . . .

It is said, in such moments of crisis, we act. There is no time to think, and that is true. I am a creature of reflex: When I see the handle of the deer-gutting knife in her belly, my only response is to withdraw that blade.

She is looking to me for help: Her eyes are wide and glassy but not unseeing. She is registering recognition, trying to say something—my name? But what comes from her mouth is blood. . . .

I grip the knife and yank with all my might. I must save her, I must. . . . And I have a sense of give, then suction, as the blade is pulled out. It is as if I withdrew a stopper: the blood does not just pour out, it is pumped.

I can tell you now that people have more blood than one would believe—that, pumped by a young heart such as Moira's, it can blast you backward to the wall and then shower you with a high-pressure spray. Arterial—that is what it is, arterial—blood, no longer stoppered by the knife, loosed and set free, as the dam has burst. Upon me.

The phone is slippery red in my grip, but I dial 911 and pray for rescue, that the phone lines are not out. "Please, someone, come quick . . . we've been stabbed."

That is what the 911 tape says this time: "We" have been stabbed. A nervous slip, Empathy taken to an extreme? Or is it some misidentification, my inner sense that the knife was meant for me? Whatever the reason for my first-person plural, this mechanism is still in effect when the police car and the ambulance careen up the drive and the emergency medic runs upstairs. I am screaming, *"We're in here."*

First at the Scene

Everyone says it is not my fault, what happened to Moira Gonzalez Gerhardt. They say the delay in getting to the house is probably to blame. It was a bad day. There were so many accidents. Trees were down all over Bonticou. There were snapping cables and popping transformers. Later the mailman, Jake Taylor, told me of the carnage—cars lifted and tossed like toys; houses bashed in, beheaded at the roofline . . .

They say it was "tornadolike." You see the splintered path along Route 27 and you wonder, if this storm was dubbed "tornadolike," what would an actual tornado do? All along Route 27, it looks as if the storm traveled straight up that road and ripped the lid off the homes that line that highway: Every house lay exposed, like a diorama.

So this is why it took so long to reach Casa di Rosas.

But I know. I know I made a mistake. The first person at the scene, the emergency guy on the mobile unit, said, "You never pull out a knife. You leave it in until a doctor can evaluate."

It was me. I made the mistake. Whoever stabbed her didn't do as much damage as I did: I was the one who caused the spurt, the blood loss. She lost three quarters of her blood supply. All that twenty-three-year-old blood spilled. From a healthy girl, with such a strong heart, pumping, pumping.

"Make it stop." they say I was screaming.

I don't remember that part.

What I remember was riding with her to the hospital and meeting Joey there—and Winsten, of all people. He saw the squad car and ambulance lights from his own house and came as fast as he could, chasing the medics to Bonticou Hospital.

I'm not glad to see Winsten. Now I am almost sure he is the breather. He is certainly the watcher. What else is he? He has a rubbernecking attitude in the waiting room, as though he wants to hear the gory details. Or maybe it is grist, or gristle, for his mill.

He writes about bloody death; he loves those mysteries. Maybe he wants to solve this one. I cannot hide my resentment at seeing him here, at what to me is a private, traumatic time.

"Getting details for your next mystery?" I hear myself greet the man. Instantly, I could bite my own tongue. "A Gideon Winsten mystery."

"John Deschelles," I hear whispered in my ear. Joey has come into the waiting room by the ICU and presses my arm. He indicates Don't confront him now.

My mind reels as it had when I suffered that brain concussion. Gideon Winsten is . . . Deschelles? The on-duty surgeon at Bonticou Hospital ER approaches me as if I am next of kin. I have called Moira's mother but she has not yet arrived; she needs to find someone to watch the twins. I have reassured her, that I will remain here, on Moira's behalf, until she can take over in the ICU waiting area. The surgeon is East Indian, in green scrubs.

"She's still critical," he reports. "The knife severed an artery. That is usually fatal." He darts back inside. Joey and I stand dully, listening to the beeps and whistles, the sound effects of emergency medicine. Carts roll. . . .

Gideon Winsten, now known to be a Deschelles, seems to sense he is now very unwelcome and moves to the far side of the waiting area, where he picks up a magazine. He shows no intention of leaving. I know I will have to deal with him later—his odd connection to me, to my house, and apparently to my grave—but for now, all I can think of is Moira, the young girl behind the closed door marked DO NOT ENTER.

So who put the knife to her in the first place?

"Any ideas?" I ask Joey, who is maybe the only person in the world, or at least Bonticou, whom I can wholly trust.

We sit in the green waiting room of Bonticou Hospital, watching the locals watch TV. It is amazing how nothing distracts from TV anymore. Even people having catastrophes are watching more catastrophes on TV.

While Moira, as they say, "clings" to life, there is a rescue mission going on across the country: A submarine, running out of air, is stranded off the coast of Newfoundland, near where the *Titanic* went down. Everyone is wondering if 112 crewmen will drown or suffocate, the way the men on the Russian sub did last year. Then there are also the missing girls, girls snatched from their own homes, girls taken kicking and screaming from playgrounds.

The other people in the waiting room carry in trays from the cafeteria, trays loaded with foods like lasagna and macaroni. I think this is unseemly, slurping Coke and eating hardening lasagna while your loved ones lie in critical care.

Winsten/Deschelles does crossword puzzles. This irritates me too. He even asks me for a word now and then. Only Joey seems to have the appropriate responses. Joey's face is somber, pale under the freckles as he takes me aside to tell me that the presumably dying Moira had, in fact, visited his father earlier in the day: that is where she went, when she took my car to town. But she had not been there to retain him for her protection and the prosecution of Rafe. She had been there to make bail for Rafe.

"What?" I say. "What?"

"Bail for Rafe," he tells me. "That's why she wanted your money—why she wanted you to take cash on the credit card: to spring him."

"She forgave him?"

"She called my dad and said, 'Someone has to care for Rafe. Someone has to love him. He was beat up awful by his dad; you wouldn't believe the burns and bruises.' "

Rafe. Did he get out?

No, she hadn't raised the money. He is still where she (or I?) put him—in the county jail. So who stabbed Moira? And—even more problematic—did the person who stabbed Moira know that they were stabbing Moira?

I have to love Joey Gromolka for the way he raises the worst doubt so gently, and while holding my hand, so the fact doesn't undo what composure I have left.

"After all," Joey says, "Moira was in your bed."

On Ice

Well, I know one person who will not be in my bed tonight, and that's me. At one A.M., with Moira Gonzalez Gerhardt listed in critical but stable condition, I leave the hospital, but not for home. The image of the bloodied bed, the slippery stair, is too much for me: I will drive the ten miles to the Northway, find a motel. . . .

I am barely two miles away from Bonticou Hospital, driving south on Lake Shore, when I notice the beams of a car behind me. Coincidence? I maintain my slow pace; there are still patches of ice on the road.

The car behind me picks up speed, tailgates; the headlight glares in my eyes in the rearview mirror. Reluctant, I press the accelerator. I pick up speed, doing fifty, ten miles over the limit for the lake road. I seem to establish a bit of distance from the car behind me. Maybe this is not a pursuit. But who would chase me tonight? The same person who stabbed Moira?

Then, worse than my fear, is the reality: The Saab slows, slows to a halt. I look down at the gauge. The electric symbols flash. Gas. I am out of gas. No, it's impossible, I think, I had a full tank yesterday. Then, I realize: Moira—the car, I have no idea how far she drove. Or did someone siphon my tank to cause exactly this event?

I am aware of my car in the dark, stopped, at the shore of the lake. There are sounds emanating from the lake. I know these sounds are the ice thawing, cracking, but still, they add to my terror. The car behind me has stopped also but has not extinguished its lights.

I have the sense that the driver will now come for me. I act on impulse: I open my car door and begin to run. The other driver has not left his car; he angles his car, tracking me in his high beams.

My feet slide on the half-melted, half-frozen road surface. There is debris, broken branches, all over the macadam. I don't know where to go, what direction to run. On one side is the stone cliff of Bonticou Crag, on the other the lake, and ahead the road. As if for inspiration, I hear a crash through the forest line, and a deer leaps onto the road, directly in my path. One Eye. By the dim moonlight I can see his shattered antler, the sightless telltale eye.

One Eye. Without even having to think, I recall his escape on the ice. The soft north end. I can run it, I think, I am light and there is a good chance that whoever is behind me is heavier, heavy enough to crash through the flawed ice. I start forth. It is almost too frightening to proceed, but the headlights on my back keep me moving forward. The ice feels weak, slick on the surface, bumpy in other places where it is refreezing in the night temperature.

I am aware of myself, a small figure transversing the narrow end of the lake. But I am making progress. Whoever was pursuing is not risking the ice. The lights remain trained, but I am escaping their full beam as I move farther and farther out on the lake.

It is only when I am at the center that I realize the remaining ice has deteriorated. The opposite shore is unreachable. I am stuck between the opening lake, with its visible fissures, and the man in the car at my back.

I crumble. I fall down and cannot rise. I curl into myself, for what body warmth I might muster, and after a few minutes I do the inevitable: I clasp my hands and pray. The Frozen Girls, I think. This is what they must have experienced. Yet, they sought this solution, and I have not. I have resisted, fought for my life, not invited "the transition."

In the hours that follow, I take perhaps my strangest journey. Do I lose consciousness, or gain it in a truer form? The cold is sharp at first, then numbing. The surprise comes with the snow that begins, almost imperceptibly, in tiny grains, then gains in momentum and size. The flurries cover me as in feather down, and the deceptive warmth associated with freezing takes over, and I begin to experience something I have only read of—the seduction of snow, the deceptive body response. The snow comforts as it begins to cover me, lightly at first, and then in earnest.

Is it sleep? The first stages of death? We know these tales of the pinpoint of light in the distance, of the loved dead waiting, beckoning. Can all those clichés be wrong? I have always insisted that they are, that we live in the here and now.

I have begun to cry, not desperately but softly, as the snow falls. Save me, I mentally call. Save me. . . . I am not coherent: I call out to "You." The snow falls in undulant veils, the arctic bridal mystery taking hold of me, and how can I not think of her, of Amie Deschelles and the Frozen Girls? I see them, almost, in their transparent chitons, swirling in the snowdance around me.

For whom do I call out? Who can save me now? Is this my ultimate test of my estranged husband? Or of myself?

Is he the man at the wheel of the car, who has trained the high beams on the lake, where I lie huddled, freezing, half buried in snow? I have some sense that it is him, it is Matt out there, in the absorbent dawn.

By what marital mental telepathy can I somehow undo the damage, reverse time, restore the lover who swam with me in this very spot? "Eternal joy," I recall—that is what the girls found when they gave themselves over. . . .

I summon the full force of my being and will him to rescue me, as he did when I was hit by the car, as I lay dying. I will him to reverse time, to erase our decline, to restore love. Maybe this has been a white nightmare from which it is possible to arise. . . .

How to explain what I experience next? The enveloping warmth, as of an embrace, the sense of love overtaking me, enfolding me, escorting me toward the beyond. In the end I agree with others who have known this near-death: There is no pain, only radiance. Is this my final dream of rescue? That I see my mother, diaphanous, without real substance, but somehow present, and it is her warmth that sustains me? Is this the final gift?

My inner voice whispers, Don't give up. And now I know the unknowable. I have fallen too far; I have been bent in supplication. My lips have melted an impression into the snow, and I know it is time to surrender not to death but to life. To get up and get on with it.

My husband will never come for me again; he is the one beyond rescue, below redemption. If he meant to kill me, he has succeeded in destroying the part of me that believed in him. I am not something he can discard with the trash or toss against the wall. Some unseen force fills me, gives me strength, and I rise and stumble onward. I turn and shout into the white light: "I am not afraid of you. I am not afraid of you." But I am afraid of whoever is there, behind the electric eyes of the car.

The isthmus is refrozen now. I may cross. I tiptoe on numbed

feet to the safety of the shore, the frosted forest, and walk the last
mile to the neon edge of the highway.

There, I am greeted by the pink and blue lights of the Bonticou
Motel, and its sign, BOW HUNTERS WELCOME.

The motel is scant shelter, yet its pasteboard walls keep out the
cold this night, and I sign up for what I sense will be the duration.
As I walk the narrow green hall, with its aqua indoor-outdoor nap-
less carpet under fluorescence, I am not cheered by the notice
posted: *Under No Circumstances Is It Permissible to Take a Dead Deer to
Your Room.*

My room is what one would expect, bleak in the modern way of
alleged comfort, with a color TV angled at a vast bed. From
beyond the thin fabricated walls come the sounds of actual and
televised argument. Someone is listening to a show that features
emergency police calls. I lie in the shallow fiberglass tub, letting
tepid water play over my red, chapped body, and I can smile.

Whatever happens next, I know one thing: I have been saved,
in the nick of time, as the expression goes. In the very nick of time.
And I know whom to thank.

A Vegetative State

A vegetative state: That's what they call the kind of coma that Moira Gonzalez Gerhardt will most likely remain in for the rest of her natural life. A vegetative state. She lost too much blood; she was deprived of oxygen for too long.

She lies, in a flannel shortie nightgown, in a long-term care facility that is part of Pewter Mountain. I visit her almost every day. I know I will stop seeing her, eventually, but I feel implicated in her fate.

She lies in a fetal curl. They keep her very clean; that's the reason for the shortie nightgown—So they can keep up with her personal hygiene. They brush her hair. Her hair is cleaner now, better combed, than when she was conscious. Her eyebrow ring has been removed: It was considered a hazard and a potential source of infection. She looks as she did at Casa di Rosas the night I tucked her in, a gesture as close to maternal as I may ever achieve. She looks like the child she once was, like her own little girls. The twins, Sybella and Brianna are cared for by her mother, who is all of thirty-six. She was only thirteen when she gave birth to Moira, so she is very age-appropriate, as they say, to be the mother of the twins. Social Services gives her some money to help with their care.

The vinyl double-wide on the mountainside sits unoccupied, like the empty Christmas box it is. Someday, somebody will repossess it, because no one is making payment. Rafe lies in his eight-by-four-foot cell in the prison, and Moira lies curled in Wing A of the Golda Fein Long-term Care Unit. Golda Fein was a woman who also spent years in a coma, and her children have immortalized her in this manner, naming a redbrick building with turquoise inset panels in her honor.

Coma is not as peaceful as it sounds. Moira's coma is agitated. They say she cries and whines at night. By day she can appear to have fits of rage: She shows her lower teeth and growls. But she never sees or speaks. She is below consciousness and expected to remain there. A sleeping beauty who cannot rest in peace.

Last week, when I was visiting Moira, my paths crossed with a man I dreaded to see—Chick Savago.

"Well, hello, Mrs. D.," he says. He is standing there in the smoking zone, a brick niche stinking of butts, by the entry to the Golda Fein Long-term Care Unit. I have the sense he is lying in wait. "Hello, Mrs. D. . . . remember me? Chick Savago. . . ."

"Supralux 699," I say, moving as fast as I can.

"Hey, Mrs. D.," he whispers; it's a hiss. "I know why you come here, and I can be of some help."

There is something so intense in his manner that I pause, almost against my will.

"I know something of real interest to you," he says. "If you meet me, I will be happy to divulge the information, Mrs. D."

"Tell me now, tell me here."

"In private, Mrs. D., in private. But it would relieve you. . . ."

No. I will not listen. "Let me by."

He stands, arms folded, as if to block my passage.

"I said, let me by. . . ."

He pauses, holding his smile, that cherubic smile. "Be my guest, Mrs. D.," he says. "Let me know when you need me."

The Investigation

The aftermath of the attempted murder of Moira Gonzalez Gerhardt is considerably more conventionally dramatic than the aftermath of Matt's assault upon me. Now, in true FemJep fashion, we do have the swarm of uniformed police, the medical personnel, the DA, the forensics. I suppose I am in shock. When asked, I repeat my testimony. I keep track of the investigation, but the details and clues register, as if on a delay.

The evidence is scant: The mud washed everything away outside. They can deduce that someone fled, but his boot prints were not good enough specimens. There was a pair of large male gloves, insulated, but also caked with mud. The knife is the main piece of evidence, and it has no fingerprints, save my own, upon the handle.

The investigation is ongoing: The *Bonticou Crier* reports the story with the sensational and misleading headline LOCAL WOMAN A NEW FROZEN GIRL? The story, contributed by an anonymous freelancer, connects the death of the woman who froze on her porch and the near-death of Moira Gonzalez Gerhardt with deaths of the Victorian "frozen angels." I know firsthand that Moira

Gonzalez Gerhardt was not frozen or naked, she was wearing a flannel nightgown.

I mention this to Joey. "Where'd this story come from?" He "strings" for the paper himself. It has crossed my mind that he might perhaps have written it.

"Came in over the transom," Joey reports, "by Anonymous."

The story is suspiciously well written. To my mind, only Gideon Winsten could have composed the prose, and only Winsten knew the complete history of the Frozen Girls. Winsten has been obsessed with me for years; how sick is he?

I am drained and shaken by the attempted murder, but I also would like it to be solved. After all, I was most likely the intended victim. I don't want a second attempt to succeed. I have played the victim for so long, I know some procedure: "Can we get a search warrant for the glass house?"

We can try.

Who, besides my husband, would want to kill me? Winsten perhaps. He is certainly showing an unhealthy interest. He is the author of *Mortal Coils,* a book that disgusted critics with its sadistic imagery and was considerably toned down for the film version in which I starred, retitled *Kiss of Death.* In his obsession he has me cast twice as a victim. He builds a house with a view of my bedroom. And now he orders a headstone with my name on it.

Yet, my sense of Gideon Winsten, or John Deschelles—whatever name he goes by—is that he is a peculiar personality of the first magnitude but probably not a killer. I feel similarly about my estranged husband: In the heat of argument, in his red-out, yes, he can lose control, I know he has. . . . But is this premeditated crime, the entry into the house with a hunting knife, Matt's style?

My own most likely suspect is Rafe Gerhardt. He could want to kill me, or Moira, or both of us. He has the motive: I have intervened and been a role model, of sorts, to his wife. I have refused to let him hunt deer on my property. I am the person who put him in jail. And some evidence points to Rafe—the hunting knife, which is being traced, his knowledge of the property, the house, the fact that his rifle was also taken the night of the attack and never recovered . . . But other clues point away from him: the workman's gloves—he never wore gloves. I distinctly remember that: His hands had become leatherlike; they were human gloves. I even remember he refused to wear the gloves Moira bought him for Christmas.

But the main and conclusive evidence that exonerates Rafe Gerhardt is his alibi: He was in jail on the date in question, and he is still there, waiting trial on his DWI and battery charges.

There's only one other person who could be considered a suspect: Chick Savago. He is certainly ominous, knew the house, and could be, in his deviant lust, interested in either Moira or me. I keep remembering the glint off his right eyeball when he said, "They come at me with sharpened spoons, Mrs. D."

Still, my sense of Chick Savago is that, odd and even deviant as he may be, he did not thrust the blade into Moira. I have quite a bit of knowledge from the better FemJep films: The ferocity of the blade, suggests an intimate. The knife is personal.

Rafe. It should be Rafe. My own gut insists: Rafe. Yet, Rafe is in prison.

I decide to visit Rafe in Pewter Mountain. He wears the orange inmate jumpsuit and seems quite glad to see me. I am interested in seeing him because I wonder if he somehow orchestrated the attack from behind bars.

I am allowed to sit across from Rafe at a plain table. He is not cuffed. A guard watches without, I must say, much apparent interest. Rafe smiles his gap-toothed grin at me.

"You don't have to smile," I say, wanting to take the lead. "I know you resent me."

"Maybe I do, maybe I don't."

"I gave Moira shelter after you beat her."

"I didn't beat her: She jumped out of my truck."

"Rafe, I know you have an alibi, but I also know it must be false. I can't affect your case. I would just like to know if you were"—I concentrate, thinking of some psychological trap I might spring on him—"smart enough to do this and get away with it."

His grin is my answer. He says, "I didn't do nothing."

"Your gun was gone when I got to the house, Rafe."

His smile shifts.

"So?"

"So you were the single person who knew I had that gun. It was your gun."

"She was stabbed with a deer-hunting knife."

God, he is stupid: That was not even in the media release. The "deer-hunting" description.

"You ain't pinning nothing on me. They got me for DWI, that's it."

"You're charged with assault and battery," I remind him.

"Yeah"—he smiles—"and where's the victim?"

His gaze follows mine out the window, toward the Spam-pink rectangle of the Golda Fein Pavilion for Long-term Care Unit.

Moira will never be able to testify against him. There is no way to make the charge stick.

His eyes taunt me. He knows I know. The truth passes between us. But how? How did he get to her? I know what happened—he stabbed Moira—but I don't know how he could have been out of jail.

I look at Rafe's hands. We are seated across from one another, at a table. There is no partition. A guard watches us. His hands are permanently discolored—the purpling skin, the unremovable charcoal-colored soil; he has long nails, untrimmed, with crescents of filth. I know, I just know, looking at his hands, that somehow he used the knife.

The mind works in mysterious ways, perhaps like a computer engine on a search. The gloves, the gloves. There's something to be retrieved, some recovered knowledge regarding those huge gloves. My unconscious mind has been flipping the files, and now suddenly our search is done: "I bought him a pair of Gore-Tex gloves, all-weather, with fleece inside and every-thing . . . and he won't wear 'em." Moira's voice. Moira speaks in my subconscious. I remember the whole speech then. "I keep buying Rafe gloves—I bought him a pair for Christmas—and he won't wear 'em." Except when he doesn't want to leave finger-prints.

"I know you did it," I say to Rafe. He has a curious eye condi-tion: He can stare at you, without focusing. His pupils seem to contract, and his focus is elsewhere. It is quite unnerving.

"I know you did it," I say again. "I just want to know: Who did you think you were killing? Her or me?"

His pupils take another quarter turn, kaleidoscopically, and he gives me a more direct look. "Maybe you, maybe her. You messed with her mind," he says, then adds, "and you can't prove nothing. You can't prove nothing."

How hard is it, I wonder, to break out of this jail?

"I want to see the head of security," I say, rising, moving away from Rafe.

"In a minute," the guard says. "I'll get you someone who would know." Rafe is returned to tier one, and the guard is replaced by a tall man with a stove-in neck, and broad shoulders.

"Can I help you out, Mrs. D.?"

It is, of course, Chick Savago.

The walls of Pewter Mountain are more membrane than barrier. The men pass back and forth, the guards and prisoners sometimes interchangeable. Many went to school together; they are friends.

"I told you I can be helpful, Mrs. D. I can relieve you and answer your questions . . . if you come with me."

What would you do? My curiosity, my need for answers, overcomes my misgivings. I am not afraid, only numb. That is what fear becomes, when you feel frightened for so long. I have anger myself now, but it is the fortifying sort: I acknowledge my fury with Moira, at the forgiveness that cost her so much. She had infuriated me when I saw myself reflected in her distorted mirror. "Why did you forgive him?" I want to scream even now. "Why did you go back to him?" Now I am fast approaching a point of no return, and Chick Savago is my ticket.

More rationally, what harm can Chick do to me here in the prison? I follow him to his office, which turns out to be cell-like, with the addition of a desk and chair. He, too, has a neat cot and a toilet bowl. But Chick Savago has a nameplate and a door instead of sliding bars, and his door locks from the inside.

"Don't close that door," I command as he turns toward the knob.

"Otherwise, I leave," I insist. These are the ground rules. I will stay and listen, but I will not be locked in with him.

"I have information that will put your mind at rest, Mrs. D.," he is saying. "I want you to listen . . ."

What is his information? I wonder. Has Rafe confessed in jail, as many do?

"I keep trying to tell you, Mrs. D., you are my ideal woman. I knew that when I saw you working with the bread dough, baking the bread. My ideal woman. And you are so beautiful. . . ."

Oh, no, I think, not this again. "Rafe," I remind him. "You said you had information."

"You are very beautiful, Mrs. D."

"Oh, I'm not . . ." I demur but his bulging blue eyes, his marbleized stare, quell any further protest. I sink into the chair across the desk from him. He leans forward and says, "Oh, you look so beautiful today, Mrs. D. I wish you would relax and just trust me. Chick Savago is your friend, Mrs. D. You can count on me."

"Then tell me. Just between you and me. Has Rafe confessed to you? To other inmates?"

"He didn't have to . . ." Chick says, but his eyes are on my face, and his gaze softens in a way I don't expect. I take a breath, and a chance. Expound my theory: see if he reacts.

"I know Rafe Gerhardt stabbed his wife," I tell him, keeping my tone as firm as possible. I want him to find it hard to deny admission. I pretend to know. "Officially, Rafe was incarcerated. I know he must have escaped. But how did he get out? I won't report you—he's in jail—I just want to know, for my own peace of mind. You promised me peace of mind. You knew him from high school. You were once friends. You helped him escape?"

"No. But I can tell you how."

"Please do."

"Mrs. D., you will think this is foolish, but I just want one thing of you. I will tell you everything—it is classified, top-secret information and could cost me my job if you report me, but I wish to give you peace of mind. I know how thoughts can worry you, keep you awake. You will lose your mind unless you know."

I keep my expression noncommittal, wondering what he wants.

"It's such a small favor in return, Mrs. D.," he says, his voice sweet. "I just want you to . . . to touch me . . . just for a second. Just touch me."

Even as my inner voice screams, Don't, you fool . . . I let his hand cover mine.

"I didn't let Rafe out of Pewter Mountain," Chick Savago confesses, "but I caught him breaking back in."

So . . . I am right: Rafe escaped and then, to secure his alibi, returned to jail.

"It's pretty easy to get out of tier one," Chick Savago is saying. "It's not maximum security, like what we have in tier four, where it's not just bars but Thermopane, 'cause they throw their shit at me, Mrs. D. They throw it and it hits the screen. Tier one is almost open. He walked out; the trick was to get back in. The prison fence is topped with razor wire. I saw him; he was stuck—his pants snagged on the barbs. He was drunk. I thought he just broke out to go on a tear. I helped him down and let him back in his cell. He was here for the bed count."

As Chick is talking, he is stroking my hand in a rhythmic way. He is breathing and I think I recognize the sound, from all the phone calls.

I am not in danger, am I? No, the door is not locked; it is ajar. I should not let him hold my hand. I pull my hand away but he seizes my wrist.

"I would never hurt you," he says.

I flinch: in a film a line like that would precede a murder, or at least an assault. For a moment, my mind screens a familiar scene— Chick Savago flips me; he holds me down. He does what? Forces himself onto me? Chokes me? I feel myself becoming paralyzed, the prey before the kill. Reflexively, my right foot moves under the desk, I am ready to kick him.

He is saying—"All I want is to help. I am not allowed to do more to you. If I were alone with you some night, I would have to keep my distance. I know that. I would have to be restrained. Held down or behind bars, but I could see you and you would talk to me. You are everything to me. I didn't believe in love, like this, until I saw you kneading the bread . . . and I knew. I knew who you were."

"You saw my films."

"Movies? Are you in movies?"

My god, he doesn't even recognize me. This is a civilian response. Conditioned by my characterizations, I expect him to banish all ambiguity. But this is life and Chick is real, and he presents himself as nothing less than a man obsessed, with me but also with the truth.

"I carry this around with me, this knowledge, that I know you need. I know it could cost me everything, but I want to give you this." In my movies, no maniac ever went soft, as Chick does. His face softens, and he does something that could not be scripted—he opens his wallet and produces a picture of his parents.

"My Mom and Dad. I want you to see . . . who I am, who I come from . . ."

They look extraordinary in their ordinariness, as if parents could be generic—the wizened dad and plump mom, sitting in aluminum folding chairs in front of a chain-linked yard. Blue hydrangeas. The sort of flowers older couples feed some metallic supplement to create color. They drink canned tea. Summer in Bonticou. Local Seniors.

"They look very nice," I offer.

"They are the best people I have ever known until you." He

fumbles in his pocket and produces a badge. "This was for bravery in the service," he confides. "I want you to know me, because I am willing to risk a sacrifice for you. My job, at least my job—this might cost me more—for your peace of mind." He touches my hand again. I think, without willing it, of the night at my house, his reluctance to leave in the snow, his walk upstairs, the breathing at my door. Did the doorknob tremble? And my shawl—it was dampened—he had used it, hadn't he?

I try to pull my hand away. I feel tainted and resist the impulse to wipe my hand on my skirt. My instinct says: Do not offend him. Get what you need, if you have to cajole or extort.

Yet, it is clear—Chick Savago is in control; he does not release my hand. I am shocked at the grip on my wrist. I flash on the last times with my husband—the midnight moments of the marriage, in the uncensored dark. Matt's sexual attitude had become troubling, in ways impossible and perhaps improper to articulate. Even to myself, I could not acknowledge the fear he inspired when his gentleness vanished. There are postures and motions that civilized people do not discuss, and I am not a prude, but something unmentionable transpired in my marriage bed, and I felt forced.

That memory had dimmed, shelved to that unconscious file where we store the unthinkable, until Chick Savago revived it. Now I recall not the images but the pressure of Matt's hands on my wrists. I would not be forced then, now, by anyone but I am still seized by this strange paralysis. My instinct to flee is strong but it is as if I cannot send that message to my legs. I sit transfixed. Maybe curiosity overcomes fear.

Run, I think, leave.

"Let me go," I demand.

"Of course, Mrs. D.," he says. "What do you take me for?"

He stands up to escort me to the door. What do I take him for?

Am I wrong? Have I always been wrong? As if on rewind, I view his visit to Casa di Rosas. What had he done that was so terrible? What could I be certain was real, not my frightened projection?

He had stayed late during a snowstorm. His car had been buried in a drift. He had waited outside my bedroom door. And since then, he had proffered his offers to "relieve my mind." Yes, he had made overtures; he had crossed some social borders. He was strange, angry, aroused but could the world be as Chick Savago saw it through his too-wide hardened blue gaze?

If so, was I wrong about other aspects of my situation? Was I too suggestible, as Dr. Hubert Lazare accused? If I was wrong about Chick Savago did that uncertainty undermine my credibility regarding my husband? There had always been something, a shadow, a synapse in my brain I did not want to occur—the final connection, the mixed message.

In film, such ambiguities can be banished; killers leap to conclusion. We end, satisfied, that we know who our attackers are. They are always captured; often killed. In the movies. But in life, nothing is so certain and it is Chick Savago who presents me with the ultimate puzzle: How much has film informed my expectation? Because he appears, bullet-headed, massive, marble-eyed— typecast to stalk me; is he, in fact, guilty of more? Or is he innocent, as he has always presented himself, his only "crime" to allow an old friend to slide back into prison?

Even if he permitted Rafe to reenter the prison, could Chick have known when he caught Rafe on the razor-wired fence at Pewter Mountain what Gerhardt had done? No, Chick could not yet have heard of Moira, bloodied in my bed. But surely, within hours, he would have surmised that Rafe had returned for a reason. So, yes, Chick Savago is guilty, at least of that. Surely, he should have come forward immediately with the information.

Instead, he has hoarded it as the gift to give me in exchange for . . . what?

"Respect. Mrs. D.," he says as if in answer to my thoughts. "I want more than anything, your respect. I have always wanted to help you, in any way I could."

The word *savior* flickers across my brain-screen. What an odd hero he is—I can never know, but I must rely on instinct, and now I believe I see Chick Savago as he is—not a villain or a hero, but a confused would-be hero, with his own dreams of saving me. His devotion is disconcerting, but he has in fact fulfilled his promise to relieve my mind.

"Thank you," I say, "for your information."

"Will you report me?" he asks, following me down the hall. He walks too close to me.

"Will you report me? I'll be fired, maybe even accused of being an accessory after the fact. Would you ruin me, Mrs. D.?" Am I misinterpreting him again? Or does Chick Savago sound somewhat hopeful? Am I an instrument then, to incarcerate him? Is imprisonment, in an ultimate irony, what he wants? To join his friends on the other side of the bars? "They come at me with sharpened spoons," he told me that first afternoon we were snowbound. Could Chick Savago want to be jailed? He is not serving his own interest to confide in me. Why is he doing this, then—to trap himself or help me? Or does he unconsciously hope to achieve both aims?

"You're nice," he is saying. "You won't turn me in . . ."

"I don't know," I say, in all honesty.

I do not know. I do not know what I will do. The final mystery is within one's own mind: I cannot fathom my intention. I must decide whether to accuse or excuse Chick Savago.

"Thank you," I say, as he presses the button that will allow me to leave the building. "Thank you for the information."

"I am relying on you, Mrs. D. I have given you peace of mind. I know you will not hurt me. I know the kind of woman you are."

Maybe you do, I think, moving away from him, but do I?

At home, with the energy of indecision, for the first time since his visit, I clean under the couch. As if to underscore Chick Savago's point, two silver balls roll forth and click, knocked together as in a decisive shot at pool.

The Decision

The truth shall set you free. That is the saying, and I must trust in it. While my case has been clouded with shadows of ambiguity, I must have faith in certain facts. I turn to these facts as my compass to true north.

No matter what the evidence, the testimony, the weight of tests and court procedure, I will tell the truth, so help me God. And I have marshaled every force of that conviction: My husband's lie cannot be proved in court, because it is only that—a lie. He may be the one who looks proper; he may even be the superior actor. I am not more or less than I appear to be—a woman of unconventional dress, untamed hair, a suggestible imagination, a young bride grown up a bit too late. I carry evidence in my purse that may compromise me.

Do I have to be completely sane or even entirely innocent of my fate? May I not be eccentric, idiosyncratic? In the structured world of cinematic truth, when one is wrong on one point, then one is disqualified on all. But I maintain that my misunderstanding of Chick Savago doesn't negate my other perceptions. In fact, the acknowledgment that I leapt to conclusions once, allows me to feel

337

more confident on what I do know to be actual incident, not con-
jecture on my part. I will tell the truth, as I know it, and hope
that, in fact, it will set me free. I believe I will walk out of court,
perhaps alone, but vindicated.

Outside Bonticou County Family Court, I see J. J. Janis in a
new cashmere designer coat, bent against the wind. As he walks
toward the entry, I catch up to him.

"J. J.," I greet him. "You have always said the flaw in my case
is—"

"Too much forgiveness," he repeats.

"No more," I tell him. "Today there is no forgiveness. . . ."

Even for you, I mentally add. He charged me an additional
three thousand dollars to cross index my file. I doubt that cross
index required ten hours. I have just done that, on my own, in less
than two hours. The process, as I have prepared for court, is now
demystified. I must take control, not accept on faith.

I return to court for the final hearing on my order of protection,
well armed with so many truths. I have been forced to look into the
mirror, albeit a somewhat distorted mirror. I have seen enough to
know that I must fight harder: I must win, or I might as well
spend the rest of my life in a fetal curl like Moira Gonzalez
Gerhardt. In her voice, I have heard the echoes of my own equivo-
cation: Yes, Rafe suffered. He was tormented as a child. And my
husband, too, had been beaten. Chick Savago has bent the law,
done me a favor and incriminated himself. Do I turn him in?

In this strange season I fight Moira's battle, and my own. I am
not unprepared and I am not alone. I have a bag of evidence. Joey
Gromolka and I have worked through the night for weeks, subsist-
ing on upstate Adirondack Chinese takeout (the lowest of the
orange, glutinous moo gooey gai pans) and a thermos of my superior Café du Monde café au lait.

The floor of my motel room is covered with stacks of documents, diagrams, maps, and file folders. For technical assistance I must thank Joey Gromolka, who thought of retrieving the electronic brain of my answering machine and for accelerating the search warrant for the glass house.

There will be no doubt in anyone's mind as to what happened on the night of December thirty-first. While motives and feelings remain open to interpretation, technology can establish chronology and I shall present the physical circumstances of The Attack. I can prove that while I am a complicated and perhaps suggestible woman, I am not the delusional, paranoid hysteric that my estranged husband claims. And Dr. Anna Shirley will support this with her own counterevaluation. After today I can also file my complaint against mental health services in this county and add it to the long kite tail of charges that may one day snag Dr. Hubert Lazare.

The final hearing is held on the ides of March, March fifteenth, a date significant in history—world history and my own. It is also the date of the bride Amie Deschelles's "transition."

On this almost last day of winter, even the light seems weak, and as I drive toward Bonticou County Family Court, a snow begins to fall. But this feels like winter's farewell: The snow falls without momentum, flake by single flake. The ground cover is gone and the earth, stripped bare, shows its wounds once more.

As I drive I can't suppress a shiver at the woodscape, the forest, bent and broken by that fatal storm. There are still bits of plastic and paper snared in the clutches of the dead branches.

The eyesores of the road are also apparent: As I enter town I see a Closed sign on the large food market, and a banner flapping the arrival of Bonticou Liquidators. At the Bonticou Diner, the Scrabble sign reads GOD BLESS AMERICA without the B. God Less

America, I think. The flags set forth in autumn are now exposed, dirtied by the endless winter; they hang, too fatigued to fly.

More obvious than ever is the square shape of the prison in the distance. It is, I tell myself, just one of those days when the bones of the town lie exposed. It will change; the course of my case will change. But I must admit, my own thermostat is dropping precipitously as I approach the gawky courthouse. I am armed, and I am not alone, but can I really emerge, from such ugliness? My spirit projects: *Yes, you must.* I enter the building, knowing my fate will have altered when I leave.

"You're dead in the water," greets MacPherson. He isn't speaking to me but to J. J. Janis.

"My client will be back in his house by tonight," says MacPherson.

Betsy West, trim in navy with white piping—her spring uniform, I suppose—nods, blond bob swinging. I wonder if she plans to be in "the client's" house with him. If so, she is mistaken: I intend to take back my life and fight for my house as I have for my life. If this woman wants a relationship with my estranged husband, she'll have her reward soon enough. . . . You will hit the wall, I mentally address her. He will hurt you, too.

On my way into court for the final session, I pause at the nursery doorway. Sometimes you don't know who you are looking for until you see that person—and there she is, her face as big as an orange, turning to see me.

"Take me," she seems to beg. But surely this is my imagination: She is only a few months old. A tiny infant. Who knows if she can even see my face? Isn't life a blur at that stage?

The grandmother is walking, rocking her.

"Would you like to hold her?" she asks. "I could use a smoke." A draft of uncertainty passes between us: the disingenuous specter of that smoke. Even the grandmother seems disconcerted: sensing the smoke contradicts the pink acrylic bunting, any aspect of maternal concern. I also pick up the woman's urgency, her need to inhale smoke in lieu of oxygen, to be outdoors, even for a moment.

I look at the clock: I have a few minutes, "If it's quick."

I accept the baby—her wrist tag reads *Jane Doe*—and I am stunned by her weightlessness: She falls into my arms like a feather, but her fingers grip. You wouldn't think an infant could hold on so hard.

Elsbieta and Nadine would say everything is written, that our fate predicts such moments. I try to resist such concepts, but when those small fingers close over my thumb, and the face turns upward, I feel the tug. I also feel the reality—the seep of heat in the baby's padded bottom. Her disposable diaper fills and expands with startling rapidity. Oh, dear. I, who have never changed a baby, fumble for the diaper bag left on the chair. It's fairly basic, and I swipe the little baby girl's bottom clean, tape the loaded diaper shut, and discard it in the proper pail. The baby looks up at me, smiles. I laugh. What a way to fall for another human being: I wouldn't call it attraction, but the sensations she inspires are new. Maybe this is the answer, I think, to wipe a baby's bottom. I may not feel exhalted, but I feel something I have not in quite a while—useful.

The warmth I felt so mysteriously, when I nearly froze on the lake last month, returns in a rush. The part of me that Matt tried to kill died that night. And so did the person who would wait for salvation. The vision that sustained me was that of my own mother holding me as a small child. There was love; I had been loved. I can love. There is a difference in this world between those who have been lavished with love and those forever starved. Someone who has been given may have something to give. I can only hope that this is true for me—that I might invert this final dream of rescue into the saving of another life. The tiny person in my arms yowls, her bid to be taken.

The grandmother returns and I ask her about Baby Doe. "I'm not really her grandmother," the woman says. "That's just a term. I'm her foster grandma, until her case resolves. . . . Baby's no relation. Babies need someone to hold them, and I'm doing that. Otherwise they get something called 'failure to thrive.'"

I am hesitant to ask if she might be available for adoption. The baby is, after all, here in a courthouse: Maybe there are parents down the hall, in yet another pasteboard courtroom, battling for custody. How dare I dream of saving her? It's almost presumptuous to think . . .

So I hand the baby to the substitute grandma and proceed into courtroom three.

The stage is a mysterious arena, and so is court. As I enter, knowing I will have to deliver my ultimate speech, my life hangs in the balance; I cannot help but feel the similarity to theater. There are occasions when an actor is beautifully prepared, recites eloquent lines with intelligent direction, under lighting that is incandescent, on a set that suits the story and yet the actor fails. There are factors, impossible to fathom, that charge the electricity in the air. There is a chemical electrolytic exchange, a force field, that draws actors and audience together.

Many performers lay blame to poor weather: Humidity, they say, is a killer, and overheating notorious and lethargy-producing. "Watch out," I have heard on wet Tuesday nights, when a cast returns from the two-day break, and the rain beats a dirgelike refrain.

I have experienced these conditions and I know a bad house when I enter, and so my confidence evaporates like the last droplet in a room humidifier when you need it most. My throat cracks, and I hack.

We are ready for this hearing, my team: J. J. Janis, Gromolka senior and junior, and Dr. Anna Shirley, with her inkblots and assessments. But I fear the room will go against us; it is in the air, and we all feel it and begin a winter sweat.

Outside, the temperature drops forty degrees in an hour. Ladybugs that had emerged in the thaw die on the courtroom window. Buds, forced to bloom, fall to the ground. Awakened horseflies buzz at the indoor window, harbingers of more disaster to come.

Creatures know a storm is coming, and so do people, if we allow the sensations to register. The lights in courtroom three flicker. Sometimes a brownout feels worse than a blackout; this dimming of light matches my expectation.

A bad house, I keep thinking, this is a bad house. Internalize it in my gut, which twists and wrings, as if in a mangle. I have played shows when the actors vomited, discreetly, in the wings, into pails held out by the stagehands. I wish for one now.

Yet, the show must go on. We are rehearsed and ready, and have our props to show. The film confiscated from the glass house should impress them: Winsten had more than a telescope trained on my window. He had a camera attached. His cinematic technique is flawed, very vérité—and the unedited footage is jumpy, grainy, and can give one floaters just by watching—but I must thank the auteur author, because he caught the moment: Matt crashing into the bedroom, swinging at me.

One wondrous aspect to technology: There is a record that wipes away all doubt. There is nothing ambiguous in the scene. The action is as I have described, maybe more severe. Even I edited out the distortion in Matt's face—the bulged eyes and screaming mouth, the swinging fists. This is real violence as opposed to staged: gawky, inchoate with a stop and start illogic.

There is pain in watching this, for it captures something I believed was private—my husband's anger, my fear, and, most tellingly, the absence of a rescuer. There is no one to stop what occurs. I watch myself running, caught, brought down like a deer . . . falling out of frame, forever. The film of course is silent, as is the court that watches it.

But we have audio, too, thanks to the ingenious Joe junior: Joey retrieved the sound from my old automatic answering machine, the one that was tethered to the smashed phone. So while the 911 tape plays Matt's finale, my old-fashioned little black box, which sat, in its blank mechanical innocence, on my bedroom floor and which I believed had recorded nothing, had in fact picked up all the ambient sound, once the phone itself was severed and broken.

Everyone in the courtroom concentrates, listens. The sound effects are here: Matt's footfalls, the splintering door, my screams, the running steps. . . . There is a brief pause during which I must have fled the house. In that interval Matt has pursued me downstairs, and the 911 operator automatically rings back. He picks up, and what else can he say? "Domestic dispute. . . . Please hurry, my wife is hysterical."

Joe Gromolka senior presses Stop, then Rewind.

"Does the court need to hear this again?"

"Objection," says MacPherson, "these tapes can be altered."

But the tapes are not altered and Judge Sintula knows that. I look over at Matt: he is glaring. Betsy West has stood; she brushes off her suit and, without saying a word, wheels her legal dolly cart out of the courtroom. I imagine she casts me an apologetic look, but perhaps not. Maybe she is simply embarrassed.

Matt's team, the remaining MacPherson and Karp, request a recess.

Even Joe, Joey, J. J. Janis, and I, clustered in the plaintiffs' waiting area, can hear Matt scream at them, and they retort in kind.

When we return to the courtroom, Matt Smythe asks to address the court: He is assuming his own defense. His legal team has been discharged. I look to my own lawyers: Will this be permitted?

"Anyone can represent himself," J. J. Janis whispers in my ear. "Of course, it is the classic—"

"—fool for a client," completes Joe Gromolka.

Matt is a patent lawyer and, having had a legal education, is somewhat better prepared than the average defendant. But still . . . how can the court allow him to take over? I look at Matt: He is discolored, mottled with rage; the slow drip of blood from his left nostril has begun. But there is no one to object. This is his legal right and he exercises it.

Second Act. Wind presses against the courtroom window, and for some moments the glass appears to warp under the pressure. I think of the tornado, the storms that strike here and shatter glass. We all huddle inward, toward the center, away from the view of a midday sky turned black.

"What you have seen and heard," Matt announces, "are all distortions, lies. Things appear one way when in reality they were another. I call Juliana Durrell Smythe to the stand."

I look to Judge Cynthia Sintula. Is this possible? My husband wants to cross-examine me?

She addresses the courtroom, for the record: "We must note that the defendant is now representing himself."

"They'll give him every break now," J. J. Janis hisses in my ear. "Loose cannons are allowed to fire, being a *pro se.*" He uses a term for client without a lawyer.

I take the stand, clutching my purse, as I have a thousand times on film and stage. Matt composes himself, approaches me. From the table, J. J. Janis stares at me as if he can direct by his stern expression. I recall his admonishments: Do not volunteer, do not elaborate. Answer "yes" or "no."

Will I follow direction? No.

Matt asks me to recite the routine facts, my name, my address. I feel myself waver: For some reason, even saying my name undermines me for a moment. Will I have to present the evidence in my purse? I don't want to, but I must not lose my resolve. He is giving me his most intimate expression, the *I love you, worship 'n' adore you* look of the past, and he will stop at nothing to score his points.

"Does the expression 'Do you like the blues?' mean anything to you?"

Of course. The first words he ever said to me: "Do you like the blues?" The date to the jazz club. The night he told truths that he never repeated.

"Yes."

"Could you tell me the association?"

"Yes." I feel the break come into my voice, the loss of control. My lip is gone. What technique I have cannot overcome this. I cannot stop, and J. J. glares as I continue ". . . the first words you said to me, seventeen years ago."

The lights in the courtroom flicker.

"In seventeen years, in any marriage, things happen, good things and bad things. There are undercurrents and blowups. It doesn't mean that there is no longer love."

Don't, I silently direct him, don't do this.

I know what I am supposed to do. I am supposed to step down from the stand, take his hand, and leave this courthouse with him . . . and do what? Go home, to Casa di Rosas.

"What about the expression 'to love and to honor, as long as we both shall live'?"

Please, I mentally beg, if any feeling remains, stop.

I don't know if I am allowed to question, but I rebut: "And 'to love and to cherish'?"

As I have a dozen times on film, I address the court. "I would like to speak."

Judge Sintula turns toward Matt: Will he object? J. J. Janis stands, addresses the Judge.

"My client should not address the court at this time, she is under stress . . . I request a recess."

"And I refuse," I say.

The Judge looks perplexed. "There is no precedent for this," she says. "If the plaintiff wishes to speak, as the defendant has already opened this line of questioning. I believe she has the right to do so."

J. J. despite his training, cannot suppress a moan. 'Don't talk' his red eyebrows knit; a scowl of sign language. I can hear his words without his voice, from past warnings: 'Don't say more than necessary; it will come back and bite you on the ass.'

Sorry, J. J. Janis, I must do this my way. If I fail, I fail, trying my best. And there is something that I must say or it will poison my future.

Matt seems surprised, as I press him to respond. "Were you ever hurt?" I ask him. "Do you know what it is to feel someone's fists? To run in fear? To be caught and fall?"

He doesn't answer but he also does not object.

"You were hurt," I continue. "I know some of the damage that was done: I can only imagine the rest." I am thinking of his parents; the unspoken cruelties of his infancy; and I am thinking, too, of Rafe Gerhardt, burned and choked as a child.

I feel the release now of my own fury. This is how abusers intimidate their victims: Being hurt by a husband is something I am supposed to be too ashamed to expose. It somehow belittles and even endangers me to take this into the open.

But I don't care. I have this—the strength of no longer caring. It is his shame, not mine. And I will not excuse him, no matter what . . . he is not the injured party here. I am.

"There are explanations but nothing excuses," I tell Matt and the courtroom. "Because you were hurt doesn't give you permission to pass along the pain. Somewhere, the chain must break." I mean to snap it here; this legacy of entitled abuse. He cannot be permitted to get away with what he did, neither can Rafe or by association and complicity, Chick Savago.

Matt colors. For once, the shame brands the one who should feel it. He stammers and mumbles through his closing statement.

Our hearing ends. Judge Sintula speaks—the defendant, Matt, is found guilty of "a family offense." The decision is in my favor. There is no joy in my victory, but relief. I walk out of Bonticou County Family Court. The order of protection surrounds me now into my unknown future as an invisible shield.

It is no protection, though, from the draft that whips down the hallway, from the open doors. Court is dismissed: the personnel, plaintiffs, defendants are leaving, J. J. Janis stomps past me, firing his farewell remarks, "Well, I hope you're satisfied . . ."

I spin around. The draft catches my coat, that Mafia lady coat that I now, at last, despite all reason to wear it—remove. "Yes, I am." I tell him and toss my costume coat into the trash.

"There's a way to do things in a court of law," he says, then to my surprise, kisses my cheek—a hard peck, as if I have been kissed by a falcon. Then he is gone. I wonder—Will I be billed for the kiss? On a filmed finale, he would embrace me, and we would leave together, victorious, and he would waive all cost. "I can't take your money," he would say. In reality, I know I will receive a new bill. And after all, why should he have traveled so many times to "Yekaterinburg" to represent me? There is no gallantry in the law. Defense costs.

In the final foyer, I brace myself, coatless, to leave the courthouse. I can feel with the marital telepathy of my past that Matt is behind me. I sense him like an animal. He is willing me to turn around. "If you turn around, I will always be here," he said. "We will never say goodbye."

I maintain my pace toward my car, knowing if I look back, I will be as Lot's wife, frozen forever in regret. Until death us do part.

Is he still watching? I recall our routine: those protracted farewells, the rehearsed turns to "see"—Is he looking? Is he? The conditioning of seventeen years decrees that I must turn to satisfy my conviction that, yes, he too has turned and stands watching. "I still love you," he will say. I know that. Love does not suffice here. Only on screen can a declaration of love wipe the slate clean.

"Don't turn around," I command myself. "Not even to see if he has turned around . . ." I choreograph my exit, one foot in front of the other. The final tie shreds as I walk out of the courthouse and my former life, forever.

I am grateful that the judge called a halt to our case, before I needed to enter my final piece of evidence. This evidence is a letter, yellowing, handwritten, from my wedding date, when those vows that now ended up in a court record were first uttered in tender earnest. The letter was written on our honeymoon departure, the very trip that led us here, to Lake Bonticou and Casa di Rosas.

The letter is an exchange between an eighteen-year-old bride and her twenty-five-year-old groom. It is an apology, one of many

I intended to submit in evidence of my husband's escalating and irrational rage.

"I am so sorry," he begins, "for the incident getting on the plane. I don't know what got into me. I love you; you are a part of me forever. Nothing like this will ever happen again. If you won't forgive me, I can't blame you. We will go our separate ways. . . ."

The incident: I had been carrying a small straw purse. It was summer, and it was an open bag that held a jumble of odd cosmetics, keys, and change. It was a last-minute carry-on, and in my haste in packing, I had not closed a bottle of red nail polish well enough . . . and just before boarding, when I checked the bag, I saw that the polish had leaked like new, overbright blood, and mired in it, were eighteen pennies. Seeing that the purse was ruined, I tossed the bag in an open trash can at the boarding gate.

Matt saw this and retrieved it. For the first time I saw the shade fall behind his eyes, and his face distort and mottle, when he looked into the purse and saw the pennies glued to the straw.

"You throw out money. This is what you do? You throw out money. . . ."

"Eighteen cents," I say. "The purse is nothing."

He is screaming at me, and now it's time to board. The plane is waiting, propellers spinning. It is a fifty seater, a puddle jumper, to take us to Lake Bonticou, to begin our life together.

I can't believe he is screaming. The other passengers turn away, climbing the ramp. "Come on, Juliana," he yells, "let's go." And that's when he does it—grips my upper arm in a vise. I know there will be a mark, but I can't think, I can't turn around. He is holding the purse, forcing it back into my hand. I follow him, blind, onto the plane and we take off.

The letter closes: "My behavior was hideous. I will never forget your eyes, your tears. How could I do such a horrible, crazy thing to you? I won't blame you if you leave me now. Guys like me are a dime a dozen."

I am relieved that I did not have to open the letter and read it into the record. Or show my reply and exhibit A, the penny, glued in red, as a seal.

"If guys like you are a dime a dozen," the eighteen-year-old bride wrote, "here is my down payment. I just said 'as long as we both shall live,' and I meant it. I love you. Juliana."

It may be time now for forgiveness of another sort—not to forgive him but myself: I can accept responsibility but not blame. The letter lies, creased and folded, in the purse I carry today. I have saved it as a reminder that we write the story. We should write a better ending for ourselves, if we dare.

Epilogue: Blooming Cherry

Seven seasons have come and gone at Casa di Rosas. The cherry tree we feared destroyed has recovered and, though scarred, blooms again.

We spend our summers here, Cerise, my little daughter, and I. To me, Lake Bonticou is, in a sense, a town restored. Its facade is reassembled, and now I can again enjoy the gingerbread houses, the cobbled streets. I no longer look behind the shutters of Duane Street or notice the legal and psychiatric offices tucked within the historic houses. This no longer seems to be a town peopled by bellicose males and fear-struck women. We see the world through a prism of our personal concerns—as alcoholics inhabit a place peopled with those who drink or abstain. As an endangered "heroine," I saw this conflict wherever I turned. To the bruised, the world is a ward of walking wounded. Domestic dramas still occur here but I am no longer the featured player.

Lake Bonticou is once again for pleasure, the ballet, the horses, the beautiful view, boating and swimming in the teardrop-shaped lake. Now I see behind another facade, the festive face of the children's venues—the puppet theater, the Adirondack playground,

the water slides and toy shops. I never drive past Pewter Mountain
or even note the bit of razor-tipped fence that is just visible above
its hidden driveway.

I know that Rafe Gerhardt and Chick Savago sit, safe and incarcerated, within its bland brick walls. I did testify against Chick
Savago. I faced his wounded blue gaze. How could you betray me,
Mrs. D.? But it was necessary. Whether he knew so at the time, or
not, he had assisted after the assault on Moira. In a film, this would
mean he was entirely evil, and I know that he is not but that cannot alter the outcome. In movies, men are good or bad, dangerous
or protective. In my reality, the men have managed to be both.
What's so hard about real life as opposed to FemJep—the actual
plot lines are murky, motivations complicated and unclear.
Characterizations and action seem unearned. Life, as does fiction,
cries out for resolution.

It has taken years to unravel the tapestry of that time, to try to
separate my projection, my fear, from what actually happened.
Because I was suggestible, I made one error in character assess-
ment. Did this make me less creditable? Because I was "wrong" to
an extent about Chick Savago, was I less credible in my account of
my husband? I would say no, but I am a prejudiced witness and
sometimes I surprised myself. I cannot say that I did not hesitate
to turn Chick Savago into the district attorney. Some nights when
I lie on my bed, Chick's blue marbleized stare haunts me. I wonder if "we are all covered with nematodes, our skin dies and is
crawling with microscopic organisms that live and feed on our
dead scales."

"Let me vacuum your bedding, Mrs. D.," I hear him whisper.
And then, most difficult to hear—"You would never hurt me, Mrs.
D. You're too nice."

Chick is no longer a guard but among the guarded. Criminal

justice, at least, has worked, almost as well as in a film—although both men could be paroled in twenty-five years.

The writer known as Gideon Winsten, a.k.a. John Deschelles, served six months' probation for harassment and unlawful tampering with a grave site. He wrote a definitive history of the Frozen Girls, which, though I mistrust and dislike the man, I will concede is fascinating. Only a man as obsessed as Gideon/Deschelles could fathom the mystery of a group hysteria that caused seven young girls to surrender their lives. The man was a distant cousin, barely a descendant of Deschelleses; Gideon Winsten turned out to be like many imposters, posturing that he was from Hollywood, and his own street of dreams. Under public scrutiny he felt uncomfortable in his glass house, sold it and moved to Oak Bluffs, Martha's Vineyard, into a community similar to the one he researched here. He received probation for harassment, as he was indeed traced as "the Breather." A court psychological evaluation was ordered and performed by none other than Dr. Hubert Lazare, who found Gideon Winsten sound, despite a history of necrophilia. Dr. Lazare did not recommend counseling for a man who preferred women unconscious (at best) and was implicated in exhumations and body transfers. To this date, Dr. Hubert Lazare practices and is an expert for hire in Bonticou County, although the list of complaints against him has grown and may one day halt his sanctioned mysogyny.

The woman who froze on her porch, Jane Baker, was ultimately declared an accidental death caused by alcohol, definitely not a Frozen Girl fatality: She had, in fact, passed out, having downed a fifth of vodka. One hopes she made her own transition without pain.

My ex-husband serves his sentence in another prison, the cell of the self, the incarceration of conscience. On some level I sense his thoughts still—and know that one day he will apologize to me. For now, he travels, on the lam from life. He lives in exotic ports of call. Betsy West sued him for nonpayment of his legal bills.

For myself, it took four years to pay off my debt to my own attorneys, the bulk owed to J. J. Janis. He has a new hip and a deck on his house in Briarcliff that was built on the bones of my marriage. I like him as much as one can like someone who cost so much in the end. On film, no one can be venal and kind, at the same time—but in Bonticou, maybe J. J. Janis managed to be both. His hatchet cut true. "A heart knows a heart."

I have chosen to live year-round in Bonticou; the winters harden me, help me survive. While I revel in the summer, it is the snow that restores my soul. Not everything can be explained: My friend Elsbieta, who passed away last year, believed in extrasensory experience and I still refuse to accept the most blatant claims of occult phenomenon. I believe perhaps what we call extrasensory is sensory—that we are all more equipped than we realize to discern the nuances of others' feelings. And who knows? Perhaps thought waves are electrical, and magnetic forces remain in locations where intense events have occurred. I don't believe in spirit photography, but I respect the power of the past, and the dual gaze of my sepia bride and groom continue to haunt me at home. I would never remove their wedding portrait from my mantel.

I have settled in Lake Bonticou, recreated a professional life here, the Chekhov Summer Theatre, performed on the grounds of the lake. I refuse to play heroines in physical jeopardy; the psychic dangers are sufficient. Perhaps as homage to my queen cherry, each season, I play Lbuv Ranevskya in *The Cherry Orchard,* even as I defy her fate, and the destruction of my own trees to stave off the annihilation of my final dream.

I was able to take over the care of Baby Doe; not an adoption—
her paperwork is forever stymied—but a foster "boarding" that
seems permanent. It was not so difficult to obtain her custody in
family court as I feared: Cerise had many problems, some physical,
such as a heart murmur and a mild form of epilepsy, the so-called
petit mal—odd moments of lapsed consciousness when my little
girl seems to vanish from her body and then return. Medication
treats this, but other problems took longer to cure. For the first
three years of her life, she suffered "night terrors" and "inconsolable crying." It was in comforting this tiny baby, in the repeated
murmurs of reassurance, that I myself was also calmed. She, my
beautiful little Cerise, is the dream so beautiful, I never dared to
envision it.

I know if this were a film and I in character, I would also
inevitably find another love. There would be a widower, most
likely a veterinarian, or a divorced doctor down the road. An available more gentle man would appear, to escort me through the rest
of my life, which could be projected as calmer.

I see him sometimes, my fictional man, in those mental forecasts that have not quite stopped: He is slightly stooped, with
thick hair, wearing a sweater, moving toward me, offering tea . . . a
bookshelf behind him. This is the last of my detailed visions, and I
discount it: I have learned my real role too well, and know that
unmarried gentlemen down the road are the stock of fiction. Yet I
cannot quite erase his hand, extended toward me. So I turn, to look
another way.

The facts of my life suffice—for now. Joey Gromolka remains a
friend; sometimes he rankles at that, and hints he could be more
than a friend. "I'm getting older," he notes, hopeful as ever. I tell
him when the age difference closes, I'll have made the real "transition." "Find someone younger, find someone your age," I say, and I

mean that. On film, he could erase my legacy, replace it with the hopefulness of youth. I have chosen another conclusion.

Each June twenty-second, my little girl and I celebrate a special day. It is not only the anniversary of the wedding for which this house was built, but also the date the queen cherry is most likely to be at her fullest bloom.

This summer, the day is the hottest I can recall, but a strong breeze wafts as if from the distant past—blows so hard, there is a blizzard of blossoms, and the earth is blanketed as in an out-of-season snow. This wind carries with it images of other times, and other people, who stood beside this tree. I can envision her, the bride Amie Deschelles and her handsome groom, so perfect on the wedding day. Perhaps they were as happy as we are—and they, too, did their barefoot summer dance, when the world went white with flowers.

Acknowledgments

I wish to thank Rosemary Ahern, Toni Ahearn, Richard and Betsy Auchincloss-Weiss, John Bowers, Paul Cirone, Judith Curr, Molly Friedrich, Frank and Ruth Gilroy and Clan Gilroy, John Shanley, Greer Hendricks, Dan Menaker, Suzanne Watson, Nina Shengold, Ron Nyswaner, Mary Louise Wilson, Zach Sklar, Joseph Kavon, Kip Gould, Karen Williams, and all the other good souls who continue to aid, abet and inspire. Special thanks to Ron, for his many kindnesses to me and so many others.